THE SNOW BRIDGE

AND OTHER STORIES

Philip Chatting

The settings of the stories in *The Snow Bridge and Other Stories* are drawn from a life spent in many countries. Several focus intently on a particular relationship: that between a husband and wife, mother and daughter, brothers, friends, partners, climbing-buddies, employer and employee; the relationship with an inner self; putative relationships that never quite begin, relationships with a location, or the inhabitants of a small town. Other stories explore the long-term expatriate's dilemma of engaging with a place not his or her own at the price of diminishing intimacy with the country of his or her birth.

Described in Philip Chatting's, 'Author's Introduction', as, "entertainment", the impact of the collection may prompt readers to reflect on the nature of their own relationships and the place we each occupy in our own worlds.

PHILIP CHATTING was born in the northwest of England in 1944 and, after brief experimentation with an accounting career, spent the majority of his working life in human resource management in the Middle East, Africa, the USA and Asia in industries as varied as copper mining, construction, newspapers and trade publishing. Since 1990 he has been employed as the Vice President of Human Resources by an export marketing company in Hong Kong.

Although an enthusiastic writer of many years standing, mainly in the area of management, he only latterly fulfilled a long-standing ambition by completing a full-length novel *Harbour Views*, published in the United Kingdom in 2014. Philip presently lives with his wife and youngest son in Hong Kong, while two older sons carry on the family tradition of global citizenry by working in Sri Lanka and Qatar. Outside work, writing and time with his family, Philip's spare moments are spent reading, hill-walking, enjoying the theatre and listening to classical music.

THE SNOW BRIDGE

AND OTHER STORIES

Philip Chatting

Proverse Prize 2014

Proverse Hong Kong

The Snow Bridge and Other Stories
by Philip Chatting.
Copyright © Philip Chatting, December 2015.
Published in Hong Kong by Proverse Hong Kong, December 2015
under sole & exclusive licence.
ISBN: 978-988-8228-28-7
Printed by CreateSpace

1st published in pbk in Hong Kong by Proverse Hong Kong, 24 November 2015
under sole & exclusive licence.
Copyright © Philip Chatting, 24 November 2015.
ISBN: 978-988-8227-82-2

1st ed., distribution (Hong Kong and worldwide):
The Chinese University Press of Hong Kong,
The Chinese University of Hong Kong,
Shatin, New Territories, Hong Kong SAR.
E-mail: cup-bus@cuhk.edu.hk; Web: www.chineseupress.com
Tel: [INT+852] 3943-9800; Fax: [INT+852] 2603-7355
Distribution (United Kingdom):
Christine Penney, Stratford-upon-Avon, Warwickshire CV37 6DN, England.
Email: chrisp@proversepublishing.com

Distribution and other enquiries to:
Proverse Hong Kong, P.O. Box 259, Tung Chung Post Office, Tung Chung,
Lantau Island, NT, Hong Kong SAR, China.
E-mail: proverse@netvigator.com; Web: www.proversepublishing.com

The right of Philip Chatting to be identified as the author of this work
has been asserted by him
in accordance with the Copyright, Designs and Patents Act 1988.

Page design by Proverse Hong Kong.

British Library Cataloguing in Publication Data.
A catalogue record for this book is available
from the British Library.

THE SNOW BRIDGE AND OTHER STORIES

CONTENTS

Acknowledgements

The cover image is from a coloured wood engraving
by Charles H. Whymper. Wellcome Images,
Library reference: ICV No 25486.
Photo number: V0025040.
Licensed under Creative Commons Attribution 4.0.

Portrait of author by Mrs Del Chatting.

PREFACE

Set in a variety of locations, *The Snow Bridge and Other Stories* invites the reader to decide if the collection is united by a single theme. Or is it rather a random exploration of the durability of relationships when the time and place in which they were created changes? Revolving through their varied surroundings, we encounter married couples, children restive under parental scrutiny, brothers choosing different paths, partners with diverging interests, employers and employees with incompatible agendas. We read of personal associations between inner idealism and outer circumstance, putative relationships which either never quite begin or are tied to particular locations. We observe the inhabitants of a small town. Each story poses puzzling questions.

One recurring thread is the long-term expatriate's increasing though superficial engagement with a place not his or her own, while intimacy with the country of birth diminishes. Where does an expatriate belong? Is a sense of belonging even important? This aspect was particularly appealing to me, having left England at the age of twenty-two and having lived in Asia for forty-four years.

Turned over and left open to the air are the dependencies of ordinary people in their plain lives, in their sitting rooms and kitchens, and in the comings and goings of plying trades, shopping for their families and in the rituals of marriage, kinship, acquaintance, rivalry, friendship, and the workplace.

Suburban London, the streets of San Francisco, the anonymous throngs of Hong Kong, Ho Chi Minh City, San Francisco and the townships of the rural Philippines are the canvas over which colourful arrays of characters act out their parts. No cosy conclusions are offered to the questions that these stories invite us to ponder.

In 'The Snow Bridge', a tale set in high, wind-swept mountains (which could belong to a dozen different countries), two friends of many years standing climb an icy crag and discover that shared adversity and danger, rather than strengthening personal bonds, shake them to breaking point and beyond.

'Turning Round' relates the history of an auditor, who, disillusioned with his dull work and duller family and hideously uneventful life, seeks escape, first in the small delights of a scruffy pub and then in a midnight train dash across the wilds of Suffolk, only to discover that breaking clear is easier thought about than done and that folly lies in fantasy and sudden impulse.

Weakening roots and the search for a sense of belonging are a focus in several stories, including 'Shades of Green' and 'The Dinner Party'. The first explores the separate course taken by two brothers. One has had a lifetime of foreign travels and enjoys allegiance nowhere. The other has never left the farm within sight of the English Channel, which was bequeathed to him by his father. Both brothers have their share of regret and envy as one slips across the surface of the places where he briefly lives and the other clings to the soil of his homeland. As they approach old age, which of the two is the more fulfilled?

Retired from the social whirl and thrust of Asia, the Hudson family are now established in the Home Counties, where Edward's wealth provides enviable comfort. 'The Dinner Party' shows the impact of this transition, the parts of the Hudsons' life that continue unabated and those that have fallen away, the impact on the couple's relationship. Edward's kidnapping and the subsequent ransom demands reveal how closely linked relationships are to the place in which they had their beginnings.

Another story, 'Lighting up the Sky' explores the same concept, but in reverse. How does the apparently perfect marriage of two delightfully intelligent and ambitious people alter when they move from the heart of commercial London to the swelter and bustle of Hong Kong?

If there is a unifying theme, perhaps it lies in the range of locations and in a variety of characters that rarely come together in a single volume. The Roman Catholic priest assigned to the South Seas, whose parishioners recognise and respond to human frailty; the young Frenchman sipping apple brandy in a side-walk café in Vietnam, in awe of the beauty and unfathomability around him; racially mixed marriage partners with children growing up among the conservative mores of Hong Kong; ambition and guilelessness set loose in Indonesia, and the chance meetings of travellers waiting for a delayed flight.

The Snow Bridge and Other Stories is a unique collection reflecting the author's varied history and his interests in the countries and cultures of the people among whom he has lived and travelled. It will appeal to those who share or would like to share similar experiences, as well as those who are curious to know about them.

Mike Rowse
Author of the best-selling, *No Minister & No, Minister – the true story of Harbourfest.*

AUTHOR'S INTRODUCTION

Dylan Thomas was inspired by the events and characters witnessed during a chaotic Welsh childhood; T S Eliot, by the twentieth century's uncertainties; Graham Greene, by moral ambiguity and Mary Shelley by dreams she experienced at the age of eighteen, after nights conversing with Byron and her future husband Percy on the subject of galvanism – the effect of electrical current on otherwise unstimulated muscles. All discovered the material of fiction in lives and the environment surrounding them, until, in the words of F. Scott Fitzgerald, they developed a burning need – a mandate they believed – to say something. Only a few – Milton say, or more recently Matthew Kneale – drew chiefly from the wells of private imaginings.

My stories, like those of most other fiction writers, have their beginnings, not in the great philosophical debates where wrongs are righted, but in the plain observations of ordinary people's ordinary lives, in corners of the world where fortune and circumstance – London, Manila, Hong Kong, Saigon, the Sussex Downs, San Francisco – have taken me; in standing at the foot of an airport escalator watching anonymous crowds; in the comings and goings of a street corner where hawkers ply their trade and shoppers buy food for their families or indulge an irresistible craving; and in the rituals and failures of marriage, kinship, acquaintance, rivalry, friendship, and the common workplace, and in piecing together the quality of relationships, which invariably are deeply wanting.

That man and woman who stepped into the room; are they happy together? How close or distant are they? Have they been fighting, or have they just come from the intimacy or the function of a shared bed? What does that daughter think of her father, walking just a few steps behind or ahead of her? Does the separating distance imply some emotional gap in their relationship? Are partnerships a convenience of time and place and does anything outlive the brief moments of their nativity? Are lives before the screen a simple exercise in rectitude and public relations? Does love inevitably metamorphose into custom and form that willy-nilly entraps, because doing anything different, especially after the passage of years, is too disruptive and complicated?

At the heart of each story is a Nietzchean suspicion that life is a tragedy, albeit made bearable by occasional low farce, with an inevitable trajectory about which we are able to do very little.

In "Endings" I have told stories following encounters with a man sipping cognac at a sidewalk café; a picture, seen on a lounge wall, of a Vietnamese woman leaning on a bicycle; a pensioned expatriate leaving behind everything his adult life had ever known for the drizzles of suburban London; a beggar wrapped in plastic bags and sheeting on the Hong Kong pavement; an aging actress on the West End stage; a dutiful Catholic congregation praying in the provincial Philippines; and two climbers swearing and arguing for all they were worth in a blizzard on the Norwegian Alps.

All of this has been a labour of love, which, although expressing a pessimistic view of humankind's lot, has kept me grounded in my past and hopeful that an entertainment of this sort will find an appreciative audience among people who can say, 'Ah! Yes; I remember how the fog hung over San Francisco Bay,' or 'the way buildings in Ho Chi Minh's Cathedral Square were coloured,' or 'how the night-time view was from Mount Butler, so black on one side and so glittering on the other,' and reflect that the enduring purpose of fiction is to explore cruelty and bliss; probe lives where nothing else touches; help all men and women look each other in the eye and explore the world's dark corners, where science and politics never reach; where seeking truth and beauty is at the heart of the grand human project.

Philip Chatting
June 2015

ONE

THE SNOW BRIDGE

"Is there anything better than being at ten thousand feet? What a sky! If you close your eyes you could imagine stars falling at midday. Why, man, we are at heaven's gate!"

There was never an occasion in the high mountains when Barton's spirit failed to soar.

"You're getting carried away again. Sometimes I think you say things for effect rather than because you believe them," Hanner replied sourly.

Over their heads the canopy was deep violet, but on the horizon it shaded away to the sort of blue street-level people might recognise. Wispy threads of water vapour rose and disappeared in the sun's hot glare and from somewhere out of uncertain distance an invisible raven's grating call floated on the sighing winds Surrounded by such magnificence, disagreement was an affront to gods and nature alike.

"There's no one but you to impress John and I know you won't take too much notice."

"Think we'll reach the top?" Hanner asked, changing the subject.

"Sure, why not? There's no more than two thousand feet to go and coming down will be a piece of cake," Barton eased into a crevice and unpacked a sandwich.

His partner chose to settle on an exposed rock before rummaging around in a black rucksack for chocolate and an apple. "You always underestimate. I don't want to be stuck out here in the middle of the night like last time."

"We got back alright didn't we? And you enjoyed telling the tale."

Today as on every day bad-tempered undercurrents disturbed their every conversation. How had their relationship lasted? Eight years to men not yet thirty was almost an eternity, especially when neither claimed real comfort in the association. Perhaps they were not friends at all and were just together for convenience and because of a shared interest in the hills?

Without openly expressing his thoughts, Hanner begrudgingly felt junior, although at the same time, he secretly admired the fractionally older man and took pleasure from being seen in his company.

On the mountainside, Barton led the climb, with Hanner trailing morosely behind. The ordering occurred automatically as if each was placed that way by external authority. Occasionally, to boost his sickly ego, Hanner took an alternative route. But the burden of leadership grew wearisome and before long he drifted back into line to follow his partner's more assured footsteps. In those humbling moments he reluctantly accepted his companion did usually know better, but, perversely, recognising as much exacerbated rather than diminished his nagging uncertainties.

When people they knew spoke about them their names were joined in exactly the same order, David Barton and John Hanner, as if an undeniable priority had been established at birth.

At university, where the two first met, Barton was the first choice of sports captains, and presidents of societies. Hanner, however, struggled to break into the football second eleven where, much to his dismay, he failed to score a single goal and was ultimately dropped from the roster after one season. At final examination time Hanner worked hard for months on end to scrape a modest degree, while Barton sailed into the top five percent without sacrificing a single second of a very full life.

Professors and games coaches had constant trouble remembering Hanner's name and frequently confused him with Hannick, an under-achiever on the anthropology course, who gained brief notoriety appearing at an afternoon lecture in a state of intoxication. Among students Hannick became known as "Piltdown" and Hanner as "the Florentine", but within the faculty, being the sort of students who passed through university and later adult life without leaving any noticeable trace, they acquired a kind of composite identity that was impossible to part.

"Let's move on. You'll be getting cold if we hang about in the wind much longer."

Retying his boots and wriggling free of the encircling boulders Barton stood up. Hanner tossed the remains of his meal into a rucksack and followed suit. Why, he wondered, was he not the one to say, "Let's go". Was he always going to wait for someone else to decide? A wave of resentment lapped around his fatigue and carried with it a few more grains of ragged ego.

Back down the slope, dense clouds, white on the upper side and dark beneath, rolled towards the stunted pine trees through which they had passed in bright sunlight, less than an hour and a thousand feet ago. Above them and under a cloak of untouched snow the mountain towered powerfully. The previously hidden raven in a clatter of blue-black wings tumbled onto rocks just above their now deserted resting place and with eyes that had kept watch in the hills for generations observed their departing backs.

Lichen-covered rocks gave way to a loose scree slope and forward movement ground almost to a standstill.

"We're going nowhere. Isn't there a better way?" Hanner's voice wailed from some metres behind.

"How about we try zigzaging? Might cover a lot more ground, but we won't skid around so much." And after a pause, "Are you ready?"

"If you say so."

"Cheer up, my lad; coming back we'll fly over this and you'll be wondering why it held us up for so long."

With no capacity to impose his will, or be creative in the face of difficulty, Hanner was consumed by floods of angry frustration and ungenerous thoughts held in check only by the knowledge he was being idiotic. In spite of the cooling breeze, effort and unreasonable passion steamed over his contact lenses and started dribbles of sweat along the length of his spine.

"Can you wait a bit? I can't see."

"Yup, sure; need help?"

"No, no. Just give me two minutes."

The shifting scree was not a comfortable place to rest, but compared with the lung-bursting ascent, it offered some momentary relief. In the slip and slide of ash, small particles ran over Hanner's shoes and trickled down into the cavities between his socks and inner soles. Repair to his white and blistered feet prolonged the delay. Above him, Barton stayed warm by moving further up the steep slope.

"How're you doing?" He shouted back through the increasingly thin air.

"Almost done."

From the advantage of a protruding rock and greater height Barton watched his companion fiddle with an elaborate rearrangement of equipment and was surprised to see how far his friend's hair had receded. Lank strands stuck together by perspiration left more pale skull visible than he remembered. Had middle age dawned before adulthood had been convincingly claimed?

To his moody friend the confident silhouette above and its floating mane of curling hair looked like a raiding Norseman standing astride a headland.

"Born for pillage and rape," he muttered through his labouring breath and clenched teeth.

"What's that?"

"I think I'm holding you back."

Hanner lurched several paces forward and Barton, chest down on his rocky outcrop, leant forward to grasp the younger man's rigid and protesting shoulders, in a handful of jacket.

"Hey! Up you come. This is a team outing and we go together, or not at all."

"Is that a polite way of telling me to shape up?"

"Come on, John, don't be such an arsehole. In your next breath you'll be telling me it's going to rain."

"It probably will, or rather snow."

"There now, don't you see how dumb you sound? We're out here to have a good time, not to convince ourselves this is a miserable experience. Just look at the mountain, doesn't it excite you?"

"Scares me more like. So where do we go from here?" The reply was more an accusation than response to a question."

Wind kept the rocks on which they stood, and next the kilometre of rising ground above, dry and clear of snow. Beyond, and seemingly impervious to wild weather, a high virgin-white dome rose sparkling in the air.

"There's no adventure without knowing we risked a bit and went as far as we could. Look, if the snow up there is hard packed we'll be okay, but if it's fresh we'll probably need to go along that line where it meets the rock face."

Over the years of fitfully shared climbs little had happened to bring them really close together; the best they could say was their partnership hadn't fallen apart. After each hike they went their several ways for weeks and sometimes months at a time until Barton, in his inevitable role of initiator, called, and a new mountain outing was planned. Hanner recognised he was in an unequal alliance that bore the familiarity of a jaded marriage, including its borderline disrespect. No longer holding any expectations they tolerated behaviour in the other, which would have shipwrecked a younger association. But seeking a better alternative called for more resolve than either was presently prepared to give. Why terminate something that functioned after a fashion and which could be followed by something less rewarding? Even among intelligent people inertia had compensations.

But, while laziness was easily admitted, it hid greater flaws of character.

Barton's natural cleverness and indolence made him both arrogant and scornful, although he accepted the adulation of minor players almost as a birthright. In stark contrast, Hanner's ineptitude and poverty of spirit had fashioned a slavish, but envious follower, who, at the very most, deserved only tolerance.

But Barton did at times wonder why Hanner had become so chronically ill at ease. Maybe the roots lay in an unsatisfactory childhood or family failings. Hanner's parents, he had heard, although not divorced, lived in near total disharmony and separate parts of a family home. Shorn of the means and the will to part, their indecision, Barton speculated, had been passed to their son and had bred bitter contrariness and malice. From being angry and unsympathetic to his parents, Hanner, by extension, had became disobliging with anyone who crossed his path, including those supposedly closest to him.

What a contrast to Barton's upbringing. He had reached adulthood at peace with himself and totally unconscious of the emotional riches heaped on him by a loving mother and a gentle and indulgent father. No millstone weight of neglect, or inadequacy hung around his neck.

The raven from lower down the valley swept into sudden view and circled inquisitively overhead. Picking up a stone Hanner hurled it roughly at the bird.

"Not impressed by the glories of nature today," mocked Barton.

"They're unlucky."

"You're thinking of magpies."

"No difference; they both eat carrion."

"All you have to do is find the pair and then, if you want, you can feel better."

Why did Hanner feel knotted in discomfort after every verbal exchange? Was it the clumsiness of his conversation, or the bluff and self-confident responses it provoked? Did Barton have any idea he always appeared to close a discussion and leave his so-called friend put-down and put out? Hanner was as widely read and knew as much about raven folk-stories as his companion, so why had he again contrived to feel driven from the field?

In the undefined distance, a growl of thunder rattled the afternoon hush, as if prowling tigers disputed territory among the farther hills. Barton again urged the party forward.

On the threshold of space, the intensity of colour startled. As they climbed higher, the dark blue sky above inched towards black, while, round about, snow gleamed whiter than an Easter altar cloth. Through one and rebounding from the other, the sun's rays pierced and scorched unhindered.

Ahead, the beckoning ice dome hid from view the now not so distant summit. If either had been worried about the rising ground's difficulty, their concerns were dispelled at the first footfall. Hard packed ice and a recent light covering of soft snow offered firm and easy walking.

"This looks a lot better than I expected."

"I doubt you spent any time thinking about what was up here."

Engrossed in the surrounding beauty, Barton did not notice still less respond to another tart remark.

"God! What a place; we, none of us, deserve this privilege."

"I suggest we get on and save romanticism for later," said Hanner snatching at an opportunity to call the climb to order and take brief, but ungracious responsibility for the party's progress.

"Huh? Oh sure, got carried away again! But just look down there will you?"

Trees and the lower parts of the scree slope had disappeared in rolling, water-laden cloud.

"That'll overtake us before we reach the top."

"Maybe, maybe not. Look at their crests, the sun's burning them off as fast as they form."

"So why can't we see the pines any more?"

The question was a fair one, but turning excitement into a problem threatening the expedition's success was an odd way to gain pleasure. Was being right, Barton wondered, more important than being safe? He imagined Hanner trapped in a burning house with the rafters falling about his ears saying, "There, didn't I tell you I could smell smoke." The thought prompted a burst of laughter.

"And what's so bloody funny now? Do you like the idea of being on a mountain top in a blizzard?"

"If I'd had the gratification of announcing it on TV in advance, perhaps I would," smiled Barton. "But I can think of less satisfying ways to die."

"Sometimes I think you're several beers short of a picnic."

At the front again, Barton stopped.

The clean rim of the dome curving away from them was so precise, so absolute in definition that the other side could contain eternity, or gaping hell; it was open to anyone's imagination.

"This is the place to get life in perspective. Think of everyone down below. What are they doing? If I were in charge I'd make the ascent of a mountain compulsory education for anyone over sixteen."

"Compulsory anything is stupid. If this," he flapped an arm in the direction of the way ahead, "has any real value you just have to show people and they can make up their own minds."

"Yep, I'll agree to that; horses to water as it were."

Acknowledgement that he had said something modestly worthwhile was balm on Hanner's prickly soul and for a while his angular retorts dried up like pools of melted snow under a blazing sun.

"Do you see that over there?"

Looking across Barton's wide frame Hanner pointed to a black clump apparently sitting on the upper edge of the white dome. As they advanced along the gradually less precipitous slope the clump grew bigger until it filled the sky in the same manner as the snow slope had from lower down the mountain.

"Jesus Almighty!"

Appearing to be at no greater distance than a short walk and an even briefer climb over the snow, a vast granite summit rose into sight. A small triangle of shadow slid slowly down one side of the upper rock face as the sun wheeled in a great cosmic arc over the peak. An awe-struck pause was interrupted by Hanner's niggling practicality.

"If we're not done in forty-five minutes we should back off."

"After we've come so far? I don't know about you, but I'm going all the way," shouted Barton as he broke into a run.

Two hundred meters further on Hanner caught up. Barton was standing where the dome ended and a snow bridge connected to the granite face of the peak. On either side of the bridge there was nothing but empty space. Far below several birds rode effortlessly on rising currents of air.

"Is that safe?" asked Hanner, his voice a little harsher than usual. "I don't see anything supporting it."

"Don't know until we try," his partner responded taking a step forward.

"Hang on! Let's think this through."

"Not much to think about except either we go on, or go back. Are you ready?"

"But....we should have brought a rope."

"We didn't. Here goes."

Placing one foot on the bridge Barton tentatively brought his weight forward. Inhaling deeply he swung his second leg round and set out as if he was going to a nearby supermarket for groceries. The dome and rock were no more than fifteen long strides apart and Hanner watched open mouthed as his companion stepped out over the void.

On the far side and well clear of snow Barton raised his arms aloft and cried "Yes! Yes!" as if scoring a goal to earn his football team a famous victory.

"Now! Your turn," he called back.

"Mother of God in Heaven!" was the anguished but non-committal reply.

In his turn Hanner edged onto the bridge and nervously planted his foot where the other had already trod. But then he drew back.

"What's the matter?"

"Matter? I'm shit scared that's the matter."

"Think of the story you'll have this time. There'll be free dinners for months."

"Not much value to a grease stain on a rock at sea level."

"Come on man, where's your stomach?"

Thus goaded, Hanner eased onto the bridge again. He thought he could hear in the emptiness below the cool up-rush of air singing through birds' wings. With mouth dry and palms cold and wet he moved sideways across the yawning gulf, thinking this inelegant posture gave the best advantage, should the need arise, for a sudden run in either direction. While he watched in horror several icy chunks the size of children's fists fell away from the bridge's edge and whistled into the void below. For the second time a rough hand caught him by a trembling shoulder and pulled him onto the rock's firm surface.

"Ha! Why, there you have it! Fifteen minutes to the top and then straight down to the largest beer you've ever clapped eyes on."

"For Christ's sake have we got to go back over that?"

"Adrenalin will make you float across."

Unnoticed the pursuing clouds had raced over the forest and scree and were now massed in billows all over the southern sky. Fluffy tops once white under the noonday sun frowned grimly and began shedding ice-cold rain in sharp stinging needles.

"Let's go back."

"Not on your life! Leave the bags; we can pick them up later." Scrambling and breathing hard, Barton set off again and was soon well ahead.

Hidden somewhere beneath Hannar's rioting nerves, the blind mole of free will still had a home. But in the face of so much strength it lay in the darkness, timid and afraid. He wanted desperately to be first at something, anything, even to the top of a climb, or an event as unexceptional as standing up at a social gathering to take his leave before anyone else. He recollected a teenager's misery of being trapped at parties and unable to say goodbye despite having ached to go for hours. The memory of an embarrassed host, wondering what was required to bring the evening to a conclusion, and the shame almost made him weep with self-pity.

A rattle of loosened granite pieces sounded some way ahead, followed by an agonisingly long interval and then from further away than he had anticipated, another unmistakable shout of triumph. Mist now shrouded the heights above and lapped around in cold, dripping curtains. The wet vapour distorted distance and he could no longer decide with any accuracy where Barton and the summit might be.

He raised his voice and realised it sounded full of the sagging spirits that were starting to overwhelm him.

"Hey! Are you there?" But no movement or sound disturbed the blanket of cloud, save for the lonely noises of grumbling wind and the thrash of squalling rain on stone.

Visibility had shrunk to a few meters and the icy dome behind disappeared from sight. Choices too seemed to be diminishing and Hanner, in the midst of mounting anxiety turned to right and left. Unbalanced questions, like those conceived in a fever, surfaced through his agitation. For safety, should he stay where he was and wait for the returning and all-conquering Barton? Or was pushing his pounding heart down from his throat and mounting the obscured boulders above a braver alternative?

The surrounding flags were as greasy and slippery as stones under a waterfall and his clutching fingers shook with cold. Handholds in the smooth and unforgiving rock seemed to be getting fewer and fewer. But whatever uncertainties lay above they did contain Barton's breath-taking confidence. He felt desperate and ready to bolt, but to the rear lay the perilous snow bridge and wild stallions wouldn't drag him back to that frightening place alone. Hanner drew a chilled and shaking breath and inched in the direction of where he thought the victorious shout had sounded. Staggering upward he wondered if his bearings were right. Was the call from straight above or to one side? What if Barton passed him in the shrouding mists? They might walk by each other and not even know. Being separated this far up with night approaching was a thought too dreadful for his suffering mind to contemplate.

Just fifteen minutes, Barton had said, would be enough to take them to the top, but in the fumble and worry fifteen turned into twenty and then thirty and still black boulders streaming with water towered above. One more rest, he thought, and a final push must carry him through. He rounded a massive granite slab and emerged onto the summit through gusts of horizontally driven wind and rain.

"Arrk!"

"Hello, mate. I thought you'd abandoned me to my fate."

On his back in a narrow break in the rocks Barton lay shielded from icy blasts sweeping out of the invisible sky. His face and satisfied smile framed by outstretched legs and boots were dimly visible in the rocky hollow and worsening light.

"Is this the top?"

"It surely is. I've walked all the way round and there is nowhere to go from here except down."

"This must be higher over here," said Hanner leaning into the now howling wind and standing on a jutting boulder.

"Well I haven't been over the stones measuring the millimetres one by one, but in general terms I'd say we were, to all intents and purposes, as near the top as we are going to get on this trip."

"Can I get in there with you?" Hanner's teeth had started to rattle and the intense cold turned his hands blue.

Barton half rolled onto one elbow.

"Christ!" he said, "You look panned. We'd better set off again as soon as you've rested."

The comparative warmth of the tiny cave and proximity of another body comforted Hanner and his eyelids drooped with exhaustion. Sleep full of wild dreams came swiftly, but lasted no more than several seconds. Though protected from rushing wind the cold crept into his limbs and hips wherever they touched the rock surface.

"This is hell," he cried with sudden and unexpected feeling.

"I'm ready to go," replied Barton and he began sliding forward from the hole into the newly ferocious gale. Once upright he thrust a gloved hand back into the gloom to pull his reluctant companion out by the wrist.

From no direction that either climber could readily discern a loud crack reverberated through the air, as if a giant tree felled in the forest had dragged all in its path to chaotic destruction. Echoes boomed from mountain to mountain and then dropped by slow-stepping degrees to a whisper spreading out in ever widening circles until the whole mountain range was engulfed. The ground shook and for a moment the wind appeared to pause. Earth and sky and everything between took breath and listened.

"What in the name of all that's holy, was that?" shrieked Hanner.

"Something pretty big."

The Snow Bridge and Other Stories   11

"Thanks a lot. I feel totally reassured."

There was little point in starting another argument if they were to descend successfully before day's end. Later, maybe, would be the time to remind Hanner that individuals had a duty to the team as well as the team to individuals.

Trembling sounds, beating almost in rhythm, faded further and further away as if retreating to underground caverns beneath the mountains. Returning rain scythed on the wind and drove the two men from the summit. Unusually and in unnatural haste, Hanner led the way and under the influences of fear and gravity fell as much as jumped from one slippery stone to the next. His hands were raw and the sinews around his knees and ankles screamed in pain in the stumbled downward passage. He strained for sight of the white dome below, but the swirling clouds blocked even the briefest glimpse. The tightening grip of fear strangled his ability to act coherently.

"I think you're off track," Barton's measured voice called from above and through the wind's din.

"What! We can't be!"

"You're drifted off to the left and the rock is sheer below here. We need to circle back again. Don't go down any more; cross round."

"No, you're wrong. I'm going to keep going."

"John, listen to me. Wait for the mist to lift a bit…see…over there…that outcrop was a long way to our right as we went up. Can you hear me?" he shouted through the raging gale, "It's still to our right. We should be on the other side."

"I'm not going."

"Just stay put. I'll check it out and come back for you."

Indecision and, on its heels, a desperate desire for a stronger hand to take control surged through Hanner's fragmenting mind.

"No, we must stay together. I can't see anything. Which way…?"

The slopes grew steeper and neither could walk as before, so they turned instead to face the mountain and used hands and feet to edge cautiously around the precipitous wall. Hanner determined not to be abandoned for a second time and trod on Barton's heels and in his footsteps before streaming rains had time to fill the marks. Momentary leadership once surrendered vanished together with his rebellion in the gusts of cutting wind.

"Over there! Do you see?"

"I can't see anything. Just get us out of here."

"Look!"

A momentary break in the twisting and gusting cloud exposed several hundred feet below and away to the left, now that they were facing the mountain, the ice dome over which they had laboured only hours – but seemingly a lifetime – ago. Confirmation that they had rediscovered their earlier route threw Hanner's distress into the hurricane and for the briefest of intervals he regained a semblance of composure.

"I'll race you."

"Hold on now, we still have work to do."

Tumbling downward with an eagerness bordering on exhilaration Hanner bounded to the edge of the summit mass on a level with the far edge of the white dome. For the barest second he felt as good and satisfied as if he had been greeted by the warm comfort of a blazing log fire and hot food in a village pub far below the mountain. But the moment was short.

"Where's the bridge?"

"Somewhere about here if I'm not mistaken. See there are our bags."

An awful realization like an avalanche swept over Hanner.

"That noise! The one we heard higher up. It was the bridge; it's collapsed."

Barton nodded, "You may be right."

"You idiot! You raving moron. I told you we should have gone back, but no, you wouldn't listen to me, you won't listen to anyone, you just keep going until we land in trouble. Now what are you going to do, eh? How are you going to spirit us out of this disaster?"

"I would say the first thing we must do is keep our heads. Are you up to that basic requirement?"

Wiping away tears of impotence and rage with the back of a chapped hand that was now both red and blue, Hanner had become a greater liability than the open chasm separating them from the long, but comparatively easy trek beyond.

"We are not going to get out of this. I warned you. How many times does it take?"

"But here I am and here you are. How to extricate ourselves is what we should be thinking about rather than yelling at each other. After this outing you're free to stay at home. I'm going to scout."

"If you're thinking of leaving me behind you're out of your mind."

"John you are the one not thinking straight. I'd like to believe you'll laugh at this a year from now."

Shuffling cautiously to the chasm's very lip, Barton peered down into the vast mist-shrouded space that smoked like a giant's ice bucket. What were the alternatives? They were hikers not real mountaineers and taking a route into the divide below would be sheer folly. To the left the ravine widened as the summit turned away and only a superman would contemplate a leap over that enormous emptiness. But to the right the remains of the snow bridge were intermittently visible. The whole middle section had disappeared leaving two small spurs on either side of the gulf. The gap was not so great, maybe six or seven feet. Didn't athletes jump twenty-five and more? Admittedly they had a long run-up and here, the best on offer, if you included the damaged spurs, was several strides. Friends at ground level might wonder why the fuss. But those clinging to a rock wall, with the elements crying like demented demons in their ears, could tell another story.

"Well! Well! What have you come up with?"

Cool reason, if it had ever been one of Hanner's qualities, appeared to have entirely deserted the human wreck grasping the rocks in the desperate embrace of bare cracked hands. Turning to look over his shoulder at Barton he appeared close to breakdown. To coax him into a desperate jump with those wildly rolling eyes would take more than a friend's persuasion, especially one as uncommitted as Barton.

"I think I've found the way, but will have to take a closer look. Just hang on there for a few minutes," he yelled to be heard above the screaming wind.

Circling again towards his left he counted out the estimated metres before lowering his body gently down to where he expected to find the near spur. Yes, there it was, just two steps further on, not a bad guess under the circumstances. But cloud descended again and hid the opposite side of the ravine and much of the remaining bridge. If the leap was really to be undertaken they'd have to wait for a break in the fog and dash onto the spur without hesitation. Practiced jumpers might well clear triple the distance, but at least they could see where they were going.

Lying flat on his belly again, Barton pulled his body forward inch by breathless inch to find more exactly the real length of the gap. The spur's end was firm, but rounded, which meant a jumper's take-off point was a foot, or a foot and a half back from the break. That translated into a five stride run and launch across the divide. In spite of himself he shuddered.

For an instant the driven mists parted and the opposite ice spur showed clearly. Rising on all fours Barton saw his earlier estimate was not far wrong. The gap was no more than six feet and if anything he had over-calculated. Yes, the route out was difficult, but open.

Slithering back over the broken snow bridge and black crags he found Hanner huddled to the mountain and caught in a kind of rocking motion as if to sooth away the horrors surrounding him.

"John, listen to me. There's a way out, but it will take some courage. Can you hear me?"

"I should never have listened to you. We will never get back. Ohh!"

"Stop that rubbish. We aren't equipped to stay here at this altitude and without shelter it's only a matter of time before we get hypothermia. We don't have a choice but to go on."

Grabbing Hanner's sleeve he pulled and dragged him first sideways and then downwards to the damaged snow bridge. Bundling him into a sitting position he held his companion of many hikes by the face and spoke straight at his eyes.

"This is the bridge. Only part of it has fallen. There's a space in the middle of six feet and we have to jump across."

Hanner pulled away, "No! Why? I can't."

"There's no choice. If we stay here waiting for something to turn up you won't see another sun rise."

"Why are you doing this to me?

"Here's what we'll do. You're going first and I'll follow. The clouds clear intermittently and when that happens I want you to run from here for five big paces and leap across. Come now; who was the star of our football team?"

With one hand under an elbow Barton yanked Hanner upright.

"Let go, will you!"

Without doing anything of the sort, Barton pulled his trembling companion upright until both their backs were flat against the rock wall.

"We'll try a practice run to get the feel and stop at four strides. Go...."

Clumsily in heavy walking boots they paced out the steps and skidded to a stop.

"Can we do it?"

"That's better, John! Of course we can. Lean on the mountain and as soon as I yell 'run' you go for it."

The wind had no one direction now and unexpected gusts tugged at their clothes, hair and their widely dissimilar strengths. From far below the gale-torn chasm seemed to reach up and pull them down into its irresistible grasp.

"Run! Run!"

Hanner's thoughts reeled between the awful leap and the empty abyss beneath his feet, but at the sudden shout he jerked as if woken from a dream. Lumbering forward for two uncertain steps he stopped. From the cauldron, mist rose all around to hide the hideous gapping tear in the mountain.

"I... can't...can't ..."

"Don't worry. It came too quickly. Let's watch again and this time I'll start you."

Grabbing both sleeves of Hanner's jacket from behind and with only his back to the mountain, Barton crouched as if on starting blocks.

"It's imposs..."

"Get your feet apart and look with me as far as you can into the fog. When the dome shows and I shout, we go. There's no coming back for you this time. Breathe hard!"

If a scaffold's trap fails to open at first pull the delay only doubles the final horror of a condemned man's plunge.

"We'll have to wait until..."

"Now, now, now!"

"Arrrrrr!"

The wet, writhing coils of fog split asunder, one half sucked down into the widening gully on the left and the other dragged skywards. A thin shaft of sunlight shot through the murk and sparkled on the white dome beyond the further spur. Without thought or discussion Barton propelled Hanner forward by the coat and on the count of five heaved him upwards across the narrow divide. With legs and arms wildly flailing and his screams piercing the clammy mist, Hanner arched untidily and noisily through the air.

The searching light from somewhere near the horizon went out as if a candle had been snuffed. Crashing onto hands and feet on the very end of the spur Hanner scrambled upright and on the same instant ran pell mell toward the ice dome's safety. The broken spur juddered behind him and a large piece of packed ice the size of a refrigerator broke away from the tip and fell with a gasp into the foggy shrouds. Clouds swept down and a cold, inhospitable embrace returned to the ravine.

"Can you hear me? John! John! Are you okay?"

Barton saw his partner stand and flee the damaged spur. But from the whipping rain and broken crags there was no response except the sounds of howling wind.

He needed another break in the weather to see exactly how far he'd have to jump. There were fewer clear periods now and the consequences of further delay did not bear thinking about. Fifteen minutes went by and then another twenty with still no lifting of the fog. Calls across the ravine went unheeded. Perhaps the clouds were settling in for the night? Lasting twelve hours in these temperatures and at this altitude was impossible. Numbness in his extremities was not a good sign and Barton resolved that while light lasted he would be ready to make the leap. He'd go on the first opening and dispense with a detailed examination, just run like hell at the first chance.

Concentrating on a point in the revolving gloom where a break needed to appear the unnatural shapes of mountain myths seemed to gather in the freezing clouds.

Without warning a sudden swirling downdraft broke to opposite ends of the ravine and opened a wide, clear view encompassing both parts of the snow bridge, the ice dome and the black rock face below.

"This is it," Barton said to himself and stood up. "The gap in the middle of the bridge looks about seven feet, but by Christ I can do it!"

Running...one...two...three...four...five! And....!

As he launched into the turning air mists streamed back from deep below. Seeing nothing he drew both legs to his chest to maximize the jump's length. Both knees struck the far ice spur and in a dreadful thud he tipped forward onto the side of his head. The bridge beneath him groaned and creaked and while still on bruised knees he crawled forward from a bright red stain on the snow's surface. Clear of the bridge he lay face down and lost consciousness.

Watching from beyond the rim of the sloping dome Hanner saw the leap, heard the impact of his companion's head on the ice and stayed still. Danger was past and nothing but a tiring ten-hour trek lay between him and their dawn starting-point at the bottom of the valley. There lay the person he had held in such awe all these years. The fallen man was no greater than any other and evidently quite as fallible; beaten down by the power of the mountain, while he, Hanner, had not only survived, but was about to return home triumphant. Taking a breath deeper than any he could remember he stood up and walked to the prostrate form. Scurries of driven snow were gathering on the back of Barton's bright blue jacket. A second red mark congealed where blood had run onto the ice. Taking hold of one arm Hanner pulled the collapsed figure onto its back; quite lifeless, like a broken puppet. Perhaps he's dead already? Kneeling down, Hanner placed an ear next to Barton's cold lips and as an after-thought searched for a pulse. He could hear and feel nothing. Taking a step backwards Hanner swung his foot heavily into Barton's lower ribs; once…bang, twice…bang, thrice…bang!

"Bastard! Bastard!" He shouted with his head thrown back, as if to make his angry cries cleave the clouds. For the first time in his memory he felt invincible.

Hanner bent down and tore open the clothing on the still body to expose cooling pale flesh to all the raging elements. From the dirty sky something, not quite ice, nor yet rain, began to fall. The gale's wind roared and Hanner, without a backward look, strode away downhill.

A story began to form in his mind as the long, waking night ticked relentlessly onward. Climbers got lost in the mountains all the time. He'd say he and his partner got separated near the summit and Barton had disappeared, which was not far short of the truth. Going straight to raise the alarm was hasty. Twenty-four hours without sleep and climbing a wind swept mountain would be a test of anyone and he didn't want to make too many slips when this outing was explained.

Campsites in the early hours are sleepy places and no one was about as Hanner slipped unobserved into the two-man tent. Over his fully-clothed and aching body he dragged the luxury of an additional, unclaimed blanket and fell asleep.

Waking in mid afternoon he took a cautious look outside. Campers, except for a couple of children playing down near the river, seemed to be out, probably hiking or climbing. He moved rapidly to the nearby lane where to any casual observer he would appear to have just come down from the mountains. The search and rescue people had a place just on the edge of the village and he'd report Barton's 'disappearance' as if just returning from a climb.

Dry stone walls edged the lane and cattle grazed in the lush water meadows. On a gatepost a raven with small glistening eyes watched Hanner pass. The bird gave a hoarse call and, bounding into glided flight, sailed effortlessly towards the riverbank. Hanner stooped to look for a stone, but when he raised his arm the target had disappeared.

At the search and rescue outpost two men and a woman were unloading climbing equipment from a four-wheel drive vehicle caked in mud. They were dressed in the distinctive reds and yellows of mountain rescue teams. Pushing through the gate Hanner called across,

"I need help to find a missing hiker. Who do I tell?"

Glances were exchanged among the group and, breaking away, the woman beckoned to him to follow. She entered a wooden building and motioned to a seat.

"Give me some details. Your name first and who is lost."

"I'm John Hanner and my partner David Barton is missing."

The woman tapped a pen on her unmarked notebook and gave a tired smile.

"Come with me, please!" She rose and walked across the wet yard to a separate building with a red cross on the door.

"What do we do here?"

"A gentleman called Barton was picked up in the pine forest, not far from here. He was in pretty bad shape, but told us his climbing buddy, someone called John Hanner, was missing. I guess you'll be pleased to see him? In you go."

TWO

TURNING ROUND

In the auditing profession, where Wallace Pifflock earned a modest living, he was known as a 'senior.' Like many of his similarly titled associates he provided support to an accounting firm's partners, while being without – other than through many unimaginative and grinding years' service – any recognisable personal qualification. Seniors were stuck between bright young men and women, who saw themselves as potential boardroom members of major corporations from their day of joining the profession as articled clerks from university, and established practitioners of some quality. Seniors were consequently disdained by the former and derided by the latter.

The firm for which Wallace worked was a small and moderately prosperous partnership operating independently in the southern suburbs of London. Clients ranged from sole-proprietorship dry-cleaners to a single high-street department store. Most clients were located in the immediate vicinity, but some provided opportunities for journeys to as far away as Slough and, early in February following a financial year-end, Grays in Essex.

In his undemonstrative way, Wallace looked forward to half-yearly travel. Unruffled predictability and regularity suited him, but within the tiny circumference of those needs, and above all else, he enjoyed the fleeting pleasure of being left entirely alone. As a man of limited invention, the leisure pastimes he favoured during these occasional interludes were reading Agatha Christie novels and taking his dinner slowly in one of the few cafés to which he had become attached over several years of repeated visits. He was, for these brief spaces of time and to the extent permitted by stillborn aspiration, his own man.

Wallace's son and daughter were in their second and fourth year of secondary school. Sometimes, he felt having children as bright as those youngsters who came to work at the practice would be nice, but, he reflected rather sadly, for undistinguished parents, the production of exceptional offspring was not only unlikely, but also potentially disorientating.

The present adolescence of the Pifflock children was the single most trying time in Wallace's adulthood and if intellectual challenge had been added to the already incomprehensible emotional demands of young hormone-riddled bodies, the destruction of his peace of mind would have been absolute.

Irene, the elder of the two, who had been named after Mrs Pifflock's spinster sister, came home one Saturday afternoon shortly after her fourteenth birthday with a pierced tongue containing a silver stud. Both senior Pifflocks regarded this as a calamitous development. The reduction of their already inarticulate teenage daughter to mumbling incoherence through temporary infection was acutely embarrassing. Not that the Pifflock's had a wide social circle to observe this youthful indiscretion. But lower-middle class values were undoubtedly offended. A female child dressed in nearly universal black from calf length boots to the tips of waxed hair was bad enough, but having her speak with the inflections of a troglodyte was doubly dismaying. What, bewailed Mrs Pifflock in the timeless prose of her antecedents, would the neighbours say? And from a distance Wallace could not help but agree.

Irene's brother George, although two years younger, encountered the first traumas of growing up at almost exactly the same time. He was not openly rebellious in quite the same way as his sister, but had, in the last year, as companion to acne, become sour and surly and spent every conceivable free minute and many that were not, stretched out on the Pifflock living-room settee. His principal activity was confined to one thumb's operation of a remote control. None of the television channels through which he continually surfed held his stunted attention span for more than an uninterested few seconds. Getting up in the morning took several calls from an agitated mother and going to bed at night the repeated directives from a weak and irresolute father. Wallace hated the moments when he had to bring authority to bear. Too often, people, especially his children, had a way of dragging him out of his hermetically sealed privacy into the harsh light of day.

Both Irene and George performed indifferently at school and – in classes of twenty-five – Wallace admitted to some relief when they ranked twentieth, or twenty-first. If they were engaged in the football league, he thought ruefully, relegation would be escaped by a hair's breadth. Their narrow avoidance of outright failure enabled him to postpone remedial decisions for another year and, if luck held, for as long as it took to complete compulsory education and get into paid employment. But what sort of work would that be, when they lacked any sort of skill or initiative? The problem, which bore down on Wallace like an unsatisfied creditor fobbed off for too long with promises of payment by post, threatened to bankrupt his treasured and diminished moments of calm.

Late one Thursday evening after an undistinguished meal in Grays, Wallace sat at a window seat of one of his preferred cafés. Condensation ran down the panes in front of him and gathered in small pools along the wooden sill. On the table beside his plate, an open, but half-read paperback was turned face down at the place where he had stopped reading. Unthinkingly, Wallace pressed a finger against the spot on the sill where water had collected. His fingernail sank through sodden wood flakes covered by thin yellow paint and the tiny pool on the sill disappeared into a decayed brown opening. Toward the end of this week's travel, Wallace found, with some annoyance, he was spending an increased amount of time thinking about his children and Mrs Pifflock. The thoughts were not those of a man keen to return to his family, but rather ones that crowded in with nagging, unresolved foreboding.

Mrs Pifflock was a simple woman with no conversation, who ran a home in a manner similar to the way Wallace performed his auditing. By any definition, both husband and wife were less than averagely competent. Charlotte Pifflock had never worked outside the home. From the day of marrying Wallace and without considering alternatives, she assumed her task was to keep house. She cleaned and cooked, not with enthusiasm, creativity, or indeed to take care of loved ones, but because it was an allotted task. Her culinary range covered about eight main dishes and a smaller number of puddings. Vegetables were invariably boiled, some would say for too long and meat inevitably grilled. In the years they had been together Wallace had probably consumed a home meal of grilled meat and two vegetables several thousand times. There was a plain uniformity of colour and content in Charlotte's menus that found echoes in those her husband sought in Grays' and Slough's cafés.

Wallace scrapped the inside of his dessert bowl to make sure the last trace of custard had been collected.

"And how will you be ending tonight, Mr Pifflock? Would there be anything to follow?"

The question was redundant, because in the whole of Wallace's adult life he had never ended an evening meal, either at home, or on his travels, without a cup of strong, brown tea.

"Yes," he said slowly, as if carefully considering a wide number of options, "I believe I'd like a cup of tea if you would be so kind."

Through the clouded window, Wallace discerned dark human shapes moving about in the evening gloom. Winter was not an attractive time of year in Grays. The hunched and formless people in the streets seemed to be there reluctantly and ready to retreat behind private doors, which, as soon as the opportunity occurred, would be slammed shut on an intrusive and inhospitable world.

Wallace stared into the thick contents of his cup. Four or five leaf particles swirled on the surface in eddies created by the circling spoon. He was not given to philosophy, but, for a moment, he could see himself as a tea leaf, unwillingly snatched by rough labouring hands from its place under the sun in the steaming highlands of Kenya, or Assam, to float meaninglessly on an unfamiliar element.

Across the street some lights went out and a green-grocer's shop closed with a noisy rush of shutters.

By late tomorrow afternoon, he would be packing up and going back to Mrs Pifflock. Fishing would be a nice way to spend the weekend to prolong illusions of tranquillity, but he hadn't had the rods out in years and wasn't altogether certain of their whereabouts. Besides, if he announced over breakfast a desire to visit the reservoirs, he would provoke incredulity and a view that his post was being unacceptably deserted. In suburbia on Saturdays residents were expected to wash the car, or weed flowerbeds, and any form of self-indulgence was counted a deadly sin. Drab and monotonous conformity was the wheel to which every commuter was lashed. Showing off was even worse than private pleasure and expressions of individualism, whether in dress or behaviour, was akin to being socially deviant.

Wallace sighed and took a long, uncomfortable gulp of tea almost too hot for his constricted throat.

"Shall I get your bill?"

"Thank you, yes."

The price, despite inflation, had been unchanged throughout his last four visits and if Wallace had wished, he could, without further thought, have dropped the exact notes and coins on the plastic tablecloth and left with his travel-stained raincoat cast around his shoulders. But the small ceremony of receiving the bill, checking the addition and counting out money with a little extra for service, was the way he liked to conclude his evening visit. The discipline of professional standards always required deliberation. Watching the middle-aged waitress with bad feet pick up the plate and limp painfully to the cashier was a ritual as essential as drinking the regulation cup of unappetizing and scalding tea.

"Will we be seeing you again next week, Mr Pifflock?"

"Quite likely, yes. I have one more week in Grays, Mrs Dilworth; prior to midyear, that is to say."

The homeward journey on Friday, by a combination of railway, underground and finally bus and foot, would usually take two and a half hours. Only at the end of a week did Wallace allow himself the minor liberty of leaving work at six o'clock. This, by his definition, was early and he was quite oblivious to the restless fidgeting of an articled assistant who ached to start his weekend. Slightly after the hour, Wallace leant back in his chair and put the top on a fountain pen given by the firm's senior partner for fifteen, faithful years' service.

"Well, I think…"

Before the sentence was complete, or the pen back in its customary left inside pocket the assistant had sprung from his seat as if propelled by explosive, closed the black audit bag with a snap and taken one stride towards the door.

"See you on Monday, Mr P."

"Yes, and please come directly without calling in at home office. I shall be here on the dot of eight thirty."

The assistant pursed his lips. He was being pressed against his will into Wallace's unthinking and inflexible routine. These dreary seniors didn't comprehend young people lived quite differently. Work was okay, but it was a means to the end of living a life of one's choice.

The door banged with nothing further being said. But an irritating and vaguely unpleasant ambiguity clung to Wallace's consciousness, like the hard-to-dispel aroma from a pot of boiled cauliflower left hanging in the air. Exactly at what time on Monday would his assistant arrive, he wondered?

Wallace picked up his briefcase and small holdall containing two changes of tie and soiled underwear, turned out the light and walked slowly along an already darkened corridor to a lift. On the ground floor, except for a seated security guard surrounded by an array of closed circuit television screens, the building appeared empty.

"'Night, sir."

"Good night."

Grays was not far from the river and the cold, damp air smelt of distant marshland. Wallace sniffed cautiously; his nose felt stuffy. Perhaps he had a cold coming on. He was feeling more morose than usual and not in a rush to go. At most he had three hours left before being expected home. Mrs Pifflock knew he would be late after a week away and would have something hot, if not particularly appetising, waiting for him in the oven. Whatever it was lying protected from complete dehydration under a saucepan lid remained to be seen, but inevitably it was part of Irene's and George's earlier dinner. The more pleasurable alternative of a separate, freshly-cooked meal did not for one second occur to Charlotte Pifflock.

The railway station was ten minutes walk away and Wallace turned in its direction with one bag in each hand. Why, he wondered, did he carry a briefcase? The best answer to this sudden and uncharacteristic question was, that it performed the same role as a carpenter's belt, or an electrician's satchel, and confirmed to those who might be interested that the owner had a place in the world, if not a particularly exalted one. But why, he asked, should those seeking total anonymity require anything that bestowed even a modest degree of identification? The absence of anything of professional significance inside the case reinforced its utter irrelevance.

The items lugged across London's underground system at some inconvenience consisted of the neatly folded Monday edition of the *Daily Telegraph* opened at the crossword page, several domestic bills collected in a plastic folder to pay at month's end and, to add force to his serious intention to shake George out of his pubescent lethargy, a brochure from an adventure school in north Wales. But each document cried out in reproof.

Late on Thursday he had sought to make excusable his so far disappointing performance of completing just a quarter of the crossword by 'week's end', by adding to that imprecise definition the time to travel home and some patches of Sunday when he would escape to the privacy of his bathroom, if not the reservoir. But later, troubled by semantic wriggling, he decided to write off his few days' abortive labours as yet another under-achievement.

Lower down in the bag, under the newspaper and another Hercule Poirot adventure, and at a depth he had no immediate wish to explore, further vacillation and indecision lurked accusingly in the express-delivered, but still unread brochure and the quantity of long overdue invoices.

Placing his briefcase and holdall at his feet on the kerbside Wallace took out a handkerchief, folded as painstakingly as the newspaper, and dabbed his nose. The cold seemed to have acquired some momentum in the chill breeze, which blew through the high street and stirred up pieces of litter and other urban debris. He looked around for relief from both the incipient cold and the encroachment of melancholy inevitability.

Traffic had dwindled to a trickle and only the Punjabi tobacconist on the corner and the dimly lit King's Arms opposite appeared to be open. Despite the overwhelming shabbiness, Wallace, in so far as he took pleasure in anything, enjoyed Grays. He liked to step away from truculent offspring and a tedious wife and find solace in self-containment. Without making any demands, Grays had given him exactly what he found most comforting.

In the pervasive gloom, an unnatural and subversive thought began forming in his stiff and resistant mind; he'd go home when he was ready and in the meantime, dammit, or at least for the next three hours, he'd do just as he pleased. Riotous behaviour to those without prior experience, or, who through neglect had lost the capacity, did not come easily. For a man with the former ability to jump six feet with comparative ease, returning after a long layoff was, in the best situation, likely to prove disappointing and in the worst, injurious. But despite the risk, Wallace warmed to a solution that would ease nasal discomfort and retain a lingering grip on his present, modest freedom. Thus fortified he crossed the road and entered the King's Arms.

There was no knowing whether a pub in the centre of a somnolent town would generate traffic likely to make Wallace's break with tradition worthwhile. At this comparatively early hour on a Friday evening in Grays, the indications were not encouraging. In one corner of the saloon bar a seated pensioner, with bony freckled hands, pressed a walking-stick firmly but pointlessly into the floorboards. With a fixed gaze he stared grimly over the top of a pint of Guinness as if carved from wax and placed there to give the appearance of regular custom. At the other end of the room, two middle-aged women in headscarves, with plastic supermarket bags under their table, chatted noisily. Not what could be called a clientele bubbling with excitement and gaiety, Wallace thought to himself, but under the circumstances, safety and anonymity was just what he wanted.

Behind the bar a woman of about forty in a heavy wool sweater hung glasses on an overhead wooden rack. Wallace didn't generally admit to noticing these things, but tonight he remarked to himself what a very full breast the barmaid had. In fact, it was quite comely.

"Yes, love, what'll it be?" she said, tugging the riding sweater back to her waist.

Lifting his eyes to the woman's face, Wallace hesitated, somewhat disturbed by the ready smile. He rarely consumed alcohol, and on the few occasions of persuasion, his susceptible stomach had been considerably upset.

"Oh... a small whisky would be fine."

"And how would you like it? With something, or straight?"

"I thought, ah, er, perhaps with some fresh lemon?"

"You sound as though you're sickening for something, dear."

"Yes, a cold, I think..."

Wallace couldn't exactly remember when he last willingly walked into a public house. These places were not part of his natural habitat and when colleagues half-heartedly invited him to join them for after-work refreshment he was quick to decline, with mumbled responses of, "Sorry; must be getting home...another time may be." Compulsory sociability, he had instinctively decided, was not in the least bit pleasant. But today the utter ghastliness of his domestic environment prepared the way for a change of mind.

The barmaid went off to serve another round to the two shoppers near the far end of the bar. Banter passed between them and rough laughter reverberated over the clink of glasses. The pensioner moved for the first time and stretched out a knotty claw towards his glass. He looked at Wallace, perched stiffly on a barstool as close to the wall as it was possible to get. The posture looked almost defensive as if taken up in anticipation of an imminent invasion by Temperance Society adherents beating drums and proclaiming against the devil and all his works. Or was Wallace perhaps guiltily picturing an entrance by the vapid and unaccomplished Mrs Pifflock?

"It's all right again, then."

"...What?"

"I said it's all right, again," repeated the pensioner in a raised treble.

"What? What is?"

"Now, now, Mr T. Some people don't come in for conversation, so you leave them be." The barmaid had reappeared and, turning to the confused Wallace, said, "Don't mind him. He's a regular...talking about the weather."

"Oh, oh... I see."

She called in a voice loud enough to overcome Mr T's deafness, "Are you going to nurse that one all night, or are you ready for another?"

"One more ...Liz," grumbled the pensioner like a dog whipped for disobedience.

Standing not more than two feet away from Wallace, Liz again reached towards the rack to take down a pint glass. He sat quite still and appreciated a second close view of the ample breast inside the wool sweater. The night was not as cold as it had been and he undid the three buttons of his raincoat.

"Are you from round here?"

"No...no I'm not. Just visiting Black's up the street...but I come to town quite often."

"Work there do you? I haven't seen you in here before."

"Yes, well, twice a year that is…I'm an auditor. But I'm not usually around in the evenings."

"Sounds a bit boring. Is it like my job, just counting money all the time to give away to the government?" The woman added with another smile.

"Some might think so," replied Wallace a little awkwardly. He didn't like his livelihood, however boring it might seem, being mocked. "But, of course, our real purpose is to ensure compliance with statutory guidelines."

"Just joking, dear. Don't get bothered."

Liz took a glass of stout across to the pensioner and could be heard chiding him in a motherly tone. That's what good barmaids do, he reflected. In addition to taking cash, they keep customers happy and free from whatever ails them in the world outside. The poor old fellow probably lived with a busy daughter-in-law who was happy to see him out of the house for a couple of hours. A visit to the Kings Arm's would be a relief for both of them.

Back behind the bar, Liz wrote something on a piece of paper.

She'll be keeping a tab, thought Wallace, quietly priding himself on acute observation of financial transactions.

"Live far away do you?"

"South London…Balham actually."

"Got family over there, then?"

"Yes. Two children, a boy and a girl." He could not immediately explain why Mrs Pifflock was omitted from his reply. "And you?"

"I've got a son, but he's far away. Charity work he tells me; in Sierra Leone wherever that is."

For a few brief seconds Wallace felt a totally unexpected and mysterious sense of disappointment. That this barmaid, to whom he'd been speaking for no more than an intermittent ten minutes, was spoken for was a source of sudden, but quite distinct, regret. For the steady, methodical auditor, the realisation that he was not just a creature of form and habit came as a sudden shock.

"…and… your husband? He found himself enquiring.

"Oh, him. He might just as well be in Sierra Leone, or anywhere else as far away."

"I see…not getting on too well?"

The directness and effortlessness of his question startled Wallace more than the woman to whom it was addressed. He was not in the habit of chatting-up bar girls, or any other women for that matter. An interest in the opposite sex had been confined to his bachelor years when he had felt a prompting, not too dissimilar from the itch of chaffed skin. Since marriage and the birth of the two children, the necessity to scratch had fallen away and was now satisfied by just seven or eight more or less joyless minutes with Mrs Pifflock every third Saturday night. He did to his credit acknowledge a special effort was required on wedding anniversaries and birthdays, even if they fell during the week. But, like so much in his life, this routine was the consequence of obligation rather than definable red-blooded desire.

The King's Arms barmaid wiped the counter slowly and looked at Wallace for a few seconds, trying to make up her mind which category of flirt he fell into. Was he a slick-talking predator with a simple bedding objective? No, not if the faltering conversation was anything to go by. Was he experiencing a mid-life crisis and likely to write letters baring his soul from distant Balham? That was a greater possibility, but more likely he was just a sad and harmless man for whom intimacy stretched no further than the warmth and comfort of a homely female presence.

"Shouldn't you be getting back to Balham?" she said, not unkindly.

"No one is expecting me until late."

The glass he was holding was empty, except for a thin sliver of lemon stuck to one side.

"'Night, Liz. See you next Friday," called one of the two women from across the room. "Got to cook supper for hisself, or he'll think I've run off with a sailor." The same earlier laughter shrilled and faded as the frosted glass door swung to with a spongy thump.

"I think it's helping the cold. Another would be good."

Removing his raincoat Wallace laid it neatly on the next stool. Customers came and went. By nine the crowd was quite dense and a noise of relaxed and friendly conversation rose and fell. A parlour's fug settled over the bar and reminded him of evenings when, not yet a teenager, he and many other members of a now estranged family gathered at his grandparents' place in Sussex.

He thought of his cousins, the two Solway brothers, who his mother once said were wild and bound to end up badly. When he last heard of them, Joe, the elder, was a pilot working for a charter company in the South Pacific and Ted had joined a film producer working on location in Trinidad. If that was where wildness carried people it didn't seem to be particularly harmful.

A man in his late fifties, presumably a landlord living over the pub, joined Liz behind the bar, to help with late customers coming in from cinemas and bingo halls. Wallace didn't like the look of him. He had a fleshy face sweating more than the night's temperature warranted. A few strands of hair lay in wet points on his forehead and several chins shook when he spoke. Wallace especially didn't like the way he edged up to Liz when she was at the till and placed a hand on her hip.

The clientele drifting in was of varied ages and dispositions. Between slow sips, Wallace watched the random and unexceptional gathering. Were they all as ordinary as they looked? At the end of the road would any of them remember a name from this nondescript crowd? Where did one go to find a soldier of fortune capable of drawing listeners in around a camp fire by the wonder of the stories he had to tell?

He called above the din for a third whisky. Liz was some way off serving another customer, buying for a large noisy group seated round the table previously occupied by the two shoppers in headscarves. Apparent inebriation was making a complicated order more difficult to communicate. Liz didn't hear Wallace, but the landlord was closer to hand.

"What's it going to be, Squire?"

I'm damned if I'm going to let that reptile pour for me, thought Wallace, and he settled sulkily back onto his stool.

"Are you done? I'll take the glass then."

"No," snapped Wallace, as if he'd been asked to cast his vote for a member of the Balham Communist Party. "I need it."

The landlord looked hard at him with round blue eyes set a little too closely together.

"Okay, okay…keep your shirt on."

Eventually Liz made her way back along the bar and Wallace got his glass refilled. As she counted the coins into the till the landlord slipped close to whisper something into her ear.

Bloody lecher, Wallace said to himself with feeling. The puffy hand was back on Liz's hip again and the landlord, as if reading Wallace's thoughts, looked back over the bar.

How can she stand letting that creep touch her?

Empty glasses began to accumulate along the bar top and Liz gathered four and sometimes five in each hand. As she passed by she murmured,

"Better make that one last if you want to stay. Guv'nor says you look like trouble and have had enough."

"What a totally silly remark, I'm as sober as he is and a good deal better behaved."

"Maybe you are, but I can't serve you any more."

"I'll stay as long as I damn well like."

"That's okay, but don't cause a scene."

Feelings of injustice, shame and anger combined to raise Wallace to a level of stifled fury he hadn't experienced since he was a boy in school and the brutish moron David Major had picked on him and provoked a fight. On that far off occasion Major accused him, as if he really cared, of taking a canteen seat belonging to an acolyte. Major was an infamous fourteen-year-old who, although accumulating grades provoking titters behind his back, held sway on football field and playground by rule of fist and boot. For the first time Wallace had felt truly victimised and alone and the lesson acquired then, along with a black eye and split lip, was that there were moments when inglorious retreat was sometimes a course to be recommended.

Under his jacket Wallace felt the vest he'd worn all week stick to his moistening skin. He wanted to jump onto the counter and kick over the pints and rain blows down on the head of that uncouth ruffian whose damp paw lay all too familiarly below Liz's waist. But instead he sat breathing heavily with waves of impotence rising under his collar.

Several stuttering intakes of saloon air tasting of stale beer and too many people packed into a small room did nothing to calm his irritation and for one not used to taking such liberties the remains of his whisky tot were thrown back far too rapidly. But, intent on leaving with as much dignity and sobriety as he could muster, he walked towards the exit with each foot placed firmly in front of the other as if negotiating a circus tightrope.

In the cold rush of night air carrying street dust in its grip Wallace felt both chilled and grimy. He gasped slightly and noticed he was less steady on his feet than usual. The last whisky lay uncomfortably on his stomach and seemed to be finding its way back into his throat.

Several aimless pedestrians clustered about on the pavement and talked in loud, coarse accents. Crossing the flow Wallace collided with a short youth who was wearing a woollen cap pulled down below his ears, and low-slung trousers into which his arms were thrust so deeply they hung as straight as boards.

"Watch it, dick-head!"

"I'm sorry. I..."

"'Ey, you pissed or sumink?"

"I didn't notice..."

"See 'im then?" the youth enquired of his loutish companions as if somehow an ill-mannered Wallace had barged through a nice family outing rather than into a bunch of vulgar ruffians.

The group passed on guffawing and swearing noisily and, with the obligations of gang membership, giving offence wherever they could. Wallace slumped onto the kerb edge with his briefcase under one elbow and his holdall under the other, and the greasy macintosh across his knees. The evening had taken a turn for the worse and was becoming quite painful. To make matters worse he was already overdue in Balham where blockishness from his son and daughter and indifference and ineptitude from Mrs Pifflock lay waiting. His entire existence suddenly seemed a towering waste of time.

And yet... and yet, hadn't he, for the space of half an evening until that unpleasant oaf from upstairs appeared at the till, enjoyed, albeit with several others, the company of a bar girl? Perhaps there was something, a small something, to look forward to beyond the spiral of daily ugliness.

A tiny flame of rebellion flickered in Wallace's frozen heart. From the cold pavement he could hear the hearty sounds of fellowship booming behind his back and he thought of the sterility of the Pifflock home. Dull, plodding responsibility was all he had been asked for and all he had known how to give. The feeling of disgruntlement was not new, but discovering he had always been truly unhappy was a seismic revelation. Sheltered from the gale's strongest winds, the candle's fire steadied and burnt in a straighter, taller light.

A lorry turned out of the yard at Black's several hundred yards along the road. Supplies were probably being delivered to a construction site somewhere on the edge of town. Huge mud-caked wheels passed within three feet of Wallace's bowed head and dark exhaust fumes and flakes from the turning wheels swirled round his unfashionable brown brogue shoes. At the traffic lights the over-loaded vehicle in a crash of gears and grinding rubber turned right out of sight and the high street returned to its deserted scruffiness. In the outer reaches of eastern London, where a hundred undistinguished towns had been devoured by the capital's greed, the days ended early.

Wallace stood up, shook his raincoat and pulled it over his faded suit and tattered ego. Without pausing or weighing the facts, he made a decision unlike any he had ever contemplated. He was going to disappear, just melt away and resurface somewhere else. No one would know where he had gone. A line would be drawn through Mrs Pifflock, the awful children, auditing and his entire present and past.

His briefcase and holdall huddled together on the kerb as if in fear of the abandonment their worthless contents deserved. What had been inconsequential in the old world, they seemed to be saying, was likely to be rubbish to the next.

Up and down the street urban fragments continued to float on rushes of winter air. On the corner next to the traffic lights and opposite the tobacconist's where the lorry had turned, Wallace observed a closed bank and cash-withdrawal machine. Although suddenly desperate for change, he was not completely unthinking; it was not in his nature. A traceable credit card, he decided, would not simplify his plan to vanish off the face of the earth, so the solution lay in drawing as much money as the situation warranted and his credit standing permitted.

Once his wallet bulged comfortably, Wallace took up the credit and cash withdrawal cards and a photograph ID from Black's office and with deliberation sawed them neatly into identically sized halves. Had the old penknife, which had lain for so many years at the bottom of his briefcase, waited for just this sort of opportunity? The thought that he had been subconsciously preparing for this hour for longer than he cared to remember left him with an intoxicating sense of destiny.

The *Telegraph* crossword, the domestic bills and the adventure school brochure were taken from the briefcase and in turn torn first in two and then in four and finally thrown onto an already full litterbin dribbling rubbish into the gutter. Wallace examined the briefcase, which for entirely unconvincing reasons, he had carried ever since Mrs Pifflock had given it as a present countless Christmases ago.

He had always avoided spontaneous behaviour, but on this rare and liberating occasion, a noise like a snort could have been heard by anyone standing within a fifty-foot radius of the municipal waste bin. Briefcase and holdall went in on top of the shredded paper and, once free of these symbols of job and custom, Wallace, in an unusually light mood, turned towards the railway station and lengthened his stride. To be without the encumbrances of an ordinary life, he concluded, was to be without the life itself.

Under a cover of clouded glass the formal lines of the arrival and departure schedule beckoned seductively. Here then, was a door opening onto more possibility than he had ever dreamed of, and all he had to do was walk through. On the near platform three passengers, separated by long empty spaces, waited for a London train. But across the tracks the unoccupied benches and waiting room were strangely enticing. The thrill of excitement surging though his veins had its equal only in the occasion when Marjorie Moon had revealed herself naked to members of the fourth year boys' football team on the occasion of their triumphant first home match.

Miraculously his cold had completely disappeared.

"A one way ticket to Ipswich, if you will."

"Last train's at …10.07, that's in twenty-five, ah no, twenty-four minutes. Cash or credit?" enquired the ticket clerk.

"Cred…no, cash will be fine." Wallace counted out the notes.

He'd have to set himself up pretty quickly with some means of earning a living. His wallet might be well-stocked right now, but, without frequent infusions, it was not going to remain that way for long.

'The night train to Ipswich', the very phrase in Wallace's, until now, timorous mind had the ring of escapade and daring and he boarded it fearlessly. He was confronting the dullness of his existence and tackling it head on. 'Pulling life by the beard,' was another line he dredged up from distant memory and repeated to himself several times on the journey east into Suffolk. Instead of George reluctantly limping into an enforced adventure outing, Wallace would vault over the laziness of his disagreeable son and embrace one of his own choosing with all the new enthusiasm at his command. He felt so elated he put his feet up on the seat in front and smiled to himself at the thought of the chidings he had given both George and Irene for similar pranks. Now, frankly, he didn't care and for his own amusement he beamed round the empty carriage at an invented audience enthralled by his roguishness.

Several pale stars appeared though the window and, behind bare trees snapping by in the dark, a large orange moon heaved into sight.

On a train journey of this length, Wallace would normally have slept, or wrestled inconclusively with one or two impenetrable clues from the *Daily Telegraph* crossword puzzle. But the magnificent decision to break loose kept him goggle-eyed and counting both the night's passing minutes and the clicking railway lines beneath his trembling feet.

Ipswich station at close to midnight was not a place where adventures are automatically born. A few immobile trains were pulled up to the buffers and public toilets were locked and inaccessible. Wallace walked out to the quiet street. There were no taxis, but even if there had been he didn't exactly know where he would ask to be driven. Getting a hotel room at this late hour was not going to be easy. A porter said a two star hotel was in the third turning to the right and Wallace set off, mildly crestfallen that this potential inconvenience had not occurred to him earlier.

A notice in the Talbot Inn window stated uncompromisingly, "No vacancies."

Bloody hell, thought Wallace retracing his steps, now what? Perhaps he should just make the best of a bad job and stay at the station until first light and then begin his new life in earnest.

In the middle of the vast forecourt Wallace located a hard, comfortless bench. Over his head and suspended from the railway canopy hung a four-sided Victorian clock and a multitude of dim lights. So this will be home for a while, he thought. A newspaper would be useful under these circumstances, but, as he patted his pockets to recall where his had been put, he remembered the ceremonious tearing in front of a waste bin in Grays High Street. Oh, well, only about six hours to go before things really got under way.

The wooden seat after a matter of minutes felt even harder and any attempt to sleep either in an upright, or horizontal position, was doomed to failure. A cleaning machine whined up and down the cavernous public space in straight, repetitive lines. For the most part its driver ignored the sleepless and cooling form beneath the clock. But on the final run a brief nod and swift top-to-bottom appraisal concluded the huddled shape was yet another vagrant relying on state welfare.

'Damn cheek,' thought Wallace. But, if many similarly miserable nights followed, this might accurately and rather shamefully describe the former senior auditor's newly-acquired status.

Cold crept upward and inward through his extremities and torso until every agonized fibre cried out in pain. He badly wanted to sleep, but whenever his eyelids drooped, numb and bloodless limbs forced him back into staring watchfulness. He tried walking and then running between the empty platforms. But exhausted and with teeth clattering, he decided to wait, bundled on the bench, for the approach of morning.

A distant clink of bottles woke him from a doze. How long had he been asleep? He could hardly turn and every raw joint felt beaten and stiff. After some uncomfortable writhing about, he got to his feet and gingerly touched the aching parts of his body. The feel of his rough chin reminded him that the basic tools of social hygiene had been deposited far away among Grays' street refuse.

The sound had come from the far side of the concourse where a not-yet-open coffee bar was getting ready for business. The window of the coffee shop was clouded with steam and Wallace could see two women preparing a large silver urn at the back of the shop. He walked across and tapped on the glass. The younger of the women saw his drawn, unshaven face and gave a start. She lent sideways and said something to her colleague who turned and eyed him suspiciously. Shaking her head the second woman indicated her empty wrist.

Wallace went back to his bench and with nothing to do except fill time resorted to playing mindless games. How far across the station, he wondered, could he walk with his eyes shut while continuing to hold a straight line? There was a huge expanse of empty space in all directions, so he started with twenty paces and, pushing himself, tried thirty. Being a modest man, he decided, forty was more than anyone should attempt, although thirty-five could be regarded as an exceptional man's outer limit.

But whenever trying for a new record he was pulled a long way to the right. The one time he tried forty he drew to a premature halt right under the awning of the closed coffee bar. As he uncertainly opened his eyes both women stared at him from behind the streaming windows. He attempted a smile, but receiving none in return retreated to the reassuring safety of the unoccupied bench.

Shops surrounding the platforms would probably open at nine. Why, Wallace wondered somewhat irrelevantly, after having seen people begin to busy themselves in the station, was there no direct correlation between the times customers were about and those offered by shopkeepers to people wanting to buy? Was retailing taken up as random employment like auditing just because it presented a line of minimal resistance? If nothing else, the change he had introduced into his life provided new perspectives on the way the world worked, or failed to work.

A one-aisle supermarket, from which Wallace belatedly purchased a packet of disposable razors, a toothbrush, a bar of soap and three chocolate bars, was almost the last shop to open. He could now clean up and really get some energy into a brave, but flagging venture. In the men's public convenience he looked at his reflection in a mirror from which large patches of silvering had flaked into a wash basin. Damn, he'd forgotten to get a comb. Well, too bad, his kind of hair didn't need much organising and he'd get by without. And now… to realise the big plan.

Getting a job of some sort was the first necessity. Later he could find a room to stay and afterwards things would really start to hum. Daylight, like whisky, had the capacity to raise a runaway's mood.

On the station's interior brick wall close to the coffee bar, which Wallace now took pains to avoid, was a map of the immediate vicinity. A couple of nearby shopping malls picked out in red, seemed to be the sort of place to begin. Both windows of the Ever Ready Employment Agency were plastered thick with posters. Hairdressers, data input clerks and shop assistants seemed to be in great demand, but on a slightly browner poster near the bottom of the display there was just what he was hoping for, a single opening for an 'audit assistant.' With a bound in his step and a personal reassurance that auditing would be only a temporary solution Mr Pifflock threw open the door.

A receptionist took his name and the code number from the window display and offered an application form on a clipboard. Possibly as a deterrent to theft by the long-term unemployed a pen was tethered to the board by a piece of string. Right, here we go; name, better be the real one, Wallace Elijah (how had his mother ever come up with such a soaring fancy?) Pifflock; address, bloody hell! What was he going to say? Couldn't put the home in Balham, or the nearby Talbot Inn. Damn! Damn! He'd just leave it blank and say he was new in town. National insurance number, current employment, sweet Jesus almighty!

What should he do?

Wallace completed the rest of the form in a lather of perspiration and anxiety and handed it back to the receptionist.

"You haven't filled it in properly," she complained.

"I've just arrived in Ipswich and only have a temporary address."

"What about all the other stuff."

"Same reason. Look, just let me speak to someone and I'm sure we can get over a few technicalities."

"Well, I dunno. Let me see."

The receptionist went away to talk to a clerk in a row of five preparing to interview candidates. Both clerk and receptionist looked at Wallace in a manner not too dissimilar from the one bestowed by the women in the station coffee bar. He was conscious of a faint odour rising from his soiled and slept-in clothes and suspected the two assistants might have seen him lying last night on the railway bench with knees pressed close to his shaking chin.

"Ms Leach will see you at number four station," the receptionist said.

Without thanking her Wallace walked quickly to the indicated desk.

"What can I do for you Sir; Mr Pifflock is it?"

"Yes, I'm applying for the job in your window; audit assistant."

"I see, but there are a lot of gaps on your application. You say here your last job was over fifteen years ago and some personal details are missing."

How could this brainless ninny, who was not a great deal older than his own daughter, get in the way? That appalling London accent fashionably referred to as Estuary indicated the height of her wit and education.

"And you've not filled in the section on references. I can't ask any company to meet you if we haven't checked up on you, especially for accounting positions."

"I'm not applying for an accounting job, I'm asking for audit. There is a clear distinction."

Ms Leach seemed to rise a little higher behind her desk and said in very precise tones, "If you leave contact details we will call when we have something for you."

"What on earth are you here for?" Mr Pifflock replied, irritably. "I don't know how you expect to make a living."

If Wallace knew how to stamp with rage this was a time he would gladly have done so. Instead, with all normal emotional outlets wasted away, his seething thoughts simply churned inside and resurfaced in starting eyes and dampness where clothes pressed tightly against his body.

Wallace made his way back to the hard station bench for what seemed like the twentieth time and took out a chocolate bar. An oily pigeon, wise in the ways of streets and people, alighted close by to pick up falling scraps and hopped a couple of paces further away when Wallace threw the compressed confectionary wrapper in its direction. Not completely deterred, however, it circled round to make sure others did not overtake its early priority.

This was utter madness thought Wallace. What am I hoping to achieve? If colleagues or family members could see me now they would be torn between laughter and pity. Poor old Pifflock, they'd say. He'd certainly lost his marbles last Friday night in Grays. Suddenly left all his credit cards in a waste bin and jumped on a train to nowhere. What must he have been thinking? He was a dreary old dog to be sure, but no one would ever guess he'd do something so completely idiotic.

The pigeon, emboldened by Wallace's lack of movement and the two remaining chocolate squares held motionless on one knee, jumped in a flutter onto the bench. Moving cautiously sideways it took an aggressive peck and knocked the remains of the bar to the ground. The sudden activity prompted four or five other alert birds in the vaulted station roof to glide down toward the unexpected windfall.

Scarcely noticing the minor commotion, Wallace dragged abstractedly to his feet. The effort and lack of sleep left him temporarily light-headed. Steadying himself with both hands on the bench he looked through the slats at the pigeons scrapping over crumbs. Some, he observed, were equipped to survive in dangerous terrain and others patently lacked the most basic tools.

"A single to London please."

"Yes sir, will that be card, or ..."

"Cash."

"Okay, next train is not until three. You've still got a lot of time."

"Thank you. Is there anywhere round here where I can eat."

"Yeah, lots of places. Pubs'll be open soon and there's a couple of caffs. Depends what you want I suppose."

"A café would be nice. Something not too elaborate maybe."

In the past oriental food had not appealed to Wallace, but today, in a final act of defiance, which fell like a dead leaf from a December tree, he deliberately walked past the "Copper Kitchen" and sought out something holding a vestige of yesterday's modest rebellion.

At first encounter, the "Red Dragon" might have been a pub with Welsh connections, but on closer inspection the curtained windows and dark interior belonged to a Chinese restaurant. Although past midday there was not a single customer to be seen. Wallace looked at the door sign for a second time to confirm business was anticipated. Yes, it did say, 'open'. Several round tables, each with a linen cloth and set cutlery testified to the establishment's intentions.

What an odd sort of place, barely lit at one end and in almost gothic darkness at the other. The menu selection too was disconcerting and, now that he read it in detail, disappointingly limited. Bean curd and noodles seemed to be in some evidence and while unattractive to long atrophied taste buds this latest inconvenience would not be permitted to face-down what was left of his tattered self-esteem.

Without warning a tall, thin, male figure dressed in a black suit one or two sizes too large for its spare frame appeared at Wallace's elbow.

"Yes?"

Somewhat surprised, Wallace turned and regarded the waiter.

"Oh! …lunch please. I'm not familiar…what would you recommend?"

"It's all good. What you want, pork, chicken, shrimp?" An economy of words matched the sparse clientele.

"I suppose chicken would be nice. Do you have a curry?"

The apparition shrugged.

"Sure, if you want."

"Okay and a cup of hot tea?"

The waiter made no notes and disappeared into the gloom as suddenly as he had arrived. No one else entered the dingy restaurant and only the occasional low hum of a passing vehicle confirmed it was anywhere near the centre of town. Can't imagine there's much business in a place like this, thought Wallace, his mind returning comfortably to matters of low finance.

An empty white plate and two small bowls, containing rice and a thick grey-green liquid were placed on the table and next to them a teapot and tall glass. Wallace looked around for milk and sugar.

"I say," he called, but the waiter had already disappeared to a part of the shop where he couldn't be heard.

The liquid, that Wallace splashed thickly onto a small bed of rice, congealed instantly into a greasy paste. There was not much chicken to be found and the few solid objects once relieved of their coating looked suspiciously like onion slices and potatoes. Wallace bit one and fumes rose through interior passages until his eyes watered and nose streamed. Dropping the fork with a clatter he poured tea into his tall glass. What in God's name was that? The contents looked like hot pond water with several black weedy bits swirling at the bottom. Wallace closed his eyes and turned his face to the ceiling. What would he have done right now for the sound of the waitress, Mrs Dilworth, painfully shuffling across cracked linoleum?

"You don't like?" The enigmatic waiter asked.

"No, I don't. You have just presented me with a total mockery of a luncheon. I will not recommend your establishment to a single living soul."

"Oh…okay…that's three pounds fifteen."

In the past twelve hours the bench on the station forecourt had become the nearest thing to a private residence. Familiarity and simplicity in a place where he was not challenged or contradicted was all Wallace presently desired. Inhospitable Ipswich had been very slightly softened by the hard wood slats, and his few forays into the town had been made possible only by the knowledge of a refuge on the concourse. One more retreat lay even further in the rear.

The three o'clock train left promptly and the entire journey across Suffolk, Essex and London took only slightly more than five hours. Street lamps in Balham lit surrounding water vapour in a series of faint halos as Wallace tugged his raincoat closer and sloshed homeward over wet paving stones. What sort of a reception would he get when the door opened? How would the missing day, lost bags and his state of dirty dishevelment be explained? Somewhere during the evening a heel had come off his left shoe and water seeped into his sock. As he limped along he could sense on one side the crinkly feeling of toes kept wet for too long.

Well, here it is, number twenty-seven. Wallace took a deep breath; still not in the least bit sure what he would say to Mrs Pifflock. He turned the key as quietly as possible as if avoiding detection at this stage would indefinitely hold off the time when he needed to make an implausible account.

The hallway was in darkness and a stale smell of cooked food writhed up from somewhere close to the carpet. Wallace stood for a minute on a coconut-fibre mat bearing the pathetic message of 'Welcome' in looping, italic script. He peered into the interior as if entering a strange place and not his home of twenty years.

"Hello," he whispered as if afraid to get a reply.

As he closed the door behind him, Wallace put out a finger to snap on an electric light. A naked bulb of no more than sixty watts glowed dimly in the grey-washed ceiling overhead. The house was empty.

Surprised, but at the same time somewhat relieved, Wallace took off his raincoat and hung it dripping on the hallstand. Gaining a little confidence he tip-toed towards the kitchen. The strip lighting buzzed and fluttered and shed anaemic white light over a dispiriting room in which many dispiriting meals had previously been assembled. On a scrubbed bare wooden table a tray with knife and fork was laid in exactly the position where Wallace customarily found his dinner on a Friday night after a week's travel. Turning to the oven he pulled open the door. A pale blue plate without any pattern rested coldly inside with a saucepan lid protecting its contents. As he lifted the lid several stiff slices of meat clung to the underside in a brown gravy glue. The meal was a lot less fresh than the usual return-home offering. If Wallace were to hazard a guess, it had been there since the previous day.

Turning about in some puzzlement he looked at the untidy kitchen for an explanation. A small earthenware pot, marked "salt" that had lost its top years ago, but still remained in use as a store for small change, had a brown envelope resting across its rim. Wallace picked up the envelope and read his name in large capital letters. Prying the flap loose with a thumb he took out a short letter written in Mrs Pifflock's plain, but recognisable hand. Wallace moved under the light to get a clearer view.

"Dear Wally," the letter began, "This will be a big shock, but I've decided to leave you. I really can't take any more. The children…"

Wallace ran fingers though his tangled hair and sat with a bump on one of the straight kitchen chairs. He looked down at the floor and the small trickle of water leaking out of his damaged shoe and wondered where exactly he had put his fishing rods.

THREE

INTERRUPTED SERVICE

They were told mechanical failure had caused the delay, but what was not clear was how long the inconvenience would last. Certainly, no airplane waited at the gate and no-one appeared to know when it would arrive. In the confusion customer service staff circulated with their own brand of mechanical dysfunction, appeasing annoyance with trained smiles and dinner vouchers.

"Will I be able to catch my connecting flight?"

"We'll let you know as soon as a departure decision has been made."

"And when will that be?"

"When we have a confirmed arrival time for the incoming plane."

"Are we to suppose it has not yet taken off from the other end?"

"We have no clarity at this moment, but, as soon as we do, you will all be advised," beamed the bearer of no specific tidings to those within the compass of her radiance, as if casting about her a feast for five thousand rather than crumbs to poorly served package travellers.

As officialdom retreated behind the collective 'we', a wave of impotent anger rippled across the gathered throng. Reluctantly and in the absence of something more substantial against which to rail, dismayed holiday-makers scattered, like worried hens, to cluck and peck at trifles.

In the drearily functional cafeteria, inert green curry and flaccid brown stew, just good enough for a one-time clientele, lay congealing under thickening skins. A harassed father with two young children passed undecided for the third time in front of the brightly lit stainless steel display.

"But Daad! It doesn't look nice."

"Well, it's either that or going 'ungry."

"I don't care and Ems doesn't care either. Do you Ems?"

His sister's appetite was more advanced than his and she had not yet concluded a missed meal to be a better choice than a disagreeable one.

Taking the part example of Ems protesting brother, Dan Starkey avoided full exchange for his dinner voucher and settled instead for a single mug of hot, sweet tea. The elderly female cashier taking his ticket bearing the utilitarian "complimentary meal" message looked at him quizzically, but said nothing to persuade him into a second viewing of the shining containers.

With cup in one hand and carry-on bag in the other, Starkey wove warily between the grumbling knots of passengers. He knew from experience that collisions in hot and exasperated crowds were capable of inflaming tempers. The days were long gone when careful manners made unpleasant situations bearable. For a reason he could not understand, a scrap these days was often preferred to soothing accommodation. If stranded passengers were any indication, refinement, after a wearying delay and a century of emancipation, had been levelled out of existence.

Under less congested circumstances, the half acre of plain, bolted-down seating might have offered several options to kill hours stretching into indeterminate distance. But, while the first groups of inconvenienced travellers aggressively occupied vacant places with their assorted bags, late-comers were denied the benefit of choice. Like a dawn flock of wood pigeons swelling beyond the ability to fly, the advanced guard devoured their free meals and flopped untidily down on every roost as if occupying a pea-field stripped clean by their incursion. Scattered personal belongings like bird-droppings established possession and held places for absentees temporarily seeking relief in bathrooms and duty-free shops.

The thought occurred to Starkey that less civilised communities conducted affairs with greater grace. What had the modern world come to? Freedom seemed to bestow the right to be unreasonable and in such hostile conditions, battling for a disputed chair was a tiresome way to begin a long wait. He lay down in a vacant corner, where a wall and roof-to-floor window met, and opened his kit bag. Wrapped into the protective packaging of several T-shirts was an eight-inch salami sausage that he was carrying to a younger brother, and Starkey wanted reassurance it was coping with the enforced delay and heated airport better than the fare-paying public. Satisfied with his inspection he dug deeper and pulled out a well-thumbed paperback. The thick novel, spotted on its cover by drops from a recent rain shower, had helped fill intervals at several earlier points along the way.

For a while, he didn't read, but instead perched his hot mug on the stout volume. His father, who hated to see a page folded as a reminder of where to begin again, would have been mortified, although he liked books to be working tools that showed a history of use. To a young son the two ideas seemed contradictory, but now, with the passage of time, they had moved from youthful disrespect into a shared truth.

And what of respect, Starkey thought, repeating the word several times with his lips moving, but no noticeable sound. The concept, he concluded sadly, was on the same path to obsolescence as that taken by chivalry a couple of hundred years ago. Just look at this assortment of people, contesting seats and food like gulls squabbling over scraps on a municipal refuse tip.

Maybe some of them were half-decent folk, but they all seemed mannered in a way to suit a coarser age, and the unexpected delay, rather than fostering stoicism, was encouraging loutish misconduct.

Time in the departure lounge began to hang heavily. Ems and her sibling devised a game to relive their boredom. The contest required vaulting the seating to a parallel aisle and running though crowded legs and luggage to gate seventeen and back. To be certain neither covered less than the full distance, the runners were obliged to return with a cabin luggage label from the stack waiting at the gate's inactive desk. Overhead the second hand of a silent electronic clock timed their rivalry.

Plunged into the sports pages and the three-inch-high headlines of a tabloid newspaper, their solitary parent gave up, or had never attempted to control his offspring's boisterous larking.

"Beat you, beat you," crowed the boy, as his panting sister, severely disadvantaged by six fewer years, clambered on all fours across the final luggage hurdle.

Mindless of grammar, or truth Ems retorted, "No fair, you cheat. I'm not playing any more."

"Cowardy, cowardy! You're just a girl, that's why."

"Waah!" wailed Ems. "Daad, tell him off, he's being wicked."

"What's goin' on with you two?" complained the father emerging from an engrossing, but essentially fabricated report of an altercation the previous evening between two football managers' wives outside a provincial nightclub.

"It's her. She's silly," Ems brother said with crushing and unarguable finality.

Drawn unwillingly from his hands-off position, the father produced a yelp of pain with a swipe at the back of the boy's legs. In the ensuing disorder of tangled limbs, loose newspaper sheets and triumphant shouts from Ems, an as yet untouched super-sized soft drink overbalanced and cascaded into family baggage and the daily news.

"You little bast..." the angry father howled, followed by, "And wait 'til I get 'old of you!" as the boy fled from sight,

On the row of seating opposite, an Asian mother with an almost motionless son of about eight impassively observed the mayhem. Dressed in a recently ironed white shirt and the tie of a fee-paying preparatory school, the boy rested both hands on top of an open exercise book in his lap. He sat quite upright, with shining black shoes suspended several inches above the ground.

Feeling the unblinking gaze on his forehead and the damp, disintegrating sports' report, the sorely-tried father turned and growled, "Oo are you looking at then aih?" in just the sort of surly manner Starkey could have predicted.

The well-polished shoes turned toward each other at the toes, but the owner's stare remained steady and expressionless. The boy's mother stiffened slightly and pressed her lips together a little more firmly.

From an escalator running down through the ceiling, straggles of passengers were discharged without pause into the already packed hall. A children's author could make much of such a theme, thought Starkey, allowing his imagination to wander. A production line in a factory runs madly out of control and drowns the town with bottles of ketchup and packets of corn flakes. Residents are forced to flee towards waiting ships, but cascading cartons follow them wherever they go until the overflow unhinges the planet's orbit.

A minor disturbance developed at the lower end of the escalator. At first Starkey suspected the restive and uncontrolled

Ems and her brother had provoked a second incident, but closer inspection suggested adults had bettered undisciplined youth.

Unable to disperse freely, passengers arriving from the upper floor clogged the escalator's exit. To avoid being thrown forward into the growing crush and without thinking, a few descending people shuffled backwards. Those following from even higher up aggravated the mounting confusion. In the midst of the packed mass, a more than middle-aged man in a silk shirt, opened to a place where a younger person might display sculptured ripples instead of slack skin folds, began heaving and pushing as if brute strength alone would loosen the pressing multitude. A linen jacket across one arm and a slender woman a fraction of his age over the other, he charged forward like an Andalusian bull at a swirling cape.

"'Ey!' what's the matta wiv you then? Can't you see it's jammed?" remonstrated a jostled would-be holidaymaker.

"Force a vay out, or someone vill be injured here."

"An' you knockin' ev'ry one over is keepin' 'em alright, I s'pose? You're a bleedin' idiot, did you know?"

Abruptly the escalator stopped and its entire human cargo, emitting a range of high- and low-pitched cries of surprise and discomfort, lurched forward. But so dense had the crowd become that only at the outer fringes did anyone actually stumble. A public announcement, appearing to come from speakers on both the upper and lower floors, stated in a bewildering echo that the escalator had been halted 'fo-for safe-safety re-reasons' and would passengers kindly move further into the 'ha-hall' to allow those still arriving from above 'free-freer' movement.

"She finks we're scrummin' down 'ere for fun," complained the now perspiring and palpably disillusioned vacationer to no-one in particular. The day was developing into an occasion for imprecise communication to be let loose on the ether, like time-capsule messages rocketed into space, which stood not the ghost of a chance of reaching any interested audience.

Empty places on the floor were non-existent now, and the crowd, to while away the cramped time, settled into a collection of individual and group activities wherever they had come to a stop. Near Starkey, a mixed male and female group of young, denim-clad adults laughed over-enthusiastically at mildly funny jokes, and played cards on large rucksacks bearing the flags of various countries. A low-level hum, like traffic on a motorway, permeated the hall.

A little further off and sitting primly upright with their backs to each other on the hard surface of a single old-fashioned suitcase, a white-haired husband and wife sipped from paper cups. Untidy tea-bag strings hung wetly and unaccustomedly between freckled fingers. Although into his eighties, the man was as attentive and polite to his wife as if he was a twenty-year-old courting a betrothed in a way learned from an Edwardian father. When her tea was done he unsteadily took the container, asked if she wanted anything else, and, hearing of her contentment, went in search of a waste-bin. They, thought Starkey, don't live in a house with disposable kitchenware or generic toilet-paper, and their tea would be loose and travel through a heated pot before coming to a cultured finale with lemon in bone china-ware.

While her husband was about his errand, the lady – she could not be identified or explained simply as a woman – looked, with limited inclination to understand, at the multitude around her. She had a view of how life should be and the surrounding mores left her perplexed and ill at ease, as if she had been dropped into the middle of a curious, but thankfully temporary, excursion to a Moroccan bazaar. What surrounded her was interesting up to a point, but she'd be glad to go home where things were so much more reliable. Her returning husband reminded her that the world she depended on was still reassuringly where it had always been. With a small sigh of relief she was satisfied by her certainties. Their lives, Starkey suspected, were so inextricably entwined and indivisible that when the time came for one to die, the other's survival for more than a few painful and disorientated weeks was impossible to picture.

At the hall's noisy centre, the silk-shirted man, previously prominent on the crowded escalator, had somehow excavated two places to sit. One arm lolled across the top of a neighbouring chair and the other, as if declaring squatter's rights, rested uncontested on the slender knees of his elaborately painted companion. Unlike the couple perched on a suitcase, this was a relationship organised in a hierarchy where the junior partner got what it could by manipulation, not entitlement. This man would make decisions for everyone with no questions allowed. Perhaps the people he attracted, Starkey suspected, preferred living next to strength, and in exchange for the independence surrendered, accepted reassuring security.

The power, which, against all odds, had cleared space in the middle of the press, was conspicuous across the long hall. Passers-by skirted the heavily jowelled figure as if encountering a restrained Rottweiler kept on the edge of starvation.

Despite the presence of his over-decorated companion, he did not ignore other young women passing through his range of vision. Thin-lipped leers and long stares came and went as if facilitated by mechanical levers from somewhere inside his unfastened shirt.

The day shaded into early evening and the fading northern-hemisphere sun slid in an oblique line behind autumnal woodland on the far side of the airport. Through the long sweep of plate-glass, a weak orange glow temporarily lit the departure hall's interior. In the waiting crowd a handful were drawn from their frustrations to watch the last glimmers of late afternoon drain away into twilight.

A woman in a straight white dress descended the stilled escalator with clicks of her high heels ringing on metal stairs. Without clearly seeing her face Starkey could tell she was Asian from her way of gliding into and out of small gaps in the crowd without coming into physical contact with anyone. An Asian's self ended where skin made contact with its surroundings; for others it extended several feet into empty air. Threading an unhurried and meandering path to the high window she looked out at the line of trees, behind which the cold sun had set only moments ago, and stared intently as if wanting to pull the great orb back above the horizon.

"Were you too late for a dinner ticket?"

Ems, full of childish directness, appeared in front of the woman.

"What was that my dear?" was the distracted but kind reply.

For the first time since the delayed flight had been announced, Ems and her brother, who was now standing just a little way off observing his sister, had ceased to hurtle about. A stuffed doll held by one leg hung at Ems' side.

"I've got one you see and I won't use it, so it's yours if you want."

"That's very sweet, but don't worry about me. What's your name?"

"It's Emma, but you can call me Ems. That's what my brother over there calls me." She extended her arm and forefinger in the direction of her older sibling, like a fencer taking guard. The mop-haired boy, more self-consciously preadolescent than his sister, spun and bolted into the crowd as if identified in a headmaster's inspection as one failing to wash his knees.

"Stop botherin' people." Ems's father, quite unaware that on this occasion no-one was in the least bit disturbed, took her roughly by the arm. With one trouser leg still stickily wet from spilt soda, he was finding nothing to objectify his thoughts. Looking over her shoulder as she was led away, Ems took with her a smile as ethereal as the last ray of the recently departed sun.

Alone again the woman cast a melancholy gaze over the dimming landscape. Her slender, erect figure and long firm limbs were as motionless and patient as those of a starving heron, waiting by a stream laid waste by industrial seepage. Brown skin and straight black hair contrasted with the whiteness of her dress and her still, pensive form was at odds with the bustle of the rough and inconsiderate throng.

Starkey wanted to give her a seat, but had none to offer. He could not quite picture this elegant woman sprawled untidily on the floor, or pushing her way into possession of a place occupied by loose baggage.

"Would you care to sit here?" The silver-haired octogenarian attempted to rise, and although succeeding in getting both legs straight, balanced precariously with one hand flat on the surface of his suitcase. His wife fidgeted about uncomfortably as if the absence of a seat had become a problem she alone was obliged to resolve.

"Do be careful, Henry," she twittered nervously, as much to show her involvement as in concern for her frail husband.

Eventually labouring upright, Henry, with face made puffy by the effort and in more real need of a place to sit than anyone in the entire airport, turned uncertainly in the direction of the woman in white.

"This is really all that is available. Please....come...I insist."

Courteously and incongruously he waved towards the forty-year-old cardboard case long thin fingers more suited to a violin player in a Viennese imperial court than an incommoded package-holiday traveller.

"You're very kind, but I couldn't."

"You will offend me greatly if you refuse," said Henry breathlessly drawing himself to a not inconsiderable height and looking down with mock severity from beneath his craggy eyebrows. The offer was accepted and the almost extinguished embers lying deep in Henry's old man's soul glowed at the success of a small gallantry. But at a loss as to what to do next, he walked around to his wife's end of the case.

"I...er... will walk a little to stretch my legs and...ah...be with you directly, my love." The last few syllables became indistinct as he turned to go.

Edging sideways through the press, Henry stepped uncertainly over the moving legs of two card-players and, after some twisting and threading came to a halt in the corner where Starkey was drinking back the last cold dregs of his sweet tea. Across the runway the outline of trees was still faintly visible and the few lights on the far perimeter fence announced the arrival of night. A van with the name "Arbuthnot's Meals of Distinction" unhurriedly circled the empty forecourt.

"It's like death really," Henry commented mostly to himself.

Being close to the observation, Starkey looked around to see if others were being included. After hesitation he rolled to his left and followed the watery stare resting on the rear doors of the departing van.

"No-one expects a great meal on budget airlines even if you were ready to pay," he chipped in unhelpfully.

"What?"

"Good grub and cheap air travel don't seem to go together if you ask me."

Henry raised his eyes back to the windows again and smiled his dignified gentleman's smile.

"Sorry, I was not talking of the motorised delivery. I was speaking generally...of long evenings."

"I see. But what is like...."

"Death? Why, the departure of a winter day. There is no one point at which you can say it has gone; it slowly diminishes in quality until nothing remains, like life itself. One neither sees nor hears as well as one did. Without noticing we slide slowly into the void, until the transition is complete. In a long life dying can take seventy-five years."

"Oh...I get it. But bit of a gloomy way to look at things, isn't it?"

"At your age perhaps, but when you are as old as I and no longer recall when dusk began, you may well come to a different conclusion."

"That's pretty sad."

"No, not really; just realistic. The young think in absolutes; prime colours, right and wrong, justice and injustice. Figuratively speaking, death to them comes on the point of a sword in pursuit of a glorious idea. But in truth we slowly moulder away, losing first one faculty then another until the moment of crossing from one state to the next hardly matters. What is sad though is to be slowly consumed and pretend it is otherwise."

"Do you often talk to blokes you don't know like this?"

"To begin with," Henry teased gently, "I was sharing thoughts with myself, admittedly outloud, but then you included yourself in the discussion."

"Is that your wife over there?" With a casual thrust of his chin from his place on the floor, Starkey indicated across the intervening and much travelled rucksacks.

In little deliberate movements that wouldn't unsettle his balance, Henry turned in the indicated direction.

"I don't like that," he remarked, rather emphatically.

Behind his wife, who was nervously beaming around her as if to reassure everyone that trusting the airline's good intentions and staying calm were the best choices at a difficult time, a balding man in a silk shirt, standing with feet planted firmly apart, had drawn the woman in white into conversation.

"Perhaps you should rejoin her; she looks a little lost."

"Who? Oh, yes, but I was more concerned for the well-being of the other lady."

Heaving onto his elbow Starkey peered through the piled bodies and tumbled personal apparatus.

"She looks intelligent enough to take care of herself, wouldn't you say?" said Starkey, noticing for the first time the source of Henry's disquiet.

"Under most circumstances I would, but we all need help from time to time and none should deny support to those on a perilous journey."

"Taking responsibility for everyone, especially when unsought, can get you into a whole lot of trouble. Sometimes it's better not to get involved."

"Whether a risk or not; it is a moral obligation. You look a decent enough sort of chap; why not assist me in distracting the lady from the attentions of one who will clearly do her no good."

"How do you decide to interfere in a conversation? Is it because some woman is talking to a guy you don't like? Why should it be your business?"

"At my age you must allow me to judge, but if you want me to spell it out, it is in exactly the way you concluded my wife was feeling abandoned and that I should rejoin her. Your name…I didn't catch…?"

"It's Starkey; Dan Starkey. Go on, I want to see what you're going to do."

In the sweating crowd fatigue was giving way to resignation. Nothing more could be wrung from newspapers, or the remains of meals stiffening on plastic plates. The drone of voices declined as conversation, dependant for stimulation on new events, ebbed to inconsequential maintenance. Card-players lost interest in their games, small children curled up in sleep on parents' numb laps and the night settled in.

"My dear, I'm so sorry to have left you unattended. I got into debate with Mr Starkly here and he detained me. Let me introduce you."

"Starkey actually; not that it matters greatly. How are you? A real waste of time this, wouldn't you agree?"

"Yes, most unfortunate. But you do meet the most interesting people under these circumstances. This is Chee Win behind me. We spoke for a few minutes before the gentleman came up. I'm afraid I don't know his name."

Glad of the opening and cupping his hand under Starkey's elbow, Henry swivelled towards the opposite end of the case where the woman in white sat.

"What a delightful name, reminds me of coming home long ago to Malaya in the school holidays. Is it Chinese?" And making sure the opportunity did not slide by ungrasped or being of an age to change what he knew best, "Please meet Mr Starkly who has become a firm friend of the last twenty minutes. He and I have been exploring matters of deep philosophical moment. And your …ah, er, acquaintance is?"

Standing with the shadow of a stoop, Henry was still three or four inches taller than the other man, but, with the weight of years and sparsest of frames, delicate by comparison. Notwithstanding the frailty, an aura of authority, as if cast by a robed judge on the bench, gave the older man weight the other might envy. Here was a man used to command and to being obeyed, not oppressively, but because he was instinctively trusted by those around him.

"Vot?" was the sour and confrontational response.

"We were making ourselves known to each other. It is always so much more agreeable to have the names of those with whom you converse, would you not agree? I believe it is called context," and adding, as if argument was futile, "Where we all start with exactly the same understanding."

From across several rows of seats a young woman, whose legs were hoisted onto her chair and folded beneath a short skirt, called out impatiently, "'Mitri! I'm getting thirsty, can I have a jrink?"

"Ah!" continued Henry, as if the answer had been provided by the person to whom he was speaking, "'Mitri, 'Mitri must be a contraction for Dmitri, no?" And, turning to the group surrounding the case, "Please meet Dmitri, from eastern Europe I suggest, perhaps Moldavia, or Stettin, or somewhere like that. I'm sure, given time, he will elucidate. This is my wife Violet and Chee Win, this Mr Starkly and I'm Henry Delaporte. There, we have all met and," he said looking firmly at Dmitri, "know with whom we are dealing."

"If you really must haf it, I'm from Salford," clarified Dmitri in an accent acquired a thousand miles from anywhere of that name.

"'Mitri, 'Mitri," wailed the voice from over the aisles.

"I do believe someone is getting a little out of sorts over there, a daughter perhaps, who needs attention? Yes, I do believe she has your smile."

An annoyed scowl met the ironic, but otherwise neutral gaze. Dmitri, without any formal leave-taking, turned on his heel and stumped off in the direction of the call, shouting as he went, "Vot's the matter wit you now? Haven't I told you not to interrupt me ven I'm busy?"

"There," said Henry, evidently feeling pleased with himself, "this is more comfortable. Should we take some refreshment? Ladies? Mr Starkly, would you be so kind?"

The crowd was a single organism with a life of its own. Cycles of resting and stretching kept the whole mass in a kind of natural balance. Close by, Ems's brother, waking with gummed eyes from a cramped, but undisturbed sleep, slid to the floor and disappeared into the swarm of humanity on an escapade only a young boy could imagine. Henry, observing the vacated space and in a manner brooking no discussion, lowered himself firmly between an overnight case and a dangling arm. But, ever mindful of proprieties, he directed a "May I?" at the dozing form of the parent, long past defending only occasionally occupied chairs. The hands on the big overhead clock slid relentlessly round.

"If this aeroplane, for which we have been waiting for an interminable length of time, were to arrive and for some reason was only able to take ten passengers, how would we pick those who should fly," asked Henry as if the thought had plagued him for hours.

"Oh, Henry, the ideas you come up with. I'm sure no-one has the least idea," remonstrated Violet agitatedly, as if such a proposition was an embarrassment and bound to unsettle the harmony prevailing since Dmitri moved out of the vicinity.

If Violet predeceased Henry, he had every expectation her last words would be along the lines of, "I'm sorry to be such a bother, Dear." Disturbing others was, apart from eating with elbows on the table, the closest to mortal sin she could conceive. The really big misdeeds didn't happen in her universe even by extension, and bringing herself to read a book which portrayed life with any colour was quite beyond her. Sexual enthusiasms and preferences, theft, or a passion to kill were unfathomable notions, which didn't actually occur unless removed by three or four centuries, or in the lives of foreigners.

"I think our friend Mr Starkly would have a view. Imagine if you will, that all of us in this hall were stranded on an iceberg in the Barents Sea and just a handful could be lifted off before the ice melts."

"But we are not, Henry. We are here, in London, and we can't drown so far inland," Violet said peevishly.

"My love, you are a…eh...practical woman, but we are duty-bound to consider the bigger picture in which practicalities should be exercised."

"I think you are talking nonsense, Henry," she chided gently and, turning for support to the others to hold her narrow beliefs intact, asked, "Don't you agree?"

"Maybe it has something to do with giving value," volunteered Starkey.

Pleased the log-jam created by Violet was breaking up, Henry took no time in refuting this new possibility.

"Inconceivable; why, look at those children over there."

In a heap of soft coats Ems lay fast asleep with the same toy clasped to her chest as the one previously dragged round the hall by a heel. Her recently returned brother, gripped by a personal fantasy, spun like a dervish and emitted warlike noises.

"No-one, with the best will in the world," continued Henry "Would say they have contributed value, but should we not give them an opportunity to fulfil their possibility?"

Ems's father, believing he had detected a faint criticism, stirred beneath his unkempt hair, and opened a bloodshot eye. Unable to pinpoint precisely the comment's origin he slipped back into a dream-laden world hanging between waking and sleeping. Among the fevered bursts of white light that sputtered in his head, both son and daughter, dressed in the stripes of opposing world cup finalists, brought to a premature and clamorous end a game inexplicably combining elements of football, free wrestling and hang-gliding.

"Should value then be redefined as potential?" queried Starkey.

"And who would presume to say with certainty where promise rests? That would be to play God and the best of us are not equipped for such a responsibility."

"I don't understand a word they are saying, do you my dear?" said Violet to Chee Win."

"Yes, indeed, I do," replied Chee Win, taking hold of the other's hand. Her unexpected excitement startled Violet.

"Oh! Then you all have the better of me. I was never very good at metamorphics," she said irrelevantly, "and shall feel like a wall-flower any minute."

"Then," concluded Starkey, "value in some form, it must remain."

"Let us debate that point; here am I nearing the end of my days and one could say a moderately productive life. Should its continuation be preferred to that of those children who have as yet done nothing, but may, if a roll of the dice permits? Or should we choose the children's father, who, as far as one can tell, has achieved no more than facilitate others' conception? Or, and this will take a bigger stretch, should Dmitri over there, who is likely to have made more money and provided employment to a greater number of fellow citizens or … ah…biddable acquaintances, than the rest of us put together, and, despite morals acquired among the creeping things inhabiting a swamp, be preferred over others? Or do we forget ideas of deserving and disqualify all others in a raw competition to save ourselves? What I am asking is not just who gets on the plane, but who, at a later date and in all seriousness, should enter heaven? Does anyone have a notion of how to deserve that honour?"

Satisfied with his peroration, Henry settled back and reflectively tapped the tips of his long fingers softly against each other. Dan Starkey, who until this moment had sat cross-legged on the floor, like a disciple at the feet of Buddha, moved gingerly from one buttock to the other.

"Then we should be content just to live good lives," piped Violet, who much to her own surprise had a worthwhile comment to contribute to the conversation, which until that moment had made only a superficial connection to her plain thoughts.

"Yes, yes," replied her husband, perhaps a little too hastily, "but what does that mean?"

Apart from the one interjection, Chee Win had said nothing. But with sudden and unexpected animation asked, "And what of those who can only wait?"

With a woman's intuition, Violet asked, "Is there is a young one who needs you?"

The suitcase creaked under shifting weight and the long line of windows vibrated in the roar of a landing aircraft.

"The urgency of what is good for them predicts who goes. It's about relieving pain, righting an injustice and bringing comfort to their suffering. That is what determines value."

"Is it a boy or a girl?" continued Violet, who quite against her expectation, found the turn of discussion completely absorbing.

"Ah! I see; we are the slaves of others and have no real value, but only what our circumstances dictate? Remember the priest who could not take rest, because his parishioners, long since deprived, required absolution one by tedious one," cried Henry, who enjoyed revolving vague concepts. But, with such deep intellect, what had given his marriage to Violet such longevity? Their lives, he realised, were almost entirely complementary except for meeting, as it were, over the teapot. The blank look of mystification had returned to Violet's face.

Landing lights lit up the passenger hall as an arriving aircraft swung into the landing gate. Engines in a high declining whine died away and a surging babble of voices broke into the monotony of the long wait.

"It's a girl and just like me, but so full of care that..." Chee Win's words ended with a catch of her breath.

"My dear, what is it? May I know?"

Falling black hair hid Chee Win's face as she looked down at her hands. A sigh, like wind blown from the empty regions of a remote desert, escaped through her parted lips. Instinctively and for solidarity, Starkey and Henry glanced at each other.

"She has so little time."

"Oh…I think…I see. But if it has been a beautiful life, then brevity leaves her undiminished. Are you called home to…to…be with her?"

"Yes, for as long, or for as short as it takes."

"I'd like to sit next to you on the way out if you have no objection. We can talk as much or as little as you like. Henry can exchange boarding passes with you and we can all meet Mr Starkly at the other end."

"Why not call me Dan to avoid any confusion," suggested the ever amenable Starkey.

"That's very nice of you. We are all good friends now," Violet announced as happily as Chee Win's revelation would allow.

A crackle of static in the high ceiling preceded another cheerless apology. The airline, of course, regretted the inconvenience, but was pleased to announce the flight would shortly be leaving and for everyone's comfort and safety passengers with small children and those holding business class tickets would be boarded first, followed by rows fifty-five to sixty-five. The rest were invited, or was it instructed, to remain seated until their numbers were called.

"Why, there you have the world's priority," groaned Henry, putting a thumb and forefinger to his brow as if to test a pulse.

Before the next announcement and to avoid being put at a disadvantage, stiff and weary travellers began to queue in a line snaking its way through the rapidly emptying benches. With hands on hips and breathing hard, Henry surveyed the lemming-like rush.

"Ladies," he said, having made up his mind about something, although still unprepared to explain, "May I recommend you accompany me? Mr Starkly! I will be with you imminently."

With one hand lightly touching each back he guided both women towards the boarding gate. Waiting at the head of the line was a young woman chewing gum behind lips that never met. Next to her, Dmitri, with a soft leather satchel slung over one shoulder, growled to left and right as if to warn potential queue-jumpers he was not a man to be underestimated. Henry as he passed gave an imperious nod in the couples' direction.

"Madam," he said, addressing a uniformed airline employee waiting at the gate and handing her two boarding passes. "I require that these passengers are boarded as an immediate priority."

The official scrutinised the documents and without looking at Henry, handed them back.

"We are not calling row twenty-three, please return to your seat."

"Madam," said Henry, a small vein beating visibly in his left temple, "How old are you?"

"Pardon!"

"I asked," repeated Henry, carefully articulating the words, "How old you are?"

"Sir, I am twenty-six, but would you please…"

"Funny, you are behaving as if you are not a day more experienced than fifteen and," looking down from a clear two feet, "If you do not accede to my request, I promise to make such an unholy commotion that the chances of your staying in your current employment until the age of twenty-seven must be held in the most serious doubt. Do you understand me?" he boomed.

"Oh, Henry!" came a plaintive wail at his back.

"Not now, Violet, I am in conference with the airline."

Faces began to turn. A supervisor was summoned on whom Henry bestowed his most gracious smile and manners. Bending low he murmured into the waiting ear, "Please forgive me for making this request, but there are most extenuating circumstance with which you cannot help but sympathise."

He went on rapidly describing in hushed tones what he had learned from Chee Win. Stepping back the supervisor radiated generosity.

"Of course, I understand. And if there is anything we can do during the flight please call on our staff. Agnes, see them through."

Violet and Chee Win followed the overruled escort onto the ramp and an annoyed call from the head of the line with an accent not from Salford was heard to say, "Oi, so vot's going on den?"

"I believe, my good man, it is what we would call, defining value."

Henry rejoined Dan Starkey and together they made their way to the very end of the long crocodile line.

"Well," said Henry, "some of us are where we should be. The rest probably don't matter too much. I hope you will agree Mr Starkly?"

FOUR

LIGHTING UP THE SKY

For a fraction of a minute I could see Jane's back and her bobbing auburn curls, which I had stroked on a thousand affectionate occasions, disappearing little by little in the crisscrossing of Queen's Road shoppers. Then she was gone. Twelve years switched off as if they had been lights around an emptying dance floor.

Before that awful afternoon in March, when summer's stultifying heat was still far away, we had reached a sort of crest in our lives. Until then many of our friends thought of us as a lucky couple in whom good fortune was seen as much for its inevitability as its accomplishment. Those were our golden years.

Then we came to the East on the back of promising careers and in a frame of mind to see our early successes move continually upward. We instinctively anticipated, but mistakenly as things turned out, an endless progression from one triumph to the next. Hong Kong was to be another step along the same sunlit highroad.

With the benefit of hindsight, I should not have been so keen to make the move. But at the time and in all truth, I did believe Asia would be good for us.

What an irony that an age after our breakup I can still recall every word of the conversation launching our adventure and the subsequent downward spiral, but cannot, with any amount of trying, identify the desperate feelings that engulfed me the last time I saw her.

Before the move to Asia, we usually returned from work separately at about seven, but on the evening of our first discussion about the new possibility, she was home well before me, and having taken a shower, was seated languidly at her dressing table. Her hair hung damply and dark streaks marked the towel beneath her bare shoulders.

"Just got in?"

"Seconds ago. Busy day?" She asked leaning back from the stool until her head touched my arms.

I stooped forward and kissed in turn her nose, lips and neck.

"Frantic. How are the boys? We had clients over for lunch. I was going to save this until later, but they're interested in having me seconded to Hong Kong."

Jane sat up. "Wow! That's a big thought. What did you say?"

"Same as I always do in this sort of situation; that I was flattered; would have to think about it carefully and discuss with you, you know."

"Have you told them I'm very well established?"

"Yes, but Dobbs must have made the request last time he was over and he's pressing again; says he wants to interview you for the counsel's job in his legal department."

"He's never met me. How would he know?"

"Oh, he's pretty well informed; seen your resume apparently and knew a lot of details."

"That's a little presumptuous of him wouldn't you say?" she was being defensive.

"I'm interested, Sweetheart. Can we talk it through?"

"Look, Pete, there's a partnership for me if I play my cards right. I don't have to go anywhere and what would we gain from a couple of years in Hong Kong? Wouldn't we just come back having lost time to others?"

"It doesn't have to be a short stay. We may like it. Why don't we get all the information together and then see how it stacks up against what we have?"

And so the subject was temporarily dropped and I went to see our sons in their adjoining bedroom.

Tony and Harry slept in that deep well of oblivion only the young enjoy. Out of preference rather than necessity they still shared the same bed. Harry followed Tony everywhere and if a suggestion had been made to sleep somewhere else he would have protested. Younger sons take their older brothers for inspiration, not their fathers. Tonight he was wearing the slightest of frowns, as if he had gone to bed harbouring a difficult thought. I touched the hair just above his ear and wondered what at the end of the day I would leave him with. The frown thawed a fraction. His brother, even in sleep, always managed to look stronger. The arm not under Harry was thrown back behind his head as if waving. He looked as if he was standing on a hill-top that slower companions were struggling to ascend. For him sleeping was a waste of time, but for Harry a blessed relief.

Over the weeks the idea of a foreign assignment gradually grew on Jane until both of us realised there was really nothing of any significance holding us back. Corporate legal affairs suddenly outweighed the petty dramas of suburban family business even for a budding partner, and her enthusiasm soon caught up with mine.

The final piece to fall in place was agreement with the company on support for our two boys' schooling. Jane greeted that news with glee.

"Private education paid for by someone else? What a fantastic idea!"

From that moment we began winding down our affairs in London and took no more than a couple of months to begin the new chapter of our journey.

Almost a year after of our arrival, Felix Freshwater, who had become a close colleague in sales and marketing, invited us to a barbeque. In London the only people we knew with experience of such events were those who had lived in sunnier climes, but here, under the brilliant sun, getting swept along by the colour and sounds of a sub-tropical afternoon was too beguiling to leave to others.

"My good friends," Felix enthused as we emerged onto his rooftop terrace, "I hope you were more punctual for your wedding day. Come on in; you will know quite a few here, so mingle as you wish, or enjoy the view. Drinks are over there at the bar. All tastes are catered for. A little different to SW19, wouldn't you say?"

To say that Felix had become a family friend would be an overstatement, but his humour and ready familiarity were nothing if not disarming.

Knots of people stood about in loud conversation and laughter floated on the gentle breeze. Glasses were thrust into our hands and Jane was pulled into a noisy group who obviously recognised her.

Temporarily abandoned, I hung over the terrace to absorb the view. The blue ocean stretched from almost beneath my feet into the far twinkling distance. Even further away, but still sharp in the clear air, were several granite islands. Softened by the miles, they appeared as if painted in a child's picture book. About me, the air caressed with the touch of an Arabian-night's garden.

A sound of wild hilarity burst from the group where Jane was the smiling centre. I dragged my eyes away from the view and looked across at her. She really was a most remarkable woman, having intelligence and beauty to envy.

One of her most appealing features was the effortless and easy way she carried her gifts; a true child of nature, a Greek nymph, who in another age would have inspired poetry. Despite the passage of time and two children she remained stunningly good looking and turned heads in exactly the same way now as when we first met, without ever, I swear, being aware of the attention she attracted.

Resplendent in flowered shirt, shorts and loafers, Felix reappeared. Following the direction of my gaze, he said, "If I may say so, you are an incredibly lucky man."

"Yes, indeed. I am very aware of my good fortune."

"You must look after her."

"I like to think I always shall."

Felix swirled the pink liquid in a glass he held before replying, "Why yes, I'm sure you will, dear boy," and then in a note of mild exasperation added, "Ahh! And who do we have here?"

Dobbs, or David O'Brien, our managing partner, was striding towards us with his young wife, Felicity, not far behind. He nodded vigorously at Felix and me.

"You look like the sports team propping up the bar. Not, I hope a signpost to the future? Say hello, Felicity."

Dobbs's wife greeted us graciously. She radiated poise and elegance and was in the starkest contrast to her husband that roughest of rough diamonds whom no-one underestimated, or expected to out-manoeuvre. His balding head and skin, bearing colours indistinguishable from the pages of a used paperback, were outward signs of the wear and tear inflicted by the years spent building a company single-handedly. Notwithstanding the name, he was of north London stock and still carried, after all these years, accents picked up in post-war state education; an original from the school of hard knocks as he frequently and proudly repeated.

"We were discussing manifestations of beauty," Felix offered.

"And this man," Dobbs indicated Felix to Felicity with the back of his hand, "speaks only in riddles. If you mean Jane, I agree with your sentiments. She does you and all of us great credit, my boy."

"Thank you, David. Mrs O'Brien, may I get you something?" I asked. "What would you care to drink?"

"Why, thank you." Felicity smiled. "A dry white would be perfect."

I walked across to the bar. Dobbs exercised his muscles a little more on Felix before moving off to chide others whose standards failed to measure up.

When I got back, Jane had emerged from the throng and, glowing with vitality and high-spirits, was in conversation with Felicity and Felix. Being in the middle of an excited group was nothing new. Her zest was infectious. Felix, eager to enjoy the end of a story he was telling, cupped Jane's elbow, which extended into a clear-skinned arm and hand with an empty glass. At the punch line he threw back his head and brayed like a mule.

"Aah ha, my dear, isn't that too hysterical," and sobering slightly, continued, "And now we will have to share you with that husband of yours who has been fetching drinks for ladies."

"Here you are Mrs O'Brien. Jane, would you like something? I see Felix has been forgetting his duties."

"How can anyone leave your wife when she lights up the sky with such dazzling conversation. She is totally wasted on you, dear boy."

"But I thought you were telling the story?"

"Chastised twice in one night by two of my guests is too much wouldn't you say? But I shall take the rebukes in my stride and retreat to a private corner with these companions while you obtain your entertainment elsewhere." Felix was never without a smart reply.

Even though not so young, he was one of the most urbane of operators, dressed to kill, with a monogrammed shirt, manicured nails and the sleekest of hair. The inexperienced young bucks about the office disguised their jealousy by ridiculing him as held together by gel and medication. But, to whatever he owed his conquests, there was no doubting his easy handling of countless affairs. His conversation entertained and charmed, and partly because of his worldliness, he was viewed by the morally correct as more than a bit of a scoundrel. At the turn of the previous century, he would probably have been horsewhipped, but in these more relaxed times his exploits attracted more envy than outrage. In all his eventful history with women, however, I liked to think he had never found love in the way I had discovered it with Jane.

Without further comment, Felix placed his soft, dainty hand, in the small of Jane's back and with Felicity on his other side steered both away from me and the subdued assembly gathered round a smoking barbeque where several guests I knew well roamed like starving jackals watching a carcase being devoured by bigger beasts. Collectively they were a project team sent out for ten days to work with Dobb's people. They looked warily around as if scenting challenges they were unequipped to handle.

"Hello, Haggard. You must be enjoying escaping from all that wind and rain?"

"Don't get much time to worry about the weather when we are up to our necks," was the dampening response.

Haggard was a heavy, morose individual, capable of making a burden out of the lightest event. Whatever the time of year, he was a man for whom the month was always November, one whose spirit had been formed under unbroken grey skies and in the slosh of wet streets. His selection to lead the team was a mystery unless a lack of colour had its corollary in steadiness and reliability.

"How come you've been put in charge of the barbeque?"

"You know how Freshwater gets by? Presents the public face and leaves grunt work to a supporting cast. A born schmoozer if ever I saw one."

"You seem displeased?"

"No, actually; I'm having a whale of a time," he said without the least hint of insincerity.

I remembered seeing people from warmer counties in London shivering in sleeveless shirts and Haggard, the inverse image with drizzle and short days in his soul, was equally unprepared.

His principle concession to the sun was an outsize pair of tan shorts that hung below his knees and which could have been acquired at a boy-scout jumble-sale. Below the shorts were unhealthily palid legs and the same black shoes and socks he typically wore at the office. Skin that had not seen strong daylight in twenty years was not benefiting from exposure, especially when accompanied by tufts of greying hair protruding unnaturally through the rolled sleeves and tight buttoning of his dress shirt.

Haggard's hands were occupied by a large iced drink, which could have been anything from water to neat vodka, and a long grilling fork. Steamed glasses slipped repeatedly along his wet nose to be as often thrust back by a clumsy thumb.

"Well, that's good. For a second I thought you'd drawn the short straw."

But Haggard was not in a mood for party jesting and squinted mournfully through the wreaths of blue smoke rising between us.

"I don't know how you people survive in this heat," he said at last, as if the effort of being companionable was just too wearisome.

"Sure makes you realize an overseas posting is not all it's cracked up to be," I suggested.

"I wouldn't want one even if you paid me," he replied, with another sticky shove at his glasses.

"We generally do, but not excessively."

Haggard tossed a charred object onto a waiting plate.

"What?" He looked puzzled, but then added after another long pause, "Uh, oh... I see."

The drink in Haggard's hand was moved to a position under his arm and he readjusted his slippery spectacles for the tenth time. Behind moist concentric circles he looked resentful as well as out of his element. The remaining items on the grill were moved around in random fashion. Standing back from the barbeque in some relief he gave his glass to a passing waiter and extracted a large, once-white handkerchief from his shorts to dab at his glasses and streaming face, before saying with deliberation, "You seem to have settled in here, especially that wife of yours."

"My guess is this transfer will be one of the best decisions we ever made."

"Well," he said as he wiped at streaks of charcoal that had somehow got onto his clothes, "I hope you don't live to regret it."

On the terrace wall an unblinking lizard felt the air with its flickering blue tongue.

Although Haggard was not someone I knew well, my infrequent contacts had led me to suppose he was a man preoccupied by personal thoughts, who didn't really exist on any social level; a man for whom life was an internal affair from which he failed to engage with any surrounding company. Perhaps what Dobbs had seen in him was this detachment that enabled a pragmatic course to be steered without getting entangled in competition or a pursuit of personal ambition.

***

In the taxi on the way home Jane, was bursting with fun and humming along with the low-volume music coming from a radio.

"Felix was the star of the evening again," I said, leaning across towards her.

"Can't imagine he ever lets the side down. Hmm, hmm."

"Do you see much of him at work?"

"Mmm? Oh! Not often, but he does have a habit of dropping by. Just wanting to chat if you ask me, and keep his contacts in good repair. Bet he does it with everyone."

"Bit of a creep, maybe?"

"Around women? Oh! Only if you let him."

Jane held my hand in her lap, but she was looking out of the window at the sweeping harbour. There was no city in the world with more skyscrapers and the dazzling array of lights covering the whole north shore was in sharp contrast to our side of the island. Within minutes of turning up over the hill the bright, concrete canyons disappeared and dense woods overhung the twisting road.

"What did he have to say after he whisked you and Felicity away?"

"Mostly inane banter. You know how he is."

"Yes, I'm starting to."

"Are you bothered by something, Sweetheart? You don't seem to be happy with the day?"

"Am I sounding grumpy? Didn't mean to when that terrace is such a wonderful spot. Did you hear the minahs chattering on the hillside?"

"Yes, I did and you are a little unhappy. I was glad Dobbs and Felicity came. They don't show up at all the staff events; too much to do, I suppose, but they are quite a pair. Do you like her?"

"After a heavy session with Dobbs, she's a meadow breeze and I'd rather listen to her than Felix's hurricane of repartee."

"Now you're being unfair. He held the barbeque as much for us as anyone else and you like his joking. You've said so before."

I could sense Jane was looking at me from under her eyebrows, but in the almost total dark of the speeding hillside and overhanging branches, it was impossible to say exactly what expression was in her eyes. The pressure on my hand did not alter, and the whip of trees passing outside the taxi, the motor's growl and the humming radio, were, for a space, the only sounds to be heard.

We went to bed soon after getting home and as usual held each other close, but there was something unfinished hanging in the air which I couldn't quite define. Jane seemed to have taken some thoughts to herself for private inspection. Her hair, which normally fell across both pillows and under my head, was pulled back to the other side. I looked at her sun-tanned neck and leant forward to kiss it. Jane in turn kissed me on the forehead and rolled away. For a while I watched her gazing into the night and then fell asleep.

The view from our flat was nowhere near as spectacular as the one from Felix's roof top, but, by any other standard, it was still quite amazing. The morning after the barbeque I woke to an empty bed. Jane, clothed in a see-through silk wrap-around, was leaning on the rail of our balcony watching the sun edge round a hill's corner across the bay.

The sea was as smooth as a sheet of glass and two yachts with slack sails hung motionless on its surface. Without an arrival time getting in the way, the best their crews could expect was a destination. Mornings such as these could persuade anyone that Hong Kong was one of the best places to live.

"Isn't it beautiful?" I said and slipped my arm about her waist.

"Yes, incredible."

"I'm glad we came, aren't you?"

"Not when we first began talking about it, but now, yes, very pleased. Too bad we have to break this early spell and go to earn our pennies."

At the end of a short ride our elevator journey from ground level to the fortieth floor office took several minutes and in the interval most fellow travellers gazed at the flashing indicator recording our progress. Haggard, who was wedged in near the back, took the opportunity to extend an invitation to a party the purpose of which he left undefined.

"You'll be joining us no doubt?" he asked as if the occasion was one he couldn't wait to get behind him. Not knowing why a welcome was being offered, we accepted more out of a sense of duty than real enthusiasm.

"Yes, yes, very pleased to come."

"Thanks, thanks awfully." Glad that he had one acceptance confirmed before anything more demanding intervened, he starred at us from behind his thick glasses as happily as such a man could.

"Poor man," whispered Jane as we turned away to leave Haggard reflecting on the best approach to the next person on his mental list. A long strand of hair, which until then had been carefully combed across his domed head, became detached from its moorings and flopped gently over his right ear, like a flag of truce.

Although the guests were essentially the same as those appearing at the earlier barbeque, the party was not a success. Conversations were polite and subdued and people fidgeted as if waiting for something to turn up. When Jane and I arrived, already an hour late, only four people other than Haggard's project team had preceded us. Dobbs and Felicity were probably expecting the worst and opted for a very late entrance.

"Happy birthday!" called a chorus from the sparse assembly. "Surprise, surprise!"

"Oh, god! How did they know?" I muttered to Jane. "And it's not until next week!"

An untidy figure peeled away from the project team's huddle and shuffled forward.

"Didn't expect this huh?" Haggard enquired. "It was Felix's idea. We are leaving the day after tomorrow and rolling you in with our farewell seemed like a...ah...coincidence not to be missed."

"You're very kind. I wasn't anticipating a public celebration."

"We try and get on top of things." Small talk was not Haggard's special skill and when Felix appeared he made off for the safety of his London team.

"Felix! We hear you are the instigator of this affair?"

"If offering a suggestion attracts blame, then, yes, I admit culpability. Ahh! Jane, how good to see you. You are looking as delightful as ever. But please tell your husband not to be the party bore this time when we are here solely for his benefit."

"Is this everybody?" I asked

"Others, I'm told, will be coming." replied Felix without turning from Jane. "Please tell a story, a joke or I shall die of ennui before eight o'clock."

"Hello, Peter," an almost inaudible voice said behind me.

"Pardon? Oh…hello and who are…?"

"Sylvia, Sylvia Mertens. Can I say 'Happy birthday'? I was told I should speak to you."

"Thank you, but it is still several days away actually. And what did they say we should talk about?"

As if acknowledging a cue, Felix boomed, "We shall return," and with Jane's willing arm held between his fingers and thumb he sailed away to a far corner of the room.

"Oh, apart from congratulating you, what it is like to move here. Whether coming out as a married person makes it harder; that sort of thing."

"I see; and who thinks I've got the answers?"

"Finnegan, Mr Finnegan – that's him over there standing with Mr Haggard at the bar. He's our engineer on the project, you know."

"No, I didn't actually, but I've seen him around and you as well."

"Oh!" she said and bobbed up and down evidently pleased to have been noticed, "Thanks ever so. Mr Finnegan says that being new here you'd know a lot about what it's like."

"It's a complicated subject, but probably moving is easier on your own if only for the reason that pleasing one is simpler than pleasing two."

"I didn't think of it quite like that. Did you and your wife both have the same interest in coming?"

I couldn't decide whether Sylvia Mertens was nosey, or just silly; perhaps it was a combination of both. There may have been other explanations and the odd way she had of screwing up her face and punctuating most of her sentences with a sniff, convinced me she did not have both feet planted firmly on the ground.

"No two people are alike, however attached. Are you married?"

The enquiry produced a riot of sniffing.

"Oh! Good lord," sniff, "no. Came close to it once," sniff. "But the man," sniff, "got cold feet," sniff, sniff.

I felt like an intruder in other's personal grief.

"Then are you contemplating moving to Hong Kong?"

"Hong Kong? Me," sniff? "I shouldn't think so."

"Then why…?"

"Why am I asking all these questions?" Sniff. She looked over her shoulder in the direction of the bar. "I thought it would be nice to talk to you. Jolly good to have all these parties, sniff. Really looking forward to eating. Missed lunch deliberately in anticipation, but I don't see much food," her head swivelled from side to side.

"How did you come to know about my birthday?"

"Oh! Funny thing, Mr Freshwater asked the project team to mark the occasion. Said it could be a sort of thank-you before we went home. Seemed to be quite insistent we should have one more celebration to bring the office together; in addition, that is, to the others you all have been providing." Sniff.

"I see. Bet you are having a great treat coming out here."

"Oh gosh, yes! My first time out of Europe. But I don't think Mr Haggard is enjoying it quite as much. It's far too hot for him."

I waited for the sniff, but this time it did not come. I wondered what would happen if Felix waltzed her away to see the bougainvillea shrubs on the balcony outside. She'd probably shriek like a hyena and sneeze all over his high fashion. Sylvia looked puzzled by my smile.

"Did I say something dreadfully stupid? My friends at home think I've travelled a lot, but Asia is something very, very different you know, not at all like Majorca and all that." Sniff.

"No, of course not. I was thinking of you people coming all the way out and then being conned into throwing a party."

"But joining in, you see, is part of the fun. Felix is so good to have suggested the idea."

"Don't you believe Felix is doing anything more than having a joke at your expense! In fact I wonder why he is not here getting the most out of his humour."

"I think you actually like Felix as much as I do," Sylvia sniffed.

I did not explain that the early pleasure of Felix's company was starting to pall and my opinions towards him were becoming increasingly ambivalent.

"These occasions are part pleasure, but they also carry an obligation to move around a little. You know, greet people with whom we should be on terms."

This observation brought on another major flurry of sniffs and she left, not to circulate, but to find a tissue. What, I wondered, had our conversation been about?

Felix and Jane reappeared. Both were laughing and a little flushed. At the dullest of social gatherings, Felix contrived to have a good time. He carried party spirit in his well pressed clothes and dispensed it liberally in every direction.

"Ah! The tedium of today's society has been saved again by your precious wife. She is a jewel to be protected from everything vulgar, Peter."

"I believe that is the second time you have urged me to look after her, so you can rest assured I have heard."

Jane put a hand to her breast as if to steady excitement. She looked at me from under her eyebrows again and I was reminded how common the gesture had become.

Voices rose near the entrance and the late arriving Dobbs appeared. Casting a restless eye over the scattering of guests, he decided where to begin and strode towards our small group with Felicity, that most feminine and gentle of creatures, close behind.

"I think the time has come for me to give others the benefit of my company," Felix whispered and slipped from view.

"Did we scare someone away?" Dobbs enquired. "I thought you were a bigger group a moment ago. Can I borrow your husband, Jane? I have something I need to discuss. Felicity, please carry on."

He put an arm behind my back and nudged me away from the growing crowd.

"Look," he began, "Oh...er...have a fantastic birthday. Ah...where was I? Yes...er...we have a chance to be involved in the development work on South Island and I want to go over some aspects of it with you."

Dobbs stood with his back to the cluster around the bar and from my obstructed view I noticed Felix reappear like a schoolboy from a farmer's orchard with Jane and Felicity in his grasp. He certainly liked to hang around pretty women.

For some men, there is no sanctity in established relationships and no ground, however hallowed, on which they fear to tread. Leaping a gate marked "Married – Keep Out" adds spice to an invasion.

Getting out of bed the next day was harder than usual; were we dulled from alcohol or sour thoughts? Jane was busy preparing the boys for school while I laboured through the morning ritual of shaving and showering. She had left a disorganised clutter on the dresser; handbag, mobile phone, cosmetics and wallet. For inexplicable reasons I undid the zipped handbag and pulled the sides apart.

A voice in the dining-room, probably Harry's, called out to say his football boots were missing.

"Did you ask Maybelle, she'll have them ready for you somewhere," said his patient mother.

The bag contained keys, tissues, various lists, an ID card and other predictable paraphernalia and, in a tiny pocket in the lining, a small envelope and card of the sort most commonly attached to a gift. Without thinking, I opened the envelope and drew out the card, which in addition to an exaggerated floral design, contained a message written in an expansive hand and startlingly sky-blue ink, saying simply, "For lighting up my life, Fey."

A door bumped to and bustle in the dining-room abruptly stopped. I replaced the card and scrambled the bag shut.

"We should get going," Jane called.

As she came into the bedroom I walked across and planted a kiss on the top of her head. The delicate smells that hung about her even in the midst of her domestic chores and my agitation were as sweet and warm as if from Mediterranean vines.

"Yep, okay. Let's start."

"Can I say something before we go?"

My heart bumped unexpectedly; had I been observed prying into the secret domain of a woman's handbag?

"Why...surely; what is it?" I replied while dreading the answer.

"Can I say thank you?"

"Thank me? For what?"

"For taking the lead to come out here, to Hong Kong I mean. You know I wasn't sure in the first place; we were so well...you know...settled. But this," she described a circle with her arms, "Has been such a revelation. Oh, it's not just the job, although that has been really exciting. But it's all the rest. I don't know how to express it, but I seem to have so many choices and there are so few...constraints. London is...well...a bit stuffy and here we don't have to conform to anything; just do as we please. We don't belong to the community, this is a Chinese town after all, and with no-one telling us what to do, or how to be, we are on our own to go whichever way we want. What I'm saying is, I've never felt so free."

"I do remember saying the change would do us good."

"Do us good, maybe, but I'm only certain about how I feel. You look astonished. Are you surprised? We haven't spoken like this before."

Was I surprised? Surely, I was, but in a way that added to my fears.

***

In the evening we sat together on the sofa. She leant back onto my chest and held my arm about her neck exactly as in earlier days. But were we in that position from habit or affection? Was this one of Jane's choices, or a hangover like eating at the same table? I wanted to ask her about "Fey", but hesitated to tell her how I came by the name. Trust is a fragile thing and like a cut flower it bruises with rough handling. The television murmured with no particular programme catching our attention. Little was said, apart from a few perfunctory words belonging as much to formality as anything else.

I wanted to cut short my mounting discontent and said, "It's getting late. Let's turn in."

But her hand unexpectedly tightened on mine and she turned to me with such a strange look in her eyes; part sadness and part absence which made me sit back. She appeared not to see my face at all, but was staring right through to a place where my thoughts might lie. A chill came over me, as if I had heard somewhere deep beneath us a heavy vault door slam shut.

"What is it, Jane? May I know?"

She let out a sigh that was not just an exhalation, but rather a breath carrying away part of her past.

"Later, when I've had time to think. Under the circumstances there's nothing we can do now."

"You sound very grim. Is there something wrong for us?"

Again she gave a sigh. Her hands that usually moved freely and naturally were held high up on her chest with palms together. They were not exactly in prayer, but had more than a hint of entreaty about them. She touched my forearm in a manner that would normally have been reassuring, but which tonight felt more like a put-off. "Under the circumstances" was an odd expression. The circumstances in my opinion dictated not a postponement, but a quick explanation to clear uncertainties. An invisible curtain fell across the room and I waited in vain for her to reach out and draw it back.

Later she sat on the end of our big double bed removing her earrings and dropping them one by one into the lap of her loose, white skirt. Her sad expression was in the craziest contrast to her sultry dress and tanned shoulders, which at another time would have tempted me to make love to her.

"Do you want to talk?" I pressed.

"Yes…no, not now. Can it keep?"

"I don't know, my love. You're unhappy with something, but I can't help unless I understand what it is."

"I need time to get it straight in my mind, before I know what to say."

"We've never in the past had a problem getting things in the open. Sharing can help. Remember it is supposed to halve the difficulty?" I said with a weak attempt to desolemnise the conversation.

"Yes, of course, you've always been good that way."

***

If Jane would not bring herself to talk, there must be something big occurring in her life to which I, even I, with all the closeness of twelve years, could not be privy. Was she in trouble at work? This was Asia; was there some corruption, some professional indiscretion? I hoped and searched for something, anything that was not a love affair.

We lay in bed together that night, not in the tight embrace to which we were accustomed, but still holding hands. Neither fell asleep immediately and from the deep breathing beside me I could tell Jane was thinking and probably looking through her eyebrows at the ceiling.

What was going on? In my mind I ranged back over today and recent weeks revisiting the clues I'd seen and those perhaps I'd missed. Oh! God in heaven, it must be that damned rapacious Felix, whom I had treated, if not like a friend, at least with decency and humour. Had he trapped my wife and stolen my peace of mind? His entertaining eccentricities and little affairs were not just a tennis club changing-room joke; now, up close, he was another grubby rake, a serpent who had intruded into my Eden.

Until today, I thought there had been no need to re-evaluate the quality of what I held with Jane. No adjustments or fine-tuning seemed necessary. Had then, our relationship's certainties been undermined by laziness and inattention?

The whiffs of instability opened my eyes and ears. What had this meant? What that? Why had she smiled, or frowned in such way? Why had she chosen exactly those words? What was the significance of an altered routine? I was racked by uncertainty and doubt.

My hand gradually disengaged from Jane's and her intake of breath told me she felt me slide away.

Anger and an immediate desire to attack and smash the thing that was wrecking my world, my love, and my sons' happiness besieged me. How would I tell Harry? I pictured the anguish in his eyes. There is nothing harder to bear than the pain of lost love on a child's face; it is worse than a striking fist.

Jane briefly fell out of my thoughts as I wrestled with the confrontation I was planning with Felix. Perhaps I'd go to his apartment in the morning and beat him until his face bled over whatever boutique nightwear he was lazing in, or I'd shave one side of his head, or yell fornicator, lecher and filthy rutting hog after him as he walked the street to the taxi ranks. The mental picture of Felix exposed and shorn of his credibility was all that kept me sane through the long, sleepless night.

Before there was any hint of day in the sky I left and drove at a furious speed into the wooded hills behind our apartment block. I had no clear idea where I was going, or why I was driving at such a pace. I'd looked in at the two boys and ran my hand over both their heads while they were still in profound sleep. Would they rest with as much tranquillity tomorrow?

From the rim of hills surrounding our home, I could pinpoint exactly where the sun should rise. But in today's morning-dark the sky wasn't ready. Would March now always remind me of the time when Jane, corrupted by the elegant and plausible Felix, left me? In future, when early seasonal winds began to blow, would they inevitably bring back pictures of her wrapped in a soiled silk wraparound and laughing in the company of questionable friends? Would the smells of veranda barbeques and the sub-tropics forever be tainted and unwholesome?

Before dawn, I pulled off the road into an empty parking area. From here both north and south sides of the island were visible. On one side, an almost endless line of office and residential towers rose out of the throb and hum of the bespangled, twenty-four-hour city and, on the other, thickly forested hill slopes spread with hardly a single light. Several cruise ships, lit almost as brightly as the city, lay at anchor to the north, and in the south, two costal trawlers with dim cabin lights were putting out to sea. This was a place of sharp and irreconcilable contrasts.

"So what now?" I asked myself. "What exactly am I doing, sitting up here?"

I took out my mobile phone and studied it for several seconds. As if my indecision carried to the other end it suddenly sounded loudly and obtrusively with its ridiculous electronic jingle.

"Yes?"

"Is that you? Where are you?"

"Out for a drive."

"But it's not even five yet! What are you doing?"

"I don't think the time really makes any difference, does it?"

"This is going to be dreadful for all of us, but we should be adult."

"Given the circumstances, remember that phrase? Being adult is hardly something you should urge on me."

"I'm sorry. But we can't do anything helpful on the phone. We must meet and start to talk."

"Jane, self-respect is as important to me as you are, or have been. If you are having an affair, I want it broken off now, or if it's serious I want you out of the house. I can't live with pretence."

There was a long pause followed by the same sort of sigh that I'd heard from her several times in recent days.

"It is serious, and you can't imagine…"

There was a wistful tone in her voice that was new to me. Do we ever fully understand the people we live with? We might get close to them over the years, but there is a time when we stop exploring and rest with what we know. This was where taking each other for granted began and decline followed. I knew I had not until this moment reached this point with Jane, but she, it was plain to see, was there ahead of me.

"I'm starting to imagine all sorts of things and none of it very good."

Again the sigh.

"Let's meet at Bruno's at six tonight, that'll give us some time to think."

Anger subsided for a while to be replaced with feelings of guilt. What had I done to contribute to this shipwreck? Had I been negligent, insensitive, unloving? Had I failed to respond to Jane's needs? For her, life had rarely imposed limitations, but I'd thought she, like me, required a foundation from which to try new things. Perhaps that wasn't true after all? Perhaps the base itself was a restriction from which she needed to escape? Perhaps there never was a way we could have led a long contented life together? Could I yet put things right? Should I apologise? But when, to whom and for what?

A feeling of violation followed hot on the heels of guilt. Something almost holy had been desecrated. That guttersnipe Felix had defecated on the altar of my beliefs. Hot breaths and lustful hands had groped their way uncaringly over beauty and innocence. Selfish lust had triumphed.

I was at Bruno's at least an hour before the agreed meeting and sought out a quiet alcove at the back where even raised voices would be lost in the evening's hubbub. While waiting, with chasing thoughts, my token beer lost its sparkle. What gives solace for such a failure, alcohol, religion, a bar pick-up? But no, there was no compensation for the great rents running through the fabric of my love.

On a wave of energy and summer wind, Jane swept in. She sat opposite me and unloaded several packages onto the seat next to her. Close behind came Felicity O'Brien. I had not anticipated our unravelling marriage being laid bare in front of a familiar, but essentially unconcerned third party. To confront a disappointing and grossly disappointed husband, girl-support struck me as bizarre.

"I hoped we could talk this through and make decisions privately, without getting into a public debate," I began, looking straight at Jane.

"Felicity's presence will cut out a lot of misunderstanding and we can move on quite quickly," responded Jane with decision.

Sometimes, after periods of deep reflection, she had the ability to be brusque even while still charming. Seeing others on the receiving end of those twin forces was once a source of quiet satisfaction. Now for the first time I realized how bruising they could be.

"I don't see why exactly, but if that's how you want it…what is the situation with Felix; damn his black heart? You said it was serious"

Jane hesitated and then laughed.

"Felix? Oh, my dear Peter, is that what you were thinking?"

I'd expected many things, accusation maybe, denial, justification, or possibly recrimination, all sorts of angry words, but not laughter. The situation was further from my comprehension than imagined. Worse still she was now starting to sound like Felix.

"Well, what's happening, for Christ's sake?"

Another, by now familiar, sigh from Jane, and then…

"Felicity, that is Fey, and I have been seeing a lot of each other in the last year"; she touched the table lightly to her side, "and we've established a relationship that we want to develop. We want to move in together soon, in fact right after I resign from the company."

"What? What are you saying? That you are, are…?"

"Don't sound so melodramatic and middle-class. Yes, we are lovers and wish to become partners. Once the divorce – yours and mine that is – is final and she has freed herself from Dobbs, Fey and I will be looking at marriage if that's possible, perhaps in London. Legal opinion is unclear on child custody in this type of situation, so the boys will stay with you for now."

"Sweet Jesus, I can't understand; I don't know what to say. I had no idea."

"Of course you didn't and that's why we are talking. We've started to share the news and prefer to let people know rather than wait for gossip-mongers to publish a different version."

"Who in Hell knows? Am I an inconvenient afterthought?"

Jane looked at me from under her eyebrows again, but this time with annoyance. Since last night she had acquired the resolution to overcome any pitfall. Indecision was left behind and her chosen path lay open before her.

"You are starting to be shrill and that won't get us anywhere."

"Well, well, talk about getting unceremoniously dumped! Remember you loved me once?"

"And still will, if you will allow me to do it in my own way."

"So who have you told? I don't want to look like a total jerk when people ask me how my wife is doing."

"Not many, but we agreed to start at the project team's party."

"That is what you'd call an insensitive way to celebrate a birthday. I suppose you haven't forgotten what was going on?"

"Dobbs knows and Felix, Finnegan and…."

"Finnegan? How in God's name did he get involved? Sorry, but you missed the town-crier."

"You're getting angry and it is not helpful."

"What do you expect? You tear up my life, discuss it with everyone you can think of and then breezily tell me to shape up. Am I just expected to 'behave properly'? Now I understand why I get lectures on 'looking after you' from Haggard and Freshwater. If Finnegan was told the word will be all over the place."

"Finnegan was not meant to know, but he saw us at the gym…"

"Saw you! You make it sound like spotty-faced adolescents getting caught fumbling under a dormitory blanket by the duty-mistress."

The conversation lurched and limped on, one speaker hot, the other steady, for the space of a further twenty minutes. But I had become so disorientated by Jane's revelation that my contribution, when not enraged, was incoherent. We spoke dysfunctionally about the boys. Jane was calm and controlled in contrast to my rage and complete emotional prostration. She wanted to see Tony and Harry and talk to them, but it would not be at what was once our home, neither of us wanted that. She would meet them outside somewhere and introduce them to 'Fey.' There were so many questions I needed answering and failed to ask. My Adam's apple bobbed up and down stupidly and my heart thumped.

From force of custom I paid the bill and walked them to the door. Felicity smiled in a way that seemed to imply sympathy. Jane, eager to start the next stage of her life, nodded briskly and with her hand gently holding that of Felicity's turned and walked away into the evening shopping crowds of Queen's Road without so much as a backward glance.

One year later, I received a birthday card written in a wide and faintly recognisable hand and unusual sky-blue ink; it was signed Jane and Fey, but I wished with at least half my being it had come from Jane and Felix.

FIVE

SUCCEEDING

The door at the end of the corridor was invariably shut and, because its occupant was an unforgiving man, few employees sought to intrude. When Ben Blikstern (or Double B, as he was called by younger elements of his staff whenever they gathered in the pub across the street) was drawn from his deliberations by external appointment he left oppressively, like a man summoned to his own funeral. On the rare occasions when he sent for people, they entered his domain in fear of their continued employment.

Double B had never confused popularity with profitability. Resorting to charm was beyond him, because, lacking it utterly, he only devoted his energy to calculating margins and weighing possibilities. Making money was his strength, and single-mindedness the route by which it was achieved; and if sensitivities were trodden on along the way, the pain inflicted went unnoticed.

Rumours of his wealth flourished, but, because he ran a private company and kept most of his cards face down, no-one, other than the accountant, had the least idea whether they were true or not. But that he wanted more was never in any doubt.

Where other captains of commerce encouraged openness and participation, Ben Blikstern sought opacity. In his opinion immature minds hadn't the capacity to cope with information irrelevant to their tasks. Distraction and hanging about in idle gossip were enemies to productivity and the thought of encouraging these horrified him.

While he hedged and obfuscated, they speculated and, in the absence of frankness, decided to give as little in return as their modest salaries deserved.

One morning Double B summoned Martin Deer to attend an unannounced conference. The old man liked employees to be crisp when handling his affairs, but not when standing in front of his desk. Underlings should, in a manner of speaking, stand naked in front of him and surprise meetings with undisclosed agendas were his way of keeping them on their toes. He'd seen a world awash with smart Alecs and he wasn't going to be blindsided by anyone making a living at his expense.

While sentimentality was not an accusation ever thrown at Ben Blikstern – no-one worried less about the necks on which he had stepped in the course of building his business – he did privately admit to two regrets. He was sorry more years had gone by than he could now look forward to and he was deeply unhappy that despite three marriages he still had no children. No son to advise and bring up in his image and no-one to carry forward a lifetime's dedicated – some would say neurotically compulsive – work. Like all old men he maintained the conceit that, after death, the world would continue to benefit, even if just by proxy, from his presence and opinion and while passing the baton was ultimately necessary the thought of retiring brought a cold sweat to his forehead and cramps to his stomach. But, at an advanced age, he could not deny some planning was inescapable.

For Blikstern's, Martin was an unusual hire. As a combined product of the best universities and business schools he was undoubtedly academically equipped to go far, so far in fact that one day, if Double B played his hand resourcefully, the office at the end of the corridor would be passed on to a qualified heir and the company positioned to continue as its founder wished. But there was a dilemma; how should this promising and exceptional young man grow from his present levels of low experience and high impatience to that of a well-rounded executive, trained to take over at a time and in a manner of Blikstern's choosing rather than his wanting?

Sharing the plan that Martin was marked for succession was, of course, completely out of the question. What would happen if he fell at any of the numerous hurdles? What of jealous rivalries, breeding like mushrooms in the dark over which there was no control? The company's few necessary servants, with their own expectations and ambitions, would desert and go elsewhere! In the manner of imperial Rome, the corporate body would be eaten away from within and fall like over-ripe fruit into the waiting hands of Visigoths knocking at the gate. Double B winced, but while his tightly curled white hair shifted, it noticeably failed to bristle. No, he thought, Deer would be progressively exposed and conditioned in a way that maintained his interest, but not to a point generating too much understanding or prematurely deduced conclusion.

"Martin...I...err...what are you currently working on?"

"The end-of-line pricing for Fairclough's light rifle, Mr Blikstern."

"Please, please, what am I always telling you?"

"Oh! Many things Sir. Are you thinking of buying low and selling high?"

"No, no! I mean yes, certainly, but take care how you express yourself my boy. In this office we refer to 'Fairclough's product.' We avoid needless specificity, which prompts too many false assumptions and unease."

"Sorry, Mr Blikstern, I forgot."

"We are simply dealers, middle-men; our task is to satisfy a customer, nothing more. In this and in every other case we do not wish to associate ourselves with the nature of the product, because we do not want the obligation of accepting its function. You understand? It's like cocaine, which, if in the wrong hands or not used wisely, can have consequences the buyer should have considered without our obligation to remind. Our role is not to seek assurances. We are not politicians who have a duty to consider the effect of certain decisions. We simply enable a seller and a buyer to reach mutual and discrete satisfaction. We do not wish or intend to look beyond that relationship. Do I make myself clear?"

"As always, Mr Blikstern. I have a lot to learn."

Martin's answer pleased Double B. Respect and acknowledgment that much needed learning was reassuring and, if time was not completely limitless, at least here was the raw material, the basic potter's clay, on which to work.

"We," Double B continued, hiding in the myth that a collective and faceless organization steered events and made decisions, when in fact no-one other than the sole and all-powerful owner initiated anything of consequence, "Have been approached, I am sure you are aware, by a Mid-East party to fill a need which could possibly be very adequately addressed by the Fairclough product."

"Yes, Sir," responded Martin; although being completely unaware any such conversation had taken place. One thing he had not failed to notice during his short corporate education in the habitually ill-informed environment at Blikstern's was that to admit ignorance, or suggest a data vacuum existed was considered perverse and obstructive. Better by far to say 'yes' and hope, as discussion went along to fit the pieces together until intelligent response replaced earlier inspired guesswork.

"We will require a reliable 'face' to meet our contact, on neutral ground you understand, to determine the compatibilities of the parties to work together." Once Blikstern allowed his preference for elliptical communication free rein his audience became obliged to interpret. Why? Martin wondered, couldn't Double B just say, "Look, Deer, go and check whether and how much these guys will pay."

"And how do you wish me to be involved, Mr Blikstern?"

"Involved? You are not always so dense. I want you to be the face, the representative if you will. Please make arrangements with Martha."

"Right away Doub...er...Sir. Will I be given the file to familiarize myself with your requirements?"

"This mission is of the highest confidentiality and therefore we do not want documents to lie around, or be observed as you digest them on the West Finchley underground. I will give you a personal briefing immediately before your departure."

Huh! Thought Martin, as he returned to the outer office. Vague, almost invisible plans were not the way to persuade anyone the future, or indeed the present, was in good hands. But whatever conclusions the old man wanted onlookers to draw, no-one, least of all the employee with a blue ribbon pedigree, believed his moderately expensive engagement had been arranged simply to fetch and carry. Months, or years, could pass while succession was nursed along without being admitted. Well, in that case perhaps there were ways to vault over the entire process and carve out a more rewarding niche.

If Double B had known his thoughts had been correctly identified, he would have been most unhappy, notwithstanding that the skill to observe, among other things, was exactly what was required in a protégé carefully selected to deal with a shady and opportunistic clientele. Ambiguity and unattributable assurances were the tools by which the murky business had always been conducted and these hidden tactics were assumed to be implicit in every employment relationship. But, however dismaying Martin's deductions might have been, the realisation that every employee, including the sub-contracted cleaners and security guards, shared identical perceptions would have been mortifying.

The owner's convoluted and indirect methods convinced no-one but himself and while he busied himself fanning smoke screens and skirting round succession the faithless noticed more than was intended.

One of the handful of employees Benjamin Blikstern regarded as loyal and thereby indispensable to his company was Martha Penfold. Her position, in terms of the organisation's hierarchy, was nothing, but, in the way it straddled conduits along which many important objectives were realised, it was a great deal. The role did not ask for massive intellect, but being at the centre of all the working parts rather like the knot of nerves in an ant's thorax, it required well developed disciplines of coordination and an ability to prevent parties to a conversation from establishing direct and free communication.

As a result of dropping out of secondary school at the age of fifteen, Martha was by some standards barely educated. But her service, shorter only by a few months than that of the accountant and Ben Blikstern himself, and a cavernous memory more than compensated for the limited time she had spent immersed in study.

Well past her prime and having never been more than modestly desirable, Martha was sour and unfulfilled. She tried to believe the intermittent physical relationship endured with a married man was what she wanted, but the summoned couplings every other month, while he travelled from home, served to persuade her in down moments that she was a convenience, rather like a public toilet, to be used as a last resort when more agreeable circumstances were unavailable. The truth was that only youth had once relieved her plainness and when that had passed she acquired the condition of an old shoe more valued for familiarity than beauty. She was a left over kept on one side in case someone woke hungry at three o'clock in the morning. But with the sleight of hand common among those despising their own conduct, she pretended the barrenness of her hole-in-the-wall relationship was a joy and sought nothing better.

Apart from the married man and one other, no-one knew her secret. Being so far from the way she wished others to see her, the matter was buried in denial. The 'one other' was Arnold Ainsley who encountered her once sharing an embrace in a corner of a seedy hotel lobby. Ainsley made sure he was noticed and allowed her to think her soiled laundry was safe in his hands.

Martha gave the disagreeable Arnold unprecedented access to information because she had to, while others she disliked were cast into an acid stew, heated over the twin burners of corrosive politicking and emotional degradation.

"Double B has told me to see you, about making some arrangements…? I don't have much detail. Are you aware…?"

Martin held everyone in contempt and spoke from imposing height. "Yes, Mr Blikstern has instructed me. There will be a plane ticket and accommodation for ten days."

"Where? …I mean to what destination?"

"I'm not at liberty to say," Martha responded in an artificially prim voice, cultivated for just this sort of enquirer and enquiry. "All briefings of this nature are handled by Mr Blikstern. He will give you details."

"Come on, Martha! Don't play the school teacher with me. I'm not asking for state secrets; I want to know what to pack."

In an irritable gesture, resulting from once having worn ill-fitting wire spectacles, Martha pushed an index finger along her nose. Attempting, many years ago, to arrest her even then declining looks she had substituted the unflattering glasses for contact lenses, but in spite of the accessories exchange her mannerism remained.

Martha's large nostrils dilated and she placed her hands palm down in the lap that cried out for honest affection.

"If you wish, and after Mr Blikstern has spoken to you, we can discuss the location. We have used it once before."

"I don't need to hear what restaurants the concierge recommends, or whether pick-ups can be smuggled into rooms," Martin retorted, without appreciating hotel rooms were a sensitive matter for Martha. "Between you and me this place cries out for some new thinking. You know what I mean?"

Back at his desk Martin reflected on the situation. He had no intention of waiting indefinitely to step into Double B's shoes, especially as there was no certainty what that precisely meant.

Knowing how self-serving the old man was, he judged that a chairmanship, or something equally contrived, would be created to allow room for underlings' new titles and for jobs to remain constrained exactly as they were now. Martin would be just another salaried hand, albeit slightly more exalted than the rest. That was not what he wanted, no sir! With talents like his nothing short of a piece of the action would do. But the way things looked right now, five or ten years could pass with still nothing made clear or more importantly gained. He would be one more time-server standing in line for a meal ticket. Well, screw old Blikstern to a musical chair; there were better things to do and the superficially secret and almost ludicrous assignment he'd been given would be one worth exploring.

If he was not to take the plodding route chosen for him, of satisfying with dull competence, he would exercise instead some imagination and seek a personal rather than a corporate understanding with the "party" he was being sent to assess. Was this then the chance to make the giant leap he craved?

Behind the ranks of office cubicles antenna hummed invisibly.

On an undefined errand, Arnold Ainsley, of order fulfilment, lounged by and put his glistening head above the partition.

"Well, Martin dear, what blessings have been bestowed on God's anointed today?"

There was nothing to be gained from establishing friendships, still less alliances, with characters like Ainsley in whom laziness and ambition were puzzling contradictions. Neither he nor Martin was above politics, but the real distinction between them, in Martin's opinion, was that only one knew how to use his head. Double B was not preparing the holder of umpteen degrees out of idle whim, but from a conviction he had found the man to succeed. Ainsley, with his gelled hair and slick ways, was no more than a Vaseline-coated lizard with a nasty, but non-fatal bite, around whom one stepped judiciously.

"If that line was not tired the day it was born it has not improved since," Martin replied without turning.

The sneer on Ainsley's face thickened.

"Now I understand. You were hired for your social grace and not the commercial brilliance we humble folk suspected!"

"Go away Ainsley, you're a dickhead."

In mock reverence Ainsley bowed and retreated into the aisle.

"We are here to be commanded. May Abu Assam and all his tribe take good care of you."

At first, the remark appeared gratuitous, a weak jest thrown away by an out-gunned Ainsley in the embarrassment of defeat. Only later, during the supposedly confidential briefing, did Martin realize the name of his contact was circulating in quarters that, had it been known, would cause consternation in the end-of-corridor office.

The "neutral ground" agreed for the undercover operation was a South East Asian tourist resort far enough from both parties' home turf to provide mutual comfort. To shroud the meeting in false trails the air passage followed a surprising western route, with several changes along the way. Martin may have been a clever man, but at the age of twenty-nine and despite chronic impatience, he remained, as Double B had determined, educated but unlessoned. In far greater minds than his, vigilance was by default the byword for such occasions. Worldliness and subtlety took time to perfect and being, in a manner of speaking, newly minted, Martin, while razor-sharp academically, was nowhere as sophisticated as he liked to think.

On the business class flight, provided to ensure the traveller arrived well rested and ready for his task, and under the attentions of sloe-eyed maidens supplying unprecedented luxury, he abandoned himself to indulgence. In the long hours that rolled painlessly by he got drunk twice and slept off one, but not the second, considerable hangover; and as he struggled at disembarkation with the stifling air that fell over him like a masseur's towel he felt distinctly unwell. Sweat, of the unhealthy kind woken up to when the previous night and the head on the next pillow were total mysteries, oozed from every part of his anatomy. At check-in the courteous receptionist ignored his bad breath and the intermittent bubblings emanating from his bowels and directed a porter to take Martin to his room.

Thankful to be alone, he collapsed onto the bed. Above and around him, in ignorance of natural laws, the walls turned. Oh! Dear God. If he could just get over this agony, he'd never touch another drop again.

A dazzling, white glare streaming in through the open windows hurt his eyes abominably. The northern sun, his fuddled brain recalled, was not in any way to be confused with the orb pulsating almost within touching distance.

Painfully edging to one side, but while still horizontal, he experimentally placed one foot on the floor and closed an eye. At his elbow, he became dimly aware of a basket of fruit tied neatly in cellophane and yellow ribbon and an ice bucket beaded with condensation. The thoughts of melon and champagne brought a heave to his stomach and with bulging cheeks and a hand pressed firmly to his mouth he reeled upright and lurched in zigzags towards the bathroom.

With scant relief he staggered back towards the bed crying out, "If only!" before falling pole-axed for a second time. Cold, wet and as fragile as a song-bird's egg, he lay without movement to sleep fully clothed and shoed for six unconscious hours.

Faint voices and moonlight seeping in through the gently stirring net curtains eventually roused him. Re-entry into the feeling world was a voyage from the deepest parts of the ocean and as he resurfaced and drew a hand over his prickly chin and gummed eyes he remembered he had known this place and body once before. With a thud of clarity he remembered the morning's drunken arrival and realised Blikstern would not be impressed, but, with his hangover receding and spirits rising, he knew, no-one this far from head office should frankly give a damn.

From the garden outside he heard tinkling music and, drawing aside the net curtains, he saw below a long dinner buffet table draped in crisp, red linen. Silver containers, exotic fruit, piles of bread, sweet cakes and pastries glistened in profusion and above the table bougainvillea and burning tapers hung from bamboo trelliswork in the languid evening air and warm smells of sea and vegetation.

Martin looked at himself in the mirror. Apart from blue lines under each eye he seemed to be in much better shape. A couple of tentative push-ups on the colourfully woven carpet reassured him that he was as normal as at the moment of accepting the airline's first welcoming glass of champagne.

Subsiding onto one cheek in the light pile he noticed, through the small space at the bottom of the bedroom door, two feet in tight Italian leather shoes. He lay still waiting for a knock, but the feet, as if caught in indecision, hesitated and then crept squeakily away.

Puzzled, but by no means disconcerted, Martin got up and re-examined the fruit basket and ice bucket. The inside of the cellophane was clouded and the bucket's surface warm and dry. The passing hours had rendered both tired and forlorn. In among the contents of the basket a blandly worded welcome note on pre-printed stationery assured him of the importance of his visit and that every service in the resort was his to command.

The message and the basket's drying contents were something new to Martin; this was not the sort of greeting given by the hotels where he habitually took packaged holidays. With the eagerness of a child enjoying Christmas he pulled back the stiff wrapping and, after some deliberation, selected a round fruit that was neither an apple nor pear of his experience and took a large bite. Hmm! Not bad and, unknown though it may be, it tasted a lot better than the still tacky residue of yesterday's whisky. Yeach! The very thought made him shudder.

Another envelope, of a flashy saffron colour, rested in the crook of the ice bucket's handle. In careful flourishes of composition there were signs of methodical preparation. Martin gave an exploratory sniff and recoiled in horror. Ugh! This was not a fragrance stocked by North London chemists, but, if he was destined to rub shoulders with movers and shakers, this might have to be the sort of vulgar taste to which he should become accustomed. He held the envelope's corner between a finger and thumb and wondered if a splash of whatever it was soaked in could resuscitate Martha Penfold's moribund allure.

Among many flowery detours the elaborate message welcomed Martin to Asia and looked forward to establishing a relationship and understanding that paved the way to mutually beneficial cooperation. The message was signed; 'respectfully and sincerely, Abu Assam.' Martin knew enough about human nature to realize professed 'sincerity' was as near a declaration as one could get to being an unmitigated scoundrel. Poo! He thought, the signatory might just as well have said, 'yours really honestly!' and have done.

Well over twelve hours had passed since Martin's last meal and, from under the diminishing cloud of his second hangover, hunger began to tug and, beyond the floating curtains and lilting music, the garden buffet beckon.

Freshly showered and shampooed and dressed in the abortively purchased white slacks and flowered shirt of last spring's holiday in the Mediterranean, Martin descended the single flight of stairs to the babbles of supper served by a tropical sea. Unseasonably cold weather on the Costas had compelled him to set aside his new kit and turn instead to an unfashionably thick cable-stitch sweater knitted by a well-meaning sister. But tonight and although smelling of winter storage, he felt equipped for whatever the world would throw at him. Was this, at last, his passage to the real thing?

In the busy garden an agglomeration of tourists and honeymooning couples talked and laughed noisily; among them several less ostentatiously dressed businessmen far from home enjoyed the company of noticeably younger women and legitimised their indiscretions by pretending nothing happened when falling trees crashed in a wilderness where none could see and hear. For Martin the resort was starting to feel like a good place to work on an unusual transaction.

Ahead of him in the buffet line several people heaped dishes higher than single meals required. But, determined not to miss out on another enhancing experience, he stood by the empty oyster bowl and, ignoring the sushi and roast meats piled in abundance, waited for replenishment.

A hand lightly touched his arm.

"Good evening Mr Deer. Welcome to South East Asia. We are glad to see you up and well. We were concerned."

"Pardon…?"

"Abu Assam at your esteemed service. We are delighted to meet the representative of the obliging Mr Benjamin Blikstern. I hear he places a lot of confidence in your ability to… ah…manage affairs."

From beneath a round and jovial face a portly frame quivered with noiseless mirth and Martin, wondering how many people were listening to this fulsome introduction, looked over his shoulder. But, without waiting for a response or slowing effusive patter Abu Hassan steered his new acquaintance towards a table on the fringes of the garden.

"Please join us; come this way. After such a long journey you will be hungry and surely very thirsty. Allow me," Abu Assam pressed Martin into a vacant chair. "Your company is most appreciated. Waiter!"

With a half-filled plate still held to his waist Martin nodded around the table at a po-faced man and two stunningly beautiful, but similarly undemonstrative, almost teenage women.

"This is my associate and the only man to whom in rare moments I entrust my wife and my Mercedes; his name is Latif, and these," he gestured with fat, ringed fingers, "are…Sonia and Sasha. In private, but, to share the humour with you, we call them the 'S' team. They are known to turn, you understand, at the greatest of speeds."

Abu Assam again chuckled inaudibly and the hitherto immobile Latif allowed a contortion to disturb features that could have been made of the same material as Cheops pyramid.

"And now we would like a Scotch on the rocks," Abu Assam continued, turning to the waiter who had stood patiently by, since first being summoned, "For our friend from overseas. I hear that is what you like, no?"

Martin was not quite sure what to make of so much chatter. Verbosity was bad enough, but noisy carelessness seemed an insane and almost comic way to preface sensitive business dealings.

Abu Assam caught at the departing waiter's sleeve and leaning sideways whispered something into an attentive ear. There seemed to be an understanding allowing requests to be made and granted that were quite outside the sort of transactional service offered in the haunts frequented by Martin.

"Look Mr Assam, can we make arrangements to…"

"My dear Mr Deer. Ha! That is a pun is it not? Let us leave business to another time. On a night such as this we should enjoy the simple delights around us. Tomorrow will be soon enough wouldn't you agree? After the rigours of the road or should I say the air, we should relax and," he continued, placing his dimpled hand on Sonia's shining knee that radiated warmth as if lit by internal fires. "South East Asia has so many pleasures does it not?" Again he laughed, and under a taut belt his wide girth bounced.

He's just a chancer, thought Martin, a bit different to that other con-artist who sent me out here, but when push comes to shove they're both playing in the same league. Well, some of us are about to be promoted to their division and without waiting for a semi-vacancy at the end of the corridor.

The waiter returned and placed a tumbler of whisky on the table. That, thought Martin, is a lot more than the double measures served during Finchley's happy hours and, quite forgetting his promise never to touch another drop, he took a mouthful and rolled it round his pallet.

"Not bad and not just another blend."

More drinks were placed around the table and the waiter, completing his circuit, murmured a few sotto-voce words towards the host.

"Yes, yes, good, very good,"Abu Assam said, before turning to his guests, and announcing, "We are to be joined, I'm delighted to say, by Sandra, an old friend who will surely augment the 'S' team with her arrival. We are indeed most fortunate." And again the muted laughter, before concluding, "Mr Deer, whose name gives reassurance to us all, deserves the very best we can offer and not to be abandoned to the solitary ways so much enjoyed by the singular Latif, now do we?"

Acknowledging the mention, but uncomfortable being centre stage, Abu Assam's associate moved uneasily on his cramped chair and, hoping not to find mockery on the surrounding faces, searched each in turn.

But, with some compulsion to emulate his master's elaborate manners, he creaked and clanked upright in the best show of civility his awkward frame and personality could muster. Next to the glossy limousine he was a building-site's back-hoe – more used to shovelling whatever he was directed to remove or heap, than in cruising at speed along a six-lane highway.

"Here, here would be perfect, next to our dear Mr Deer," soothed Abu Assam, "I'm sure you will have much to discuss; travel, youth, opportunity perhaps. Latif you may sit down now. The ladies prefer you to be more comfortable."

The request further inconvenienced Latif and he rumbled back into his seat gracelessly with a bony knee brought up close to his chin. Across the table Abu Assam slouched between Sonia and Sasha as if every minute of every waking day was spent in such indolence. Crocodile skin and silk sat easily on one, while even the best tanned Italian leather, paid for by his employer, tortured the other's feet beyond endurance.

If Ben Blikstern took the trouble to go on the road, Martin thought, he'd know what a business trip to South East Asia really meant. Getting an assessment, of whether clients would pay for a container of the so-called 'Fairclough product' was something any errand boy could achieve, even the sly-witted Arnold Ainsley. But getting in with these guys and working out a special arrangement required a bit of finesse and some give and take. Rushing along and spoiling the relationship before negotiations got under way was not the place to start. Loosening up and taking a longer perspective, yeah, that was how to begin and with a return flight still nine days away, or almost as long as the average annual holiday, there was plenty of time to use your smarts and make the most of something that had the makings of a rather pleasant situation.

"You have sufficient on your plate for only a very small man. Latif, what are you doing? Look at our guest; he lacks even one oyster. We must not be found wanting in our hospitality; nothing is more regrettable. "

The aide unfolded for the second time and set off stonily for the buffet spread, while Martin turned to Sandra.

"Can I get you something?"

The reply was warm, almost intimate.

"I expect Latif will find enough for both of us. I'm sure he can take care of things. Let's wait and see."

"I was thinking of a drink. Want me to order for you?"

"A green mango juice would be fine."

"Really? Is that what you normally go for? Then let me see if…"

He raised an arm into the air and looked around for help.

Sonia and Sasha watched, but said nothing.

"And these ladies will have the same again, unless I'm mistaken; but allow me," Abu Assam said addressing first his dinner party and then the waiter who had again appeared like a genie at the turn of a magic ring.

How much tipple, Martin wondered, do those two put away in an evening when not disorientated by gripping conversation. Not what I'd call a sharp pair, compared to Sandra. A glass of fizz may be better than an empty one but, personally, I'd go for the malt any day, especially when it's sitting right alongside.

Sandra was so attractive and inviting, Martin suddenly realised he was staring.

In his circle of friends he was used to women who were often just a bit too overbearing and not nearly as feminine as this raven-haired beauty. What exactly was it that made her so delectable? Was it the short mauve dress that showed her legs and shoulders; the thin silver chain that contrasted with her olive skin, or just her straight back and dainty figure?

The small space between Martin and Sandra was suddenly obstructed by Latif's ponderous frame precariously juggling two large dishes, heaped with crabs, prawns, oysters and other assorted sea food, some of which was completely unknown to an infrequent traveller. Latif's load was shoved without fanfare into the middle of the table and he took one pace back to pause and wait for approval, or permission to return to his place at the crowded table.

"We still need a mango juice, green I believe," Martin said looking at Sandra. Without indicating he had heard, Latif turned and lumped back in the direction from which he had only seconds before arrived.

"Then she shall have two or as much as she craves," said Abu Assam, enjoying the jest and the waiter's approach with a tray of fresh drinks, including an iced green mango juice complete with a cocktail umbrella and slice of mango on its rim.

Close behind a journeyman trio of musician, a weary photographer, aware his rental payment was due, followed, winding among the tables and singing yesterday's songs, which, regardless of culture or continent, were known to everyone from the year they were born.

Spotting an opening, Martin gestured to the photographer and in the sudden white flash pressed close to Sandra.

Food was eaten, empty plates departed, Latif returned with yet more green mango juice to set beside Sandra, glasses drained and the moon disappeared from sight behind thatched roofs. The clamour of diners fell away and soon only two or three tables remained occupied.

The cameraman reappeared and offered Sandra a large slightly unfocussed portrait in a cardboard frame.

"Oh! That's nice."

Martin put a hand to his hip.

"How much?" he enquired.

"Special price, Sir, as it's late in the evening; twenty-five dollars."

"What? That's a special price alright!" But, seeing Sandra's raised eyebrows, he leant forward and extracted a few compressed notes from trousers that were so tight, getting them out hurt his hand. "Here," he said, before adding to himself, "bloody crook."

The cost of paying for anything not for himself always felt like a total loss to Martin. But in a way perhaps even this outlay had a selfish purpose. He took the photograph a little too brusquely and wrote in one corner, "To Sandra Savanathrop; in memory of a beautiful evening, with warmest regards, Martin Deer."

Throughout the long dinner Martin had fallen into her almost exclusive company; Latif, save for intermittent glances in the waiter's direction, sat as detached and inelegantly as a pile of concrete blocks dumped by a house builder and, pursuing a separate agenda, Abu Assam wove a web of sticky entanglement around the frivolous Sonia and Sasha, the two summer-born fruit flies lolling on a steaming buffalo pat.

"Well, it is high time we sought our beds," eventually boomed the ever-affable host, rising to his feet and coiling reptilian arms round the waists of his companions. "We to ours and Latif to his…ah…own devices and you, my guests, to yours. We have much to accomplish tomorrow. May you all sleep if not as much as you should at least as well as you deserve."

With his two companions tucked close to his side Abu Assam rolled away into the darkness. Was it that simple? Martin wondered; just eat the fruit ripened by sun and showers?

"Would you like to show me the beach?" he said turning to Sandra. Without speaking she turned and walked away towards the sounds of tiny waves slapping on the shore. 'I'm in, I'm in,' he crowed to himself and rubbed his hands with glee."

The returning intoxication and mood of his outward flight persuaded Martin he could side-step any hidden ambush and, with the agility of a tree-top monkey snatch the bait planted by Abu Assam and make off with it unscathed.

He'd made up his mind Sandra was not as the other two. Entirely different material, yes, he enthused, and as a resort employee, rather than a freelancer, merely making important guests comfortable with their surroundings. Serious right of access would be available only to those she liked, not to those offering reward, however well-heeled. Her full red lips and wide black eyes had carried him in the space of an equatorial heart beat to a place beyond recall.

Palm fronds rustled overhead and the ocean sighed. Away from the resort's lights the Milky Way sparkled like diamonds in the black and unfathomable sky. Enchantment in the night and spirit in his glass had turned Martin's senses and he sat on a fallen tree and kicked off his shoes.

"Let's watch the sea," he said stupidly and dusted the trunk beside him encouragingly. "Isn't it fantastic?"

"Yes, but I do live here and see it every day."

"Of course, but plenty of men have been lost for this."

"Are you going to be one of them?"

He turned and looked at her sitting next to him. In her eyes, which were as deep and dark as the night sky, he thought he could see the stars' reflection and leant forward to kiss their lids that smelt and tasted of hibiscus and frangipani, cinnamon and sandalwood, salt sea breezes and the warm red earth, and his veins throbbed in his head like steam-piping.

"I think may be I..."

He looked down and saw the mauve dress clinging to her glistening thighs and without a thought put his hand between her knees. Sandra didn't recoil, but, not being the girl he surmised, nor did she dissolve into a jelly at the sudden intrusion.

"You're suffering from the heat," she said, taking a grip on his wrist, but leaving the hand exactly where it was.

"I wouldn't doubt that for a second. Have you ever wondered how far comets travel?" Sandra's soft, smooth skin under his finger tips and the lack of outright rejection persuaded him she was going though the customary female response of not wanting to appear over-eager, while being as ready and fired-up as he. So he pushed a little more vigorously.

"Please don't think I'm here just for the taking," she said, more firmly than he expected, before taking his arm with both hands and pulling him away.

"But isn't a man and a woman being together a beautiful thing."

Sandra smiled, "And you thought that I was ready to be 'beautiful' with you? Really? So soon?"

Standing up she flicked wood particles from her dress, while he, sensing ambiguity, clung to his hopes and the palm trunk. But when she made a step towards the garden he scrambled for his discarded shoes and, snatching them up in the hand made warm by her thigh, ran after her.

"Can we meet tomorrow? Are you working? What do you do for lunch?" His questions tumbled out as rapidly as sand falling into a broken dyke and he scrambled sideways with his socks catching on thorny vegetation. "Look," he said, coming to a halt and calling after her, "I want to see you again."

She stopped a few paces further off and looked back at him, "I have a busy day ahead of me and midnight has already past. I'll let you know."

"Is that a put off?"

"It's whatever you believe. But I have to sleep or I can't earn a living."

He caught up with her and studied the exquisite face that was a good twelve inches below his before stooping for a shared kiss. She did not back away, but, turned and offered her cheek. Scorning such a modest victory he bent lower to touch her neck with his lips and in that spicery discovered again what he thought were all the fragrances and mysteries of the islands.

"You're unbelievable; do you have the least idea?" he breathed, without opening his eyes.

"Yes, I have heard men say this before, but I try not to get carried away," she replied, before turning and sailing gracefully away.

"I'm in room 201, if you want to leave a message," he called after her.

"I work here, remember?" she threw back over her shoulder and disappeared from sight.

The crossing of multiple time zones, midday's drunken unconsciousness and now the pounding hopes of tropical romance plundered him of rest. Not until six o'clock when the eastern stars faded into a backdrop of approaching day, did he slip into anything approaching real sleep and in jumbled dreams, fractured at the end by an early morning cleaning service, he returned to the end-of-corridor office. Ben Blikstern demanded a report on the eastern mission, but was dismayed to find his protégé attending his summons without shoes. From behind his oak-wood desk the old man observed damp green stains of crushed vegetation on Martin's polyester stockings. Noisily tapping a gold fountain pen that had been the gift of a gratified buyer, Double B angrily demanded why socks were being worn several shades lighter than the accompanying suit when everyone knew such trimmings must be darker.

"When will you ever learn!" he thundered, his tiny eyes shrinking to pin-pricks the size of melt-water drips in snow. "I did not get where I am today by ignoring the basic elements of dress."

***

Waking with a jump the earlier tapping escalated into banging and Martin thrashed about trying to remember where he was.

"Room service," a disembodied voice called.

"You must be joking; not now!"

"Can I clean your room, Sir?" the voice's owner enquired from outside.

Yanking angrily out of bed Martin flung open the door.

"I said, not now!" he yelled at a middle-aged woman wearing a dust cap and toothy smile.

"Certainly Sir," and on noticing Martin's unshod feet added, "Would you like slippers? They are available in…"

"No! Dammit I would not."

"Very good Sir. May I place this notice on your door? When you require servicing please turn it over and your room will be cleaned. We are proud to have you stay at our resort."

Many uncharitable thoughts whirled through Martin's sleep-deprived head. But at a loss to express them adequately, he slammed the door shut on the sunny matron and aimed an ill-advised kick at a stand holding the warm ice bucket. The stab of pain that ran from his toe to the nerve centred in his right buttock produced a yelp heard by the chamber-maid as she pushed her cleaning trolley away towards more agreeable visitors' rooms.

"Not used to premier service," she confided to a meal-service waitress passing en route to a luxury suite at the end of the floor, with a delicately poised tray bearing three grilled breakfasts. And, as the lift opened beside her, she repeated the message to the duty medical officer rushing to attend to an emergency call made from room 201.

While Sonia and Sasha slept in twisted sheets and pillows on the luxury suite's gigantic bed, Martin endured the smart of an anti-tetanus injection and the waitress, being familiar with the unconventional sleeping arrangements that often followed busy nights, placed her tray in a tangle of brown limbs and abandoned clothes and left unheeded.

Emerging from a steaming shower in the folds of an enormous bath towel encompassing his ample proportions Abu Assam examined the tray's contents. The eggs had hardened on the long journey from the kitchens and were not to his liking. To make matters worse, Martin, whom he had marked as ambitious, had not bothered to call. Weren't young men supposed to be in a hurry? Was it possible he had misread this emissary and was, even now, dealing with one of no more complexity or motivation than a salary-man delivering a message?

If Abu Assam disliked anything it was the commonplace. Unexceptional people, like unexceptional events, left him unmoved. Up to this point the business deal and subsequent female surrender, before a serious barricade had been stormed, left the quality of both much in doubt. For a man such as him the week was so far singularly unstimulating. Would Benjamin Blikstern's colourless envoy step up to the plate and alleviate the burgeoning sense of disappointment? Well, well, he'd just have to wait and see.

A partly visible, but unidentifiable article of blue-laced female clothing protruded from beneath crumpled pillows and a head of cascading black curls. Tugging it free and holding it over his nose Abu Assam inhaled deeply. Ah! Even when laid out on a plate the seductive power of satin impregnated with a woman's scent took some beating. He drew another breath and reflected on the morsel that lay concealed beneath this taut fabric late last night. Too bad the mountain top had not been at the end of a more exhilarating climb! He screwed the garment into a tiny ball and thrust it down into the folds of his towel.

A muffled telephone ring and grunts from the neighbouring room half roused the two untidy sleepers.

"Answer that will you!" Abu Assam shouted at anyone who cared to take note.

After a great deal of unidentifiable shuffling, the ungainly lieutenant pushed the inter-connecting door open a fraction.

"I think it's in here."

"What! Well find it, find it. Don't expect me to do everything."

Dressed in boxer-shorts and somebody else's Disneyland tee-shirt, the bulking Latif edged forward and nervously turned over miscellaneous items littering the floor.

"What's happening?" enquired a husky voice from the adjoining room. "Don't forget I'm on again at twelve."

"Get him out of here, snapped Abu Assam."

Latif, who was peering under the opulent bed that would not have been out of place in the Court of Caliph Haroon al Rashid, heaved himself into a semi-erect position and reversed back towards the adjoining door. Exposing the full length of his sinewy legs to a female audience, including one that slept, was more than his self-confidence allowed.

"Where are you going?"

"You asked and I'm going to…"

"Not now, you incompetent. Find the phone first and then get rid of your…friend."

Crouching again Latif pointed to the bed. "It's under there."

"Well, get it out, get it out. Am I cook, driver and laundryman?"

Huddled on his knees Latif tugged an exposed cable with one hand and held his frayed tee-shirt in place with the other. The telephone receiver and console separated at Abu Assam's feet and the ringing abruptly stopped.

"Oh!"

"You imbecile, you useless thing…Tell me why I keep you? Why? Huh?"

Abu Assam raised a hand high in the air to slap the unfortunate assistant, while Latif, with the stoicism and humility of a martyr prepared to receive his punishment; but the passion of the moment froze in renewed clamour from the telephone.

"Don't you dare touch it," screamed Abu Assam and, then with a voice as soft as a mother's whisper to an infant born that morning, cooed, "Hello, Abu Assam speaking."

Latif scuttled back to his room and noiselessly pulled the door into place behind him. Sounds of frantic scrabbling followed by a pause and the click of a latch falling into place filtered though the panelling.

Among the rumpled sheets and on both sides of Abu Assam's pudgy knees Sonia and Sasha yawned into wakefulness.

"What happened…? Did…?" Sasha began before giggling and stretching out a manicured hand to search the voluminous towelling above her.

"Not now; can't you see I'm talking? Be good girls and eat your breakfast; then get along; I'll call you later in the day. For the moment I have work to do. Yes, yes," he purred returning to his interrupted caller, "I was not expecting to hear from you. But we are moving well, if a little slowly. We will be in contact as we proceed. Please thank your colleague for making such gratifying arrangements; we are all truly, truly honoured."

Replacing the handset with a thump Abu Assam scowled. But, observing the twin naked forms forking waffles from the tray at his feet, his annoyance subsided. The grind of work did, after all, have some compensation and if this journey had not yet overflowed with joy one had to be grateful for the smallest of mercies.

Further along the floor the medical attendant confirmed Martin's toe had been dislocated and began laboriously encasing the damaged foot in plaster-of-Paris. Being effectively immobilised and something of an exception in recent guest-management experience, the patient was left for two hours while the whereabouts of a pair of crutches was discussed. Eventually equipped and eager not to lose further momentum to his ambitions, Martin hobbled uncertainly into the garden in search of Sandra.

If a note, bearing traces of a familiar and not very attractive perfume, had not been thrust into his hand by last night's waiter, whose cheeks were hollower than yesterday, the light rifle negotiation would have remained a footnote to the day's programme.

Damn and blast! And if this messenger, who lent closer than absolutely necessary, was allowed to walk around a stylish resort with what looked like bite marks on his neck you could wonder where standards of customer service were heading?

"Good day, Mr Martin." He read, "We hope you are enjoying your glorious visit. Abu Assam takes tea on the terrace at sixteen hundred. Please to join him. Your obliged, Latif."

In the conditions of his upbringing Martin believed arriving five minutes late was an admirable way to make your host aware you were not there out of necessity or desperation and were, in all things, your own man. Abu Assam, however, was of a different tradition and at a quarter past four and, indeed, at four thirty he was still nowhere in the terrace's vicinity. After ordering tea, which, in his opinion, arrived somewhat oddly as a pot of just warm water and several bags on a saucer, Martin wondered what else he was expected to tolerate.

At about four forty-five Abu Assam swayed into sight, but instead of joining his guest directly, spent several minutes in close consultation with the waiter who had delivered the message. Remembering the steps of negotiation instilled into him at Blikstern's, Martin wondered whether a successful outcome was as firmly in his control as he had felt a few hours ago, or was the issue no more than that people in this part of the world were an unreliable lot, who didn't know how to keep their own appointments.

"My dear," coxed Abu Assam ingratiatingly as he belatedly heaved across the terrace and, upon noticing the heavily plastered foot lying beneath the table, continuing sympathetically, "My unfortunate Mr Deer, what has befallen you?" Without waiting for an answer and as a knowing smile spread across his wide round face, he continued, "Did she, how do you say? Lead you a dance? Were you given the thrill of a chase? Ah! You are indeed twice blest," and with a sigh, "Whereas I alas, had a miserable, yes, most miserable evening's pursuit."

"I'm not sure what you are talking about, but if you are referring to Sandra," Martin replied stiffly, "We broke up early; she is working today."

"You mean, oh, I see, that's too bad. Well," he said brightening a little, "I can't believe you will be unlucky again and if you are I could ask Sasha to pop over and..."

"No, no! Please, I don't need any more help" and continuing after a calculated pause, "...can we discuss the Fairclough product?"

"The what? Oh, you mean the light rifle?"

Martin looked to see if anyone was listening to their conversation other than the waiter who had followed close behind Abu Assam.

Yes, yes… if you like."

To eliminate liability and costs of storage Blikstern carried no inventory. He was an intermediary who arranged deals and took a margin on the transaction, but in all other ways he stayed out of sight. The over-run production line at Fairclough's, which added up to several thousand "units", would consequently remain in the manufacturer's warehouse until the right buyer was found.

When events in the Middle East had again turned sour several urgent enquiries had come his way, including the one communicated by Latif Imad, acting on behalf of unidentified principles. Only with the last request had Double B taken steps to evaluate his options and knowing from a reliable source that the manufacturers would accept a per-item selling price of five hundred dollars he rapidly calculated the handsome profit an oil-money arrangement was likely to deliver.

Despite his instructions to undertake a careful scrutiny, Martin was not overly concerned about Abu Assam's ability to pay; in fact so carried away was he by the prospect of personal gain and a romantic dalliance, no real doubt or critical analysis disturbed his thinking. On the flimsiest of evidence, he decided, Double B would get what he wanted and a little bit extra, but that instead of slapping down more than was really needed on the desk at the end of the corridor he would skim a slice off the top and, as icing on the cake, charm the woman out of her wits. Nothing could be better.

By the simple expedient of over-charging he would take his own "turn" and, as necessary insurance, impress his employer beyond all expectation. A move of this magnitude might even persuade Double B there was no reason to hang on grimly until he dropped dead behind his desk and that the company could move swiftly into safer hands. Martin's unshakeable faith in his own ability and the gullibility of others convinced him a prodigious opportunity lay within his grasp.

"I'll come straight to the point," he went on, "we can offer five thousand units. Are you in the market to buy?"

"We are always open to possibilities, but of course I would need to test a sample."

"One can be made available in London at twenty-four hours notice. The cost in advance would be ten thousand dollars."

"Ten thousand? That is an unexpectedly high figure! Why should a single unit be worth so much?"

"Because we have what you want in volume and paying for a sample at the level I propose will indicate how serious you are. The bill would be adjusted on final shipment and after we've agreed unit price." In spite of his aching toe, and inability to sit down for periods of longer than five minutes, Martin felt he was getting into his stride.

"You are a very abrupt young man, but it could be arranged. A full transaction will depend, of course, on the cost of each unit."

"I was coming to that and…" Martin wavered and hopped up onto one leg. Other than minor matters of unsubstantiated expense claims, this was his first deliberate attempt to swindle Blikstern's and he was taking care how to frame his question.

His potential buyer, familiar with the ways of a shadowy world, and observing hesitation, took from his pocket an exotically-laced blue handkerchief and, bringing it close to his face, took a long satisfied breath with his eye lids half-closed, before continuing.

"Aha! Ahem, yes…in my country we expect to reward those who facilitate important agreements. Please sit down. Why, I myself began as a simple government agent and many of your big companies have seen fit to extend a hand of gratitude for my modest assistance in reaching…finality. Could it be that I may be in a position to thank my good friend Martin Deer?"

"Well, I have put in a lot of effort to bring the Fairclough product to a preferred client and have facilitated a very reasonable selling price. If you feel service to you should be a subject of recognition I would not stand in your way."

With no effort and, because imprecision suited the occasion, Martin had started to ape the convoluted form of expression employed by both his distant mentor and first serious client.

Agreeability began to flow between the cups and into the conversation like syrup. Each Fairclough unit, they decided, would be priced at eight hundred dollars, including a one hundred and fifty mark up for Martin's "enablement" charge. Fairclough would get their asking price and Double B one hundred and fifty. The ten thousand dollar advance for the sample would be handed over tomorrow as a demonstration of the buyer's good faith and then there would be nothing more for the "face" to do other than bank his receipts. Martin was overjoyed.

In a little over the day and a half since his arrival he had accomplished every business goal he had set out to achieve, and that had been the purpose of his journey. He had entered the heady realms of mega-deals and proved to his own satisfaction he was equal to any who fancied themselves as wheeler-dealers. Let Arthur Ainsley and Martha Penfold play their games and pretend they influenced events; they were stuck in the starting blocks breathing the dust stirred up by his flashing feet.

Late afternoon gusts from the sea swayed dusty palm tops and Abu Assam called to the ever-present waiter.

"A bottle of your best champagne if you will. We have much to celebrate."

Luck favours the bold, thought Martin smugly. There were a few pieces to put in place, but nothing insurmountable. Congratulations were entirely in order and he could afford not only to rejoice, but to devote his remaining time in South East Asia to the task of pursuing the delectable Sandra and salting away the down-payment of his considerable financial coup.

The fee, of course, needed a depository far from home and away from the eyes of prying auditors and tax collectors. If he were clever, this and the interrupted romance could neatly dovetail into one another. After a third glass of champagne and with resurfacing hopes of happily concluding yesterday's conversation, enlisting Sandra's help appeared the next obvious step.

Deals in the Blikstern environment, Martin knew, were concluded with an understanding and handshake, carefully leaving implicit the many issues others would have considered critical to a contract. In this half-lit world mutuality, rather than honesty, ensured the transaction.

The effusive and bear-like embrace Abu Assam threw around him with a cry of, "Brother Deer", was entirely of the tradition expected and, although not at all appealing, taken as ink on parchment.

With the bottle empty and expressions of eternal friendship ringing in his ears Martin limped uncertainly out of range to seek out the ravishing but still unpossessed Sandra.

Abortive enquires at the reception desk left him temporarily disconcerted, but while considering his alternatives, he observed Sasha's dripping and robed form cross the lobby.

"I say," he called jerking forward, "Could you help?"

Alive to the possibility of even the most tangential inquiry, Sasha stopped and looked at him from beneath her moist eye lashes, "And what help could I give a young gentleman?"

"I'm looking for Sandra, have you seen her?"

"Oh, oh…yes, yes I have."

"Do you know where she is? It's rather urgent."

"She's working tonight," she hurriedly explained, as if an errand as immediate as Martin's called her away. "People to entertain; you know how it is?"

"Really? And tomorrow?"

"Try at the business centre," Sasha suggested as she moved away, "around ten, or thereabouts; she should be in."

As she left, with little wet patches marking every tiny footstep, Martin noticed her glossy skin hadn't got the dulled appearance usually left by swimming pool chlorine. She must have emerged into the lobby from an unusually timed shower and on her way to another encounter with the beaming Abu Assam.

Aches in his toe and sensitive buttock persuaded Martin he should conserve energy and eat in his room. Not under any circumstances did he want his injured foot, or lack of rest, to impede plans for achieving the grand finale his personal triumph deserved.

A dish of tiger prawns in thick chilli gravy and another unknown item from the fruit basket was enough to ready him for sleep and, as daily baths were not his habit, he lay down stickily and with a firm round belly and hoisted his damaged foot onto a stack of pillows.

He had experienced physical attraction many times before, but this was starting to feel like something different. With each minor decision he found he was thinking to himself, "this was for her." The chill in air-conditioning was noticeable after the humid garden and he wondered if he was developing a fever.

"I couldn't find you yesterday," he whined to Sandra when he found her in the business centre next morning.

"Oh, were you expecting to?"

"Well, you know, I was thinking we could carry on from where we left off."

"And where was that exactly?"

"I'm sorry, I got carried away. But you are pretty irresistible."

"Holiday romances may suit some people, but they're not for me."

"Look, I like you, I like you a lot and I want to see more of you."

"That isn't very original and besides you'll be gone in a week. What then?"

"I was planning to come back."

"Most men say what they have to for a limited objective. How do I know?"

"If I showed you that I'm ready to trust you, would you do the same for me?"

"Depends what you have in mind?"

Martin took a deep breath and laid his plan at her feet.

"I want to open a bank account and need guidance from someone local."

He stared at the impassive face and tried to read the workings of her mind.

"Why would you need a bank account?" she said in a whisper, "when you'll be gone next Wednesday?"

"How did you know?"

"Because I wanted to find out."

For the first time since being rejected Marin felt his heart skip a little faster.

At the bank next day a tidal wave of red tape engulfed his enquiry; do you have a reference? Where is your residence certificate? Who is your employer? Where will deposits come from and how often? And on and on until his enthusiasm sagged.

"This is disastrous. What do we do now?"

"Is an account that important?"

"More than you can believe, so where do I go to from here?" he said giving her another searching look, "Unless... unless... look, can I really trust you, even more than just showing me the way?"

"Am I here helping you, or did I say go and look for yourself?"

"Yes, yes, alright, I know, but I'm going to suggest something that should convince you without a shadow of doubt."

"That's not another invitation to be beautiful is it?"

"No, no, this is business."

Again he took a deep breath.

"Can I make a deposit into your account, for you to look after?"

He had come to a conclusion that funds held by her would bind her to him more surely than anything. Some wedded couples he knew never even went that far and maintained separate finances for a lifetime. Wasn't this then the highest declaration of intent he or anyone could offer? If she was not persuaded by a shared interest deeper than a marriage vow then nothing would move her.

"Is that what you want?"

"You can't say afterwards I'm not genuine."

"Well, well...."

And this time when he bent towards her she did not offer a cheek.

His remaining days in South East Asia passed in a whirl. He had obtained everything his fantasies and calculation had imagined. Financial independence and a woman, who was a paragon of beauty, virtue and good sense, were, he believed, his. The gods must surely have chosen him at birth as one of their own.

On the morning of his return flight they went together to the airfield and amidst embraces wet with tears and promises to be together again within three months he took his painful leave, reluctantly turning at intervals to wave and look for assurance she had substance and was not a creature of a dream.

Later, in the cold grey light of a northern autumn, Martin planned his next moves. He'd have to get the sample to Abu Assam's man who would be contacting him in the coming week, and then, with examination complete, arrange carriage of the main consignment to a Spanish fishing trawler arriving unscheduled at a port along the Cornish coast. And after that he'd have to make up his mind whether to hang on at Blikstern's, or move out on his own.

Now that his foot was no longer encased in plaster-of-Paris he strode confidently between knots of people resisting the coming day's work. He should have noticed the interest in his reappearance, but, dismissive as always, he jeeringly labelled them nonentities. Had any the courage to choose a better way? Had any recognised the multiplicity of roads around them, or said I'll take one untrodden by the rabble? They dully went about their lives with none asking why or why not and − like chickens laying eggs for others to fry − they were governed by the cooking pot.

"Mr Blikstern will see you at ten," Martha said as he sailed by.

"And the agenda will be…? Or should I bring my own?"

He mistakenly read Martha's expression as one of incredulity and laughed out loud.

A free hour before important discussions with the company's owner might usefully have been spent in preparation. But Martin, sure of his ground, raised both feet to a window sill and opened his computer. An incoming rush of messages flooded the screen and save one marked "ssavanathrop" he deleted the entire mailbox. Only this, he decided, was worth his time and effort.

The single name remained on his screen. Should he open the message now or let anticipation build with the contents savoured later?

"Our saviour returns and we poor tillers of fields wait for an invitation to the harvest." Ainsley's oiled head rose over the partition. Beads of undefined moisture that could have been hastily drunk coffee or perspiration, dotted his long; some would say too long, upper lip. Thank God for natural selection, Martin thought. Repulsive creatures such as this had little chance of passing on their disgusting genes, when they were thankfully destined to die out in a single generation.

"What do you want, Ainsley? I don't have time for your babble."

"Would congratulations be in order? We all know the twists and turns of Asian negotiations are mastered only by a few. In fact you could say the Orient's ways are full of ess-bends."

"What's that? Look, just get lost will you?" Martin snapped and spun away.

"Please, be careful taking your feet down from the window. Extremities must be protected from what may be left around."

Ten o'clock came and Martin passed, as he had on the day of receiving his assignment, past the ranks of hidden antenna tuned to detect the faintest hums emitted at the galaxy's end. He had suddenly become a little anxious, without being quite sure why.

"Good morn…"

"Enough already," snapped Ben Blikstern throwing a document across his desk, "What do you know of that?"

Looking at the blurred piece of paper Martin saw what appeared to be a scanned copy of a bank deposit slip for a large sum of money deposited in the name of S. Savanathrop."

"Where did that come from?"

"That's hardly material. I asked you what you know of this… this…transaction."

"I… why, nothing…I don't know who she…er he…"

"Is that so? I would say you are attempting to lie your way out of broken trust," Double B's voice rose to a shriek. "And I suppose you have no idea who this is?" He hurled the picture of Martin and Sandra and its very personal inscription straight at his former protégé's face. "Simply put, my boy, you have failed the test and become a stunning disappointment. Your desk is being cleared. You may expect to hear from our solicitors. Now get out."

"But, let me…"

"I said get out!"

In private conversation many employees held the view Blikstern's was a totally inflexible organisation. But on the occasions that really mattered Double B changed course as vigorously and unexpectedly as a door blown open by a cyclone. Pulling the telephone towards him Blikstern punched in an extension number.

"Send in Ainsley."

Before the handset was back on its rest a knock as timorous as a child's on a Victorian father's study brushed the door.

"Come in…come in. Sit down. Tell me Ainsley, what are you working on?"

"Slightly routine task Sir; advising suppliers preparing the Bogota shipment of the entirely avoidable complexity of customs paperwork."

Double B smiled bleakly, "Yes, yes, you can probably pass that to someone else. We have a transaction that has recently run into difficulty. The person to re-establish contacts and develop negotiations needs to be exceptional. Your recent investigative work persuades me you may be the man for the job. The company does not forget loyalty to its interests."

"Yes, Sir. When do you wish me to start?"

"Soon. And I'll brief you before you set out. There is some preparatory work before we move ahead; a small matter of the 'goodwill' payment which may have to be written off as expenses; to keep the customers' full engagement you understand. But, I can tell you Arnold – it is Arnold isn't it? – if this deal is saved there is no knowing what may be achieved in this company for those executing to plan."

"I'm very gratified," replied Ainsley rubbing damp palms on his trouser leg, "That you place so much confidence in me."

At the door Arnold Ainsley stopped with one hand on the brass handle. Blikstern, whose attention had returned to the documents on his desk, was shaking his head.

"Sir, if I may make an extraordinarily presumptuous request?"

"What...what is it?" Being asked for anything always put Double B on the defensive.

"I... I'm actually getting married, to...to a lady I met during the work I did overseas for you...er...the company, last year. We've been in contact ever since, but now we have...ah...been able to save a bit, yes, quite a bit and we want to get together permanently. Could...could I ask if you would be so kind as to consider attending our wedding. It would be an enormous honour, but of course we'd understand if you felt, you know, too busy."

Blikstern straightened from the crouch he'd assumed at the start of Ainsley's speech and, with some relief, smiled dourly again; it was not a gesture that came easily. "Why, yes, I'd be happy to attend and..." he added, in an uncharacteristic afterthought, "If the bride needs someone to give her away in a foreign land where she may not have relatives, I am ready to lend my services."

"That's awfully generous of you, Sir. My fiancée and I would be most incredibly grateful."

"Yes, yes, that's alright. Just tell Martha as you go out to put the date in my book. She will make sure I am prepared. And Ainsley…"

"Yes, Sir?"

"This is one of those occasions when you wonder how far a comet travels."

"Indeed it is, Sir."

SIX

O'CASEY'S CONGREGATION

The weathered mass of San Javier's parish church leant precariously into the township's undisciplined street and from among its broken masonry and the seasonal puddles, collecting in holes on the forlorn bell tower, grass and tiny mimosa saplings sprouted. At street level the mossed and crumbling brickwork looked picturesque, but Father Patrick knew a sturdier construction with less vegetation would bring him greater peace of mind. But until the miracle unholy chastisement of local artisans was all that stood between today's half-ruin and disaster.

Dead insects, leaves and, from the upper rungs of a step-ladder leaning on the outer wall, a bird's nest several seasons old filled just some of the yawning spaces. The problems, he could see, originated deep in the masonry, but recent earth tremors, which caused the church and land to groan together like men and women embracing in sleep, had pushed more damage through the outer surface. How many more shocks would this old building stand before being reduced to rubble in the chaotic streets? Under the ample frame of Patrick James O'Casey, the ladder shook.

"What is it ye are doing now, Frans?" he called down in affected sternness to a thin, bare-footed man. The irony of God's well-proportioned representative being held aloft by an emaciated assistant was lost in familiarity and the gulf of offices.

"Padre, sorry."

"I'll give ye sorry, my boy. Who'll be holding Sunday mass if I were lost to ye all?"

"...Brother Reyes?"

"Are ye being cheeky with me now? What's that rogue got to do with San Javier's, I'd like to know? He belongs where he is twenty miles away and with Bartholomew's. Now, run and get that idle cousin of yours with his tape measure before I get really cross wi'd ye, do you hear?"

"Yes, Sir Padre."

As Frans let go, the ladder shook a second time.

"What in the name of all that's holy are ye doin'!" exclaimed Father Patrick clutching at the stones in front of him. Caught unprepared his native accent became as thick as music hall jokes."

"Fetching Raul Father, I thought you…"

"T'ought? Who was askin' ye ta t'ink? Wait 'til I get down from here and then ye can go and do as much t'inkin' as your leisure time allows."

The cloth and his undeniably foreignness combined to elevate Father Patrick to a status that few in the islands, other than ostentatious landowners, enjoyed; indeed, although unlike them and far from financially comfortable, he was in an enviable position, which some would describe as being on the edge of magnificence. The seminary of his youth and early work in the slums of Cork were a million miles away and lived on only in sketchy recollections. So much so that the idealistic young man who shared the same name and preached the Word with such fervour up and down O'Connell Street could almost have been another person.

Right since those days twenty-five years ago, after leaving his native shores, he had been at the disposal of his brotherhood, as a teacher and priest, for this remote rural community on the eastern margin of islands dotting the Pacific's rim like emeralds. Now approaching fifty, he hoped to end his days in this distant outpost, where the townsfolk with their contradictory virtues and vices, clung determinedly to the old faith like vines around a Spanish belfry.

His flock ceded to him complete spiritual and temporal power and, for this absolute acquiescence to his authority, he was duty bound to provide future deliverance and present protection. Grace, heaven and occasional earthly employment lay exclusively in his soft, pink hands.

Father Patrick shook street dust from the hem of his frayed, white cassock and entered the church's nave beneath the worrying bell tower. Today, as on every day, his worries were dispelled the moment he felt the tranquillity and serenity of the house he tended for his God. Outside, the town might be hot and distracted, but inside calm transported his sore spirit to the distance of cloud-mantled mountaintops.

Only outside was he assailed by sad reflections that, if God was indeed everywhere, why was equanimity not constant instead of a fitful visitor, like the condescending bishop who rarely toured this remote corner of his scattered diocese? Perhaps the stifling market's vendors, who routinely cheated their customers, were able to shuffle between contradictory states, but a priest, holding to a higher calling, should be blessed at all times. For officers of the Church, peace – like love – should either be all around or nowhere.

His parishioners' believed a priest was half way to heaven and through him lay the only route to the celestial kingdom. His fat hand was on the gate's handle and Father Patrick's person stood astride the road. But, he protested, where was the justice that allowed them to wallow in squalid and repetitive transgression, while he, obligated to pardon, was unable to find rest for his own flawed soul?

"Father, forgive me, for I have sinned."

And the weary preamble to absolution, "Are ye truly repentant, my son?"

"Yes, Father."

"Then say three 'Our Father's' and two 'Hail Mary's and let me be seeing ye take communion more often." The release was mechanical as if a curative for headache had been given and not free passage to an endangered soul. "Are ye understanding me?"

"Yes, Father, thank you."

On both sides of the long nave, windows were thrown back and hot, dust-laden air floated in to sparkle in beams of tropical sunlight. A pair of squabbling sparrows flew by, sparred briefly on the stone-flagged floor and departed, one in hot pursuit of the other. Would the cause of the dispute be a hen? Could these road-side spoilers of the bird kingdom, who cared not a jot for the consequence of their sins, be any more virtuous than those cast in their Maker's image?

Near the altar two women trimmed flowers and placed them in burnt earthenware pots. Four arrangements stood on wrought iron stands in cascades of white and yellow; the shades of purity and chastity best suited for God's mansion. The priest instantly recognised six or seven different varieties, but after all these years in the islands he still could not put a name to any other than the lily. He didn't have the same trouble with his congregation. Each face and name, along with all their grubby little secrets, was imprinted indelibly on his memory alongside his own, as if contained in the Lord's judgement day ledger.

The older woman was dressed in a print frock with faded frills edging her neck and elbow-length sleeves. A loose bun and diagonally placed wooden pin held her grey-streaked hair in place. The priest remembered her as having always been old, arthritic and widowed even on the day he arrived. If there had been any change in her life, it was not visible in the degrees of her infirmity or in her condition. Today, like yesterday and the day before, she stooped stiffly and scuffed uncomfortably over the stone floor. Maria Rosa had made the church her sanctuary; her shield against an unkind world. Like the surrounding damaged monument, her brown, sinewy hands spoke of passing years and privations endured. In her honest and unsteady grip the floral displays' stalks rustled.

"That surely is a sight to gladden the hearts of God and sinners alike, Rosa. Ye're doin' a fine, fine job again," Father Patrick, with feet spread wide and fleshy fingers lightly held behind his broad rump, boomed from the far end of the central aisle.

"Arranging them is easy, Father; the beauty is in their creation." If all his parishioners were as reliable and responsive as this humble woman, the Padre's credits would show a very satisfactory balance. Saint Peter himself could not but be impressed.

"Ah! Rosa. You're right and ours is but to glorify the Lord and pray he'll take the offering from unworthy hands."

"Yes, Father."

Swaying backwards and forwards in his sandaled feet and pomposity, O'Casey was by turn proud and disturbed. Pride was an undeniable sin, but hadn't he steered his flock with devotion? And couldn't the Church count on him, to deliver it well-shriven, and almost to a man and woman, at the gates of eternity? Wasn't the priest of San Javier's the one person who had kept them on the path of righteousness for twenty-five long years? But, if the small sin of smugness was pardonable, what of the other more deeply buried one he could scarcely bear to name and which stood between him and the Hallowed City?

The two women, each bending low with one arm placed in the small of their backs, brushed away cuttings from the flower arrangements in the manner daughters inherited from their mothers. And, at the other end of the aisle, a cool church-air breeze bearing thick floral scents floated down to Father Patrick where he paused in mid-sway on the tips of his toes.

"Will ye both be helping with evening mass tonight, Rosa?"

"We will Father, you can count on us."

Yes, for sure he could. The ever dependable Rosa and her daughter Celine were always there, asked or not. Their attendance was ever a comfort.

The local custom to collapse a beautiful name to a single syllable plucked at random from nowhere in particular had, among those who knew her, reduced the exquisite Celine to a tediously unoriginal "Lin". Father O'Casey had never quite been able to bring himself to utter what seemed to him a banality and little better than a number.

"Perhaps we can call upon Celine to carry the Book tonight?"

Although she had done this many times before the Priest's request had the power to confer distinction.

"Thank you for the honour Padre," said Lin.

"Those that work in the service of the Lord shall receive his blessings, my child."

Subsiding onto his heels Patrick O'Casey let out a long, pensive sigh that seemed to disappear among the spiders and geckos in the cracked tower overhead. Dear, delightful Celine had been in the front row of his congregation for his first service at San Javier's. Then, she had been little more than eighteen, or thereabouts, and he eager and full of a young man's instincts. That he had loved her from the start was unsurprising, but that he had contained nature's promptings and loved from a distance was remarkable. She was now in her early forties with three children but his ardour for her, while controlled, was still as strong as when he first saw her.

But, during many sleepless nights, he believed a test had been set which he had failed by being unable to repudiate feelings and deny a pleasure. Thus, of all the town's people, he alone was not fit to pass into the everlasting sight of God.

And yet to be tempted was not to break God's holy law. Had not the Son of Man himself experienced as much in the desert? Yes, but he had rejected the offer unequivocally, whereas Patrick O'Casey had not. If theft was a sin, then stealing a hundred pesos was no better than embezzling a million. The act of robbery was the offence and its size was immaterial and the same must be true of sins of the heart. He desired her and whether he had kept that to himself was neither here nor there. He could pretend honesty, but in truth he had touched her when he should have pulled away.

Love for a woman was just about pardonable, but to wilfully seek one out for no better purpose than to be in her company and take her hand in spite of his sacred undertaking crossed a line he could not excuse.

He shuddered at the recollection of how many times he had deliberately patted her lips as she took the host from his raised hand and how he'd brushed against her hair as she moved back. He had sullied the holiest of his duties in unpardonable desire. In his mind, if not in fact, he had committed adultery on a thousand separate occasions.

The knowledge burned his secret heart, but if he knew his parishioners half as well as he supposed, he would have realised his shaking fingers and appealing eyes while she was at the cup were noticed and the subject of nods and understandings among the township's market wives. Only Lin was entirely oblivious to the Priest's hidden pain.

Over the toll of years and through the rough, rural existence Lin's good looks and O'Casey's passion should have moderated, but to anyone other than a casual observer and no one observes casually in a country town, the opposite was true.

To Lin's earlier fresh and unrestrained beauty could now be added the inner strength of a good person who, with intricate laughter lines around the corners of her eyes, had a generosity of spirit not present in the younger woman.

Unlike her mother, Rosa, Lin stood perfectly straight and today her thick black hair was held in a simple ponytail showing a slender brown neck. While staring at the mildew-spotted ceiling in his lonely room at the dead of night, Patrick O'Casey imagined planting an unchaste kiss on that warm, supple nape as it leant towards the altar. Such thoughts pierced, like poisoned darts, the fragile structure of his worth and sanctity. Holy vows, duty, congregation, and the life he had committed to were all turned to dust in the solitary confines of his cell. The devil, he believed, was laying siege to his weak soul and all he could do to keep from the final crime of abandoned licentiousness was to pace the floor and read aloud passages from the Bible.

Father Patrick suddenly ceased rocking to and fro and with hands held aloft sank to his knees.

"Great God in Heaven, save me!" he cried in a voice that echoed around the high roof and brought down a tiny shower of sand particles from the bell tower.

From a long interior prayer he opened at last his eyes. Beside him, Lin knelt with a puzzled expression. She was so close he could smell the warmth of her skin, like papayas ripening in the sun.

"Father?"

"My Dear, I..." He squeezed a proffered hand more than absolutely necessary and rising left the church with a moan that seemed to travel the length and breadth of San Javier's.

He pushed absent-mindedly into the noisy street and collided with a man carrying a brown leather satchel under one arm. Reeling back, the man asked, "Father?"

"Why, in the name of t'under and lightnin', is it no-one in this God-fearin' town ever asks anything else?"

"You sent for me," explained the man who had a lead pencil, stuck for convenience in his matted hair.

"What? Who?"

"Raul, Father. Frans said you wanted me to look at some work."

"Ah! Of course; my apologies. It's a hole in the wall I'm wantin' ye to look at and the work ye can perform. Where's that no-good fellow you call cousin?"

Momentarily detached from waves of self-doubt by the immediate troubles of a priest's daily work, Father Patrick quickly resorted to gruff command. He indicated the damage in the church's outer wall and Raul, who already knew of it, for he too attended mass and took communion and held conversations with his cousin, calculated numbers on a dirty notebook.

"It's deep damage. The best way is to pull down the whole front wall up to the tower and rebuild from the ground."

"If I wanted advice on erecting a new church I'd be callin' the Holy See itself, not askin' you for a price on a bit o' brickwork."

"The whole tower looks unstable to me."

"Patchwork man, patchwork is what I'm after. We just need somethin' that will hold us all together."

In spite of his hope for a more lucrative project, Raul went away to quote for the price of breaking out rubble around the crack and replacing it with red stone, or, if the fee held firm, substituted lower-cost concrete. And Father Patrick left for a substantial meal prepared by his housekeeper and to make notes for the evening sermon and reflect on the many sins within the compass of man's invention.

Rolling a pencil round his thumb O'Casey starred at the blank piece of paper. What his manhood wanted to cry out and what was expected and permissible were worlds apart. The congregation would, as usual, be looking for common assurances that, after lives spent suffering, the Promised Land offered bliss eternal; a destiny to which only he in the town held the key. Typhoons and mudslides and the burden of want would melt away and they would rise on angel's wings to meet their Lord. Open-mouthed wonder and trust would be evident in every pew and radiate from every hopeful face.

How could he tell them he was a phoney, a fraud who had heard their confessions and interceded between them and their God, while stubbornly clinging to the imperfections heaped on his back? None could set him free because he had no wish to repent. The steep road to everlasting heaven was his to seek like all in his congregation, but to get there he would have to abandon not loving this woman, but the pleasure of her kiss on his unholy fingers. How could he do that when she burst into every waking thought and filled his heart with unconfined rapture? Wasn't taking vicarious enjoyment in imagining an act more depraved and sinful than its perpetration in an act of selfless love?

Closing his eyes over the empty paper he struggled and failed to prepare high-minded thoughts of deliverance. Instead, Celine, like torrential rain sweeping in off the Pacific, rushed into his emptiness and carried all before her.

"Oh, my dear God!" he exclaimed and fell back into his chair with arms hanging limply beside him.

"Can I get you anything, Father?" a middle-aged female figure enquired at the door.

"There is nothing ye or anyone else on this weary planet can give that would be of the slightest help to me in my condition."

"I'm sorry for that, Sir," the enquirer said despondently, as if her professional competence, after years of unimpeachable service, was being called into question.

"Away wi'd ye. I'm alright now," he said dismissively.

"Yes, Father, if you say so."

As the nearest thing to God in this parish his "say-so" was never in doubt. But what would he give right now to forsake the cloth and be as immoral and pardonable as they.

Ah! Celine, Celine, Celine. Why did you ever erupt into my life? From the moment I saw you in that front pew, my soul has been in turmoil. At every service I look out for you and become by turns elated and cast down. Chance encounters in the town when I'm about my duties are such a whirl of unconfined pleasure, like waves surging freely over rocks on the seashore. When I smile and wave, parishioners say, "Father Patrick is well today." Joining people in conversation, blessing babies, teasing over absences from mass; they all occur with renewed energy, new enthusiasm. Am I not at those times, a better man? And his answer came back, "No, not while you take lascivious pleasure in her touch."

Like many rural women in the islands Lin had married early. Her family and Sonny's, although knowing each other for maybe three generations, never got on well. But, despite family discouragement, the children were often together, first at school and later at church. Among friends and relatives, the eventual marriage provoked a feeling of resignation, rather than jubilation. At a distance beyond the extended network of cousins third and fourth removed, some preferred to believe familiarity and a kind of tropical torpor had as much to do with the decision as affection. For his part, Father Patrick knew nothing could remotely equal his seething, forbidden passion, which, in his fevered and self-serving logic, was plainly absent from Sonny.

The priest's deep and suppressed yearning was painful enough, but later to witness and officiate at the marriage was agonising almost beyond belief.

At the words, "Do you Sonny, take Celine to be your lawful wedded wife?" O'Casey fixed the groom with dull grey eyes, willing him to say no, fluff his lines, or drop dead on the spot of a raging apoplexy, or from divine and just intervention by lightning bolt from Sinai or even Olympus, anything, it didn't matter much which, as long as this damnable miscarriage of justice was prevented. But alas, nothing happened and although both groom and priest sweated profusely and struggled with their parts, Celine was married to a man whom O'Casey, God forgive him, loathed from the very bottom of his anguished heart.

During the night of the wedding's consummation, the priest took first one and then a second glass of whiskey. The wedding had been an ordeal of participation, but this was ordeal by conjecture. Medieval witches burned at the stake didn't know how lucky they were. Tortured bodies were nothing compared to a tormented mind in which a rustic's hand with black and broken fingernails groped in the velvety and abominably sensual dark.

Almost nine months to the day a first child was baptised. While drawing a thumb across the sleeping infant's forehead, Father Patrick could not help but think disconsolately that in a perfect world this would be his son and someone else splashing water on the tiny head.

In O'Casey's estimation, Sonny was not too bright, but hard work and a certain dogged application did go someway to maintaining a decent family life and, although no longer his direct business, the Priest was by turns gratified and appalled by Celine's early happiness. After the birth of the child, Sonny got a contract job as a seaman and returned home only once a year. During a space of six years and after every second visit he fathered another child and then returned to sea. Since then the frequency of his visits declined and circulating rumours said he had acquired comforts and obligations in other towns visited by sea-farers.

For his sermon that night Father Patrick chose the text, "The way of the ship in the midst of the sea." That the proverb ended with, "And the way of a man with a maid," he did not feel inclined to extrapolate and wanted his audience to appreciate only that, while he and they were tossed about seemingly at random, there was a hand steering them all to calmer waters and safety. The homily was not a success, for neither his heart nor head were in it. Each man and woman too, was a ship lost at sea, but whether they ever reached safety or peace of mind, in his opinion, had tonight more to do with where they were blown by capricious winds, than steered by divine hands.

On his return to the vestibule he found Rosa putting away the vestments. Grimy lines of dust disfigured the white material.

"Really, Rosa, we must get this place cleaned daily."

"We do, Father, and sometimes twice, but there's no keeping away the dust from the old stonework any more."

"And isn't that the truth too. But shall I look for you again tomorrow around eight?"

"We'll be later Father. Sonny is coming home and Lin is expecting him to arrive on the early bus."

"Ah! Is it that time again? How could I forget? Will this be a long visit?"

"We'll see; Lin misses him so and is hoping this time he is back for good."

"Does she? Well, well, I suppose that's as we would want to hear. A good husband's place should be close to home wouldn't you say?"

"A good husband, yes."

Sonny did come home and although still in his forties and strong, he decided not just to stay, but to retire. Let others take their turn to man the world's ships cheaply; he'd done his share and was ready to take some rest. He sought out friends from earlier days who lacked either the will or opportunity to pursue the life he'd had. They were habitual pensioners, surviving on the sort of remittances he and his kind had sent home over the decades. Now, with some money in his pocket, it was his turn to entertain and enjoy a few idle pleasures.

Unlike activity, indolence does not require a plan and the Saturday cockfight and bars at the south end of town filled the void with easy and shallow fellowship and provided the main alternative to sleeping away hot afternoons.

The few pesos Frans obtained from labouring for his cousin were spent on visits to the same dimly lit collection of nipa huts where men dulled their senses with cheap alcohol and scarlet women. Indulging his several weaknesses often kept Frans confined to bed until late the following day. For the sake of family Raul had learned to live with the inconvenience, but Father Patrick, to differentiate his public persona from the private one, was never so persuaded.

"May all the saint's preserve us! Did ye see your own face this morning, Frans? You're a disgrace to humanity and the light of day alike."

Too thick with gin to think or answer clearly, Frans could do no more than take the verbal beating.

"Padre, sorry…"

"Sorry! Sorry! Don't sorry me. Wi'd eyes as bloodshot as your's, how will ye be able to see the gutters from on top the ladder? Ye knew we had work to do today."

"Pad…"

"Don't. I don't want to hear any more. Go and see Rosa at the back and get something to eat. Ye look as if ye'd spent a fortnight in an ginebra bottle and not eaten so much as a spoonful all that long while."

The mention of food caused Frans' face to go pale beneath his dark, farm-labourer's skin and he hurried away, not in the direction of the tiny kitchen for the poor at the rear of San Javier's, but somewhere, anywhere where he would be out of hearing of the ringing reproof rattling his aching head. Breaking into a cold, dizzying sweat he slid down between a brick wall and palm tree and with an arm about each threw up what remained of last evening's revelries. When returning sailors were freely buying, declining their hospitality and comradeship was unpardonable. Wiping his damp mouth and chin on the tail of a torn vest he stood up and, although still undeniably delicate, went in search of Rosa and a little fried fish and rice to settle his sensitive stomach.

With a ball of sticky food warming his lower ribs and moisture slowly returning to his palate he stepped out of the kitchen shadows. If chance, at that moment, had unexpectedly offered him an hour's sleep in an out of the way nook, he would gladly have accepted. But, rounding a corner, he saw Raul, Father Patrick and Celine gathered across the street from San Javier's. Frans decided to wait for his summons, or until those opposite left on their various errands. With his back to the stone fabric he settled onto his haunches and watched. Father Patrick was waving both arms in the air and Raul apologetically, but obstinately, looked at his notebook.

"Outrageous! Unconscionable! How can ye contemplate robbing the Church?"

To steady the Priest's hot temper, Lin put a hand on his arm. She was playing a part in a ritual, learned from the ways of the islands and long experience of the participants. O'Casey, red in the face, knew Raul would overprice, Raul knew the priest expected as much and Lin, accepted by both as the moderator, ensured the rules of negotiation, of giving something and in return taking, were kept, so that ultimately both sides could leave appeased.

Two troops of macaques, noisily contesting territory, swung about in the high branches of the nearby acacias lining one side of the shabby street right down to the edge of town. From adjacent trees the shrieking and bared teeth of the separate packs rose before subsiding into grumbling consent.

"I'm offering it at my cost. I have to cover expenses."

"Have ye not forgotten what Christ did to the merchants in the Temple? To their eternal shame he drove them forth. What should I be doin' with ye now?"

"Father; Father." The gentle hand at his elbow was oil on a turbulent sea.

"Look now, I'm wantin' ye to give me a price I can live with. Without it the work isn't done. It's that simple. The Church isn't made of money ye know."

"Seeing it's for San Javier's, I could ask my suppliers to provide their material without a margin," said Raul, affecting a token shift.

"There now, that's all I ask. We don't want the bells fallin' in the street and every one pointin' a finger now, do we?"

Calculatingly mollified, Father Patrick threaded a way with Celine though three-wheeled taxis, pedestrians and a couple of water buffalo to the entrance of San Javier's. Drawing abreast of Frans, who shuffled his bare feet nervously, the Priest, with both fists on his hips, was again quietened by a restraining touch.

"Well? Well? And how will the gutters be cleaned wi'd ye now sittin' on the floor waiting for them to perform a miracle on their own?"

Hesitatingly coming upright, Frans avoided meeting the Priest's gaze.

"I'll get the ladder, then?"

"And wouldn't that be a grand idea. I suppose ye remember where ye put it?"

Without waiting for an answer, Father Patrick strode into the church with Celine close behind. In her presence he was a different man. He wanted her to know the power she had to turn his anger to calmness and mellow his excess. In her company his virtues blossomed, he became gracious, witty and confident. Short of the one fatal step he would take any risk, perform any task and mend any characteristic for her good opinion.

Save for a couple kneeling in prayer and a few people idling at the door, the church, pausing between services, was empty.

"I'll be taking confession for the next hour for those in want and need," he announced to Celine.

"Yes, Father. There will be some."

The rite of confession in a town this small was an odd affair. Inevitably the priest knew every man jack of the population; knew what they had been up to the previous night and often what they could not or would not share with their husbands or wives. Anonymity was assumed, but nominal; a plagued conscience from a voice heard a hundred times was a powerful insight into the intricate and overlapping jealousies, rivalries, loves and hates of the town. He heard when Raul supplied sub-standard cement for the school extension; knew in detail which municipal councillors were on the take; who slept with which easy wife and whose husband in a drunken fit beat almost to death the woman he'd sworn to cherish. In all its shabby tawdriness the town stood naked before him and he, contrary to his own assumption, stood similarly stripped.

"Father, I haven't attended mass for two weeks in a row."

Ah! That was the baker from Villa Pedrosa Street, who – with a reputation for mixing pig meal into his flour – was apologising for lesser errors and hoping larger ones were swept in general absolution under the carpet.

"Father, I have not respected my parents and... and... Father, I let a boy touch me, what should I do?"

Yes, that was Marlyn Espiritu. Everyone expected her to come to a sticky end and no doubt the gossip was being fulfilled. How trite, how dreary, how commonplace and, with the handy apology kept snugly in a back pocket, how conveniently escaped.

"Father, what is the right thing to do for a husband?"

Jerking out of his apathy O'Casey sat upright; that was Celine speaking!

"Are ye posin' me a riddle, or have ye something to say, my child? How can I help?" Through a voice quivering with anticipation, he strained all his senses to draw from her a story, a revelation that allowed him to embrace the inner secrets and feelings of this dear, dear soul.

"My husband has been away for many years."

"Yes, yes," said O'Casey hurriedly. He knew that bit and wanted to move rapidly forward to new events.

"He came home recently."

"U-huh! …and?"

"I am not a good wife."

"Oh! My…" A chill like a shadow crossing over the sun clutched O'Casey's heart. Was this going to be a familiar and dismaying account of sexual impropriety from the only woman he'd set on high and desired beyond reason? He tensed as if to receive news of a dearly beloved's death.

"Although I love him and, after years of separation he is all I want, he doesn't have time for me."

O'Casey wanted to leap up and cry, "The blackguard!" But the cramped confessional inhibited wild demonstration and, as he sought more information, the angry rush of blood subsided.

"Would ye like to be more specific, so I can be offerin' particular advice? In what way have ye sinned?"

"Didn't the Lord say love one another? How can my husband do so if I am unlovable? Son…my husband… hardly looks at me and spends all his time drinking and gambling with people, such people as he meets in bars. He's all I want, but there is not even a kind look from him any more." Muffled sniffs came through the booth latticework as if a sleeve was pressed to a wet nose.

"Well, this is a pretty kettle of …, but if you're keepin' the commandments and love and honour him then perhaps he should be sittin' here in the box and not ye?"

"Father," the hidden voice said impatiently, "I need forgiveness and help."

"Ye have a wounded heart my daughter and surely need someone to talk to, an older woman, a priest mmm…maybe, but there is nothing I've heard to forgive. Do you pray?"

"Yes, often."

"Continue as long as the pain lasts and trust in the Lord, he will be merciful."

Duty demanded that a priest's time was there for every member of the community, saints and sinners alike. Sonny, however, was not a man for whom Father Patrick had consistently kind thoughts or patience, how could he? But because Celine's happiness weighed so heavily on his mind, O'Casey resolved, while respecting the privacy of the confessional, to pull whatever stings he could lay hands on. If Sonny was a drinker and an habitué of bad company, the very person was on hand to bring back details of the transgression and clues for its reformation.

"Look now, I'm not encouraging your dreadful habits, in fact ye are to stay at least half sober. But I want you to watch out for someone for me and bring word of what he's doin' with himself. Tell me what I'm askin' ye to do."

"Padre Sir, you want me to watch someone. But I don't know who he is or where I find him."

"Will ye stop blatherin' for a second, Frans, while ye hear the rest?"

"Yes Sir, Padre Sir."

"By all the Powers, listen will ye! It's that Sonny Bautista who's living the life of Riley. I want to hear where he goes, who his company is and what he does. If ye're a good lad I'll be takin' care of ye. Are ye understanding me now?"

"Yes Sir Pad…"

"Stop that this instant before my head breaks and get away wi'd ye."

News in small rural towns is either on everybody's tongue or non-existent. Those excluded from a circle of the informed might just as well be isolated on the moon's dark side. To Father Patrick's knowledge Frans disappeared, suddenly and utterly off the face of the earth as if spirited by demons. There had been occasions in the past when he was unavailable, but usually for no more than a day or two while he slept off an exceptionally bad hangover. But to be gone for so long was entirely unprecedented. Enquiries with Raul, Rosa, or any of those usually in the know, produced baffled looks and shrugged shoulders. A week passed, and then two, and without warning a dreadful thing happened.

While moving a ragged herd of goats in the early morning from one over-grazed pasture to another, a youth stumbled across a body. The goats had torn off and begun eating shreds of clothing before the boy understood what they had uncovered. With loud cries of "clack, clack," he drove his charges to a slightly greener patch of scrub and hurried back to examine what lay under the wild thorn bushes on the side of the track.

On the slender evidence of its long trousers the body appeared to belong to a man. It lay face down with arms stretched out above its head as if frozen in an act of diving. Prodding roughly with the long stick used to shepherd his goats the boy edged closer, half expecting the still form to suddenly jump up and run screaming into the fields. He could see a dark patch of dried, blood-matted hair and wood ants scurrying in stops and starts over the fallen figure. Holding the stick under one arm the boy knelt down and patted the body's legs. Testing a slight bulge in one pocket, he extracted a sodden wad of bank notes smelling of vomit and stale beer. To make sure he was unobserved he looked to left and right before rapidly transferring the damp mess into his own tattered shirt. Rising abruptly and with another cry off "clack, clack!" he chased the unruly goats back along the path over which they had sauntered just moments ago.

On reporting the discovery to the police, the goat-herd's uncle, being the immediate source of information, was held overnight for questioning. A stonemason's mallet found in nearby bushes and bearing traces of blood and hair was presumed to be the murder weapon. The victim was identified by the investigating officer as Sonny Bautista. Provincial policemen are apt to know everyone, innocent and guilty alike. Early suspicion fell temporarily on Frans. Not that anyone had heard anything significant to link him to the victim, but because he had been seen drinking in the same bar as Sonny and had now vanished seemed reason enough. But as days passed investigative interest slowly moved to more pressing matters.

Buying endless rounds of drinks in the dirty nipa huts at the south end of town had bought Sonny fleeting popularity in some quarters, but, with one exception, none mourned, or unduly regretted his passing. Lin, however, wept endlessly and felt her failure to bring him back into her life and away from the bars was the route by which he had met his unpleasant end. Father Patrick was a whirlwind of mixed emotions. His Christian duty to love everyone tripped over the more human satisfaction, lying like a lead weight on his conscience, of witnessing a long-standing rival's downfall. But that too was compromised by the pain of Celine's despair.

Frans' exploratory reconnaissance and the embryonic attempt to tame Sonny by a back door had come to naught. If Frans was implicated in Sonny's death, surely the answer lay at the bottom of a gin glass and argument over a trifle?

As weeks came and went Celine was seen helping less about the church and more frequently in solitary prayer. The trauma was aging her prematurely and her face had become tired and drained. Although effectively a widow since early in marriage, the actual death of her husband had destroyed at a stroke the work her life had sought to make perfect. Making bearable her family's existence, coupled with devotion to God, was for her the surest way to secure peace in the hereafter. Now from desolation, the spiritual world alone beckoned.

"What can we do for her, Rosa?" Father Patrick asked.

"Only time and prayers can help, Father."

Summer rains lashed the empty streets outside and water dripped into the nave from the broken bell tower. A tiny bat, unaccustomed to day, flittered down into the echoing church, before dodging and turning away into the roof above the altar rail. High rafters groaned and creaked in sudden rushes of wind.

"We must surely get that repaired as soon as dry weather returns. I'm hopin' we have enough time to keep the roof over our heads."

"The Lord will find a way."

"Aye, we must be faithful to the end."

"I'll take Lin with me, Father, and be back tomorrow."

"Yes, yes, of course. I'll wait a little longer to see if anyone comes for confession and then I'll also be making my way."

Seated in the last row of pews, Father Patrick looked first at his hands and then at the lighted altar. In all the years, what had he achieved? He helped the flock keep faith, performed the services his office demanded, but was there any unique or lasting contribution distinguishing his life from any other? No, not much, and in fact he had tarnished the priesthood and his holy duty. The sins he had committed were legion; he was proud, vengeful, venal, corrupt and had a lot less to offer the Heavenly Father than many of the simple, uneducated people who surrounded him every day of his waking life with their small, almost ludicrously pardonable offences.

A thin figure, hidden under a dripping waterproof, stepped into the church. As he hesitated, drops gathered in pools around his bare feet. Half turning the Padre raised his eyebrows in question and the visitor, motioning to the confessional, took a seat while waiting for Father Patrick to join on the other side of the booth.

"Father, I ask for…"

Before the sentence was complete the Priest butted in, "What in the name of all that's holy are ye doin' in here?"

"Father…"

"Don't ye be fatherin' me, now. Where have you been these many weeks since?"

"I've to confess a great sin."

"Great God Almighty, what have you gotten into?"

"Father, you are bound to hear and forgive."

"Don't ye be teachin' me my duty, ye waster, ye…."

"I did it for you, pleaseee…ah!" The last words trailed away in sobs of anguish.

An icy grip squeezed the priest's beating heart almost to a standstill.

"What in God's fearful name, did ye do?" the Priest demanded in an awful whisper as if he was held by the throat."

"I killed Bautista," and then a torrent of words, "I've seen you look at her; we have all seen. I've known since you first came. You are not a normal man; others would have taken her and kept silent. You have shown us the light, the way of a priest."

O'Casey rose as if to flee the madness that was sucking him down to destruction

"And for that you murther a man? Did I not ask you to watch Sonny and that only?" he breathed through tightly shut teeth.

"Forgive me!"

"You must get away from here; as far as you can."

"Father, I've confessed my sin. Save me!"

"Look, I'll give you money. You must be leavin' tonight…"

"I did it for you. I cannot leave without your blessing."

"No, no…I can't…who will help me?"

"Without your word, my soul will be lost and on your conscience. Is that what you want? Father, you are duty bound…"

O'Casey was trapped, so with tears streaming over his fat cheeks, he raised his right hand and with two fingers made the sign of the cross at the invisible face in shadows behind the grill.

"In the name of the Father, the Son and the Holy Ghost, repent and be saved," and he clattered out of the box.

The rain-soaked Frans tumbled out from the other side of the confessional and, dropping to his knees, clasped the priest's ankles.

"Bless you, Father. You are San Javier's saint."

Wrenching free, O'Casey fell back several paces and with hands over his head ran out into the teaming rain.

Wind wailed on an approaching typhoon and rattled the ancient bells in the church tower. Beneath the broken and trembling stonework the crack shuddered and widened. Sheets of corrugated iron torn from nearby roofs cut and sheared their way through waterlogged streets and into the whipping acacia trees. In distant barrios the crash of San Javier's belfry rang and pealed as if the last judgement had galloped in among them on hoofs shod with steel.

SEVEN

IN THE NEWS

Lights blinked green and shoppers poured over the pedestrian crossings blanketing Central District's main street intersection. Vehicular traffic held back as the surging pack leapt from its marks to claim places at the head of the queue. For those wanting everything fast, access to high-end buying was a necessity and the flush and impatient were not to be denied. Carrier bags of every description adorned well-fleshed arms as purchasers sped determinedly from boutique to boutique in a spiralling and mind-numbing ritual of acquisition. Meanwhile, the poor heard the city's heart beat and, huddling on the pavements, got by with what they had.

Sufficiency, because it failed to dazzle, was no longer enough. The out-of-control frenzy, drowning large parts of the town in a sea of promiscuous ownership and disposable packaging, had assumed a rationale entirely its own. The moneyed class's new mantra, regardless of requirement or logic, was, one is one's brand.

The withering propaganda of the new order had become, "Oh, good Lord! Don't say you got it there!"

The prosperous no longer slimmed down to thread the eye of a needle, because, being discriminating citizens, they had decided that, as having beyond all reasonable need was good in this world, it must, by extension, be equally esteemed in the next. Seats on the right hand were to be reserved for those spending and owning at the most ostentatious and self-indulgent level and Saint Peter, instead of scrutinising records for virtue and humility, would give, in the manner of an airline business-class check-in clerk, preferment to those who, however sinful, had paid. Henceforth paradise was open only to those with premier credit ratings and convincing evidence of irrational consumption. The out of luck destitute, denied cake during their unfortunate lives and, having seen the best stores only from the outside, were thus forbidden entry to the kingdom of heaven where only the profligate had earned rightful admittance.

"Sorry, Sir, you can't come in here with a history like that. What were you thinking; just shopping for what you needed?

Not a bonus point or a VIP membership in sight! Heh, heh! I expect you'll receive a call from the other place. I hear they're taking all the folk without a credit card, there, these days. Since the new regulations came in, there's no ambiguity or shuffling anymore."

Above Mundy's grimy head October sunshine touched the glass and steel canyon summits and sparkled; around him the shameless throng seethed. Being without material comfort himself, other than for his single change of shirt contained in a soiled rucksack, ironically referred to as his social outfit, he considered himself entitled to a point of view. And observing the garishly lit pretension of obsessive purchasing paddling and dabbling among the shoes, bags and fripperies, like famished ducks in a frog-filled pond, he decided his weeks and months of impecunious idleness needed no effort of justification.

At the pedestrian crossings lights changed to red and shoppers massed on the pavements like Israel's tribes waiting for Jehovah to divide the sea, or migrating wildebeest held up by Serengeti's flooded rivers. Vehicles nudged stealthily forward into temporarily unobstructed space as if entering territory not quite their own; here, they seemed to acknowledge, incontinent customers took precedence over purposeful public and private transportation.

Alone among the hesitant intruders a yellow Italian sports car, whose owner knew exactly where he stood and where he was allowed to drive, growled round the corner and into knots of undisciplined taxis picking up precariously-loaded shoppers in the middle of the street.

Denied smooth and privileged passage, any millionaire with manicured nails and bad teeth was permitted contempt for the mob and this one vented fulsome displeasure by leaning heavily on his horn until blasts rang and reverberated up and down the surrounding concrete walls.

Close behind the showy and pointlessly overpowered vehicle an open-sided blue pick-up truck, on its way to a distant fish market, swung violently to avoid contact with the silken coupe's suddenly arrested paintwork.

Imprisoned at a low but still gratifyingly streamlined level, between a dawdling taxi and the sea-food carrier's chipped body, the yellow car's owner could neither open his swallow-winged doors, nor see clearly into either driving cab and, in mounting exasperation, he thrust his well-groomed and sunglassed head through an electronically controlled window to yell abuse. Inside the taxi the preoccupied driver counted his afternoon's takings and waited for a passenger and in the pick-up three bare-chested and tattooed young men exchanged looks and wondered how to extricate their load and meet a scheduled delivery.

Along the busy pavement the unfolding street drama passed unnoticed until the moment when the pick-up, with racing engine and a few inexpert hops, bounced back into the main traffic flow. Several uncovered tanks of salt water and the morning catch sloshed about on the van's greasy loading boards and, to the escalating fury of the trapped sports car driver, discharged their contents over his spotless vehicle's gleaming sides. With the final bound an unanchored tank struck the tailgate and ejected into the street a medium sized garoupa. Shoppers, momentarily diverted from their consuming passions stopped and watched the incongruous flapping in a quickly drying pool.

A decisive businessman in a neat three-piece suit stepped off the pavement and caught the fish by its pulsating, red gills. Thrusting the slapping creature into his tissue-wrapped purchases at the bottom of a signature Versace carrier he departed briskly into the maze carrying with him the certainty of an early and cost-effective supper. Shouts of, "Hey! Hey!" from the stationary sports car driver fell ineffectually onto the crowds' wondering ears.

Perhaps, thought Mundy, economic fixation had more permutations than might be supposed and, if that was true, then hanging about on a bustling street corner was as good a way as any to observe the options addicted minds contrived.

The crowd, like a stream reclaiming lost space after a fall of rock and sand, rapidly forgot the incident and resumed its irresistible flow towards the sea of a collective destination.

Not far from the ingeniously configured crossing straddling the intersection, where wheeled traffic's free movement was intermittently strangled, a line of automated cash-tellers lured holders of fast emptying wallets from the passing human torrent. Like drifting detritus floating momentarily on a conflicting current consumers needing replenishment of ready money swirled to restock before being born away again on the flood with hip pockets and hand-bags bulging comfortably.

An inert beggar, lying on a sheet of cardboard torn from discarded television packing cases, accepted the swarms for what they were. Wound up in a mass of oily rags and lying like yesterday's sticky-rice on a cold dish, his considerations were not so much about what to do, as on which days and for how long to do it and that hadn't changed since primitive skills had first been thus employed. Mundy, mistaking a lowly life with one fallen from grace, wondered how long ago the blackened hand that shook a cracked enamel cup had last held dim sum in the safe and boisterous company of friends.

The coursing shoppers arced around the prostrate form and, breaking apart into smaller rivulets, ran into individual boutique doors lower down the sloping street. The trickles that had turned away in search of ready cash washed clumsily over the prone shape and without summoning any reserve of will or scruple, or giving a sideways glance, remained steadfastly on course. A paltry few reluctantly dropped coins into the damaged mug before being saved from further heresy by the next seductive window-display.

The bundle of dirty rag ends that could have been heaped hospital refuse waiting for disposal had no age or gender as far as Mundy could decide. The possibility of sickness or handicap stirred no thoughts of mercy on the bustling pavement and, other than the smattering of donations, few of charity. Was destitution and incapacity shameful as well as disadvantageous? Were there others like this hidden from view in an underground place or back room where family skeletons lay buried? On this side of the harbour in a clambering, hustling city, dereliction was an unmentionable transgression best left unacknowledged. Was that why no-one ever made eye contact as they passed by and why rush and inordinate wealth were the only palliative to three thousand years of insecurity and the appalling prospect of coming second?

Mundy watched the horizontal figure. It was pathetic to be sure, but not as completely lifeless as might be supposed. Without visibly counting, the value of each coin was rapidly assessed. At a heavy clunk there was tightened anticipation, like a blue-rinse matron grimly holding down levers on a Las Vegas slot machine. How many more of those for a dish of fried noodles, or a can of cheap, local beer? At a lighter tinkle and as a well-clothed back departed, the disappointed wrappings exhaled. No more than five coins were kept in the cup at any one time before being ravenously scooped back into the bundles' dank, ragged entrails. Meagre generosity was not to be taken for granted on these polished streets and anyone in circumstances similar to the beggar's and who might be thought to have more than was suitable for a person in his station, would do well to avoid losing the hard won sympathy patiently squeezed from cold, dry eyes.

Above the congested streets electric lights blinked on one by one to overtake the departing sun's weakening reflections. Shoppers with their newly acquired feathers fluttered back to apartment blocks, like roosting starlings, to preen and strut and prepare for the next day's voyage through the bursting malls. Mundy, leaning on a steel crowd barrier that kept the shrinking throng from self-destruction under passing wheels, had no home to go to and spun out the hours before seeking his night's repose.

Divorced, unemployed and homeless, he had less at stake in prosperity than anyone, including the street-side beggar. Once, not so long ago, he'd held the view that his condition was just temporary and normality would follow soon after work was found. But, as weeks passed and seasons changed, the idea grew on him that destitution was not so dreadful after all and had as much legitimacy in rationalising inconsequential lives as shopping. Now, after eleven months on the streets, he had acquired a stable routine and in a perverse way had grown to accept the person he had become.

The five-star hotel next to Chater Square tipped out its day's kitchen garbage at eleven in the evening. Timing his arrival to five minutes later, when the cleaners had disappeared and rats still waited in nearby drains, he could unload enough unspoiled food to get him through a couple of days. But the booty had to be pastries, or pies, something cooked and unlikely to go rotten in humidity and heat. Eating something from the skip a month ago had sent him to the community hospital for a night and he wouldn't want to repeat that purging experience. Not that the hospital bed, clean white linen and slender nurses had been entirely bad, but ill health made a vagrant's life too precarious and difficult to organise.

The cash-teller beggar appeared to be in a nearly identical situation. He worked a territory and system and played on the single string of misfortune until none were left on the streets to give even token alms. And as darkness drew in, his trade's tools, the enamel mug and cardboard mattress were stuffed into a crevice in an alley wall and then, just like Mundy, he left in search of food and shelter.

Distant clanks from an unloaded skip being readied for accumulated cordon bleu waste echoed among the emptying towers. Other city noises faded slowly from Central's earlier hectic streets and moved westwards to where shops stayed open all night supplying late essentials, not of high fashion, but shark's fins, screw drivers, dried fish, fuses, durian, disinfectant, light bulbs and ground tiger bones. Swinging his rucksack onto one shoulder Mundy looked up at the electronic clock spread over an entire third floor block. A slow walk, he estimated, would bring him to a timely dinner.

From the outer road the skip was dimly visible in an unlit tunnel running along one side of the hotel's rear entrance. This, he'd noticed, was a spot much favoured by policemen preparing to pull over lorries entering an area reserved for pedestrian traffic and he wanted to keep his semi-functional habits simple and avoid a brush with the town's inflexible constabulary. Looking to left and right, for reassurance that no blue uniforms lurked in building entrances, he walked briskly across the street and into the dark tunnel colliding almost immediately with a body leaning into the skip.

"What the fu…?"

A stream of incomprehensible invective and an uncouth push sent him staggering back against the tunnel wall, but, prompted by instinct rather than bravery, he swung the weight of his dirty rucksack into the shadows where he supposed a head might be. A dull thump stopped the abuse as if a hole had been plugged and, knowing he held the advantage, Mundy swung again. A cry of pain was followed a few seconds later by a long hacking spit. The rucksack, in addition to the shirt, contained a battered vacuum flask, which, if luck were on his side, had struck a sensitive spot. With blood rising, from the sudden and unexpected exhilaration of administering a thrashing, he prepared for a third blow, but the indistinct contestant, deciding enough was enough, surrendered claims over the skip and fled into the street. Not wishing to terminate a rare victory Mundy hurled the rucksack and his few earthly possessions at the fleeing figure. Curling into the gloom the bag and contents landed somewhere close to the mark and produced a puncture gasp.

"Oof!"

With considerably more alacrity than might have been expected from their earlier dead weight on the pavement by the bank's cash machines the mummy-like figure and trailing rags burst at speed into the lighted street.

Breathing hard Mundy paced to and fro. In the last year his enthusiasm and pride had taken a severe down-hill turn and while the decline had been gradual there was no denying he sometimes let his moderate day-time optimism dissolve after dark into thoughts of abject and irredeemable failure. This was especially true when he stood at the junction in Central and watched the departing armies flash new acquisitions on society's public stage. But a successful pounding, even on an impoverished tramp, left him pleasantly and surprisingly elated.

Glossing over appearances he was momentarily convinced he was no less a person than those crowding Central. Excluding the beggar, what could they claim that he could not? Expensive apartments filled with more possessions than they could use? What about some peace of mind? Weighing the joyless evidence of ceremonial income disposal he felt no envy. Spending was, in all truth, no less fatiguing than earning. Freedom lay in choice, but if the only option was tedious and competitive exhibitionism that either argued poverty of imagination, or distorted values. Did any of the po-faced shoppers, he wondered, go for a free walk on the hills above Central, or, away from the urban crush, stop and marvel at the equally inexpensive bird-song that filled every morning? More likely they'd hurry in luxurious limousines from air-conditioned residences to high-pressure offices, and when eventually released from late work, speed home in time to put a child to bed. Wasn't everyone too busy making money to enjoy a family of no more than one expensive offspring, or to wonder where they were going? In this city romance and the stuff of poetry didn't exist in any noticeable form. Through windows Mundy had seen diners' intimacies saved for mobile phone applications and not the person sitting opposite. Perhaps sex, when it wasn't interfering with the priorities of making ever more money, was arranged on one of those electronic planners?

"I can give you fifteen minutes between nine forty-five and ten and then I have to fly to catch my ten thirty. No time for foreplay, we'll just have to get on without it. Bang, bang; can't do a cuddle after, time's too short, but are you okay for the same again on Tuesday week if nothing important crops up?"

Mundy sucked in a long breath. The fracas in the tunnel was not a particularly edifying incident, but it had given him a rare feeling of being in control and not at the mercy of society's imposed standards. If this city provided only misery on the grand scale it had mapped out then it was welcome. A raw punch-up over some random odd-ends of food refuse was just the thing to get adrenaline pumping and remind the victor what really mattered. Walking to the end of the tunnel where the glare of white lights rebounded from glass shop fronts Mundy, with his jaw thrust a little further forward than usual, scanned the street. If the beggar was still around he might be worth another couple of whacks.

But scuttling sounds behind reminded him that the night's main business remained untackled and that further delay would give uncontested benefit of his spoils to the rats. He felt like a solitary leopard standing astride a slain springbok on the forest's edge. Packs of hyenas buoyed by the courage of numbers were circling to rob him of his due. Well, just let them try!

From earlier expeditions to the tunnel he knew a single low-wattage light bulb, serving the late night shift, lay somewhere close by. To the right here somewhere, he remembered, and groped along the wall. Ah! There it was! At the sound of the flipped plastic switch a noise like the drawing back of waves shrank into the darkness. The rats, visible only by an occasional green reflection on a retina, slid away to watch and wait.

In the gloom Mundy pulled a none too clean plastic bag from his rucksack. As he leant over the skip a smell combining opulence and decay rose heavily to meet his nostrils, like the stale perfume on a tart's sweaty neck the day after application. Stirring about in the ruins of exotic meals he turned over an unappealing mess of chicken bones, fish and wet broccoli.

Aha! But wait a minute; what was this? With sleeve rolled to his elbow he drew out a thick paper carrier, of the sort he'd seem exhibited on a score of stylish arms that very afternoon. The swollen bag, with neat cords, hotel name and marketing logo, belied its fallen state. The encircling rats, cowering in fluids seeping from the skip, breathed closer until the sound of a stamped foot sent them scurrying back into their bolt-holes for a second time.

There was almost no need to transfer the contents from one soiled bag to another, but while the origins of the stains on his plastic were well known those on the paper carrier were open to speculation.

By the modest measures of destitution the evening was becoming an outstanding success. Not only was he supplied with two clear day's food from a fashionable bakery shop patronised by the city's gossiping elite, but the primitive tussle in the hotel tunnel had given him an unfamiliar feeling of cheerfulness. Who cared that the food was past its sell-by date or that the beggar had presented limited resistance to a man who was only recently in his physical prime; when the sides of your stomach touched, minor achievements loomed as large as milestones on a grand trunk road.

For a while Mundy felt he could take on the world and was justified in his scorn of Central's spiritual wasteland, where mindless consumers trod the wheel of their class and found no contentment. Their horizons were no more elevated than a chain gang breaking stones and starting and stopping on every command and blown whistle. He might have been poor, but at least he was free to choose what he would do at the dawn of each morning.

Having provided for his evening meal, Mundy's next thought, such were the uncomplicated exigencies of survival, was where he should sleep. Of the several necessarily rough locations mapped out over the months, he most preferred the civilised arches of the Culture Centre, partly because they were far from the throbbing insanity of Central's squanderati, but also because they afforded incomparable views along the full length of Victoria Harbour. Not many of his contemporaries woke to such a spectacle. Most were cooped up in drab four hundred square foot bed-sits with no better outlook than the grey stone wall and hanging laundry of the next identical block.

The rucksack was heavier now with the plastic bag and its contents stuffed deep inside, but it was a weight he carried lightly as he set out towards several dejectedly splashing fountains opposite the Post Office.

Except for a few government employees and messengers emptying company post boxes, not many passersby visited this back-street, although on an elevated walkway an hour ago the herds deserting closing stores and offices had flocked to their aerial rookeries to chatter and scrap over the day's plunder. In their regular flight the inconvenience of small change was sometimes cast sporadically into the fountains below, with, Mundy liked to suppose, a wish for more bargains and better luck avoiding handouts to undeserving tramps. But, thankful superstition lived on, he mustered an enviable effort of economic concentration to fish for the one dollar and twenty cents crucial to a lower deck ferry crossing.

With his sleeve rolled up for the second time that night he slid his skip-soiled fingers into the green growth at the bottom of the pool. Each visit had taught him to dredge a different few square metres; to be sure recently trawled ground was not over-fished. The technique had become almost infallible and, if his estimate of three months for a complete circuit of the fountains was accurate, he was assured of fare expenses for as long as they were needed. Tonight was no exception and after fifteen minutes he'd done even better than usual having harvested enough algae encrusted throw-aways for both an outward and return journey.

A traffic warden, patrolling metered spaces nearby, watched Mundy's dredging impassively. To an old man, destitute foreigners were a new phenomenon and a sign that something puzzling had happened to the world he'd grown up in. Once, gweilos were assumed to be privileged, so how come some now shared the lot of those at the bottom of the heap? The rules of the past had been much easier to understand. Shaking his head he licked the end of his pencil and wrote a ticket for another over-staying limousine.

With his clutch of wet coins, Mundy passed though a turnstile onto the ferry. Sitting next to the bulwark he took out a wheat bread crayfish sandwich, which, according to the sticky label on its underside, was for purposes of human consumption dead and buried last Thursday. But, be that as it may, there was no doubting, in the midst of this wide black harbour lit with cruise ships and lighters ploughing though the swell, he was king.

"And," Mundy rejoiced, "I don't care a toss about tomorrow. Who, for crying out loud, needs to agonise over what the next text message will bring?"

Rustling down into his plastic bag for dessert he took out a Portuguese egg tart. On inspection the filling and pastry had gone hard, but, for all that, it remained an egg tart and he wolfed it down in two greedy bites.

The last passenger to board, before a deckhand winched up the gangway, sprawled untidily on the bench supporting Mundy's outstretched feet. An unusual collection of cloth pieces randomly wrapped the person's whole body. There was no sign of normal clothing except for a sort of linen cap tied below its chin and covering the entire head. The effect was to make the figure look like a Victorian doll, or Egyptian mummy. Mundy squinted and looked for a split lip, but could identify nothing more than a blue contusion above one half closed eye.

"Next time, you bastard, it'll cost you a tooth," he said out loud.

Unmoved, or uncomprehending, the bundle thought its own thoughts and looked out over the rail at the approaching Kowloon shore.

Unlike those who lie every night under the same roof, homeless people sleep when circumstances allow and from where they are unlikely to be moved. Around the Culture Centre a few indistinct grey shapes emerged from the shadows as patrons of the evening's show dispersed and security guards gathered behind locked doors. The building's interior was in the hands of trained officials and its outside, under trees and in dark corners, was surrendered to the elements and night. By midnight the grounds were deserted except for a few abandoned dogs and the dispossessed. In the shelter of unforgiving walls bedrolls unfurled like the drooping colours of a defeated army and, on stomachs that had mostly failed to discover the joy of hotel leftovers, the faded standard bearers fell asleep.

If a person was tired enough he could sleep anywhere; over a steering wheel, lashed to the side of a mountain, on a rock or stone floor, the location made no difference. Huddled heaps sank into instant, but watchful repose, like hens on a rail with foxes prowling at the gate. Mundy, however, continued to bask in the glories of his day and slumped open-eyed against a thick glass door. The light of a distant security station dribbled palely over dotted mounds and for a while he was convinced of his exclusion from the surrounding despair.

Under the domes and awnings of the Culture Centre Mozart and skid row rubbed shoulders. Was this a place where opposite ends of the one spectrum circled round to touch, until extremes had no distinction? Can a man with no certainty of the next meal experience the unconfined rapture of a classical symphony? Looking at the surrounding heaps he doubted the possibility, but then again, even before falling on hard times, appreciation by some may not have been within their capacity. A lout remained a lout whether he was force-fed culture or not. But, for his part, if the strains of the Requiem unexpectedly filtered through the doors at his back there would be a short-odds chance he would weep over the remaining crumbs of his five-star menu.

Hunched and deliberating, Mundy slipped into confused sleep and dreamt he was walking up to a conductor's rostrum. Instead of being resplendent in black jacket and bow tie, he wore his society shirt and smelled of mold. With arms spread wide like a martyred saint he addressed the orchestra. Immaculately clad to a man and woman they sat, instruments across knees, with raised eyebrows and unconcealed sniggers. Undismayed and inured to ridicule, he gently brought both arms together to launch onto the expectant air the ephemeral notes of Mozart's immortal first movement. But the violins stayed silent and at the back of the pit someone hammered a monstrous kettledrum. Glancing up, Mundy furiously flapped his baton at the drummer ridiculously attired in a patchwork mass of dirty rags. Leaping from the rostrum he vaulted stairs three at a time towards the percussion section and threw a punch at a soft pulpy head in a cloth cap. Spotlights above the royal circle and in the ceiling swung round to pick out the brawl developing behind the woodwinds and, in the stalls behind, the dinner jackets and evening gowns roared with laughter.

Snapping out of sleep he was baffled by an assembly of bright arc lights not ten feet away and two wide-eyed young women talking at him unintelligibly.

"Sorry to wake you, but we have a deadline to meet and wanted to get…."

"Who…? What are you on about?"

"Can you answer some questions? I'm doing a piece…"

"Look, I'm sleeping. Bugger off!"

"Oh!"

"See, I'm not a nice guy living a not-so-nice life, so get that light out of my face or I'll hit someone."

Discountenanced, the first woman sat back on her heels and called into the darkness behind her. The lights whined and went out.

"My name's Breezy, Breezy Chou; shall I explain?" the second woman, who was no more than a girl, asked.

"You'd better, if you intend hanging around," he said recovering some degree of self-control, "But I must say the lot of you are in danger of spoiling my day. Hope you've got something worth saying, Breezy"

"That's the point," interjected the first woman.

"Shh! Let me," insisted the other, "I'm from the Social Welfare Department and…"

"Good God in Heaven; am I on the end of a government intervention. What do you want to do? Have me put away because the harbour front is getting untidy?"

With a professional and natural patience the young women described what she did; just offer help where it's wanted, no more than that. Now a television station had become interested in the department's "outreach work" and wanted to "raise concern" and "highlight the plight" of the growing numbers of homeless people in Kowloon, which everyone agreed was an "affront" to a city priding itself on its "civic awareness." Consequently, "Cloudy Wong," that was the other woman, had been sent along with her "crew" to see the "suffering" and "do a story" on the "intolerable" situation.

"Then talk to all those layabouts over there," he said gesturing in the direction of some of the piles of human compost covering the Centre's pavement.

"The television people have already spoken to some of them and recorded interviews, but wanted to include you because...because..."

"Because I'm a foreigner and we aren't supposed to live like this? Is that it?"

"Well, yes, if you like. It is unusual."

"Okay, okay...who's taking notes? You?" he said, turning to Cloudy. "There's a lot of weather about here. I hope there's more to you than an absence of sun, or there won't be many boy friends waiting to take you to dinner tonight," and then with resignation, "Go ahead, ask me something."

Ignoring, or more correctly failing to understand, the humour, Cloudy waved to her crew and the whirring lights started up again. Taking a microphone from her sleeve she turned to a portable camera.

"We are here tonight under the majestic arches of the Culture Centre to share with you the blight of homelessness in our great city. Deprivation is no longer the preserve of the old and sick, but extends to those from all walks of life who may simply be the victims of unfortunate circumstance. We are talking to one such. Sir, please tell me your name and what brought you to this situation?" and swaying back from the camera she thrust the microphone into Mundy's face.

"Christ Almighty, what do you expect me to say?"

"Just tell us your story."

"I'm...uh... the name's Mundy and well, actually...in the summer... I...er... quite like it here."

"Huh? I mean, you do this out of choice?"

"No, no, not exactly. Things went wrong a while back, but now I'm used to it...not being tied down and all. It's quite liberating if you think about it."

"But how do you live, where does your money come from?"

"How do I live? Well, a bit of this, a bit of that. Look, I don't want to be specific and have a bunch of derelicts invading my patch."

"But do you plan staying this way?"

"Unless something better comes along, I'll get by."

"I see. Thank you." And after a pause, "That's rather weak, but let's wind down, edits will come later; we can work this in with the rest."

Preceded by another whine the strobe lighting popped out and the crew, gathering up generator, camera, cables and other paraphernalia, strode off with Cloudy in the direction of a van parked on the main road. The human flotsam littering the stone floor had not caught their imagination for as much as a second. What did matter, however, was what was in the can on its way to the studio and the kudos surrounding tomorrow's prime-time show.

Breezy's interests took a different direction and she patted Mundy's arm.

"Don't mind them. But, you know, TV has the power to touch consciences and ultimately help people in need…Would you benefit from our involvement?"

"You don't seem a bad girl," he said ignoring the question and placing a hand on his face to prevent the odour of discarded crayfish offending her. "Shouldn't you be on a catwalk or wining and dining the press instead of being out here in the middle of the night chatting-up down-and-outs?"

The intoxicating presence of a young woman, who carried on her scents he'd long since relegated to another existence, tugged at distant memories. He was like an aging dog, blind and deaf but still able to smell. A bone had been buried somewhere nearby and, whether gnawing it would do him any good or not, he was compelled by inexplicable urges to exhume the rotted remains. Remembering where this line of thought and first conversations went, he tasted again the bitterness of entanglement with the wrong woman and divorce.

"Being there for people is what I like to do. What about you?"

"I'm fine; just need to be left alone."

"Take care," she said and, stood up.

Did some people really understand after all? A current of air sighed like a sob through the arches and tugged her cheesecloth skirt tight round the shape of a warm thigh.

Oh God! he groaned, I'll take care alright, or put out a hand to touch and then there's no going back. The madness of what drives a spider's mate to be eaten in the act of coition tugged at his reason. Dragging his few clothes close to his body he turned to the wall and willed himself to cold, celibate sleep.

At the Culture Centre three nights later and just at the moment when Mundy's head sank onto his soiled rucksack a man dressed in cream slacks and an open patterned shirt stood up from a bench on the far side of the arches. Although the attire was expensive, the couture was more that a shade too haute for the middle-aged figure it contained. Snug hipsters emphasised slack buttocks, and collar points, extending beyond the reach of unusually narrow shoulders, betrayed a man of fashion but limited taste. Sunglasses at this hour suggested either affliction or affectation. Hesitating as if unsure what to do next, he waited while Mundy wriggled into a position of more of less comfort.

"Are you Mundy?" he asked, crouching a little closer, and then without waiting for confirmation continued, "My name's Chan Peng."

Stirring from under the arm crossing his forehead Mundy replied stickily, "So, good for you. What do you want?"

"I…I saw you on the television last week and…Ms Wong – you know, Cloudy – she's my …ah…fiancée. She said I'd find you down here."

"And?"

"It occurred to me that you could use some help."

"What makes you think I want help? And pardon me, but you don't look like the sort of person who offers charity to anyone."

Smiling in a way that raised one smoke-stained corner of an upper lip Chan Peng exposed a row of unbrushed, brown teeth.

Searching for an association and thinking Cloudy was every inch as mercenary as she had looked, Mundy pulled his arm back a little further and asked, "Have we met?"

"Not very likely."

"Meaning we don't move in the same circles?"

"Meaning I have interests that occupy my time."

"Ah! I remember," said Mundy, recalling the swallow-winged sports car and a street altercation, "How's the fishing in Central?"

"Uh?"

"Never mind. Can't imagine there's much I can do for you. What are you after?"

The lop-sided smile, which, on closer inspection was more of a leer, spread to include both sides of the unattractive face.

"I'd like to offer you employment."

"You don't know what I'm fit for. Why on earth would you want to do that?"

"Concern for my fellow man perhaps." The sunglasses blocked any insight into the thoughts behind. Apart from the periodically curling lip there was nothing revealed, least of all a proclivity for kindness.

Scanning the squatting figure, Mundy wondered where on the planet flaunted wealth and liberality met, or was this another circular theme where black and white became the same. Making up his mind that, in this case, there was no connection he replied sourly, "What's the matter with you people? Aren't you too busy grubbing your way to the top to want to stick your nose into my business?"

"We could help each other."

"But I don't want your help; don't you understand? You haven't got a clue how someone like me thinks or behaves. We hate it to begin with, but later it's owned and we can't let go. Have you heard of learning to love despair? You suck something from it, it's like alcohol and you can't, won't, give it up. You might not realise but I'm enjoying myself and the last few days have been better than most. Even if you were genuine, which I doubt, I don't want your offer."

"I…see."

"My guess is you don't see anything other than your flashy possessions."

"There's no harm in making money."

"If your performance in Central was anything to go by, there's plenty of harm."

Realising they must somewhere have been in contact, Chan Peng replied, "I can only help others when helping myself."

Mundy sat up as if suddenly remembering something. The unexpected movement caused Chan Peng to topple over onto his thin buttocks and expensive trousers.

"Mind your clothes they'll get dirty on this pavement; it's not scrubbed as well as Central's."

"I'm not here to save you, just seeing if we have the possibility of cooperation."

"Look, here's the fact of the matter. There's a handful of Buddhists round town who may understand, but, unless you're one of them, which would amaze me, I don't expect the same insight has struck you. We are all trapped on a wheel, and there's no way off. My wheel is no job and no money and there is no way out because after a year it is me. Just like all the poor sods, you included, over in Central. You are too engrossed in your own greed to see other people as anything more than someone, or rather something, to overtake; your humanity, if it ever existed, has deserted you. Your wheel is making money and spending so as to look better than all those others doing exactly the same thing. There's no joy or redemption and it's worse than all the political isms, because the compulsion comes from within and struggling against it, even if you wanted to, has become impossible. It's like saying I don't want to be me. Well, hey buddy, guess what, you may not like the package, but there ain't any other, it's in your blood; the same way as it's in mine."

"Perhaps we like it that way."

"Why, there you have it! Next time you're in Central on a Saturday afternoon look around, instead of waiting for the rest to marvel at you. Ask yourself or anyone with a boutique carrier bag if this is how he or she wants life to be. When the lights go out at the end of a futile existence, do you want all the people with whom you never had a meaningful relationship to say 'he was a fine shopper and owned the fastest car in a city where driving more than twenty miles an hour was impossible.' How's the Almighty going to pick anyone for the hereafter? Not that there is a heaven, but if there was, who would stand a better chance; an enslaved person of your type, or mine? The worst I've done in the last year is bash a beggar who got between me and my supper. I'd say I was as well off as anyone. Now fuck off, I'm busy."

Without a further word and against the inclination of unexercised joints Chan Peng detached his body from the pavement, turned and walked away. But before his stiffened limbs were fully at ease a voice called out from under the arches behind him.

"Hey! If you really want to help and are meeting up with Cloudy sometime soon ask her to tell Breezy that when she's round here again I'd like to discuss my situation. That's all."

And turning to the wall he watched his condensed breath gather and stutter uncertainly down the cold grey facade in front of his weary face.

Chills in the night air replaced the clammy heat of summer and as the season moved so did the destitute. Mundy located an alley in Western, which, at day's end, was usually piled high with cardboard boxes from nearby factories. With scavenged newspapers stuffed as insulation between his clothes and skin he nightly scared away prowling cats and climbed in among old cartons to sleep the sleep of the forsaken.

Late one night, while methodically screwing twists of newspaper into his disintegrating shirt, he noticed on one ragged sheet, a column entitled 'Inside Destitution' written by Cloudy Wong and with a black and white print picture of a beaming Chan Peng.

The article was on the editorial page and referred to the recent work of that well known "business man and philanthropist Chan Peng", who spent "freely of his time and fortune", to bring "hope" to the "vagrants" sleeping on the city streets. In "conversations" with the "investigative reporter from the newspaper's affiliated television station RTVO" he was able to conclude that, although the minority, through "ill health, age or drug addiction" were in need of "society's help", some were homeless "by choice." It was in fact a "lifestyle decision" and even able-bodied foreigners who were an "unwelcome disgrace" were refusing "meaningful and rewarding jobs" to live off "social service and taxpayer support".

Well, well, so that was the game, free publicity for Chang Peng laid on by a partner in ambition that fitted like a bespoke yachting outfit and with the rampant immoderation that left human wreckage stranded far behind. Whether the offered jobs were real, or not was beside the point. Columns of praise enhanced two carefully constructed reputations and careers. Instead of the reflected glory of brands purchased at the most exclusive stores Chan Peng and Ms Wong had leapt over their rivals and, in the middle of the daily news, contrived a high-recognition self-branding none could hope to copy. For a day and until another ingenuity overtook them, the greasy-pole's priorities had been satisfied and the city had set new standards in competitive irrelevance.

Wrapped warmly in cardboard and newspaper Mundy sank into sleep and against his will and in spite of the cool night air dreamt of taut cheesecloth pressed tightly to Breezy Chau's golden limbs.

EIGHT

FIFTY PERCENT OFF

The view from thirty-two floors above street level was majestic. On the right a swathe of green sports fields fringed the sea and to the left sheer cliffs bathed warmly in the Pacific Ocean's languid breezes. From out of the overarching blue sky kites stooped to within inches of the hillside treetops before sailing away on motionless wings towards the hazy profusion of stone islands scattered along the Pearl River Delta.

Small freighters, avoiding the congested harbour, unloaded in the nearby roads and throughout day and night tugs and lighters chugged with stacked containers between ships and ragged shoreline.

During early morning, when the sun was still hidden behind encircling hills, the sea was green; at noon it was blue; and after sunset and during the moon's solitary governance of the firmament the black, undulating waters sparkled like a magician's cloak dashed with silver.

From his luxurious penthouse and oblivious to food and sleep Fuk Choi had spent many recent hours gazing blankly onto this changing sweep of beauty.

The deal to buy Lok Tau's open-air market and develop the site into an exclusive brand-name shopping mall had run into difficulties. Despite the obvious business case for demolishing minor local tradition and replacing it with shiny profitability, re-zoning permission had stalled, loan interest had begun to pile up and the latest calculations were falling short of first projections made for investors just a few short months ago. To make matters worse, threats of public enquiry rumbled ominously in the distance, like typhoons before making landfall.

Could he or anyone else have anticipated the clamorous campaign to hinder and challenge the venture at every conceivable turn? In the past, every project he'd pursued and brought to profitable conclusion had produced its share of awkward people, but without exception their objections had been carefully soothed and smoothed away. Why then had this one become stuck on a rock of intransigence thrown into its path by an unimaginable alliance of youthful environmentalists and local traders impervious to the sort of solutions he was accustomed to deliver?

What prompted young people these days, he wondered, to take their displeasure onto the streets? Had they no fathers, no mothers, no older relatives to guide them in proper behaviour, or had they been corrupted by the sort of ugly foreign influences he knew only too well?

Immature feelings were unreliable things at the best of times and should be dealt with behind closed doors and under the weight and supervision of a family's inner circle. The restive traders, who had similarly deserted society's correct ways, were another lot who would have benefited from the wisdom of their betters before seeking to undermine benefits mapped out for the wider community. But no one was listening. Disagreement as spectacle, he concluded, was so unproductive and so un-Chinese.

In better times, an astute combination of *guanxi* and string-pulling had spirited away inconveniencies, but today, with woolly and impractical idealism converging on the neighbourhood from every point of the compass, these silent and ancient mechanisms of facilitation had almost become liabilities.

With some effort the traders might have been bought off even at this late hour, but romantic defenders of the dirty and inefficient market were another story altogether and, as it turned out, quite beyond temptation. If activists accepted only one outcome, how could they be encouraged to accept what would amount in their eyes to an unholy compromise? They were, he decided disconsolately, little better than terrorists with suicidal tendencies against whom none of the usual levers of authority and coercion had the least effect.

Once these rebellious and unreconstructed elements joined forces and spread disorder the banks had begun leaning on Fuk Choi and his company to get the project back on track, but he, incapable of breaking the deadlock and surrounded by the collapse of his standard terms of reference, was for the first time in his business career grappling in the dark.

In the commercial world Fuk Choi was a shadowy figure known to just a few who saw him as an instinctive and trusted organiser; a man to get things done. His way of negotiating away obstacles by secretly and unobtrusively oiling rasping wheels had until this minute enjoyed great, although quiet favour.

Never before had he achieved, or desired, the near-celebrity status thrust on him now, or been dragged under glaring spotlights by irresponsible students who may have trekked the Andes and visited Roman ruins on the financial support of wealthy parents, but who knew nothing of working ten or twelve hours a day to raise a family's material comfort to acceptable levels.

At the beginning his difficulties appeared to be minor and well within control, but quite unexpectedly this full-blown crisis had erupted, calling into question every aspect of the unhygienic and decrepit market's redevelopment. And now, with debate raging around the formerly invisible crannies of his business dealings, the stalls and interconnecting back streets of Lok Tau were experiencing unexpected revival with the outward flow of trade and residents to newer middle-class areas, inexplicably reversed.

The hip and upwardly mobile, for whatever reasons that guided fashion and set trends, began shopping there, followed soon after by the festoons of red and gold bunting hung up by the merchants and green banners and placards of environmentalists, ignorantly proclaiming, "Hands off our livelihoods" and more seditiously, "People before profits". And, if that was not enough, the atmosphere of raucous gaiety and entertainment soon drew in all manner of outsiders keen to join the fun without needing to express a point of view.

The government, television and press got hold of the story and, in Fuk Choi's opinion, spent an inordinate amount of time conducting fact-finding meetings and filming and interviewing students and fishmongers, who, with linked arms and sympathies, were turning the again thriving streets of Lok Tau into a jamboree. All the ballyhoo really let the side down and was simply not the way business should be conducted. Offering inducements and making behind the scenes arrangements were the accepted ways to overcome blockages, not civil disobedience and riot. But, if the possibility of reducing regrettable publicity through private intercession or collaboration still existed, even at this late juncture, and should the consequence be a further redrawn revenue forecast, he would still gladly have accepted the offer. Faced, however, with noisy street disturbance fingering him as a community pariah, he was at a loss to know where to turn and what to do next.

In almost every way Fok Choi was a traditional man valuing hard work and filial duty. Throughout his life, more or less consistent dedication to those two themes had enabled him to amass an enviable fortune and bask in his mother's cherished but nagging pride.

Since first establishing himself as a businessman, burgeoning wealth had been the means by which he created yet more money and acquired countless symbols of achievement, although, from the time when cost no longer mattered, his diet remained steadfastly unexceptional and his vacations infrequent.

Spending lavishly on his mother, even after the time when she became too infirm to venture far from the family home, fell partly into the category of symbolism. The other part was the familial obligation inherent in being a good son. Inordinate satisfaction overwhelmed him, when, decked out in fine jewellery, with her wrinkled skin as smooth as any beauty treatment could pretend, she sat resplendently in brilliant colours, like a prize mare at ease in the paddock long after her last race was won.

Under the tower block overlooking the roads he parked, with elaborate conceit, a gleaming top-of-the-line European saloon car, which from time to time he took out and drove sedately, to the annoyance of other highway users, along the fast lanes of the city's busy expressways. The lane positioning was intuitively selected as the best place to flaunt an outsized vehicle and, less thoughtfully, because he was a very poor and short driver who needed, in addition to a cushion's artificial assistance, a great deal of unreasonable space to navigate safely the many street perils inseparable from a rushing population.

With his father long since dead of overwork and starved affection, Fuk Choi's natural bond to his mother had increased and the respect and duty he had always shown her became obsequious and fawning; while she, a matriarch by right, grasped the opportunity to bully both her son and the many servants he'd hired for her to run his extra-large home.

But, as his fortunes blossomed and she basked in his prosperity and grew old, he contrived, just once and with her unwitting agreement, to taste the forbidden fruit of independence.

At the relatively late age of forty-five, he decided to replace the haphazard reading of business magazines with direct experience of foreign methods and, to add legitimacy to position, by acquiring an overseas post-graduate degree. The North American residential course selected separated him from his beloved mother for eighteen long months and during this painful period, he learned the varied skills of organisational, operational and people management, the modern principles of finance and accounting, marketing, how to "push the envelope"; and – underpinning everything – the mind-blowing wonders of socially acceptable, as opposed to hole in the wall, fornication. But, being frequently distracted by extra-curricular electives, his academic accomplishment gradually lost momentum, until the ultimate embossed certificate, which eventually hung in his mother's private lounge for her aging friends to discuss, was obtained with the lowest possible grade awarded that year.

The freedom encountered throughout his long absence from the maternal bosom led for the first time to a decision her presence and guardianship could and should have prevented.

To say that he fell in love would be an exaggeration, but the whirlwind of frequent and open sexual activity left him unbalanced and indecisive. He had not previously been aware that sleeping with a woman could be a natural progression of acquaintanceship rather than something paid for in the dingier parts of town, or the consequence of marriage. The year and a half passed in a flash and the reality of returning home to be without the regularity of on-request relationships filled him with dismay. The solution, he decided, would be to take with him one of the companions on whom he had come to rely.

A casual suggestion to a casual woman to cross the Pacific might well have been enough, but for the sake of the Fuk matriarch he believed there was a paradoxical necessity to formalise the arrangement, or revert to the unreliable seedy habits of pre-business-school days. Alternatively, the successful candidate could have remained unwed and live out, but that would increase his expense to a level his parsimonious nature for expenses unconnected to vulgar show was not prepared to contemplate and, if present experience was anything to go by, held the potential for compromising unequivocal right of access.

Fuk Choi consequently decided that before returning home he would marry.

With the lessons of his barely scraped MBA lodged insecurely at the back of his head he fell to rapidly devising a plan for his domestic future and to enthusiastically staffing the position he had declared vacant. Poring through his diary, which looking back held more social appointments and associated telephone numbers than the times of lectures, or study meetings, he decided somewhat disappointedly there were only two candidates realistically worthy of a short-list.

One was a neat, fastidious woman who worked for one of the major accounting firms and who, while decidedly liberated and well qualified between the sheets, was apt to talk too much. All women where Fuk came from were inclined to shrill verbosity and it was not a behaviour he found attractive. His mother had enough opinions to go around and, in a prophetic insight, he could imagine what it was like getting wedged between two differing points of view and suffering for being present as much as for doing anything to displease. What he needed was someone not over bright to complement his vast assembly of material possessions and with imagination keep him and his mother satisfied in the different ways they required.

That left Natasha or Nats as he called her. The whispered diminutive caused her to pucker up her well-bridged nose in a mock-offended sort of way, which he found totally irresistible.

They had met, in a manner of speaking, at a party welcoming participants to the business course. His only view of her that night had been from the rear and he was struck by how tightly delightfully rounded hips squeezed into her pants. Later on he heard malicious descriptions of "sprayed-on" clothes from another female student and his perception that Nats had many enviable qualities was reinforced.

She, in addition to being voluptuous, further piqued his interest by being a little bit of a mystery. Fuk Choi was used to identifying people in categories. Knowing the framework, he felt, helped determine responses. All the nationalities of Asia were clearly different and consequently deserving treatment fitted to their background. But with Nats he could not at first tell whether her origins were of any particular continent or country. Her accents and colour failed to speak of one place and this both disturbed and excited him. She was something he had not previously encountered, which by extension gave him freedom from obligation to behave as if propositioning a woman from his own world. What he overlooked, however, was that the virtues contributing so significantly to her allure in North America rendered her almost impossible to assimilate into a conventional Chinese family. The limitations of a hectoring accountant were easy to spot; the incompatibility of exoticism was not.

With just three months to go before returning home and in an exhilarating climax to his American adventure Fuk Choi asked Nats to accompany him to the East as his wife. Although they had spent many nights together the possibility, or desirability, of a long-term relationship had not for one second crossed her mind. Their relationship, she had assumed, was not of that type. But on the back of Fuk's careful preparation and her understanding of his substantial commercial interests the proposal's value started to acquire appeal. Being game for an escapade and mindful that union to a wealthy man held possibilities exceeding any she had so far enjoyed with other male friends, she accepted, while not forgetting a properly set up marriage was as easy to get out of as into.

On the road between Sacramento and Reno there is a drive-in chapel where a very affordable marriage can add no more than fifteen minutes to a traveller's journey. And so, on the acceptance of a credit card, Fuk and Nats began their formal partnership. Later that same night the distant matriarch was informed by long distance telephone call from a motel called the "Mono Ski," which from Fuk's initial point of view augured well for the future. His mother, however, believing the union to be no more than planned rather than consummated in word and deed maybe fifty or even a hundred times before, during and after the event, absolutely and loudly forbade the marriage. The free and easy Nats heard the noise of disapproval jangle from a handset held a good foot from Fuk's dejected head. Preoccupied by the red-blooded intensity of the chase he had been slow to realise how thick were the clouds confusing his brain and how enormous his transgression.

"Is she mad?" Nats said swaying backwards and forwards in a semi-naked and cross-legged position on the luxurious king-sized bed.

What a figure of unrestrained fun she was, exuding unabashed ease with herself and her surroundings. The sort of woman who felt no reservation in running barefoot, or in living without thought or obligation, except to touch and taste and move on again. Her nature flew wherever it had a mind to go. She knew no loyalty, no guilt and no shame. In an unpremeditated way she was amoral; one of Pan's wild companions dancing in flower circles and shaded forest glades. There was nothing intellectual or self-serving in this view, it was not a posture, but simply the way she was. In this she was Fuk Choi's opposite. While he was suppressed and tortured by inner doubts and the chaffing shackles of an inflexible and intolerant culture, she floated like the open-sky kites above his far off homeland.

As the tidal wave of imperial female wrath gathered over his head, Fok Choi wondered whether similar censure had once contributed to his father's early and rarely discussed demise.

Why tonight, he asked, were the moist tentacles of Nats' entwining embrace more than usually welcome? As his mind struggled with the question and his breathless and perspiring body sought the most fundamental of all relief, he realised for the first time since discovering the glorious Natasha that his ship had collided with a reef between two distinct and irreconcilable geographical hemispheres.

If the matriarch's control was, by virtue of her absence from the marriage celebrations, less than she required, her former fearsome grip, she determined, would be restored once her son was safely gathered back in her embrace. Not that Fuk Choi's peccadilloes brought her dismay; indeed in the world with which she was familiar it was the duty of a close female relative to ensure men were provided with every conceivable comfort their dispositions required. But the fact that this liaison was outside her community and permanent filled her with grave disquiet. At the very least customs would be re-established and ensuing offspring lashed to the native barque.

To maintain the integrity of his marriage offer Fuk Choi carefully avoided direct untruths. But, because accumulated omission painted a flawed picture, his amazed wife was soon convinced of extensive and craven deceit. The matriarch's occupation of not just a near-by granny apartment, but all the rooms of the house, including an out-of-bounds private area reserved for her and her servants, was only the first. Servants, Nats discovered, were instructed by the old lady and consequently the content and timing of meals, her son's clothes, who visited for majong games, the extent of a wife's authority, Cantonese communication and traditional holiday gatherings, were all prescribed at her pleasure. In the eyes of Fuk Choi's mother the unexpected out-break of foreign marriage, like a boil, on the family's countenance would not under any circumstances be allowed to disrupt, still less dilute, the rightness and radiance of her exclusively middle-kingdom views.

Nats had no idea an inner circle, defined by blood, language and a three hundred year old provincial origin, existed; for which, despite her nominally important position, she held the very weakest kind of membership qualification. Given her open and forthright character, her first impulse was to write off the first few weeks as a bad mistake and go back to where she had been at liberty.

But not only had Nats arrived in Asia uncomprehending, she also came pregnant. Maternal instincts, even among the previously carefree, quickly become all-consuming and consequently Nats paused to consider. If her child was carried to full term both she and it deserved the very best Fuk Choi could provide and, unless she was palpably mistaken, he was in a position to provide a lot. The provision of love, time and tolerance might not be major gifts at his disposal, but riches would be accepted as alternatives and in just payment for the wild nights and lack of frankness along the road to Reno.

In the next few years a kind of civil war engulfed the Fuk household as rival groups contested the single plot of ground. And, in between, cut off from safety, Fuk Choi paid in double kind for the loose months in North America with the increasingly sedentary, but uncompromising Madam Fuk on one side and the disarmingly untameable Natasha absorbed by the task of motherhood on the other. To his face he endured ridicule from a wife who wouldn't be marginalised and scorn from a maturing, but over-privileged, daughter, while at his back his mother's prodding never rested. The fearsome trio left not a crack or crevice, no bolthole or resting place in which he could hide or draw peaceful breath.

By the time of Jessica's teenage years, Fuk Choi had long since abandoned hope of a harmonious family. The only times he now chose to spend at home were when others were away, or when he was permitted to lock the study door and immerse himself in work. The continued accumulation of yet more wealth, however, rapidly lost meaning, but, because it was all he knew and dulled his ache, he could no more stop than fly with the birds circling outside his airy penthouse. Only once, he reflected sadly, had he enjoyed the freedom of those soaring wanderers and it had cost him every last contentment.

As years drifted miserably by he saw the universe solely through his mother's wisdom and became, if more certainty was needed, convinced of her infallibility. A local girl, one who maintained the cultural themes of the household would have suited everyone better. The awful reality surrounding fractured domesticity was that only his money kept it under one roof. If tomorrow impoverishment dawned, the various pieces would fly, like a punctured tyre on a wildly driven racing car, in as many directions as they numbered.

Scrapes on the wood tiles overhead insinuated their way into his wretched thoughts. The matriarch, having slept lightly and irritably for an hour after lunch was ready to be bathed. Her two white-coated attendants supporting every feeble step would later descend with her to the living area and, acting as intermediaries, give directions for the household's afternoon.

A fresh wave of anxiety rose in Fuk Choi's troubled chest when he should have been concentrating on resolving the debacle at Lok Tau. Now there was nowhere to run or lay down his head, or recall the small pleasures of turning a business scheme into good profit. Once, not so very long ago, he had still found meaning in a worker bee's enslavement to the accumulation of honey for others to plunder. Today, all he had left was a crippled vision and the ashes of what might have been. He loved his mother dearly, but feared what she would say when news of the development's collapse reached her ears. How he hated her constant reminders that he should have done something, everything differently.

In the roads below a tiny sampan buffeted though the wash of an inbound freighter. The tiny craft and bees, he mused, had much in common; both were unfit for their chosen elements and while one tossed perilously on the water the other was cast about by the demands of vexatious queens. By any law of nature neither should have survived their day of creation. Please God, an inner voice whispered, next time let me come back ready to be a eunuch.

Drained of confidence in the powers that once guided his forays into commerce he crumpled into massed cushions on the hideous sofa provokingly purchased by Nats prior to last year's autumn sales. A flood of incomprehensibility rose around him and in a desperate search for order and reason in an increasingly turbulent day Fuk Choi turned to the financial pages of the *South China Morning Post*.

Under an immoderately gleeful banner headline declaring "Developers Ambitions Demolished", he saw, with desolation and fulsome rage that moved his face though many contortions and deepening colours, a newsprint photograph of the fishmongers and butchers of Lok Tau. Unhygienically dressed in singlets and rubber boots, the tradesmen were surrounded by a sprawl of student activists proclaiming environmentalist credentials in uniform green shirts. At the centre of the flag-waving and chanting mob he was appalled to see his only child.

Fuk Choi sprang to his feet and then, with hand on throat, fell back among the heaped cushions. What had he done to deserve such ingratitude? Had he not lavished clothes, electronic gadgetry, international schooling, overseas holidays and everything money could buy on this wretch, this pestilence, this thankless brat? In return for his care, she mocked his existence and the very effort sustaining her comfort. This latest antic was not just another crude teenage joke, but a gun aimed at his vitals and the means by which he paid bills and manifested his and his people's historic values. Never had he felt so devastated, so betrayed.

His mother's shuffle in the doorway broke into his reeling thoughts.

The old lady grunted forward to her preferred seat from which she commanded a view of the room, the roads and all they contained. With one veined and palsied hand grasping a stick and the other the chair's hard arm she lowered into position. Without inclination to do anything but tyrannise she tugged her embroidered jacket tightly to her chest and prepared to issue commands.

"No, not those slippers. Fetch me the black ones," she scolded in the piping cadences of extreme age. The reproved servant, as if anticipating imminent termination of service, hurried nervously away to an upstairs room in search of more acceptable footwear.

Unlike her despised daughter-in-law the old woman's skin was dark and criss-crossed with myriad lines owing nothing to character, but all to an absence of muscular tension on a very old and fleshless face. Her still strong grey hair was drawn down on both sides of her head in severe straight lines like curtains in a Taoist retreat. From under a fringe of uncompromising cut she looked disapprovingly around with the sharp eye of a house lizard hunting moths beneath a porch lantern. In the absence of necessity an empress manufactures opportunities to complain.

"What's the matter with you," she said addressing Fuk Choi.

"I was about to go out."

"Why? I've only just got up."

"You'll be looked after. You have the servants."

"I don't want to be looked after by servants, I want my son. And where is my grand-daughter? She is not as a good child should be."

"She's fifteen and likes to be out."

"That is not a satisfactory answer. She should be at home practicing her characters. Mark my words she will be lost to you and us if you forever tolerate her laxity."

Long ago Fuk realised all the women in his house, yes his house, believed in different things and excluding the bond between Nats and her daughter, disliked each other intensely. They were like bands of Madagascan lemurs shrieking at one other among the treetops to maintain territorial advantage through mutual enmity. His domestic duty had degenerated from the titular head of the household into explaining and apologising for all of them and providing the funds to fuel bad habits.

Commanding anyone other than employees had never been his proclivity, nor under the merciless grip of the present totalitarian regime, was it an opportunity that had ever arisen.

"You are like your father; afraid to beat naughtiness out of a child. She'll go bad if you let her…and that mother of hers is even worse. Why you brought her here I'll never know. What are you going to do?"

Do, do? The question screamed in Fuk's head, why should he have to do anything? Why was everyone and everything his responsibility? The smiling face in the *Post*'s open pages and marks of printers' ink left on the sofa's artificial suede seemed to join the chorus crying, guilty, guilty! Even without his mother's harrying, he realised, something had gone further out of control than usual and forces building like a tropical storm were on the brink of washing away the few remaining strands of an already fragile self-esteem.

Instead of moderating, tension crackled and flashed round the extravagant apartment like electrical discharges under a rain cloud and were boosted to an even higher level by the inadequacies of the returning servant.

"You are hurting my feet, silly girl; stop that. My son will show you how."

Without further instruction Fuk Choi knelt in humility and obedience and eased the tiny stockinged feet into their felt slippers. What, he wondered, would happen if he just turned and bolted into the street? Without strength to make a serious challenge or disappoint, the thought was no more than a sour idea shrivelling like an addled egg exposed to cold air. Frozen in an abject position he did not raise his head at the howl of boisterous laughter that swept unexpectedly in with the return of his wife and daughter.

"What are you doing down there?" queried Nats as she flung a collection of bulging carrier bags onto the floor, "looking for something to fit a glass shoe?"

A second peel of laughter convulsed the returning shoppers. Servants exchanged uncomfortable glances and hurried from the room. Intimate insults, they decided, were as delicate as terms of endearment and none but family should bear witness.

"Where have you been? " Fuk asked as reproachfully as he dare.

"We have been saving you money dear boy. Instead of paying full price we have taken advantage of the sales. Not a single item we bought offered less than fifty percent discount. Aren't you pleased we have learned your lessons so thoroughly?" Nats eyes were full of mischief, but her lips showed no hint of humour.

The old woman stared fixedly at her son as if transmitted thoughts alone would be enough to bring him to action. Blinking and perspiring behind glasses and still in a supplicant's position he said nothing.

"Come to me child, I want to look at you."

Unafraid, Jessica looked to her mother for consent and at a slight nod edged nearer to the stern and forbidding figure stacked in its wooden chair as rigidly as a pile of bones.

"Yes, Grandma?"

"You are not a respectful daughter to your father. When I was your age we were taught to give duty to our elders." The comment although spoken to the girl was meant for her mother

"Is that right, Grandma?"

"And what sort of a reply is that? If I say it was, why should you question?"

"Because she is a modern child and has been taught to think," said Natasha with no hint of warmth.

Renewed battle lines were being marked out like trenches across the fields and, anticipating an artillery barrage, Fuk Choi lurched clumsily to his feet.

"I have an appointment and will be back late."

"That's first-class nonsense and you know it. You don't want to be involved again. Isn't that the truth?" Natasha did not mince words at the best of times and today she was in no mood to be gentle.

The wife and daughter looked at Fuk Choi with a mixture of pity and contempt. The mother, completely unaware her crushing control had emasculated him beyond any hint of self-sufficiency, bestowed on him a honey-comb cloying smile as sweet as any in her arsenal.

Perhaps the remnants, the rags of his authority, resurfaced in business dealings. Could what had been denied at home and at Lok Tau return with vigour in better regulated bargaining? Above the busy shipping lanes, on the thirty-second floor, there was no evidence Fuk Choi still held in his persona the sharp tools necessary to maintaining a thriving commercial empire, nor that he had ever arrived at any semblance of complete manhood.

"Cook will wait up for you," soothed the Matriarch.

"Before you go, Pop, I want to tell you something."

"Not now child, your father has work to do and we must not detain him."

"Say what you want Jessica," Natasha urged, "Tell him what you told me."

Turning to the still abject, but now vertical, figure the girl, with the assurance inseparable from a full-grown and spoiled adolescent, possessing the verbal exactness that had won plaudits in school debating contests, said "I've joined the protest at Lok Tau. We've stopped the development."

"Such nonsense," countered Madame Fuk, who was not disposed to let a child rise above its station.

"You wait and see," the girl retorted with hot teenage passion.

In the swell of squabble each rejoinder bettered the one before and Fuk Choi's eyes spun from one to the other in growing horror. He was a wide-eyed stag standing on a crumbling precipice with ravenous wolves circling in nearby woods.

"I...I must go," he stammered. No one prevented him from leaving, or spoke a word as he grappled with the door and so, with their combined gaze piercing and burning his neck, he scrambled into the elevator. The faintly droning motor allowed his thoughts to re-order, but his furiously racing pulse banged like New Year fire crackers all the way down to the basement.

In the half-light of the car-park high ceilings echoed to his dragging footsteps and the sound of condensed water dripping from overhead waste pipes. He was overwhelmed by self-pity. The women's staring faces haunted him. They were accusing, and scornful of each other, but most especially of him. He had built his life around the twin objectives of a healthy, prosperous and united family and as much hard work as was required to look after it, but inexplicably he was rewarded with dust. Had he not given all that could reasonably be asked and more? Why then, was he so despised by his wife and child and fenced in by his mother, who had unwittingly crushed every ounce of liberty until his unrebellious heart could not move but surreptitiously and evasively. Was her legacy to him no more than a lesson in dishonesty? His only real freedom had been when he was far away and that one occasion had ironically snapped shut the prison grill and condemned him to a life-sentence.

The airtight door of his massive sedan closed with a barely audible whisper and, hiding behind the steering wheel, he slid from sight. Outside the windscreen, painted and numbered spaces lined both sides of the basement and, dotted among them, like chess pieces late in a game, other expensive and glistening cars waited for ostentatious owners to claim them. Several signs forbidding skateboarding, inexact parking and laundry hanging shared places on the damp walls with limply hanging fire hoses doubling up as car-wash facilities.

The hoses caught Fuk Choi's attention. With the sudden cold clarity of a star seen above the roof of the tower block on a winter's night, an idea struck him. Stepping from his car he threw back his head and yawned; it was one of those yawns, which seemed to crack jawbones and in the emptiness of the basement, needed no disguising. From a beautifully equipped toolbox in the huge boot of his shining limousine he took out an unused hack saw and ran his smooth, round executive's thumb over the edge. Satisfied, he walked round the vehicle and, with the detachment of a samurai warrior beheading a criminal, he sliced from the dangling pipe a length of about six feet and, after measuring it in outstretched arms, he rammed it into the open end of a chrome exhaust pipe.

At the turn of a key the precision engine purred into life and only a gentle vibration gave evidence of a running motor. Fuk Choi dropped the loose end of the severed hose into the boot next to the toolbox, scanned the length of the basement to be assured he was alone and clambered over the lip onto soft, felt carpet. Grasping the underside of the lid he pulled it closed behind him.

Later the following day a cleaner, who had been sent to prepare another vehicle for a visit to the city's inexhaustible shopping malls, noticed the length of hose and the turning but unattended engine. Not wishing to be involved, she called a security guard and watched from a discrete but curious distance.

***

In the minds of the police sent to investigate there was no doubting the motive; beset by financial worries precipitated by the Lok Tau development fiasco, Fuk Choi had run out of options and rather than face the consequences of a failed venture that threatened to engulf his company he resorted to taking his own short but well-intentioned life. He left no explanation for anyone to consider and those that knew him would not have expected otherwise. His colleagues and business associates recalled him as a man of few public appearances and one who busied himself in the single-minded pursuit of work. Without bringing any private matters into open view, Fuk Choi in their opinion had fought a good fight for commendable goals, but at the end had lost his gamble and chosen an honourable exit. Others, under the same pressure, would be applauded for doing as much.

After her son's sudden end only the bitterly isolated matriarch, who continued to nag and chide her servants into behaviour of her choosing, stayed on in the apartment. Natasha and Jessica returned to North America and never wrote or called. They disappeared as completely as Fuk Choi's coffin into the crematorium furnace and Jessica never again practiced her Chinese characters.

NINE

ON THE HILL

Half way up the hill on the corner of Haig and Ford was a line of brightly painted and variously coloured row houses. Early in the day and under every window, boxes of hydrangeas matching the red roof tiles flourished in sea mists drifting across the peninsula. Later on, but long before the sun began to set, the last traces of fog burned away and the wind-flecked glory of the Pacific Ocean filled the entire western horizon. Above the steep streets, seagulls clamoured and their raucous cries tumbled into the city far below.

A blue house at the end row nearest the summit, with white framed doors and windows, was the home of Steria, who been named Wisteria by her stubbornly conservative parents, and her companion Madge.

Wisteria had spent a miserable childhood in New England wishing she was someone else and her later assumption of the name of Steria became the beginning of a solution to an agonizing dilemma. Retaining any link to the times of her greatest distress had been a close call, because disaffection towards her family had once been so consuming, she had been prepared to accept anything from Brandy to Xantha, but had been persuaded at the end by a sound lacking any apparent gender distinction. Her father's pet name of Wist, which attached to her psyche like a leech bleeding away self-assurance, was never again uttered, not even in jest, once she was free of her childhood home's suffocating constraint. Like lavender soap, now substituted in her hilltop retreat with Madge by "Woodland" and, en suite "Tropical Nights", she modified or purged every debilitating association.

Her struggle for identity, manifest in the search for a bearable name, originated in the certainty she had never, on any level, fitted her parents' view of her place in their orthodox world. And they, not wishing to hear details of the condition they regarded as an affliction, hoped to wake one morning to find it had simply gone away. But, as that day never dawned, they were left to regret the ill humour, bad taste and, as she grew, political inclinations of their frequently brooding offspring. When a college and subsequent career were selected precipitously and without consultation on the opposite side of the country they felt rebuffed, although, without admitting as much to their like-minded friends, they agreed her decision was in the best possible interests of all concerned.

Free of her upbringing, Steria developed from a thin, angular and ungracious teenager into an opinionated and uncompromising woman. In less defensive moments she was intelligent and owning some physical grace. If she had allowed her more attractive qualities free rein she doubtlessly would have become both professionally and socially much sought after. But, because she retained a suspicious and querulous disposition and almost wilfully rendered her best features redundant, many promising possibilities were turned away and, instead of enticing the bright and glamorous to her acquaintanceship, she drove them into the arms of more congenial company. Left with a marginal circle of friends, she became, in the words of her estranged mother, everything her parents had suspected.

Steria's brown and grey costumes could occasionally be stylish and pleasing, but when unfailingly repeated without highlight or contrast and in poor tailoring, she was perceived as unimaginably dowdy and no-one, either out of conviction or empathy, ever felt compelled to throw away in her presence the platitudinous praise of, "Hey! Nice suit."

Plain attire, often one or two sizes too large, an absence of make-up, and blond hair, which her father had once thought so beautiful, now close-cropped to a bristly two centimetres, made Steria's sex from any cursory angle a complete mystery. And that, because it did not matter, was her intention. If there had to be a motivation for not looking well, it was because she could not stand the thought of people regarding her as feminine. Ugh! The very word made her flesh creep. Under no circumstances would she be confused with one of those silly women who used their looks for advancement and about whom men devised self-promoting and largely false stories. She demanded indifference, while forgetting the world craved judgement.

Recollecting the asinine corridor conversations she'd interrupted, where only the "guy-thing" had permitted participation, made her cringe with revulsion. Crude references behind her back to someone called "Cereal" and remorseless

Neanderthal guffawing filled her with trembling rage. How she hated the mindless, one-dimensional male view. Well, she'd show them and, given a chance, thrash the lot. Let them choose the ground and she would be their master - no, not another one of those hideous words! For her own and, if he was a woman, for God's sake too, she would be the mistress of them all.

Despite the occasional office "water-cooler" incident, her life at last became more or less to her liking. From the beginning, Madge created the environment in which Steria became, if not wholly fulfilled, at least able to enjoy long patches of tranquillity. Their three years under a shared roof was the rock over which the boiling tumult of adolescence broke and wasted its strength and became more rewarding than any Steria could recall.

Unlike Steria, Madge was a huge, hearty woman with a fondness for slapping people on the back until their glasses spilled and teeth rattled. With a roar of laughter, she enjoyed distinguishing herself, in the wake of Steria's explanation of her own origins, as being from "Old England." At first hearing, the joke, if not hilarious, was engaging enough and Steria, with the indulgence of a long established relationship, smiled supportively through its many repetitions.

Madge and Steria fitted together like pieces from the same broken plate. That they were of the same utensil was clear, even if differently sized and shaped. One was small, spare and cutting and the other, large, round and accommodating. The fabric of this single partnership gave Steria her new-found, but fragile, strength; but for Madge, who was attached by previous existences to old social circles, it was delightful, but not the only offering in town. Mutual bonds were strong, but only for Steria were they indispensable to her equanimity.

Ideal weekends for Steria consisted of summer hikes on the eastern bay's brown hills, followed by slow dinners full of shared confidences in which she found nearly total peace. Madge too looked forward to the outings, but with less robust enthusiasm. She was not built to march, free of discomfort for eight hours on the dry, crackling slopes, and felt her mottled and blotched skin at the end of an outing was testament to the exceptional effort she expended on behalf of joint experiences. And, should that not be enough, weren't the two and sometimes three hours given to a protracted meal confirmation of her commitment?

Sometimes Madge was left wondering whether their relationship was perhaps just a little too exclusive and insular. Men didn't have to be universally beyond the pale. She could distinctly remember meeting two or three whose friendship, in the loosest sense, she enjoyed. Music and shouted conversations at mixed parties stimulated her and she regretted the cerebral and mono-dimensional Steria's instinctive dislike for such events.

Toward the end of their third summer together, when salt sea breezes and smells carrying all the way from the Arctic icepack could be detected on the currents of air sweeping up from the sea, the property next to the blue row house fell empty. An old Greek immigrant who had lived there for as long as anyone could recall died for no apparent reason other than his accumulated years. Until the very day of his death he and his wife had managed with questionable profitability, but a great deal of friendliness and engagement, the imported provisions store lower down the hill. The widow, not knowing how to live alone after sixty years of marriage, moved many hundred miles away to be with her daughter's family and, over the space of a single week, the shop, once housing sacks of cinnamon and nutmeg bought in markets on the fringes of the orient, was replaced by a twenty-four-hour convenience store. Cured hams that once hung in blackened rafters, gave way to empty, but hygienically whitewashed ceilings. Pre-cooked meals in chillers overtook the one thousand ingredients that, for generations, had found their way into exotic dishes unassisted by a recipe's printed page.

Not that anyone had purchased goods at the Greek store more than once or twice a month; its casual availability rather than fast turnover being a part of its charm; but up and down the street people were saddened by the unexpected closure. With the departure of old Stephanopoulos and his soiled black beret and rusting bicycle, a tenuous connection to a more romantic and leisured age disappeared and the hill became that much poorer.

The house next door to Madge and Steria, once predictably quiet, except for the night-time creaking of drying shingles, became home to an incessant hubbub generated by assorted gaggles of transient and excitable young men. First attempts by vaguely curious neighbours to identify permanent occupants, or those who might have purchased the property, were at first lost in the various comings and goings. But, after the passage of a few weeks, there appeared to be just two men, one older than the other, who conducted to all intents and purposes and with no visible interlude, a nineteenth-century soiree. Noises, escaping from open windows and through permeable walls, suggested the unifying topic of art, in its widest possible sense, was what attracted so many visitors. Like gaily plumed birds attracted by fallen fruit on an orchard floor, callers twittered into the throbbing recesses of the row house to leave hours or days later tipsy with poetry and unregulated fermentations.

The adjacent whirl was much to Madge's taste. But the total absence of female participation deterred her from an overt attempt at involvement. Instead she hovered intermittently on the fringes, hoping an entrée could be stage-managed through apparently unpremeditated contact. Steria, however, who was appalled by the sudden eruption of a loud and unrestrained all-male enclave on the doorstep of her sanctuary, felt violated. Wild behaviour, she thought, was like tobacco smoke, permissible in the private acts of consenting adults, but unacceptable to those wanting to remain untouched by its influences. Braying laughter, loud conversation and a female-free zone did not remain behind dividing walls; they spilled out onto the street and ran along the edges of the sidewalk and into open doorways until the character of the neighbourhood began to change. If old Stephanopoulos were unadvisedly to pedal his bicycle back from beyond the grave and up the slope to the coloured row houses, he would have scratched his chin and wondered whether he was anywhere near the junction of Haig and Ford.

As Madge thrilled, Steria inwardly groaned. While one opened windows, the other closed them. The screech of tyres, announcing the arrival or departure of yet another group of hedonists, produced unabashed giggles, and cries of, "Oh, I say," from Madge and grinding teeth from Steria.

Like beetles contesting rights to a dung heap, an untidy clutch of vehicles, of colours and models not seen on the staid parking lots lower down the hill, gathered and jostled for places. An automobile, of a distinctive yellow and red dual tone and more often present than absent, was presumed to be owned by the new occupants and deserving of first precedence.

Even while the two women lay in bed lazily reading Sunday newspapers the whines and discords of music unknown to any instrument under the sun, seeped and insinuated over, under and through the blue house, until it seemed to be kin to the plasterboard and drapes. The very walls embraced the invasion that overwhelmed every prior form of privacy.

Inexplicably, Madge discovered needs at obscure times of day and night for the type of consumable available only in the twenty-four hour convenience store half way down the hill, in contrast to the time when the purchase of household provisions had been confined to a joint Friday evening after-work visit to a vast supermarket on the outskirts of town.

Careful attention to the house's weekly needs had until recently been one of Steria's elected tasks, which Madge, a much more spontaneous shopper, had cheerfully handed-off. A list, attached to the kitchen refrigerator by magnets given away at a nearby gas station, was available for any sudden flashes of inspiration not catered for in the regular bulk-buying foray to stock the provisions room and basement freezer. Such was the thought given by Steria to her task that the blue house could in extremity have withstood a siege or almost any unexpected catastrophe emanating from the San Andreas Fault. But, while the house's collapse on their heads remained outside Steria's range of control, any other eventuality was unlikely to find her wanting, thus allowing Madge's involvement in shopping expeditions to be purely supportive.

So why was it that Madge would announce at eleven in the evening an absolutely essential need for a new brand of coffee to take to work the following day, or had such a clanging headache that only an alternative type of pain-killer was worth contemplating?

"If your head is hurting so much and you don't like what we have here, let me go buy something," Steria said with a note of exasperation creeping into her voice.

"I wouldn't dream of being such an imposition and besides the walk will do me good; clear my mind, you know."

"No, I don't know, but if you insist, tell those people next door to tone down the racket. They don't realise others live on this street as well."

"They're just having fun. We shouldn't mind."

"They're having fun! What about the rest of us? I haven't been able to think since they moved in and took over the whole neighbourhood."

"We must expect artists to be exuberant."

"Artists or whatever, they should show respect." Steria grumbled herself into a knot of discontent on the sofa, like a scolded child seeking refuge in a corner.

The store was no more than three hundred yards down the hill, but Madge was gone for an hour and a half. Steria, grappling with the twin emotions of concern for her partner's safety and burgeoning jealously, ventured into the street to see if there were signs of the round and comforting form returning. She could see all the way down the slope to the shop's green neon light flashing, "All Nite," in endless repetition, where a group of men, holding cans of drink and blowing cigarette smoke into the currents eddying along the street, huddled on the sidewalk. But there was no sign of Madge.

Freedom to take whatever route they chose without rules or obligation was a founding principle on which Steria and Madge had formed their partnership. A formal union was not for them. There was no compulsion to stay together. If affection went inexplicably cold not only should release be expected, they must demand to be pushed through the door. That was what they had believed.

In spite of the ringing declaration made at a time of certainty, Steria, with mounting dismay, felt she was showing signs of hysteria of a variety belonging to mawkish housewives, not free women among whose number she had proudly counted herself and flown her flag.

Surrounded by sofa pillows and continuing anxiety, she pulled at random a magazine published for the women's market from a stack beneath the dark coffee table, which had been their first joint purchase. The page that fell open screamed the headline, "You and Your Relationship," and began, "Are you really getting what you deserve? Don't you think you should ask yourself whether...?" She couldn't bear to go on, and to make matters worse the muffled drone of synthetic music began again, oozing indistinctly up through the carpeted floor and down from the pelmeted ceilings. Tiny vibrations rippled in the cold liquid in a cup standing on the coffee table and the whole house pulsed invisibly to the low sounds of external rhythms. Without knowing quite what she intended, Steria grabbed a wooden steak mallet from the kitchen counter and, throwing open the heavy white door for the second time that night, rushed into the street.

To her complete surprise she ran straight into the back of Madge in the midst of a coterie of apparently simultaneously talking men who, judging by the affected furrows between their eyebrows, were hearing fascinating and profound commentary dealing with the most gripping questions affecting the art world.

"Oh!" exclaimed Madge falling forward with a small yelp onto a man distinguished by flashes of greying hair at his temples.

"Hey!" was the light-hearted protest. "What's goin' on?" and on noticing the white-knuckled grip on Steria's mallet, "I hope we aren't about to be mugged? We heard this was a classy district."

A murmur of mirth rose and fell across the assembly. Breathing hard and feeling ridiculous, Steria looked at the circle of tanned and confident faces.

"Bryce is one of our neighbours, dear and he's been showing me their place. It's been completely redecorated since…" And on noticing Steria's expression, "Is everything alright?"

"I've been worried why you took so long."

"Guess getting home late for dinner deserves a ticking off," said Bryce, his smile broadening over a display of large white teeth.

"Look, I don't think I have to…"

"No, of course you don't. That's exactly the point," and turning abruptly Steria went inside and closed the door behind her with a click as apologetic as a mouse's cough in a cathedral.

Suddenly feeling quite weary she went upstairs and without washing, or brushing her teeth turned the lights out and went to bed. An hour later Madge pulled back a corner of the comforter and like a berthing ocean liner eased heavily alongside. Steria faced the window and although wide awake stayed exactly where she was.

"Do we need to talk?" Madge asked, recognising the tension lying between them like heat on a night heavy with thunderclouds.

After a pause, stretching into minutes, a voice from among damp pillows asked, "Are we going to last?"

To Madge, the question was shocking and irrelevant. But she knew the frailty of her partner's personality. For Steria, their relationship was the centre from which everything became possible; it was the one thing she could look at and say, 'this was what defined me.' Madge too had purposes around which she built and the partnership was a part, an important part, but not the whole. Expressed in her own fashion she would say her objectives, if that word was not too trite, were based on a community, in which her partner was the key member. The centrality, however, lay on a broad base, not the tip of a needle.

While Steria settled into disturbed and fretful sleep, in which the disapproving and nagging figure of her mother made frequent head-shaking appearances, Madge listened, with hands clasped behind her head, to the indistinct sounds issuing from the street and neighbouring house. Noises of vehicles, voices and entertainment mixed into a symphony, which in her imagination were like sounds calling children from blocks away to an approaching Mardi Gras.

Neither Steria nor Madge were in the habit of taking breakfast. One, because her austere style and slender frame did not count it a necessity; the other, on false assumptions that missing a meal was beneficial to weight control, even when lunchtime salads coated generously with mayonnaise, more than compensated for earlier savings. Thick, dark coffee, brewed by the first person up, however, was always plentiful.

Next morning Steria was showered and down to her mug's last half inch before Madge, in a billowing robe encompassing her wide proportions like a lawn marquee, bumped down to the lower floor. Last night's strains had almost completely passed from Madge's recollection and in her jovial, thigh-slapping manner she sailed rudely into the new day and Steria's tortured thoughts.

"Up in time to catch a worm?"

Beneath her thick unshaped eyebrows Steria's gaze ran the length and breadth of her partner.

"Hmm! tastes as though it's been standing a while," Madge continued unabashed. "What's the programme for tonight, shall I pick you up at six?"

With another question unanswered, Steria turned away to the sink to wash her cup and look through the window. Outside on the street people had begun moving. The majority plodded downhill towards the city's financial district, some, having no apparent purpose, just milled about.

The yellow and red car was pulled up next to a fire hydrant on exactly the spot where old Stephanopoulos had been in the habit of padlocking his bicycle. Two men, one whom Steria recognised as Bryce, and the other, olive skinned and dressed in faded denim, stepped from the next door house. The visibly moving features of Bryce's companion injected a note of agitation into a few seconds' of conversation until, sliding low onto a front seat he was caught by Bryce at the shoulders and gently kissed in his dense crop of curling, black hair.

Whether pacified or not, Steria couldn't tell, but she did know that if she had received such an early morning gesture the day would have had an entirely different outlook. Dissatisfied and ill at ease, she left with the weight of change lying on her chest like heartburn.

Despite the lack of clear agreement Steria was waited for at six on the edge of her office's parking lot. Madge, revving hard to keep the vehicle's air-conditioned interior chilled, thumped her hand on the steering wheel's rim in time to booming music. A wave of gusting noise swept out as she threw open the door.

"Hey! Had a good one?" roared her enquiry from above the amplified thuds of songs favoured by people twenty years her junior.

"Okay," Steria replied, giving no more away than that the smart of yesterday remained unalloyed.

Madge drove without debate to a supermarket on the freeway, where long lines of shelving packed with fresh produce, juices, frozen goods, bakery and delicatessen cold meats and at the furthest end, as if hidden from temptation and those with limited self-control, alcohol, stretched in a dizzying range of choice. Knowing the layout, Steria armed with her itemised list and organised rationale stalked from aisle to aisle piling high the cart pushed by an incessantly talking Madge.

"…And I said to her, over my dead body and she gave me the slyest look you'll ever see…and…oh!...isn't that Gustavo over there?"

"Excuse me?"

"Gustavo, you know…the musician…lives next door…with Bryce."

The details of her shopping list were suddenly more than usually absorbing and Steria chose not to look up, or respond to the suggestion they should follow the figure that had moved from sight behind massed ranks of cleaning fluids and wrapping foils.

"I forgot lemons; we'll have to go back."

"Do we have to? We'll miss him."

With surprising tartness, Steria snapped, "Is it so important to chase after people whose voices we hear without invitation every hour of the twenty-four? Anyone would think you were a love-sick teenager."

There was nothing new in her partner's acid words, but the sharpness of the attack caught Madge by surprise. Faced with the inclination to blow a disagreement into a fight, she settled instead for flabbergasted and silent annoyance.

Their few remaining purchases were loaded onto the cart and the two women took their place at a congested checkout lane. With feelings of sore pride and vexation they contrived to look in every direction except at each other. Their pain was beyond discussion. To wait for the other to speak became for the first time more important than settling their differences.

After several minutes in the line and with repeated glances at her watch Steria said through teeth clenched like a vice, "I'll get the dry cleaning." Being able to turn her back and walk away, she decided, was half way to repayment for the climb-down implicit in the release of a few choking words.

Moving some time later from the crowded line with packed brown bags, Madge wondered what was taking Steria so long. Should she wait, or load the car? Where was Steria? Wasn't this just too infuriating!

The dry cleaners' was tucked into a corner at the far end of the long shopping-mall strip. In between were a jeweller's, several clothes and shoe outlets and a department store, but in the entire distance there was no sign of Steria. Well, thought Madge, that's it; she's gone to the car and continued her sulk while I do the heavy lifting. I'm damned if I'll let this childish nonsense continue.

Striding resolutely in the direction of the parking lot she paused at automatic doors trying to recall exactly where she had left the car. From behind and somewhere above her head an authoritative male voice called out, "The woman in mauve jacket, please step back inside."

At first, the command made only a limited impression; such was her preoccupation with recent domestic friction. But gradually, as if by third party report, she became aware other shoppers had slowed to stare at a developing incident. What, she wondered, were they all looking at and why had Steria left her to cope with what was traditionally a shared task.

"The woman in mauve," the harsh call repeated.

Suddenly aware of the intimidating approach of a security guard the palms of Madge's hands grew damp with unease and inexplicable feelings of guilt. The blue pants, beige shirt and various symbols of office attached to a barrel chest persuaded her she was about to experience a serious exchange. If only law enforcers realised they were dealing with human beings rather than misdemeanours numbered in a rule book, there would be wider acceptance everyone was batting for the same team.

"Yes?" Madge felt she was shrinking under the scrutiny of irresistible and infallible authority.

"Please return to the security office. We have some questions to ask."

"Why?"

"We can do it here, or inside; your choice." The stern and unsympathetic reply from behind a copious and stiffly turned moustache left no room for negotiation.

"But, what about my groceries?" she pleaded weakly.

Her father or brothers would not have permitted a woman to struggle alone under such harassment, but here egalitarian principles were different, or was it just that officials knew no discretion. The guard marched briskly at her side, while Madge, feeling failure to keep up might land her in even more trouble, heaved and panted along at a far from natural pace.

The security office was a bare white room furnished with an interview table, two plain, upright chairs and, along an inner wall, a discoloured window, presumably permitting vision from only the opposite side. The grocery cart was dragged inside, and, upon instruction, Madge sat down. A massive female guard with feet planted wide and a thousand yard stare took up position by the window.

"ID please."

Madge offered her driving licence. "Will you tell me what's going on?"

"I'll ask the questions if you don't mind."

"Is guilt presumed as the starting point?" Madge asked, her resentment drowning out fear.

The guard raised his head from note taking and looked at her as if he would bore a hole through her soft, flabby mind and, with the intensity of his gaze, burn away any hint of opinion detrimental to his duty and certitude.

"Empty your hand-bag on the table please!"

Not the slightest hint of charity, humour or doubt disturbed the guard's impassive features. The man was his work, but, Madge thought, would he revert to some sort of normality if, compelled by circumstance, he took employment as a truck driver, or, perish the thought, an accountant, or were the breast pocket sunglasses and thick brown belt as much a feature of character as the bovine and desensitised face?

"I'm not sure about the legality of this, but if you expect unqualified cooperation at the very least you owe me an explanation."

Annoyed by the distraction, but convinced of his position, the guard replied in a level voice, "I have the right to hold and search suspects within the precincts of the mall," and then as a crumb of concession, "There's been a theft from the jewellers, we've had a tip off and want to eliminate you from our enquiries."

If policemen and security guards had ever sucked mother's milk, Madge told herself with a temporarily returning smile that must be a line absorbed along with nursery rhymes.

"Well! That's ridiculous; I haven't been anywhere other than the supermarket. You'll be pleased to hear that I've been with someone for all..." then adding, after the merest hint of hesitation, "Almost all of my time in the mall."

"Uh-huh."

"Ah, I see. Do you want to start with a witness, or the vegetables?"

Realising his grasp and control of events was not as complete as he liked, the guard stood up and said, "We'll just start with your bag and, if necessary…ah…move to the groceries and witnesses after if necessary."

After twenty stressful minutes and with puddles from melting food spotting the interview table, Madge indignantly reloaded her cart and huffed and puffed her way back into the mall shopping strip.

A parting shot at the overbearing guard was irresistible. "I doubt how-to-apologise is written into your robot's operating manual?" she stormed.

More thwarted than crestfallen, although a suggestion his moustache was not as firmly in place as it once had been, the guard responded, "It's the job."

"You can tell your boss this civic customer thinks you're a buffoon," she replied and, not wanting her attack's sting to be diluted added, "If you know what that means," before marching angrily away with her supermarket cart rumbling towards her car and a similarly unappeased Steria.

Madge's humiliation continued to rankle throughout the journey home and during the evening she complained loudly and indignantly at the incompetence of mall security personnel, the injustice of a system permitting arbitrary detention and the lack of the principal offender's contrition.

That night, while she sank into puffing, noisy slumber, like a bear sliding into long awaited hibernation, Steria stared inertly at the patterns of passing car headlights on the bedroom walls. Her identity's construction, carefully assembled out of the traumas and dysfunctional splinters of youth, seemed to be falling apart. Forces, over which she held no influence, had regrouped to wreak havoc on what, until a few days ago, had been near perfection and now she was being dragged back to the days she thought she had escaped.

In sleep as in wakefulness Madge was difficult to divert and Steria's stealthy departure, admitting no cold air into the huge bed, passed unnoticed. The street door, detached from tight insulation, opened with a gasp and in the pause that confirmed her companion slept as if drugged, Steria backed onto the sidewalk. Concentrating on pulling the door into place behind her she became dimly aware of faint but hurried movements by the now unencumbered fire hydrant. A scan of the deserted late night street revealed nothing. Some undefined and muffled sounds came from the next-door house and lower down the hill neon lights above the all-night convenience store blinked. Further on still an intoxicated form with wildly gyrating movements wove uncontrollably in the direction of the empty city.

The excruciatingly familiar yellow and red automobile, partly lit by a street lamp opposite, was drawn up on the patch of road once preferred by old Stephanopoulos. Only a self-proclaimed exhibitionist, Steria thought, would drive such a thing. Talking down a rival, she decided, was the next best thing to hearing an unlikely confession from Madge that her judgement had been sadly at fault in believing Bryce held the slightest merit. Any two open eyes, including Madge's, should see how shallow his attractions were. He wouldn't stand by her in times of trouble or sickness; he wouldn't do all the daily chores of shopping and laundry or of keeping her life in order. Nor would he worry if she was out later than expected.

Steria lengthened her step and with face pulled close to her chest, as if encountering smoke from a factory chimney, she strode past the car and neighbouring house and through the seemingly polluted air surrounding them. With the safety of distance she looked back to take stock. On the left side and compressed in black letters covering half of the flamboyant car's hood, someone had spray-painted the still wet and dribbling word "WHO", just that, nothing else, to leave the shining vehicle as disfigured as an inner-city subway train.

An odd nervous sensation surged up from somewhere near the soles of Steria's unstockinged feet. She couldn't decide whether to run quickly from the scene, or slink undetected back into the safety of the blue house. In muddled trepidation she retreated backwards down the slope, contriving to remove herself from implications of complicity.

Each additional stride in the cool night air stimulated her thoughts. Did the enigmatic statement mean something? The colourful car would certainly attract attention from louts never totally absent from any big city, but why the cryptic "WHO" in bold lettering? Would either Bryce or Gustavo, who singly or between them owned the automobile, understand the significance?

Was this something, unlike her present three o'clock street wanderings, to discuss over morning coffee?

Getting lost in a grid-patterned town was almost impossible and Steria, while allowing her bitterness to be overtaken by speculation, navigated intuitively for the space of an hour. She walked at a brisk pace along three and a half sides of a great square emerging onto a familiar street with the row houses a couple of blocks lower down the hill. In the pre-dawn hush only a cat, bounding into a damp alleyway and a solitary speeding car confirmed life on the planet still existed. Far off and somewhere near the docklands a police siren faded from hearing as if it had followed the rest of humankind over an edge into the abyss where all the others had perished.

The blue house and hydrangeas stood still and wet in wisps of morning fog. Steria watched and wished with all her heart the spot next to the fire hydrant, instead of being occupied by the ostentatious car dripping moisture into the gutter, was once again home to an old, rusting bicycle belonging to a Greek grocer.

Reluctant to return and pick up the intractably tangled threads strangling her very existence, Steria slowed until barely moving. The sloping road had taken on a ghostlike quality with watery vapours undisturbed by wind forming and dissipating in the increasingly sodden gloom.

Obscured flashes from the convenience store's neon sign ceased their regularity and blurred into a less steady beat. Shapes and shadows hovered in the street and, for a second, Steria thought she saw a head bob at the furthest end of the yellow and red car. She watched as the form disappeared and then reappeared with undeniable substance and, if she was not completely mistaken, a head of black curls.

The alley where the prowling cat had sought refuge opened next to her and she slipped in sideways with heart and curiosity thumping. A clatter, carrying over the distance of the block separating her from the row houses, sounded as if something had fallen into the gutter. Steria opened her mouth to steady her hissing breath. For the space of five long minutes and with her back and palms pressed against brickwork she waited, but heard nothing more. Slowly, with one unblinking eye, she peered round the alleyway's corner. Over thickening fog the upper floors of the row houses floated detached from all earthly existence.

Another much louder crash, from a place not ten feet to the rear, almost brought a shriek from her parted lips. The cat's hurried departure from disturbed refuse containers calmed her panic and with her mind made up she brushed down her clothes and resumed her nocturnal walk.

Her key in the blue house turned silently and she squeezed the white door ajar. A familiar sigh drew her back into an embrace without which she felt destitute, abandoned. Silence and the remains of peace lay over the entrance and on the thickly carpeted stairs leading to the second story bedroom.

Out of after-work habit Steria placed her keys on the corner table in the hallway. Still desperately inquisitive about Gustavo's activities in the foggy street, she peered up the stairs for the lightest sound of Madge's trembling sleep. Again decisive, she stepped back into the street and cautiously edged towards the yellow and red car. Stepping off the sidewalk and edging round the hood she saw an extended spray-painted message howling to the obscured stars the word, "WHORE!"

Recoiling in disbelief, Steria trod on a can lying next to a wheel tyre. She turned the object with her foot and realised it was an empty aerosol container. Ahah! This was the evidence and triumphantly she bent down to pick it up. Black paint dripped from the nozzle and stained her fingers. So that was the answer; Gustavo too was feeling jilted and he, almost without doubt, was behind that fiasco at the mall; Madge had seen him. Now in a strange twist he was out to vent his suspicions on all of them. What a lowlifer! I don't care about Bryce, he deserves what he gets, but no-one will hurt Madge, not while I'm around.

Dropping the can from her hands Steria stood up. An early morning gust of wind came sighing over the hill and down the wide street and the door on the blue row house breathed to with an emphatic "phthut."

Two hours later under opaque, grey sky and as Steria shivered morosely on her doorstep, Bryce stepped out of the old immigrant's house with Gustavo on his arm. Both were laughing loudly, but in spite of the coolness of the hour and a reluctance to move rapidly tiny droplets of perspiration had gathered along Gustavo's hairline.

The Snow Bridge and Other Stories   191

"I'm still as sore as hell," Bryce said with feeling while looking down at the hand he was holding, "If you'd wanted a ring like that I should be the guy to get it for you. It's not the sort of thing you go out and do on your own. We're a team, remember?"

"But I don't always want to wait and sometimes I have to do a few things to make me feel good."

"Okay, okay; let's not talk about it any more. Elmo will be out any second to get you to the studio and the guys will be over by the time you get…geez, will you look at…what's happened?…my car!"

As Bryce circled the hood of his hitherto immaculate, if gaudy, automobile the complete spray-painted message became clear.

"Whore? Whore!?" He stormed, "What son of a…a whore? And my beautiful…"

Hanging back Gustavo said nothing and Bryce, beside himself with rage ran twenty yards down the hill and twenty back up. On the return journey and with passion rapidly overtaking reason he snatched up the recently discarded paint canister from where it had come to rest by the fire hydrant and flung it at the row house's open door etching a semi-circular skid mark across the shining white paint. Not satisfied with the one demonstration of fury he picked up the can a second time and hurled it at the much abused vehicle. A hub cap dislodged by the sudden impact sprang free and rattled unevenly across the street in the direction of the far off convenience store. Several early pedestrians turned in the direction of the disturbance, but like urban dwellers anywhere, they continued their paths after only the briefest pause.

Seated on the doorstep of the blue row house, Steria, wondered why educated people caught in emotional extravagance were unable to construct a grammatically correct sentence. No-one could say she had not experienced turmoil, but her choice was to articulate or be silent. Incoherent blather stuck her as immature, and even more damnably, a male thing.

Bryce's peregrinations up and down the street brought him abruptly to a conclusion. Steria became aware he was standing in front of her with bulging eyes looking down at her blackened hands. What exactly he was saying she was not quite sure, but the clear inference was somehow she was responsible and that he would get even. But having nothing left in his hand to express his considerable outrage he threw a punch in the approximate direction of Steria's head. But the blow, steered by temper rather than steady nerves, thumped the wood a good foot above its intended target.

The unusual collision reverberated inside the blue house and brought the lumbering and barely awake Madge enquiringly to the entrance. The tableau, of Bryce's purple-faced anger, the suave, but unreliable Gustavo standing slightly offstage, and Madge in ballooning robe and fluffed slippers floating accusingly over the wretched and white-faced Steria, would have been impossible for an outsider to explain.

Madge, who moments ago had woken to an unshared bed and a false but convincing realisation that the unexpected dry cleaning errand was taken to make a false report at the security office, absorbed the accusations being thrown at her partner's seated form.

"Oh Steria!" she intoned, as though a favoured pupil had been caught with examination answers written on her sleeve, "How could you?"

Realising a tide had run out leaving her stranded on isolated mud flats Steria turned to Madge.

"Is that what you think, after all this time? Then we have nowhere to go." Standing up she added, "I'll send for my things," and without turning walked away down the hill. As she passed, Gustavo stepped out of her way and, Steria noticed, even though the morning was getting warmer his hairline was no longer damp.

TEN

VISITOR TO THE BARRIO

July rains were no heavier than in previous years, but after two decades of rapacious logging the empty hills were unstable and each new downpour brought earth slips closer to San Juan's eastern barrios. Aware of the increasing danger local officials should have ordered evacuation, but self-interest calculated risk in missed opportunity not in threatened lives, and besides, other than turning poor people into the rain, where could they go?

Near the end of the season, when the problem was close to being postponed for another year, one slide larger than the rest swept over the barrio of Magalindan and buried the flimsy shanties huddled closest to the bare, water-drenched slopes under a great swathe of mud and filth. If the tragedy had occurred during daylight loss of life might have been less, but at three in the morning Magalindan was unprepared and almost acquiescent in its fate.

No-one knew how many people died; maybe there were dozens, or scores, or even hundreds, but certainly the burden fell disproportionately on old and young, now that the community's heart and vitality had leeched away in the migration of able-bodied men and women to employment in other countries. San Juan and more particularly Magalindan had taken a generation to bleed to death and then in the space of one night and in an act of near finality it was buried beneath twenty feet of impenetrable black clay.

For just this once the impoverished barrio acquired recognition in the international press. But the disaster, like any temporary novelty, left the giddy world's consciousness as swiftly as it entered. San Juan and its tragedy were briefly on everyone's lips, but in the short space of three months, or as little time as it took an American factory worker to forget a summer vacation, there were none outside the town who recalled the name.

A short flurry of foreign concern and the arrival of two planes carrying tents, corned beef and a search and rescue team raised hopes in the shattered slums that someone had heard and something at last would change. But, even before the mud began to dry under the harsh tropical sun, attention turned elsewhere.

After days of desperate digging and, finding nothing but the wreckage of broken lives, the rescue men and women left as suddenly as they had appeared. Leif Stromsen, however, did not go home, at least not immediately. He had seen desolation in the eyes of Magalindan's diminished number of children and was haunted by the pathetic lives that only the fatalism absorbed at a mother's breast made bearable.

Before returning to the security of its own country, the search team, such was its training, had camped with military precision at the seaward end of the short San Juan airstrip. Once the team had packed and gone, only two tents, speaking of the short, abortive rescue attempt, remained amid the patches of trampled grass.

Now that he was alone Leif planned to use one tent as his living quarters and the other as a first-aid station. Offering his minimal health care skills to the devastated community, however, was not uppermost in his mind. While working below the black scars disfiguring the once verdant hills and in among the few remaining corrugated iron roofs of eastern San Juan, he had decided that there was more important work to be done.

Some way off from the hissing camp-stove and a pot of boiling water that occupied Leif's attention, an impassive boy of about five or six years of age squatted in the safe cover of a few ragged bushes dripping with early morning rain.

"Shouldn't you be in class at this time of day, sonny?" Leif called out.

The boy did not respond, but continued staring. Across his narrow chest a handed down tee shirt, as if in denial of the nearby catastrophe, displayed the faded message, "Tampa Bay Rocks." Hunched on his bare heels he was as much a part of the impoverished landscape as the stunted vegetation and browsing goats. What possible future, Leif wondered, awaited such resignation?

"Does anyone know you're here?"

"Ano?" was the noncommittal reply.

"What are you doing out here at the airstrip on your own?"

Pursed lips and an upturned chin indicated a tiny, untethered cow, cropping straggling creepers. Leif stood up and the young herdsman, startled by the movement, scampered away into nearby undergrowth. Trust was not automatically bestowed on even the most well-meaning new-comer and, as if in reinforcement of Leif's disappointment, a poorly aimed stick arced over his head towards the nearby river.

From the airstrip's elevated position the huddled bamboo and concrete houses of San Juan were visible, held together by a random network of twisting earth roads. Secondary sets of tracks, marking the forlorn plod of ragged livestock to and from over-grazed pastures, connected the roads to a nearby beach and riverbank. Near Leif's encampment the airstrip and beach converged and, soon after his arrival, he had discovered the easiest way to reach the town's municipal office in the dusty central plaza was by using the route along the seashore. During the course of the hot days and moonlit nights that followed, negotiating the river and beach paths became as easy as if he had been born to them.

At the municipality, conversations and the attitudes surrounding them were hard to classify; to begin they were neither helpful, nor hostile. But, when raising his voice in excitement, or pressing for a decision, Leif felt the ground give way beneath his feet. Conclusions were as hard to define as the air borne sounds of bats hunting at sunset and for reasons he could not at first understand officials did not see the problem in the same way. The mud slide had happened and there was no purpose in asking what failings had caused them; that was the way things were and nothing could be done about it.

Logging and stabilisation of the slopes above Magalindan were activities beyond the local authority's control. How, they asked, without requiring an answer, did he expect to make these change?

"Isn't it obvious?" he protested, "Move everyone out of what remains of the eastern barrio, seed the hillsides with mahogany and build a barrier to divert future earth slips, that's what we should do."

"Yes, yes, of course, but from where would the money come to support such a large project and what about the agreement of landowners?"

The municipal officials exchanged glances, as if to imply Leif had not considered even the most obvious difficulties.

"But, if you have access to relief funds, we could, for the sake of efficiency, channel them to needy families through this office. We will let Mayor Linganan know how concerned you are for the welfare of San Juan's citizens."

Indeed, Leif thought, there was no doubt about the need for efficiency when financial assistance was being discussed. Too bad managing funds was a more engaging subject than initiating the dreary and back-breaking work of digging muck out of survivors' homes. Half of the problem was that no-one in office understood public service as anything other than an opportunity for personal gain. The other and complementary half was that the town lived under the spell of abject and debilitating consent. How could a system be changed when even the poor owed what little they had to its continuation? Only a saint could be persuaded to act differently.

Ricardo Linganan, the mayor of San Juan was seen twice at Magalindan on the day following the hillside collapse. His first arrival was with several junior officials at eleven in the morning when the rain was easing and he had asked to be shown the destruction. A labourer in bare feet offered a back to carry the administrator along the periphery of the flood which divided damaged houses from those completely buried. The slum dwellers watched in silence as the official train wound its way through the quagmire's misery.

Satisfied with his tour of inspection, Linganan was hoisted onto the ruins of someone's veranda to make a short speech expressing empathy with the displaced and promising his government's immediate involvement to rebuild the district.

His second visit came later the same afternoon and this time, clad in rubber boots, he escorted the manager of a building materials supplier to observe the extensive damage he had witnessed earlier in the day. Linganan was not seen at the scene again, but on enquiry and for the next few days until residents lost hope, they were told he was coordinating relief work from the municipal hall on the northern end of San Juan's central plaza.

On the steps of the same government office Leif sat despondently thinking about how much chance shaped personal destiny and happiness. The random fact of birth blessed some with plenty, while condemned other to hunger; some to be with and others to be without. How could anyone in this country, he wondered, believe so devotedly in God, when all were abandoned to hardships no elected official sought to mitigate?

Along the opposite side of the rain-spotted square stalls in the pathetically under-stocked market the meagre wares attracted scant attention. No-one had money, or inclination to buy. On an upturned cardboard box made soft by repeated showers a withered woman as brown and worn as betel nut and of any age between thirty and sixty, such was the toll of rural life, laid out several small, dried fish, half a dozen mangos and three tins of corned beef. That someone along the chain of distribution had diverted a charitable donation added to Leif's growing sense of frustration.

"How much for a mango?" he enquired.

The stall vendor eyed him up and down carefully. "Ten pesos."

"Oh come on, that's ridiculous. I could buy one for less where I come from and that's half a world from where they grow." Leif returned the several coins to his pocket and turned to go.

"Then eight pesos."

He continued walking and a shout came from behind, "Two for fourteen."

"Look," he said, starting back. "I'll pay a fair price, but don't mess me about. Here's ten pesos, but I'll take two."

He dropped his money next to the dried fish and picked up the slightly green mangos. The old woman did not touch the coins, but nor did she protest. Stoicism born of faith, habit and penury accepted, but was aggrieved and she hoped he understood.

Half way across the plaza Leif stopped. This is crazy, he thought. I've come here to help and yet deny this woman with nothing a chance of making a few miserable pesos. Both she and I know she was trying to rob me, but if survival alone is the goal and only cheating can make it possible doesn't that then become a greater morality? In the absence of order aren't her wits all she has to feed herself and who knows how many dependants? There comes a point where thievery is a kind of honesty, which mercy must allow.

Retracing his steps to the dilapidated box and its meagre display Leif took a soiled one hundred peso note from his pocket and dropped it on the cardboard display. He was not sure what reaction he expected; gratitude was one possibility, but if that had been his expectation he was to be disappointed. He hadn't yet grown used to the idea that reminders of destitution and dependency are even worse than its reality.

Subsequent visits to the municipal office were as inconclusive as the first. Polite hearings gave way to difficulties in making contact. Officials, he was told, had been called away on unexpected business and their time of return was unknown. The only justifiable activity in this crisis, he thought, was to dig the barrio out from under the mud, but no-one seemed to be making that the single, screaming priority and, in the meantime, the community was being left to recover on its own.

Later, not even an excuse was offered. Attempts to meet the Mayor were fruitless. Neither he, nor anyone else, was ready to talk, still less cooperate. No-one was even bothered to say, "Make an appointment." The realisation that he was being left to sink into a sand trap, where his involvement in the workings of San Juan was effectively neutralised, came slowly. An even more difficult notion to accept was that the whole hopeless mess was held together only by the oppressed's tacit agreement.

Decisions in San Juan, he realised in a flash of understanding, did not flow from a desire for solving problems following factual examination of obstacles, but emerged from one of just two related sets of circumstances.

The few who held power used it as their means to make an extraordinary living, not to provide stewardship for the community's well-being. Officials in San Juan did not concentrate on the calamity because no benefit lay in alleviating misery, and besides, they might say, only those with no means to pay lived in the slums under the hills. Outside the inner circle of those in charge a vast, swirling, disenfranchised populace, el Masa, was left without rules, governance, or opportunity, plundered by the powerful and left to fend for itself against the ravages of man and nature alike. God and government were both beyond comprehension or influence and in the face of such unarguable strength, what else could anyone do except lie down and ask for pity.

Don't impose conclusions, but work with local institutions. Hadn't he heard that refrain a hundred times before setting out with the relief team? But what if those same institutions wanted to keep inadequacies exactly as they were? Was he to wait for one of those moments when a critical mass formed like a shoal of sardines turning in unison at the sight of approaching barracuda?

The short walk back to the airstrip was hotter than usual. A group of young boys, including the one with the "Tampa Bay" shirt, kicked up wet dust and laughed loudly as he passed. Wearisome calls of "Hey Joe!" and "What is your name?" pursued him along the beach until the gang, bored by its prank, melted away into the nearby backstreets.

Out on the shimmering sea a small costal steamer belched black smoke over billowing cumulus cloud and, in a rush of chain and loud shouts, dropped anchor.

Leif sat down on the almost white sand. If he was to take direct action, without waiting for official help, what form would it take? Answers were not hard to imagine, but more willing hands would be necessary. Next morning, he decided, he'd go straight back to the mud-slide and talk to anyone prepared to listen.

From around the point where airstrip, river and beach met, a native *banka* riding very low in the water and with outriggers sloshing in the running swell chugged towards the steamer. Leif, who remembered his childhood on the Baltic, guessed she was carrying a heavy load, maybe a cargo of coconuts below decks? But, in a sudden snap and shower of sparkling water, a towrope leapt up from the sea and he realised the banka was towing something still out of sight.

Fifty feet behind the labouring *banka*, three log floats, strung out one after the other, slowly laboured into view. Leif jumped to his feet and rushed down to the water's edge, but, still unable to see clearly, he quickly ran back again to the higher ground. In the sun's heat sweat ran over his face. Excitedly, he mounted a bamboo trellis erected by fishermen to dry their nets and ignoring its ominous creakings watched the two rapidly closing vessels. Over sounds of slapping sea and a growling engine he could hear seamen shouting.

Instructions appeared to be passing from the steamer to a bare-torsoed sailor balancing on the banka's plunging outrigger. With the end of a coiled towrope in his grasp the seaman waited for the two vessels to draw alongside and then leapt the gap. The snaking line was snatched from him and secured in the rolling stern by the steamer's crew. Freed from its load, the banka surged away in a foaming arch and sped back towards the river mouth.

The cluster of men surrounding the towrope dispersed, some to haul canvases and others to engage the ship's rattling engine. Another burst of smoke plumed across the face of the sun and the vessel turned, as ponderously as a carabao wallowing through water-logged ditches, into the ocean's currents, with the pontoons of floating logs stretched out behind. Before she sailed away into the wind, a short man, wearing a wide-brimmed hat and white slacks, emerged onto her deck and, beneath an awning strung out amidships, ran his eyes over the naked hills and the one person on the headland.

Beneath Leif's static weight the bamboo trellis sighed and buckled. Why did everything in this county lack definition? Even wood didn't break in the sort of sharp snap that was natural elsewhere; it just bent and swayed beneath an oppressive burden before adjusting to a forced deformity. He stepped away and the twisted structure groaned and swayed ineffectually.

Down by the water's edge, the sand was hard-packed and firm and he set off at a run towards the river. As he climbed to higher ground, where the dunes were hot and blown and covered in purple-flowered bind-weed, he began to toil, with his breath coming in quick, short pants. Sweat darkened his shirt and a pulse thumped in his ears.

At the top of a ridge he could see down into the river basin where, half beached and half afloat, the banka lay hemmed in by dense clusters of water-hyacinth and mounds of dry, grey silt. Several of the crew sat on boxes playing cards in front of a doorless cabin; in the shadows of tilting bows others slept. Leif wanted to rush down and remonstrate, but remembering how little had been achieved by a similar display at the municipal office, he struggled to contain his outrage.

"Boy, its hot today," he called out as he approached the banka. "You wouldn't have any water there would you?"

The card game paused and a few crumpled peso notes stirred in the hot breeze. Except for the sleepers, who lay as still and warm as candle wax, the seamen fidgeted and said nothing until an invisible barrier as impenetrable as plate glass slipped into place around the *banka*.

One sailor older than the rest half turned and spoke over his shoulder. "What do you want?"

"Some water if you have it."

No-one moved until the speaker with an upward flick of his face, gestured towards the youngest person in the circle. The still teenage boy held his unplayed cards in one hand and reached beneath his legs with the other for a plastic bottle half full of tepid water lying in the oily bilges.

After taking several gulps Leif handed it back. "Thank you" he said, "I needed that." The youth replaced the bottle under his seat and the crew waited to resume playing.

Leif wanted information, but knew by now that deprived people cared nothing for the numbers of trees on the hills, except for the price they might fetch from a ready buyer. Why would any of them share his concern when their bellies were empty?

"How far inland do you have to travel now to find a full grown narra tree?"

Again, the bruised looks, but this time with a hint of anger. Who was this foreigner and what right had he to question anyone?

As much to himself as the seamen, Leif continued, "In six months, or a year there'll be none left in this province and you'll have to go as far as the Maginloc Mountains."

"Bahala na," said the older seaman with a shrug and then after a pause, "Maybe you should go."

"Yes, perhaps I should, but how much does he pay you, that man, the one in the white slacks and fedora?"

The futility of the conversation was depressing. His bitterness had achieved only the alienation of the very sort of people whose support would be essential if he was to ever to help San Juan recover or acquire new self-respect.

Back on top of the ridge there was no sign of the steamer. She'd disappeared with her cargo to a place where obscene luxury awaited some and the pennilessness of others was left far behind.

With the sun directly over-head, the glaring sands were almost too hot to walk on and he ran quickly down the burning slopes and into the thankfully cooler sea. The country was so full of contradictions and the biggest of all was that paradise and despair lived alongside each other. On one hand so much splendour and on the other a crushing burden none should be expected to bear.

In his tent on the airstrip Leif lay on his back and gazed at the canvas over his head. His thoughts drifted to a time, which seemed years ago, but was in fact only several weeks before the rescue mission had set out. He had returned to his night camp in the high hills and latitudes of his homeland when the summer sun still shone like a cold yellow ball behind lines of conifers. After a long trek he had slept for hours without moving and with no more than a waterproof sheet separating him from the mountains' stones.

But wasn't courting hardship like that a perversity, when people here knew nothing other than pain, which, above all things, he sought to relieve? Even the one-man tent over his head kept him on the upper end of comfort, when at the bottom of the slope in Magalindan, survivors had only what they stood up in, or if they had been unluckily caught naked by the avalanche, not even that small relief.

The few tents brought by the rescue teams were insufficient for so many homeless people and provided no more than a bandage to wounds flowing with blood. Erected on the opposite side of the airstrip and giving shelter without water or electricity they spiralled within days into another insanitary, rat-infested slum. The conditions and the call of community soon drove families back to the mud-ravaged barrio where the one thing left to claim was a birthright. Only that they were Magalindans set them apart, and retaining that distinction allowed resurrection on precisely the place where it lay buried.

Their wisdom did not come from any attempt to make the barrio a good and safe place for grandchildren, but in maintaining the continuity of who they had been for untold generations. Part of the family may have been taken away in the dead of night, but the only way to do it justice was to restore its rightful place on the grave where there was nothing to drink but rice water.

In the days following his encounter with the *banka* crew, Leif laboured among Magalindan's dispossessed. His hands were soon hard and calloused from making makeshift repairs to wrecked dwellings, blocked wells and broken dykes that had escaped the full force of the flood. In the few intervals of rest he argued with all who would listen, and there weren't many, for a collective effort to plant saplings on the slopes above the town. Some heard him patiently, but most were too tired, or crushed to care. And in any case those problems belonged to tomorrow when God would take care of his own.

The parts of the town unaffected by the tragedy continued as San Juan always had. At whatever hour Leif walked from his tent to the desolated eastern slums, activity in the winding dirt streets varied only by degree. On street corners, bare-chested youths gathered with no particular purpose in mind other than to associate and be know by their association. Children, more than he'd ever seen, despite the loss of so many in the mud, ran back and forth, clothed and unclothed, treating every house as their own. The interior of homes and their surroundings were closed to none and society met spontaneously wherever it would. Chickens and small dogs as numerous as the children chased each other through refuse heaps and ditches in search of scraps. Women everywhere shared laundry and the rough preparation of vegetables, while indolent men in tee shirts, pulled up to cool flatulent bellies, observed without interest the chaotic streets and in every lane and alleyway one isolated house with a fresh coat of paint or a new fence proclaimed an exiled son or daughter's overseas employment. Day and night in San Juan was the same and time had only the present's dimension.

In the shell of a Magalindan house where walls closest to the mountains had been torn away several soil and sweat begrimed men with hands blackened and bruised by labour ate fish and rice from two tiny, plastic containers. Their little food, like mud and work, was shared.

"Land on my side of the airfield is unoccupied and needs no clearing. There is enough fresh water from the river and, as soon as we are done with emergency repairs in this area, we could start planting a nursery." Unrestrained excitement was one of Leif's more endearing qualities, but in the sadness and apathy of Magalindan it was not infectious. A man repeatedly beaten by circumstance, or by those wishing to keep him poor, will hide in a corner until relief comes. Rage and outright rebellion were unknown among the ruined shanties.

"Let's go down there tonight; who'll join me?" he continued, looking hopefully at the circle of dispirited faces.

Another voice, which also failed to ignite a flicker of optimism in others, replied hesitatingly, "Okay," and, as if to provide better grounds for joining the airstrip inspection, added, "We're running out of wood here and there'll soon be no more help we can give."

"Running out of wood? How can we with rows and rows of broken buildings? There should be enough to repair dozens of houses. What about the other gangs? What are they doing?"

An uneasy shuffle of bare feet was followed by a painful explanation.

"The lumber merchants are paying one peso for each clean foot of plank delivered to their yards and..." The speaker's words trailed into silence.

"You have to be joking...? And then they sell it back at ten times the cost or more to people patching up their homes?"

"But money is needed to feed our families. And... we can stand a few holes in the walls."

"Ah! I see....so if not you, then someone will be giving ten pesos a foot?"

Shared misfortune should develop understanding and, although Leif would never know true suffering, joining in the daily labours and arguments had produced a kind of bond. Dirt and work did not make everyone the same, but it narrowed differences.

The return walk with his weary companions through the congested lanes and across the plaza to the moonlit beach brought some relief to Leif's tired muscles and, as the nameless street noises subsided with nightfall, to his fretful mind.

"Will you show me where the lumber supplier has his yard?" Leif asked Ramon, as if the thought had suddenly occurred to him.

Ramon, a man of about his own age, in whose mat of black hair streaks of grey already showed, pointed a finger.

"Down there, a block from the plaza market."

"Show me."

The street was wider here and material could move in and out of the merchant's yard without hindrance. In front of the compound, but separate from other buildings in the row, was a wooden shop with what appeared to be a living area on the floor above. Just to the right, a pair of heavily-padlocked gates in a high, wire fence gave access to an extensive rear yard. By San Juan standards this was a very large enterprise. Below the lighted windows of the upper rooms and above the shop entrance a hand-painted sign, with stylised lettering, bore the message, "Linganan Building Supplies."

Leif turned to Ramon. "This might sound simple-minded, but would your mayor own this company?"

"No."

"Who then?"

"His sister."

"Oh! I see. Nothing like keeping everything in the family. Just look at all the timber in that yard; there's enough to repair a hundred homes. Are there any other suppliers in town?"

"Yes."

Leif waited for Ramon to continue.

"Just one."

Sometimes he liked to think he was well thought of in Magalindan, but no-one seemed to want to say more than just enough to be civil. Even Ramon, after weeks of shared toil and the beginnings of a friendship, answered only in the briefest of terms; little, or nothing was added to illuminate a monosyllable.

"And what might this business be called?"

"Designer Builders."

"Huh! That takes some beating and can I ask who owns it?"

"Maylenne Linganan."

"Not that it will make any difference, but let me guess, is she the same, or another sister?"

"The same. Giving another branch a different name just makes it look unconnected, but they're really all one and everyone knows."

"God in heaven! And I bet both yards are bursting with timber needed in the slums. How do you let this happen?"

The question was unfair. No-one let anything happen, but collectively all were to blame."

Power, Leif thought, should be conferred on those who earn it and forfeited whenever trust was broken. End of story. That at any rate was the theory, but did it ever work quite so easily? Not, alas, in these beautiful islands and among these sweet, ungoverned and ungovernable people.

Leif and his companions turned and made their way towards the plaza. Behind them, in the rooms above the hand-painted sign, a light went out. In among the fishermen preparing for the night's work and some farmers returning from the fields, a few housewives searched the market's meagre offerings and a single carabao with a cord in its nose was led by a mop-haired child who could have been either a boy or girl. Above the shop, a curtain moved and a short, bare-chested figure in white slacks twirled the twisted gold chain about his neck and watched the foreigner and his companions cross the square towards the beach.

A huge orange moon rose over the horizon and Ramon paced out an area near the rescue team's bivouac. Leif wrote down the distances called out, while others in the group cut and trimmed bamboo stakes to drive into the ground at intervals. The mahogany nursery, which would be stocked with seedlings found on the hills, began to take rough shape, while the effort of finding enough plants in the receding forests was saved for another time.

Every recent day had been long and arduous, but this one had been longer and harder than most. The two tents' flaps were pulled back and the previous night's cold fish and sticky rice was taken out and distributed a little to each waiting hand. With young appetites partially appeased, three men squeezed into the first aid station, leaving Leif and the rest to pile into the other. Packed bodies needed no blankets, so they slept warm and exhausted until the approach of dawn.

"Why don't you vote him out?" The sun hadn't risen, but heat from the paraffin stove and the conversation's subject started a moist sheen on Leif's forehead. They were starting later than planned and instead of being at the barrio by first light were still struggling to organise their day. Ramon's answer was brief.

"No need. His term ends in November and he can't stand again. He's had his time."

"Then you need someone from Magalindan to stand."

Ramon laughed the unaffected laugh at once so common yet so pathetically misplaced in the midst of disaster and daily deprivation. "It's not that simple. To be in politics you need money, lots of it. Elections aren't won by offering appealing policies; you have to make promises to people with interests who then deliver votes. You need to be a name. No-one in the barrios can claim anything recognisable, or has money to get through the day, so how would you expect any of us to win an election? Don't confuse what we have with democracy. We don't have the means for that sort of luxury and are obliged to be dependants with no ability to influence."

This was the longest speech Ramon had made on any subject since Leif first met him. Even when smiling he appeared to be just an averagely awkward and taciturn youth, but under that casual surface he had many reasons to be unhappy. Preventable landslides, apathy, greed, corruption and latterly Leif's unintended, but inescapable condescension, all contributed to his sense of hopelessness. In the face of a tidal wave of problems, he was driven into withdrawal.

Taken aback by the unexpected rush of words Leif looked at Ramon's wide, black eyes.

San Juan and its people had become a splinter under his fingernail that was impossible to remove. One day, in the future, his children would ask where the marks on his hands had come from and he would be forced to relate how he had acquired them when he travelled to the far side of the world and laboured for weeks and made no difference to other men's problems.

In a lower voice he asked, "Then who is likely to become mayor?"

"A wealthy business person with good connections; one who knows which people to satisfy."

"There can't be many in a town this size."

"There will only be one candidate with any real chance."

"And...who will that be?"

"Why, Maylenne Linganan, there aren't any others."

Breakfast was more cold rice, but this time, mixed with the contents from a can of vegetable soup. Hot, sweet tea made with powdered milk followed and was passed round the circle of patient hands in the one available mug.

Every day was starting later than just a week ago and when Leif and his companions walked up from the beach and re-entered the plaza the time was already after seven. No-one in San Juan measured hours with precision, but nor did any in the group doubt they had stayed too long.

Half way across the square Leif with Ramon at his side stopped to knock sand out of his shoes.

"Bare feet would be more comfortable."

"If I had nothing on mine I'd soon be a cripple."

On the plaza's edge two fishermen dragged an open crate into the market. Four or five youths, gossiping with idle tricycle drivers, lolled at the corner of the municipality building.

The sun was high enough now to colour buildings facing east in a gentle pink, while the narrow lanes untouched by the morning's rays still trembled in darkness. Out of one leading towards Linganan's lumber yard a short, thickset man emerged. He was dressed in white slacks unfashionably wide at the foot and a gold chain in the space created by a mostly unbuttoned shirt.

"Will someone tell me who the hell is that person?" Leif shouted angrily at Ramon who was standing no more than a foot away.

"Who?"

"Why him; that man, there, dressed like a playboy. Where's he going, Christ it's the municipality and if anyone cares to know he's not making social calls to an elderly relative."

The figure mounted three town hall steps and at the top turned to survey the plaza's pedestrians. Before stepping into the gloomy interior his gaze fell on the few surrounding Leif and his forehead furrowed.

"But nor is it our business, so don't get involved."

"What are you saying? That's the guy who's cutting down the trees and bringing landslides into your homes! If that isn't your business, I don't know what is; don't you understand?"

"We understand what we can do and what is not going to help."

"Well, I'm damned if I'll sit here sucking my fingers."

Leif shrugged off the restraining hand and ran across the plaza.

Jumping the three stairs in a single leap he ran down the passageway into which the figure had disappeared.

A slouching guard with an automatic rifle slung across his knees called out, "Hey! You can't go down there!" but made no serious effort to intervene.

The first few doors on both sides of the corridor were locked, but the third on the right flew open at a touch. If he had been in less of a hurry, Leif would have noticed the words, "Mayor Linganan", cut so deeply into the doorway's centre panel, that permanence appeared unarguable.

Only the upper half of the Mayor, draped in an open green shirt, was visible and, although not an old man, slack skin hung around his face and soft, spongy bags dragged down the lower lids of his watery eyes. A few grey-at-the-roots threads of hair fell over his forehead, but blown back at intervals in the warm currents circulating under a slowly-turning ceiling-fan. Undisturbed by the inconvenience of documents or files, the metal desk, on which he leant, was a model to the art of delegation.

The white-slacked visitor rested his feet on a corner of the Mayor's desk and took no notice of Leif's peremptory appearance.

Ricardo Linganan moved forward on his elbows and stopped opening and closing the clasp of an expensive watch held in his hands.

"Yes?" he asked, turning his eyes, but not the heavy head in which they were set.

"What, in God's name, are you people doing? You have an unimaginable disaster on your hands, but offer no help and stand by while others strip the hills and make conditions worse."

The visitor re-crossed his legs and left a film of sand on the end of Linganan's dull desk. The opening and closing of the watch began again and the Mayor sat back on his creaking armchair.

"And who are you?" he asked.

"That hardly matters. What is important is making lives bearable and stopping tragedies from happening."

"And what do you have to do with it?" A faint sound, as of a tyre decompressing, came from the visitor.

"You're all criminals riding on the backs of the poor." Leif's blood was rising in the face of so much injustice.

"Are you here to tell us how to run our country? Leave, go on, get out!" the Mayor snapped.

"I'll be dammed if I'll go without some answers."

"Guard!"

Without his cap the reluctant guard appeared in the doorway. Linganan held the open ends of his watch strap in two hands as if examining an unexpected malfunction.

"Take this man out and make sure he doesn't come back. Do you understand?"

"Yes, Mayor. He just walked in; I tried to stop him but..."

"If you want to keep your job, just do as I say; clear?"

"Opo Sir, opo, opo!" The guard leapt out of his lassitude and, with the urgency of the instruction understood, waved the rifle at Leif.

"You heard the Mayor. Out!...now!"

Ramon and the others were waiting in the lane on the far side of the plaza.

"So what happened; how far did you get?"

"Ramon, sometimes I despair. The solutions are so obvious, but no-one wants to change anything. What do we do?"

"Well, yelling at the Mayor won't help, unless you want to get us into bigger trouble."

No day had been worse than this. Leif felt he was sinking in quicksand, where every twist and turn dragged him ever deeper. Once, in spite of the misery, willingness to get something done had fanned out across the community like a hot grass fire, but now, faced by the scale of the disaster, it had not only cooled, but had almost become forgotten. He could make excuses for achieving so little; the people's poor diet, the absence of tools and money, but there was really no justification for lethargy and the sense of inexpressible surrender. Until now Ramon had appeared different; he'd been strong and people listened to him, but now he too was faltering under the weight of so much responsibility.

"If we want to head to the forest for seedlings tomorrow we'd better start early."

"I...we...can we delay for a day? There's something we must take care of and...we won't be ready."

"If we still want to get this done, can we make a commitment?"

Leif looked around at the sullen faces. He was disappointed. The "something to take care of" sounded like another piece of sidestepping.

There was just too much work to do and that night his companions left before him. They seemed eager to set out on with what they had planned. At the end of another draining day he hoped something pleasant awaited them, maybe even the company of girls. In the midst of poverty there were few consolations and sleeping with a woman could for a time lull the most desolate man into believing his misery was not total.

Night fell quickly and from the streets some of the children and women drifted away. Dogs and cats having no particular owners sought shelter in wood-piles, baskets and under any convenient clutter. Behind windows oil lamps stuttered into life and in the yards cooking pots and wood fires were prepared.

Why, Leif wondered, did people never fail to disappoint? Was he expecting too much when San Juan, and maybe the whole country for all he knew, had been this way for an eternity? What forced the world to make the choices it did? Was it self-interest only or inertia? Was there a place for simple idealism, or was that just another myth? Perhaps there was no place on the planet, he concluded, where indigence and morality could be reconciled?

Of those he'd met in San Juan and Magalindan, only one had given cause for hope. The great disenfranchised mass was simply too unaware to care, and let themselves be carried along by events and on the giant wave of fatalism. Others, such as Mayor Linganan, the string-puller in white slacks and the so-far invisible Maylenne Linganan, under whose windows he was now passing, were, to a man and woman, beyond the pale, gorging themselves on food grown by the poor.

In the dimly-lit upper rooms over his head a red glow rose and fell. Movements, like heartbeats, deepened the colour almost to crimson. From somewhere in the direction of the plaza and the Municipality buildings, an unidentifiable odour drifted along the alleyways. Involuntarily Leif shuddered; did depravity too have a smell?

The streets, which had never until this moment been free of rowdy and aimless traffic, suddenly seemed deserted and only an unexpected sound of timber falling somewhere behind the tall fence broke the silence. The yard gates, he noticed, were unlocked with padlocks hanging loosely on their rings. Was someone working late between the lumber stacks to scrape an honest living in the service of a dishonest mistress? Or had a poor man, under cover of darkness, decided to steal back what was rightfully his? Could the night's dark beauty not only cloak recent horror, but at last set free one person's will to say enough was enough?

Leif walked across the sandy plaza and turned right onto the beach. Light from the full moon palely picked out surrounding roof tops and tree branches. On the sea's face there was barely a ripple except for a few wavering concentric circles. How strange that those born to this wonder were hardly aware of its existence.

He could usually see his two tents once he'd crossed the sand spit at the end of the airstrip, but tonight, for reasons he couldn't immediately explain, neither was visible. Yesterday they had been visible from the tenth marker of the mahogany nursery, but, tonight, as he passed and counted off the stakes one by one; seven,…eight,…nine he realised the tents were no longer there, or at least no longer where he had left them. Unexpectedly disorientated he found he was standing in the middle of what had once been his camp. The tents had been hacked from their pegs and lay on the ground with great gashes in their fabric and contents scattered in every direction. Bottles had been emptied into the sand and smells of chloroform and lighting spirit hung in the damp air.

Leif sank to his knees and closed his eyes, his hopes collapsing as swiftly as Magalindan's impoverished gaiety had under tidal waves of mud. Neither he, nor anyone else, he now realised, could bring change alone, because no-one in San Juan, in spite of what they said, wanted to do anything differently. Change for the better was just another pointless fantasy.

Only returning rains would make matters worse and the heavy trails of cloud that had begun obscuring the moon's twinkling images on the sea threatened more calamity to San Juan's blighted barrios. But a sudden burst of angry red sparks rushing into the billowing vapours dismissed thoughts of rain in an instant.

The blaze was not coming from Magalindan, but somewhere near the town's centre and close to where he had left his friends. Staggering upright he raced back as fast as the shifting beach sands allowed and up through the dusty plaza before realising the fire was in Linganan's building supplies yard.

In front of him a crowd had gathered in the street, jostling for a better view.

San Juan's resources didn't stretch to a standing fire service and, in the ramshackled back streets there was little anyone could do to fight frequent accidental blazes. Most were allowed to run their course, but ones closest to the river were rated as the least unfortunate, because buckets could be filled and passed from hand to hand. But, although the blaze in the lumber yard was near the river, no-one rushed to fetch water.

Poor people bore each other's tragedies together. But disaster on a rich man's property prompted hints of fiesta and a voyeur's fascination, until, that is, the Mayor's breathless arrival from the Municipality with several labourers in his train interrupted the collective commotion.

"You men there, bring buckets, form a line!" he shouted in a voice made hoarse by smoke and whisky.

Several spectators broke from the rear of the crowd and melted away into nearby alley-ways. Others gravitated in a knot to a position further along the lane.

"Let me through," Leif shouted, as he rushed into the heat and glare. But no-one took any notice, except Ramon, who caught his shoulders and pulled him away from the growing throngs.

"This time don't get involved."

Ramon was not often so insistent.

"But there are people in there, I heard them working. We should get them out."

"There is no-one in the yard," he said. "I know because I was the last one out."

The fire appeared to have started near the back. Several sheds standing on the far perimeter had already been destroyed and their smoking collapse was what precipitated the huge shower of sparks seen from the airstrip. Flames, growing in intensity, had begun to leap the narrow spaces separating methodically-lined stacks of lumber and were now moving closer towards the office premises.

Ricardo Linganan's gang of government labourers had dwindled to just two or three as others eroded away on errands, they said, to find water. In the face of this creeping mutiny, the agitated and sweating Mayor was left to rage alone.

"There are lights on in the house! What are the people inside waiting for?" Leif shouted.

"Maybe they are expecting the fire to stay in the yard," Ramon shrugged.

"But that's stupid. Isn't the house and yard owned by the same person and shouldn't she be out here helping, or taking charge? As a candidate for office she's not making much of a showing."

The Mayor took out a mobile phone, but discovering San Juan was not well covered by satellite services, he needed several attempts to make a connection. Huddling into a corner of the street and with a hand cupped round his mouth he spoke urgently. Several times his voice rose and several times, following angry looks at the massed townsfolk, he lowered it to a whisper. The glow of electric light in the two upper windows above Linganan's shop abruptly went out.

Fanned by hot winds fire swept across the piles of dry timber and, gusting through the chain link fence, drove people back in body as if they had been one individual.

Above the rush of flames crackling sounds erupted from behind the two-story building and with it another column of burning debris shot into the night sky. Writhing coils took hold of the house's framework and licked and curled towards the building's front and upper floor prompting a collective, "aah!" to rise with the roaring updraft.

The shop door should have crashed open in the emergency, but, rather than being driven to desperate evacuation, it edged apart almost invisibly as if no-one inside wanted to attract too much attention to their presence. At last, after a great deal of vacillation, three figures emerged cautiously, while the fire-storm rained cinders and ash over their heads. The first, a girl of no more than sixteen, but with a well developed figure clothed in a blue leotard, tip-toed out carrying in one hand a pair of stiletto-heeled shoes matching her costume and, in the other, a man's large white fedora. Her natural prettiness was made ugly by gashes of scarlet lipstick and black mascara scarring her face. She moved timidly, as if worrying where dainty feet should be placed.

At her back came the young seaman from the banka, who had offered Leif water when they met at the river basin. He was wearing black from neck to foot and his trousers were so tight every youthful fold and mound was shaped into the material. His shirt scattered with silver sequins covered a muscular chest that one day ago had earned its keep pulling ship's ropes. On a stage his appearance would have entertained, but in a provincial barrio abutting a builder's yard, God-fearing folk looked and were ashamed.

Some way behind, as if he was not a party to the general exodus, the man with the gold chain and white slacks followed. A low murmur welled up from the watching crowd and Leif turned to Ramon.

"What in heaven's name is going on? It looks like a joke."

"I can tell you there is nothing the least bit funny in any of this," Ramon replied, before turning to several men who had appeared from the alley and added, "Go, don't let him slip from sight."

Maylenne Linganan was the last to step from the building. But, so belatedly, the name board over her head bearing the message, "Linganan Building Supplies" was already wreathed in flames and, as she ducked through the whirls of smoke, one end of it broke free and swung down in a heavy arc. Her head took the full blow and she staggered forward falling spread-eagled into the black ashes. The watching crowd gasped and again moved as one. Several men and women took hold of Maylenne and pulled her to safety, while the Mayor, from a doorway in the building opposite, shouted instructions.

"Not that way, over here. Are you blind; can't you be trusted with anything?" he bawled.

Nothing in San Juan, Leif decided, was ever quite what it seemed. But, if he had learned anything at all, it was how great the generosity and sympathy of the people of San Juan could be. Their magnanimity sprang from undeniable Christianity and the knowledge that for Maylenne they, or anyone else, would have done exactly the same. She was, in her moment of danger, and at the very least, one of theirs and as such entitled to forgiveness.

Ricardo Linganan marched stoutly in front of the small procession crying out, "Clear the way! We have an injury here." Behind him, four men, each holding an arm or leg, carried Maylenne face down to the home of the only doctor in town. Leif felt he should have offered help, concussion being exactly the sort of injury his training was equipped to handle, but the suddenly changing events and San Juan were passing him by.

He, the crowds and the people from the burned-out builder's premises scattered in several directions, while Ramon and his friends went to implement a local solution to a local problem. What right had he to an opinion? There was nothing he could, or, more exactly, wanted to do any more.

Leif didn't see his companions from Magalindan again. No-one knew, or chose to say where Ramon had gone. God knows what happened after the fire, or in the pursuit he'd been told not to join. But if nothing else was clear, there was a sense that one of those indefinable moments had occurred when a critical mass came together and ocean fish had decided which way to turn.

The weekly flight in and out of San Juan was scheduled for tomorrow and Leif prepared to leave. What he had on his back was pretty much all he wanted to take. Most of what he once claimed was scattered over the airstrip, or now in more needy hands.

The incoming flight only had room for twelve passengers and only half the seats were taken. What business had anyone in San Juan, unless a son or daughter returned to the black clay and bare hills to which they were tied by blood and sacrifice?

Leif settled into a seat two rows behind the pilot. There was a delay, but no announcement. Away across the fields he could see a few glinting corrugated iron roofs. From this distance the town looked at peace, but he knew too well there was more below the surface than he or anyone should care to know.

Behind him there was a commotion as a final passenger climbed aboard. The small aircraft swayed as the last arrival's weight made its way from the rear to a front seat. Leif glanced up and encountered the face of the man in white. Blood and mud had dried in patches on the once immaculate shirt and, although an attempt had been made to arrange his hair, parts were torn away. The man's face, bereft of its former confidence, was a mass of blue and red, except for one firmly-closed black eye.

The rear door banged shut and the aircraft turned onto the taxiway. Through the window at his side Leif could see the remains of the rescue team's encampment and, standing in the middle, a solitary figure with black hair with some greying strands. The young man didn't wave, but followed the plane with

The Snow Bridge and Other Stories   217

his eyes until it vanished over the scattered palm trees and deep hillside scars.

Three years later Leif received a letter, postmarked Rio de Janeiro. Ramon hoped he was still remembered and wanted to let his friend know he had become a seaman. In fact he had been working on container ships for the last twelve months and was expecting home leave in another two. San Juan, the letter related, had not changed a great deal since the mud slide and night of the fire. Maylenne Linganan had survived her accident, but had retired from business and politics. Her face bore the marks left by the falling board and she never fully recovered the poise, some would say arrogance, of her earlier years. After Ricardo Linganan's term in the Mayor's office ended, his youngest nephew Pablo, who had been studying overseas, took over; everyone agreed the election was untainted and that the town's best interests continued to be served by safe hands.

ELEVEN

IN HER SHADOW

In early childhood, during countless hours waiting for her mother to be transformed in neighbourhood beauty salons, Mildred Clingford leafed through the pages of one glossy magazine after another. The images of luxury and beauty, theatre and fashion fascinated her, until little by little she conceived in her young mind the idea of escaping from provincial drabness to the fantastic world displayed in her lap.

When old enough and no longer expected to accompany her mother, she read extensively in books found in dusty profusion under her mother's side of the parental bed that spoke of heroes and heroines for whom a happy rainbow ending always waited. The repetitive diet of fraudulent glamour progressively developed into a reality greater than the trudging boredom she witnessed in the mean and crowded streets outside. The conditions of her birth to parents, who had met over a production line assembling Korean television sets in a northern city and an unpromising schooling, she determined to put from sight and memory.

On the first occasion she and other aspiring teenage-girls attended an audition for places in an amateur chorus line she came ready to present her newly devised persona of Rebecca Janes. The name had come to her after many hours juggling combinations found in the pages of what later turned out to be the heart of her education.

Fifty years on and long after her hopes had been granted the star that had risen so high began to fall, until all that remained were sad dependencies on an album of faded newspaper cuttings, dimming memories of appearances on the boards, her nomme de theatre and a faithful husband. The magic that once lit every step dimmed to a point where the slightest breath would extinguish it forever.

Through the brevity of her heyday she had whirled among the sophisticated and, in moments of effortless make-believe, felt herself to be in possession of the very qualities she recreated for the wonder of others.

Once, she remembered, theatrical agents sought her out for the timeless, classical roles she had determined to play from the very first day of becoming aware of their existence. Her Desdemona and Titania, in particular, were stunning successes reverberating up and down the critics' columns for weeks after opening night, until her face became as well known in public as it was to patrons of the stalls and upper circle. She gloried in the throng's adulation and, in her vanity, believed it would have no end.

But now, in the evening of her career, when only rare cameo performances and bit parts left of centre stage came her way, the crowd dwindled. The eternal celebrity of her dream retreated before a thickening waist, deepening crows' feet and the audience's desire for fresher talent.

"It is such a slight thing, Jeremy," she complained peevishly to her husband at the offer of a minor walk-on role. "I would not appear until the second act! How could I accept?"

"But Becks your name will be heard again and new dimensions added to your repertoire."

"Don't use that appalling diminutive and what, pray, are the dimensions I lack?"

Rebecca, even as Mildred, had been testy, but the thespian instinct to act-up any situation exaggerated an innate tendency.

"In the right hands mature roles are as vibrant as those of young leads, my love, and yours would be the right hands."

"Uhh! Not to a gallery thirsting for enchantment. I would simply die playing a woman of over forty."

"Cleopatra was older when she captivated Anthony, my dearest."

"I don't believe that for a second and I wish you wouldn't be so pedantic; it doesn't dignify older men."

"Yes my dear, if you say so."

No one knew by how much, but casual gossip widely believed Jeremy was older than Rebecca by one, two or more decades. They had met when she was at the height of her career and he a successful businessman and politician. Their affair caught the interest of tabloids and weekend press and frequently fuelled the sotto voce conversation of social gatherings.

At first she resisted his advances, but eventually, succumbing to persistence and a fascination with his position, she surrendered, as only she knew how, with a sigh on her lips and a hand to her brow; a besieged maiden overthrown. He had scaled the ramparts and taken her captive, which, in view of her love for none but herself, was a remarkable achievement.

Jeremy Pilkton had indeed undertaken the courtship in a manner resembling a castle's siege and threw into the fray every weapon at his disposal. He bombarded her with flowers, expensive gifts and letters; he attended all her shows, sometimes the same one for several nights in a row and, on the evenings she made herself available, he took her to fashionable restaurants and into celebrity circles where she enjoyed the ministrations of famous hostesses and maîtres d'hôtel.

He may have been, and in fact was believed by many, to be a besotted old man willing to compromise his reputation for steadiness by throwing a considerable amount of energy on winning an object of his fancy. But with the commendable determination characteristic of his entire career he brushed aside innuendo and tenaciously mounted the ladder rung by rung.

The detractors, however, never stopped whispering that her interest in Jeremy was founded on his access to the highest in the land, rather than her love for him, or his autumnal enthusiasm for performing an escort's function. Even after several years, they still said, how could such an unlikely union survive longer than the average ill-stared entertainment romance, which, for the purposes of the times in which they lived, included in its broad description, politics, business and theatrical performance.

The gossip sometimes prompted younger, more handsome pretenders to contest Jeremy's position, but he swatted them aside with the peremptory disdain of a man used to total control. From the beginning, Jeremy ensured the relationship by indulging Rebecca's every whim and in taking time to lavish nearly total attention on his acquisition. He spoiled her so utterly that, should any niggling doubts surface in her mind of life as Mildred Clingford, they were dispelled among the vaulted ceilings and chandeliers as quickly as applause from last night's audience.

Throughout the years of Rebecca's glittering success he kept her court like an experienced chancellor, allowing only those he considered acceptable into her presence and by forbidding entry to the rest. His sure grip kept her free from worldly worries, until now, with only the shell of her once soaring achievement remaining, he sought to protect her from the knowledge of her decline.

When minor parts were all the profession had to offer and her off-stage questions multiplied, he remained the one staunch and dedicated fan striving to preserve her legend and perpetuate her belief that she remained the stage's eternal queen, even when the months during which she had been unmentioned in society media stretched into years. He loved her unwaveringly and demanded more discerning observers see her through his eyes, as still the summit of womanly perfection and theatrical accomplishment.

Not that Jeremy was a fool, far from it. Junior Home Office ministers in Her Majesty's Government were unlikely to achieve high office by self-delusion or incompetence. The simple fact was he knew what he wanted and spared no effort to cast it in the guise and colours none could mistake.

The one factor that Jeremy failed to anticipate in an otherwise carefully laid plan, occurred just seven years after marriage and while Rebecca was still ascending to the stars in her silver chariot. She gave birth to a daughter, which immersion in the great romances had failed to predict. In her mind, love and conception, rather than one being a consequence of the other, were entirely different matters. Her universe, the only one she chose to recognise, consisted of heart and style, art and performance without ever stooping to mere function. Child-bearing was grotesque and child-care appalling. Feeding and cleaning an infant were events belonging to Mildred Clingford and her sort of people and were simply not recognised activities in Rebecca's realm. No one in gorgeous palaces changed nappies, simply because nappies and the reasons for them failed to exist at her rarefied altitude.

Jeremy, in his considerate way, employed a nurse whose secondary duty was to care for the child. Her primary task was to do it at such a distance that no hint or suggestion of the nursery intruded into Rebecca's consciousness. At first Jeremy was drawn to the child, but, feeling his time and duty restricted, he gradually allowed the nurse to become substitute father as well as mother.

After pregnancy's initial bafflement and delivery's later humiliation Rebecca contrived to put the whole ghastly matter from her mind. Hannah, for that was the girl's name, consequently grew through infancy at the far end of the house, enjoying only occasional contacts with her father and almost none with the mother. A delicate and sensitive child would have carried the scars of parental abandonment into adult life, but Hannah, inheriting the steely single-mindedness of her father, thrived on emotional neglect and in time became a determined and formidable young woman.

Early schooling was provided by the nurse, but because her personal qualities centred on the provision of physical comfort, she fell at the first hurdle requiring serious intellectual stimulus. A private boarding school rapidly became the obvious solution and Hannah soon left with minimum fuss and even less concern. Jeremy wrote the cheques and felt his responsibilities were discharged to everyone's satisfaction. If an audible sigh of relief at such a painless and agreeable conclusion to raising children had been heard, no one, if they had been listening, would have been in the least surprised.

"I will reject the part, because it does not thrill."

"May I advise, my love?" Jeremy interjected and, without waiting for a response, continued, "We are approaching summer, which we know is quiet. Your admirers haven't seen you cross the stage for twelve months and more. They should not be disappointed further. Let's give them this morsel; it will be crumbs from the rich feast of your work, but starving men deserve as much."

"As much, or as little? I should not be tempted by your siren persuasions," replied the weakening and artificially reproachful Rebecca.

"I could not be a siren my dearest, because they…"

"Don't start that, my nerves simply would not stand it," Rebecca replied, her voice and jowl trembling over what had once been a firm and shapely chin.

The show was not a success. A planned run in the West End was quickly scrapped when the out-of-town trial drew poor houses. Not only did the public fail to respond, but the few critics who bothered to attend were in complete agreement the play deserved to flop. To make matters worse Rebecca's contribution was not even mentioned by two columnists and a third unkindly referred to her as "the late Ms Clingford." Rebecca was mortified.

"Ahh! You see, I was right; I should not have involved myself in that too ridiculous production and become a figure of scorn for the sensationalist press."

"Tastes have changed, my sweetheart, and we have to experiment with what is available."

"I am tempted to say you no longer remember the parts I played best. I glory in grand drama, not in kitchen theatre."

"You are a great actress and can therefore play all parts admirably."

Rebecca, although inclined to disputation as well as irritability during moments of disappointment, paused to weigh the significance of Jeremy's comment. More than her fondness for being admired, she relished the sort of lavish compliment that allowed pride to exceed her inordinate shallowness.

"In this instance you may be correct. I shall allow you the benefit of the doubt, but only this once, mind."

"Thank you, my love."

While her myopic mother ignored approaching twilight, Hannah progressed with scarcely a filial thought or backward glance from boarding school to her first choice university. And from the businesslike privacy of his study Jeremy continued paying school fees and a monthly allowance in exactly the same manner as he settled water and electricity bills. His daughter, preferring to spend time with friends, only very occasionally returned home during the holidays. Home, however, with its suggestions of intimacy and warmth, was altogether an incorrect word. Nothing, other than discussion of the lingering financial link that was destined to disappear on her day of graduation, brought Hannah back to the place where she began. Her willingness to show affection to her first guardians was directed almost exclusively towards the old nurse who, although long in retirement, was spoiled with frequent visits and telephone calls. Estrangement from her parents had its roots in the past, but was preserved in aspic by Jeremy's and Rebecca's inability to find anything to say to Hannah, or she to them.

After the disaster of her tiny second-act part in the provincial production and the cruel reviews, Rebecca never performed again. She fooled herself by saying she could afford to wait and be selective, but in the absence of a perfect play containing an ideal role, her career was ended by her own hand. The bar was set beyond reach and her comfort lay in the absence of excuses needed for declining the jump.

As the years continued to roll on, Jeremy's business activities declined and gave him even more time to be with Rebecca. She, with almost nothing to occupy her, took to gardening and reliving the triumphant occasions gradually receding from view. If only she had made a film, something tangible would remain. But an insubstantial theatre speech, she reflected disconsolately, died the moment it was released onto the air.

The worn and well-turned pages of several scrapbooks filled with cuttings and show programmes, excepting the last one that was erased from mention and memory just like her history as Mildred Clingford, became the daily oxygen that kept her from the bitterest finale of all.

"Jeremy, do you recall the royal visit to Drury Lane? The Prince and Princess of Wales themselves came to watch my Miranda...I've often wondered, is it correct to call them the Wales, or the Wales's? I'm sure it must be the Wales, but I don't know why."

"They are not often referred to collectively."

"But we always talk of the Kents, do we not? What can be the difference?...Wasn't Miranda dazzling that night? Flowers filled the dressing room from side to side and end to end."

"You were beautiful, my dear. And besides you can't add an 's' to a word that ends with one."

"I used to love the way stagehands created the storm's thunder; rattling those metal sheets."

"I don't believe they do it the same way now. Recorded sound effects are much more reliable."

"Really? I wonder what the Princess would have said."

In the middle of the following summer Hannah completed her course with an honours degree and was recruited directly from campus by an international oil company. She was to join them in September as a management trainee and move to one of their subsidiaries in south-east Asia. Jeremy and Rebecca had nothing to say on the matter and, in a manner of speaking and with some finality, the file and cheque book were closed. Hannah, however, who felt neither anger nor obligation towards her indifferent parents, made one of her rare visits to state her plans and acknowledge the conclusion of the funding that had underwritten her education.

A young friend dropped her in the narrow lane at the rear of the Pilkton residence. As his car sped away in a shower of gravel fragments, she wondered why youths took such delight in dramatic and unnecessary acceleration, when the rest of the world moved at an altogether different pace.

In front of her, the high brick wall, with ivy creepers trailing along its upper edge and the wooden gate set in its mossed side, was at once familiar and remote. The extensive garden on the other side and its warm rural secrecy enclosed her childhood home, but laced in with happy, snapshot memories, was the question of whether fortune had favoured her quite as much as other girls.

The wide lawn interspersed with flowerbeds ran all the way to the back of a white house. How dense the garden had always seemed to be, whatever the time of year, and especially as it was now in the early summer when shrubs and trees exploded with greenery and budding life. She remembered being home from boarding school and playing games with the nurse in and out of the bushes while her parents toured and she wondered when next a child's voice would break this strongly-scented stillness.

In one of the ornamental beds something moved. Rebecca, not quite upright, but looking straight ahead, was kneeling on a blue towel and wiping the back of a hand across her forehead. From behind, Hannah tried with difficulty to imagine how this portly frame, with a muddy trowel on one hip, had once moved as lightly as a minstrel's fingers over a lute's strings.

"Hello, Mildred."

Since her mid-teens, first as a joke, but later as a choice consciously to demonstrate the equality of their roles, Hannah called her parents by their first names. And in any company, but especially her mother's, she shunned the fraudulent theatrical accessory.

As stiff as a stage prop, but without letting go of the trowel or any of her dramatic instincts, Rebecca feigned physical difficulty.

"I...come round to the side, I can't see..."

"Hello Mildred, how are you?"

Adding to the several already permanent lines, a new furrow creased Rebecca's brow. She seemed to be struggling to remember something from the very distant past. Then, as if a light had been turned on, said, "Aah! Yes, Hannah. We haven't seen you since...to what do we owe this visit?"

"I've finished university and wanted to let you know what was happening."

"Univ?...and what have you been doing there, my child?"

"Yes, your child! Do you ever stop performing Mildred? Can we go in and talk to Jeremy?"

The long-limbed young woman reminded Rebecca of herself when she was twenty-two. How ironic that all the qualities of grace and good looks had deserted her aging figure and slipped into the form of a daughter she didn't really like and who, when given half a chance, preferred not to recognise.

"Gardening is such a revealing hobby. You tend the most beautiful plants only to see them wither in spite of extravagant care. I don't know why it attracts me so."

"Perhaps you are trying to recapture something," Hannah said frankly, if a little brutally.

From her knees Rebecca studied her daughter inch by disdained inch; the resemblance was a mirror image of that other hateful person, Mildred Clingford who also possessed the sort of middle class views that could have been fathered in the back of a Friday night taxi cab on the return from a public dance.

"Jeremy is out," she snapped.

"Then I'll wait for him to come back if you don't mind," Hannah replied brightly before turning towards the house.

"And leave me here?" the voice was starting to tremble.

"But aren't you doing what you enjoy?"

"Yes, but now I want to get up and need help!"

"Really Mildred," said Hannah holding out a smooth, naked arm with a gesture of exasperation, "You are too much."

Seeking support for her full weight Rebecca leant to one side. But, creaking stiffly and with pouting annoyance, her outstretched fingertips barely touched the waiting hand and she stumbled forward breathlessly. A large straw hat, brought back from Barbados a decade ago to protect her even then age-blemished skin, slipped over one eye.

"Oh! Does one ever expect the sacrifices of motherhood to be repaid in the small change of a child's ingratitude?" she gasped.

Out of robust good humour, but not bitterness, Hannah smiled at her mother's self-deception. How, she wondered, could a parent totally ignore its child yet remain convinced everything had been given? Was it possible for a thought to be repeated so many times it became a fact? Perhaps this was exactly what had once made Rebecca a remarkable actress? Words spoken with ringing conviction from a script were after all just deceptions by another name.

"I think I should leave you to your cuttings and borrowed lines."

Rebecca had acquired definition only through the roles she played. Without a part to enter, only a husk devoid of any real personality remained. She had no depth, no principle, no insight and, other than selfishness and vanity, no character. Ephemeral lines thrown to an audience were what gave her reality. She was like the branch of a rose bush, which came to life only when grafted onto the stock of a more vigorous plant. A biographer, even one painstakingly instructed to preserve her unique legacy, would unearth no more than a tedious catalogue of performances. There wasn't anything else.

With the handle of her trowel Rebecca raised the sun hat slightly and deposited a thin smear of mud on her dampening forehead.

"Jeremy will not be back until late."

"For the next three weeks I have all the time in the world. I don't suppose he'll be as long as all that."

Hannah smiled again, but in a way that didn't change her eyes except for the shadows that momentarily deepened beneath them. Her visit was turning out to be exactly as she had anticipated.

Thin muslin curtains moved gently on currents of air wafting into the lounge. Most of the furniture was white except for two large chinese porcelain jars that stood on the floor at either end of a fire-place. Framed photographs of Rebecca and other actors and actresses, many long since dead, covered every surface.

With arms spread wide and tousled hair spilling over her shoulders, Hannah fell into the cushions of a long settee and wondered whether her mother had any concept of keeping house, or experience of dusting ornaments.

"Does Mrs Finch still do for you?"

"Really, I wish you didn't sit like that…legs wide apart, so unladylike. Is that what they teach you at school these days?"

"University actually and they don't have anything to say about how close a woman's knees should be. You really are hopelessly pretentious. If I were Jeremy I would have dumped you years ago."

Rebecca's scalp tingled. But with nothing to say, she sat down and pulled sharply at the soiled ends of the gardening gloves still on her hands.

"We have a live-in," she said reaching for a tiny silver bell on the coffee table. A woman in her late fifties wearing very dark clothes answered the ring. Afternoon tea was ordered and the heavy figure retreated from sight.

"Good Lord," remarked Hannah, "you've travelled even further back in time than I remember. I didn't realise such relationships still existed in this country. Where did you find her?"

"I'm troubled by this conversation and your tone, there is no…"

"Oh, come on Mildred, you might be able to fool Jeremy, but he's the only one. Everyone else knows you are a phony."

"If you have come here just to be hurtful, I suggest we end this meeting now."

"I'd like to have the sort of conversation with you that's possible with most other people, but we inhabit different parts of the planet and apart from a few random genes we have nothing to share. How do I begin talking to you?"

Turning to the mantelpiece above her, Rebecca saw reflected within the space of a vast gold-framed mirror the blinding green of the sunlit garden and the gentility of her spacious house. Right in the middle of this precious picture in jeans and unpressed shirt and sprawled across the settee, lay Hannah. She looked as if she had been poured there from a broken jug to stain the spotless furniture. But, thought Rebecca begrudgingly, there was no denying she was a very good-looking woman and if one concentrated and discounted the positively ugly clothes, which could as easily contain a man as a woman, one might even say she was beautiful. The light shoulder-length hair was not exactly blond and for a short spiteful second Rebecca hoped the origins were a bottle. But that, alas, was clearly not the case and the unaffected cascade was an expression of Hannah's languid and enviable personal comfort with herself and her surroundings.

The unnamed "live-in" returned with a jingling tray to lay out teapot, cups, scones and jam. Without offering a word, she withdrew again to a place where instructions acquired form. Rebecca continued to gaze disconcertedly into the mirror. In the glass her face and her daughter's were side by side. The images combined past and present and, in a muddled way, were both sources of regret and dislike. The world that had once given Rebecca identity was passing and leaving her behind. Like a champion mare at the end of her racing life she had lived to see the foal she momentarily suckled become the odds-on favourite to win next year's Derby. How she hated arriving at the finish and having no purpose but to wait out the remaining months in meaningless time-filling hobbies. The sight of her muddy garden gloves now tossed over the handle of a wicker basket by the fireplace suddenly appalled her beyond reason.

Unlike her daughter's fresh, smooth skin, which glowed with youth and vitality, she could see hers was a lattice-work of creases and, against the finger raised to her cheek, they had the soft, spongy feel of fruit left forgotten on a kitchen shelf. Some faces, thought Rebecca, were enriched by events and surely, if Ophelia had lived as long as this, her unkind love would have been imprinted on her features. Why then, did her likeness look back at her and speak only of age but not virtue and experience?

But hadn't she given something that had entranced, which, if not wholly her own, had at least shed light on others' brilliance? If the mirror revealed images of a damp and empty dungeon instead of the majestic garden, would its value diminish like hers? Her life seemed spent and the acting career that once soared among the cloud tops was brought as low as her beginnings. The final scene in her tragedy was of having outlived her time.

Rebecca's nose started to feel wet and, taking a small embroidered handkerchief from her sleeve she turned away and sniffed.

"After you've seen Jeremy, please don't stay too long. It isn't that you are not welcome, but seeing you so capable and intelligent, with the entire world at your feet, I simply can not bear to watch. You do understand, don't you?"

A single tear from Rebecca's left eye ran jumpily across her tiny wrinkles and stopped at the corner of unsteady lips.

Hannah sat up.

"What is it? Are you going?"

"No, it isn't that. It's just... Well, you were for a second different and sounded almost... Let me pour tea."

The small door of opportunity for Rebecca to share some of the inner workings of her heart, however trite, with her only daughter, closed as quickly as it had opened and she slipped back into her habitual part.

Fitful and irrelevant conversation limped back and forth as late afternoon shadows gathered among the garden's trees. At around six o'clock the "live-in" was called to close the French windows against a rising breeze.

"You should be ashamed to ask an old woman to do a little task like that; let me."

Hannah reached up to close the curtains and the setting sun's horizontal rays made her hair shine. Standing to the light with a shirt pulled tight by the effort, Rebecca observed a trim, rounded figure and narrow waist. The outlandish clothes contrasted sharply with the sensual body and against her wish Rebecca drew in a long breath.

"Oh, I say, I think that's Jeremy coming in the back gate. Gosh, he's wearing a hat! I thought only Russians and cowboys wore such things these days."

Hannah held back the doors as Jeremy picked his way carefully between the flowerbeds. Neat to the point of fastidiousness, he avoided treading on things that might stick to well-polished patent leather. A route into the house through the garden did not appear to be the obvious choice for a person as well-dressed and finicky as he.

"I wanted to surprise you my love," he explained, "I thought you would still be tending the plants."

As an afterthought and as if there might be some doubt, he added, "...oh...and who have we here?"

"Hello, Jeremy. Your beloved daughter, that's who."

Several thoughts occurred to Jeremy, which together caused a puzzled ripple to cross his countenance. For the space of a few seconds he looked not unlike a baby whose feet were being tickled and had yet to decide whether it was something enjoyable or not. But as he was a practiced politician, the confusion soon passed.

"Ah," he began, with a smile as flawless as any executed on stage by Rebecca, "It's been a while and to what...er..."

"...do we owe this pleasure?" In spite of the mockery Hannah's directness was attractive. One of the qualities that brought her many friends was that everyone knew exactly where they stood in her estimation. She was observant, but not disparaging; she could be and often was sardonic, but never maliciously. To be underhand or devious was for her impossible and in the sharpest contrast to her father who had got where he was by taking on the world in a game he played better than most. Both parent and child were sharp, one with native shrewdness, but the other with disarming frankness.

"If I remember correctly, this is your last year at university, is it not?"

"Indeed it is and I've come to thank you for supporting my education and to let you know my plan."

The thin, horizontal line of Jeremy's mouth stretched a little wider. He had anticipated a sense of release when the moderate financial burden and minor emotional investment in his daughter were concluded. But this unscheduled interview gave him an uneasy feeling it was he and Rebecca who were the millstones being cut away. Not knowing whether he should comment, or wait for an explanation, he glanced towards Rebecca, who had absent-mindedly returned to the mantelpiece to contemplate her unhappy reflection.

Across the cavernous space of the room and in the few words exchanged between Jeremy and Rebecca there was a connection, like the pulsing of intermittent sparks of electricity. But from Hannah to her parents and more especially to her mother, there was nothing, not even the sterility of an icicle hanging in the afternoon air. The magnetism, with which Rebecca once held audiences spellbound, was neutered in the shock and annoyance of parenthood.

Hannah looked at the pair in front of her and was reminded of old sepia photographs that held the movements of Victorian groups frozen in starched poses. A tray of fresh tea, brought in by the aging domestic at the sound of Jeremy's voice, stood cooling and untouched on the coffee table.

"Well, I'll do my best not to break up the party, so let me be brief and I'll be on my way."

In short, quick sentences, Hannah related that she had graduated and was leaving for overseas work in a few weeks time. She thanked them for their financial support, but added she would manage independently from now on.

"But, the dormitory…? Won't you be expected to move out before your…ah…foreign venture?" Jeremy asked as if a sudden suspicion had dawned on him that important parts of the story were being withheld and he might receive an inconvenient request at some ill-defined moment for a bed under this very roof.

"You've forgotten of course. I haven't been in residence for two years. The chap who dropped me here; he started well before me and has been my roommate since finishing his degree."

"Oh!" Rebecca appeared to wake up with a start. "I wouldn't do that if I were you."

"In case it has escaped anyone's attention, I am not you. Look, I didn't come to debate. I'm here out of courtesy and to thank you. That's all. And then I'll be on my way."

Rebecca and Jeremy, seeking conclusion, looked at each other again.

"Well, we are sure you know best," Jeremy, always the ingratiating diplomat, eventually said after a silence as total as any endured by a monk in holy orders. "…And now…?"

"And now," continued Hannah, picking up on a trailing sentence for the second time and rising from the settee, "I'd best be going."

Her parents did not embrace their daughter, or accompany her to the door. A dutiful shake of hands over cold tea and the sort of formal goodbye offered to first-time visitors was as much, or as little, as they could muster.

Hannah walked out into the lane through the back gate and, as the bird song of a still summer evening and wisps of wood-smoke rising from a nearby garden fire gathered around her, she hastened away.

Ten months later Jeremy died. In other families the news would have reached a far-away daughter through a mother's urgent and distraught telephone call. But in Hannah's case the discovery came from a short inside-page article contained in a week-old London newspaper picked up in a local coffee shop. The announcement was curt; "Jeremy Pilkton died suddenly yesterday at his home in Surrey," followed by a paragraph on his political activities and a comment from a former Home Secretary who remarked on his "ability and integrity." The article concluded with a comment that his wife, the former actress Rebecca Janes, and a daughter survived. There was no elaboration on the circumstances of Jeremy's death or of the shock and horror that had so traumatized Rebecca in the days following his collapse in front of her.

She had been working in her garden preparing for the rush of spring growth. A row of canes had been set out to support the purple clematis flowers, which in her imagination were not just plants, but vessels holding reserves of nectar and mystery in their deep, fluted trumpets. Shortly before midday, the ever-attentive Jeremy had come down from his room on the first floor, where he worked on household papers, to collect a lunch tray from the live-in. He thought he would please Rebecca with his attention and give her a break from her self-imposed labour.

"My love, it's time to rest and regard the beauty of your work. Every artist should stand back at intervals to contemplate and absorb what has been set out on the canvas."

"Do you think we should have somebody in to help with the heavy work, while I concentrate on choosing and arranging?"

"Whatever my dearest desires I shall endeavour to…" Jeremy's face turned deathly pale and he winced with pain. His hands let loose the lunch tray, which together with the cutlery and a delicate bone china plate fell in a crash at Rebecca's feet.

"Oh! Jeremy, how careless of…"

"Sweetness, I think I'm…not at all…"

Half turning Jeremy dived headlong into the clematis canes. His reading glasses, which until that moment had rested on the end of his nose, fell free and one lens cracked against a flint. Rebecca's mouth opened wide and she looked at the fallen figure lying chest down on the flowerbed. Both of Jeremy's arms were twisted behind his back and a thin dribble of saliva ran onto the ground from his parted lips. The man who had been so precise and particular in his tastes and manners had damp compost smudged along his white collar and Rebecca in her confusion and desperation leant forward and flicked it away.

The event of unexpected death in one so near numbed Rebecca to her core. Up to this moment the only place where she had experienced tragedy had been on stage. On those occasions, however, when the curtain fell in the evenings she had been able to hang up her most profound emotions with her costume and the garlands thrown over the footlights. But now confronted by real personal loss she stood on the edge of an abyss and saw beneath her the most unspeakable depths. This was something she could not put to one side like a recalcitrant daughter or spare bottles of makeup paint.

Superficially, the loss was of Jeremy's steady hand in the many roles he had played in her affairs, which in number almost equalled those she had lavishly performed on stage. He had been her champion, her cheer-leader, her manager, her advisor, her protector, and long ago, when she had allowed, her obedient lover. But more crucially he had also been her myth-maker and, although her career had effectively terminated years ago in a manner as abrupt as his fall onto the clematis canes, only he had sustained the make-believe that closed her ears to the sound of harsh reality's footfall on her doorstep. Now the shocks underpinning her glorious delusion of resting on shore in readiness for a new voyage had been knocked away and she lurched uncontrollably into unknown seas.

Financial provision for Rebecca's future was not the issue; even from the grave Jeremy's devotion was apparent. The house, funds and investments, to which she had given no consideration, were in the sort of order expected of a scrupulous businessman. He, knowing Rebecca's limited practicality, had engaged a solicitor to administer and manage the estate after his demise. Her needs, however, went a long way beyond timely meals and cash in hand. She needed the constant accolades only Jeremy had been willing to provide long after the fickle public had turned its back and gone on to other entertainment.

"If you will permit me," said Mr Lepper, the cadaverous partner visiting from the solicitors' firm one morning, "I will engage a person to tend your garden. Two days a week should suffice. To keep it in good order you understand."

"Whatever you decide; I no longer have the patience for it," sighed Rebecca, without showing the least interest in either the control of the now unkempt garden, or Mr Lepper's solution for its maintenance.

After the death of her comforter and guide, Rebecca's remaining enthusiasms dwindled rapidly away and nothing, least of all the flowers and shrubs, held her for more than a few unfocused minutes. Never a wide reader, other than in the adolescent rubbish found under her mother's bed and for the dramas she was rehearsing, Rebecca had little to anchor her mind and she drifted all day from room to room as if in search of someone or something. Occasionally, the leaves of her scrapbook caught her temporary attention, but without Jeremy to praise and overstate the contents and the events they recalled, they became increasingly more difficult to believe. Was that really me, she often found herself wondering, so young, so beautiful and, yes, so irresistible?

Next to her bed, Rebecca kept a single photograph of herself taken, she couldn't exactly recall the year, at a time when she was still single and becoming a toasted celebrity. The once black and white photograph had yellowed with age and in two or three places had stuck against the cover glass and let several pieces fall to the bottom of the frame.

The occasion, she remembered now, had been a first night and a press photographer had stepped alongside her, as she entered a waiting car. The tossed hair and fine, white teeth were a stunning image. Her long evening dress clung seductively and a bunch of open, white lilies rested in the crook of her pale arm. Now alone and in the depth of winter nights she frequently woke with a start to scents carried over the space of years from the long dead bouquet.

"There were some documents from my daughter; sent I believe just before she went abroad. Do you remember what became of them?" she suddenly asked the live-in one October morning.

"Yes M'm, they'd be in Mr Jeremy's old office unless that Mr Lepper took them with him when he sorted through the papers."

"Can you find them for me?"

The domestic help returned an hour later with a thick brown envelope showing Hannah's bold, uncompromising hand. Rebecca looked at the handwriting, which held such confidence and certainty in every bold stroke. There were no flourishes, just plain strength, not, she thought, like her own elaborately cultivated curls and sweeps. The difference was that from the start she had set out to impress, while her daughter never sought or lived by the good opinion of anyone.

The envelope contained a letter of some eight or ten lines long, a copy degree certificate and several colour photographs, which, explained the letter, were taken at graduation celebrations and on the conclusion of Hannah's academic experience and were the least she could leave her parents. Rebecca had to confess the envelope and its contents had not been devoured with any eagerness and Jeremy had taken it away to be dealt with very much in the manner of a begging flyer from an undeserving charity. Until this day the letter had been opened on just one occasion.

Spread out across the glass top of her coffee table, the photographs stirred no thoughts or warmth of a distant child, except... except....Ah! There it was! – A picture of Hannah leaving some sort of social function and about to step into an open-topped car, presumably the one owned by that university boyfriend of several years ago. Casually held over one arm was a bunch of variedly coloured flowers. The young woman's head was thrown back and had on it a smile that her mother instantly recognised as identical to her own.

As a consequence of rough storage, the photograph had become bent across one corner. Rebecca put a finger in the edge of her sleeve to smooth away the crease. Four or five passes seemed to produce the effect she desired and with her head slightly on one side she looked with satisfaction at the fresh and sparkling face rising from the table in front of her.

With an effort Rebecca stood up. She no longer moved with the ease of a girl over a dance floor and climbed the curved flight of stairs to her bedroom with difficulty. At the head of the stairs and without letting go of the photograph or the heavy wooden banisters, she paused and looked down. Hurriedly and without much care the live-in below was scooping scattered photographs back into their envelope and clearing away the afternoon tray.

"Shall I return these to the office M'm?"

"Yes, I have what I need, Juanita."

The domestic looked up. Was this the first time Rebecca had called her by name?

"…is everything alright M'm?"

"Yes… I'm feeling very well."

The large bed in Rebecca's room had an odd shape, unlike the one in the neighbouring room where Jeremy had slept since Hannah's birth. From hours of bearing a body that was uncomfortable elsewhere, her preferred side tilted towards the door and this afternoon, as happened every night, the mattress creaked under her familiar weight.

Next to a glass of water, placed on her bedside table in anticipation of a customary afternoon nap, was Rebecca's faded photograph. She examined it with curiosity. The images that were still intact were blurred with age, just like the faded gaiety of that distantly remembered evening. She desperately wanted to pull her triumphs back into the present and recollect them in all their original colours. But her memory would not let her and she realised her golden years had been as transitory and forgettable as her very last ill-fated performance. The road to death starts at the second of nativity and no amount of wishing could overcome that hideous truth.

Once Jeremy had told her a story of the time he had gone in search of his grandfather's grave. He had arrived at the cemetery to find the local municipality digging up the older end to make way for those more recently deceased. Even the desire to preserve a loved one's memory appeared futile. But, she urged herself, we should try, we must try.

The clips on the back of the photograph frame were corroded, but with a rub of bathroom soap she worked them back and forth until they slowly came free and the frame opened. As she pulled away the glass small particles of dust and bits of crumbling paper fell onto the white bed cover. A larger fragment bearing the lilies and a corner of a smile stuck resolutely to the glass.

Rebecca was as careful in scraping away the pieces and polishing the glass as she had been in removing the crease from her daughter's graduation photograph. Quickly and surely she slid Hannah's picture over the top of what remained of her own and snapped the frame shut. Later in the loneliness of the night and before sleeping the last thing to meet her eyes was the steady gaze and smile from the bedside and their implied confidence in the future.

In the autumn, when short wet days kept the neighbourhood indoors, Rebecca fell sick. Mr Lepper, now a little stiffer and a lot less upright than he had been in the first years of administering Jeremy's estate, concluded his client should be taken into care. The live-in had been useful, but tending to the needs of a frail, old woman required professional skill, which she was unable to provide. Juanita was therefore paid off and allowed to retire to her native Portugal.

Late one morning an ambulance parked in the lane at the back of the house. A number of untidy schoolboys taking a short route home to lunch stopped to stare and point. Drizzle hung in the air and the big trees, which in another season towered in green proliferation, dripped darkly. Two medical attendants helped Rebecca into a wheelchair and steered her between sodden flowerbeds towards the rear gate. Except for her hands, which moved in a continuous knitting motion, Rebecca sat quite still awaiting her fate. An attendant unfastened the latch and Rebecca looked back with her one good eye at the home of many years.

"I used to be a famous actress you know," she said to the young nurse who helped her from the chair.

"Were you, my dear? Well, you'll find lots of good company where we are going. I think we have a gentleman on your floor who tells us he knew Dylan Thomas."

Rebecca's room was very small and only a few of her possessions made the journey to the home. None of her furniture came; it was just too large. She took some clothes and four or five personal ornaments. What the residence was prepared to provide consisted of utility furnishings passed on from a previous guest. Although the tiny bedroom was more or less private, meals and entertainment were shared with other residents in the noisy and strangely odoured community rooms. Beside her bed on an all-purpose chest of drawers, bearing marks of wet glasses and the burns of surreptitiously smoked cigarettes, Rebecca placed her favourite photograph and a crystal-glass figure given her by Jeremy, which she liked to pretend, was a likeness of Titania.

She knew she had once played in *A Midsummer Night's Dream*, but couldn't remember any details and was not at all sure who, other than herself, had been in the cast. Next to the figure were three or four books containing pictures of actors and actresses from the generation immediately preceding her own all of whom had once been her idols. Another gift from Jeremy long ago, a Venetian mask, was confined to a drawer because nothing, she was constantly reminded, could be hung on the walls. The home's staff seemed to be very strict and Rebecca, not being used to scoldings, grew daily more listless. She spent her time waiting, but couldn't imagine any occasion that would make the days more agreeable. Perhaps, if the few occupants to whom she had chosen to speak were not replaced so quickly, she would have felt more settled.

A very elderly gentleman in the next room attached himself to her early after her arrival and listened to the faltering stories, which depended more on his ability to listen than her accurate recollection of events. The contents of her scrapbook, descriptions of both real and imaginary occasions, the bright lights and glamorous people intrigued him. An audience of just one old pensioner, who took pride in being a "working-man", was the remnant of the best years in her life.

She got in the habit of sleeping longer. But extended hours in bed diminished the quality of her rest. Once eight hours of fathomless oblivion brought a sparkle to her eyes and bounce in her step, which together gave her the springboard for creative energy. At the home, eight extended to nine, then nine to more, but sleep no longer came from the same deep, ravishing well. The slightest noise disturbed her so that she hung for long periods in semi-conscious limbo and in the grip of increasingly disturbing dreams. One night at about three in the morning she woke with a start and called for Jeremy, until realising there was no longer anyone to bring her comfort at God-forsaken hours.

Every day after breakfast, a nurse took her from her room in a wheelchair. In fine weather she was pushed onto a balcony with several other inmates to overlook a poorly-tended garden and gaze into the hazy distance. If rain threatened, or there was a bite in the wind, she and the others in the intermittently changing group were parked in front of a common-room television, which none could see or hear with clarity.

At the Pilkington residence there had once been a kitchen knife without a handle that Juanita, who was familiar with its years of service, hadn't the heart to throw away. Rebecca too was a broken utensil, lingering until time and chance decided when she would be let go.

The illness that brought Rebecca into care was imprecise. Her doctors concluded only old age afflicted her. But in truth, she had lost the desire to live and, by slow degrees, sank gradually to her grave.

The end of life, unless by accident or deliberate design, lacks the clamour of birth and in place of a loud rap at the door, there is a gradual winding down as light slowly sinks behind distant hills, until the actual point of departure is almost impossible to discern. So it was with Rebecca, as only her faintly fluttering heart registered her time was not quite over.

Tracing relatives proved difficult. Hannah, though remaining in far away Asia, had left the oil company and set up on her own some while ago. Eventually located and advised of her mother's imminent demise she wondered whether to return or not. But, surrendering to the better aspects of her nature, she decided on one last act of magnanimity.

The home lay in its own grounds at the end of a long driveway where gravel crunched under foot. Wet mists drifted across the tops of surrounding plain trees and a long laurel hedge splashed disconsolately onto a blackened lawn. Shivering in the damp embrace of late afternoon that was neither day nor night, Hannah quickened her pace. The inhospitable cold extended even into Rebecca's room.

An attending nurse got up to leave as she entered.

"How is she doing?" Hannah asked.

"The doctor will give you details, but she's been practically unconscious for days and hasn't spoken for several weeks now. You're probably just in time."

Hannah looked round the cheerless institutional room and almost immediately noticed the only picture Rebecca had chosen to display. The photograph was propped against a drinking glass holding a brush with strands of grey hair matted at the bottom of its bristles. In spite of herself, an overwhelming feeling of pity swept over Hannah and for the first time in adult life she cried, first in silent tears running hesitatingly over her cheeks, but then in great heaves onto a quickly wet sleeve.

Seated on the side of the bed Hannah took Rebecca's thin, veined hand in hers and pressed it to her chest. Did this old woman, who had shown so little interest and no love for her daughter throughout her life, have fond feelings after all? There was no real evidence of Jeremy in the tiny room; was the daughter then the last affection? Moving closer she put both arms round the frail, almost skeletal figure and pulled her close. Unabated tears dampened the old head beneath her chin.

The day slid into evening and light outside the home drained away. Tall, leafless trees above the home scattered water drops onto the windows in flurries, and night, like a cat crossing the roofs, crept in unnoticed.

Still lying in Hannah's gently rocking arms Rebecca suddenly emitted a faint sound of escaping air. There was nothing else, no grand exit, no fanfare and no ovation, only a low hiss as her last breath departed. Hannah laid Rebecca back on the pillow and saw how very small her mother had become.

The few personal articles scattered about the room were all that gave testament to moments on the stage and now how pathetic and inconsequential they looked. Nothing would find houseroom anywhere else or acknowledge a life of any value... except...except perhaps the daughter's photograph. Hannah took up the picture and stared at it as if she wanted the smile it contained to continue keeping her mother company. That no relative, not even Rebecca, had attended her graduation was, for the present, forgotten.

The room filled with bustle and Hannah was gently escorted to a reception area.

"Would you like someone to be with you," the nurse asked.

"No that's alright, I'll be fine... thanks."

Still clutching her university photograph, Hannah watched the rain-lashed trees through a window. A doctor bearing the weight of daily death on his shoulders came to speak with her.

"We were fortunate that you arrived in time to be with her at the end."

"Yes, one more day and it would have been too late."

"She always seemed such a thoughtful person, one might say almost wistful."

"You'll make me cry again if you're not careful."

"Ah! I'm sorry…can we…relatives usually make arrangements following a guest's decease, but, if you wish, the home can make preparations should you prefer."

"Thank you that's very kind, but I'd like to take care of this myself."

"Will you be taking her possessions as well? I see you are holding her photograph. Such a beautiful lady in her early days and, if I may say so not at all unlike you."

"This? Oh, this was me when I left university."

"Really? She always said it was of her at a gala of some description. Perhaps she had become confused."

Starting with a chill of disappointment, a slow realisation crept across Hannah's thoughts.

"…Perhaps, let me think about this, what help could the home provide for…for a funeral?"

Rebecca was cremated three days later. Several wreaths were sent by acquaintances from the theatre world and a bouquet of white lilies came from Juanita. Hannah had gone straight back to her work in Asia and did not attend.

The crematorium was a busy place and the hearse's driver was told to take his time, or he would quite easily overrun the previous service. He knew his business and calculated arrival to perfection. As he sped away from his twenty-minute visit another hearse turned slowly in through the grounds wrought iron gates. He nodded professionally to the man in the incoming vehicle, but also to himself at another job smoothly handled.

TWELVE

A WOMAN PASSING BY

Since disembarking from the Paris plane two years ago Jacques Decamps had been confused. At the beginning he assumed his frustrations were those of any newcomer to a foreign country. But as day succeeded day his feelings for Ho Chi Minh City became gradually more disorientated as he groped through unending fog towards a town that was at times irresistible and at others beyond reach.

Ho Chi Minh and Saigon, he'd discovered, were two distinct places, with both owning contradictory capacities to enchant and unsettle. If he knew little of either when he arrived, the succeeding months had done nothing to give a better understanding. Each minor insight, instead of adding to a developing picture, shifted the entire construction further from sight. The two cities lying one on top of the other were simply unfathomable.

Without being welcomed or rejected he felt like a trespasser in a holy place, where aloof gods laid down unknowable laws. There were no open rebuffs, but the entire community was closed to his expansive Gallic curiosity. There was no connection to either heart or mind. Was it just language? No, he didn't believe so. Plenty of younger people, as in the world over these days, spoke English; an older generation, French; and he, with some embarrassment, a few travellers'-book phrases of Vietnamese. And through the mixture he strove to gain acceptance. But, rather than encouragement or admiration for his brave attempts, he encountered shrinking puzzlement which left him abandoned like drift-wood on a forgotten shore.

Some misunderstanding, he realised, was expected, but the almost complete opacity came as a shock. He found no common ground, and after pondering through many months, over how or where it might be revealed, he had lately begun to ask whether there was any point in knocking at a door that remained firmly closed.

A few foreigners he knew had made Vietnam their home and affected to have found the answers. But as far as he could see this was a fraud perpetrated on any patient enough to listen. Oh, yes, maybe some could eventually speak the language and were living outside the clustered overseas communities, but they, like any other visitors, achieved at most a courteous, but meaningless nod. And long before their arrival weren't these same people self-selected loners escaping home's constraint for third world licence, who wouldn't know true brotherhood when it stared them in the face? They were society's scrap-ends for whom a used bar girl was the chief solace in low-life escapism.

But all he had ever wanted was the freedom implicit in a welcome and the chance to move without suspicion through anywhere he chose. Vietnam had been the choice, but deep exclusion and his innocent wish to hold something of his own kept him fatally excluded.

The stink of the river, the motorbike mayhem, the sun beating like a hammer on the sidewalks and metal roofs, the intensity of colours in the blinding light and dripping humidity weighed heavily. In his daily walks to and from the language institute and a teaching assignment, Jacques felt especially burdened. The oppressively stewed air hung upon him and the stunning chaos and filth like a wet shroud.

Frequent stops at a pseudo-French café on the corner of Cathedral Square, where tables under chequered patterned cloths spilled onto the street, kept him tenuously linked to a distant homeland's sanity. But still the early morning espresso and croissant was without the taste and texture of those in far off L'Oudon and Caen. How could a croissant, made to a recipe unknown throughout the length and breadth of continental Europe, compare to what he remembered of a true baker's complex art? Was any restaurant business so inept? But, then again, why should anyone in this country think of making one differently to the way it was? The travesty was by turns a joke and reinforcement of the feeling that he was left out and only the later afternoon's slow calvados and cigarette saved him from real despair.

Except during an indeterminate four of five hours after midnight "Le Quatorze Juillet" was always open for custom and throughout long days its roadside tables lay unprotected from frequently blistering sun and the occasional squall of rain. In today's withering heat and strength-sapping afternoon that sucked oxygen and energy from every living thing, the once bright umbrellas dotting the forecourt lost a little more of their already faded colour.

Across the square and in peripheral competition with the mock-French café, several elderly country women, selling deep-fried insects and other arcane delicacies, crouched on cracked farmer's heels.

Unassisted by the waiter, Jacques lugged a juddering, almost-too-hot-to handle iron table into shadow and gingerly sat down on its hot, flaking slats.

In the horizontal distance and just over the heads of passing motorcyclists, billowing thunderclouds signalled the dry season's approaching end.

The Quatorze waiter, although familiar with this customer's twice-daily visits, treated him nonetheless as a total stranger. There was no word of casual greeting, no acknowledgement of their many previous encounters and no expectation or desire for any intimacy. Untrained, charmless and with only a miserly readiness to perform, he conducted one half of an employment bargain a single notch above unacceptability. Ly Cam was identified on his name tag as number seven.

The badge was a puzzle; could the designation belong to the last in a line that had passed unremembered into Saigon's seething crowds, or did it hold fateful significance? Orientals were a superstitious lot, Jacques had decided, who saw good or bad fortune lurking everywhere; in the way furniture was arranged, how an ear sloped, and in the suggestive sounds of words. The number did not for one second suggest six other staff were in attendance, or on shift rotation, to cater for the needs of the daily clientele, which at no time, in Jacques' memory, had ever exceeded four.

Whatever characteristics Ly Cam boasted, none could deny his qualities as a minimalist. Next to minimal efficiency was minimal cleanliness, minimal effort, minimal agreeableness and, no doubt to the proprietor's utmost satisfaction, minimal cost. But in demonstration of a double-layered personality, his affinity for humour did not reach the level of other attributes and resided, frozen and unexercised, at zero.

Habitually dressed in an ad hoc assembly of soiled black bow tie, green flip-flops and a shirt that was neither white nor brown, but had in its fibres and dry odours the substance of the man it contained, Ly Cam positioned himself in the café's cool interior behind a dark glass door. Often without movement he stared for hours at the streams of traffic and flowing pedestrians. In hands clasped behind his back he held a round metal tray and an unhygienic wiping cloth bearing the stains of the too few meals he had served over the course of recent weeks.

While Jacques fidgeted on the still uncomfortable seat a yellow cardboard menu appeared on the plastic table-cover in front of him. Pushing the worn menu card away with the end of his thumb, as he had done in a ritual that hadn't changed throughout the four months of patronising Le Quartorze, Jacques requested a calvados. The waiter listened without expression and in silence dragged from sight as if slouching towards his grave. The brown feet and short round toes that had grown hard over long seasons ploughing in the wake of an equally stoic buffalo looked oddly out of place on Saigon's concrete sidewalks.

Across the steam of motorcycles spewing blue smoke into the fetid air, the kerbside women fitfully scooped up cups of crisp crickets and secured them in twists of cheap recycled paper. Their sudden, piercing, almost feral laughter reminded Jacques he had no idea what it took to make a Vietnamese countrywoman smile.

The waiter's back disappeared behind the dull glass door's thud. What manner of man was he? Had he any idea who or what he was, or, like others, was he unable to say with certainty? Created by an apparent mishmash of competing forces he should have been no more than a collage of pictures taken randomly during and after the revolution and without any unifying theme. But stuck in bottomless apathy and lacking affinity for Ho Chi Minh, Saigon and his work at the French café, Ly Cam still remained of his time and place and in that, if nothing else, he was Jacques' brother. Vietnam had painted him a particular way just as the broad brush strokes of France had rendered Jacques. For both a die had been cast long ago from which there was no going back.

Glumly, Ly Cam returned with fingers of one hand spread wide under his tray in a fashion not too dissimilar to the way his weight was supported by stubby toes on flat rubber slippers. A glass of water, a tiny rack of thin tissue paper, a single dish contained several oily snacks sprinkled with red chilli and smelling not unlike the nearby Mekong, a grimy bottle with a peeling label and an empty brandy glass rattled together unsteadily. With the glass cupped in both hands, Jacques watched the disinterestedly poured measure of thick spirit swirl and cling.

There had not, in his recollection, been a first time to experience calvados. The brandy was not quite as every-day as wine at the family table, but, for all that, it was as familiar as the apple trees from which it sprang. In particular he recalled the autumn days and the long rural lunches that stretched past four o'clock when the bottle passed from hand to convivial hand and relationships deepened in the orange and yellow glows of September.

The discovery of calvados in Ho Chi Minh had been unanticipated, almost startling, like encountering strawberries during a European Christmas. Being, as he imagined, the only aficionado for miles around and with none interested in the single bottle's existence, he acquired an odd sense of personal attachment, like the proprietary feeling over a young woman in hot-breathed male company. Of all the people on the streets, or in the whole compass of Indo-China perhaps, he alone had found and been reminded of an umbilical attachment to a distant corner of northwest France. Up to the moment of discovery, neither proprietor nor waiter, if either cared, had been aware the dusty and unopened bottle, standing high on a wooden shelf, was of the smallest value to anyone. Lying unnoticed through changing ownership and employment, it had taken on the status of a decoration, in the same way as the collection of international bank notes pinned among the café's racked glasses.

The first slow trickle of clear, warm liquid crossing his tingling pallet carried him in a heartbeat from the afternoon's stifling warning of rain to golden afternoons in Normandy and the surprising thought that young men too had memories. Did he by chance know the orchard, or had seen ten or fifteen years ago the very apples from which this calvados had been distilled and brought to perfection?

Recollections of long moist grass, laden fruit trees and Etienne his first love, whose eyes were as blue and wide as late-season cornflowers, jostled aside Saigon's clammy grip and led him down steps off the burning edge of Cathedral Square to a dungeon of disappointed spirits. Did postings to distant places, he wondered, inevitably find expression at the bottom of a drained glass?

"S'il vous plaît." The French courtesy with its smooth, round sounds would not let his reflections go.

On the raised finger's signal the waiter sloshed a second measure into Jacques' waiting glass and without knowing released another burst of fragrance from a distant northern farm. Tiny fragments of paper from the bone-dry label fell like dust onto the table to be inexactly flapped away by the multi-purpose grey cloth carried more as a symbol of office than to clean tables. The bottle, Jacques noted painfully, was now more than four-fifths empty.

Somewhere in the direction of the delta indistinct thunder rumbled and on the pavement opposite the snack sellers huddled closer.

Were a home and concurrent enjoyment of the open road irreconcilable aspirations? To possess one completely, the other had to be abandoned. Committed travellers did not need an anchor, because for them only the voyage existed, without beginning or end. Jacques' problem, he decided in a flash of realisation, was that, while France remained his rock and Vietnam a stop along the way, he had no immediate compulsion to abandon either.

In the midday heat humanity and nature paused. The few tourists retreated to air-conditioned bedrooms and lay down spread-eagled under grunting ceiling fans to sleep off unnecessarily elaborate lunches. Streets rapidly emptied and the few remaining motorcycles, still bearing as many as four passengers, now sped unhindered at greater and greater speeds. With reduced risk of intersection annihilation they departed noisily into the shimmering distance as if pursued by demons.

Hawkers of fake brand-name watches, school children in spotless white uniforms, pimps and petty criminals whose business kept them in the open sought out tiny patches of shade under the sweltering boulevard's big plain trees. Chatter among the insect sellers died away and their conical hats settled lower over crouched and dozing forms.

Near the end of his second glass, Jacques, with both heels resting on a neighbouring chair, wondered what he would do when this solitary bottle was drunk to the lees. Local spirit, regardless of touristic popularity and once animate content, had never quite struck the same cord. Houseguests back in distant suburbia might be impressed for a while, but novelty provided no solutions for Jacques' jaded pallet.

There was little likelihood that somewhere out of sight in a forgotten or uninventoried storeroom more calvados waited concealing scents of kinder climes. Perhaps, once the flavour of French brandy had departed, his enthusiasm for Le Quatorze Juillet would also disappear. But, there was no denying that the café's position, roughly midway between his rented rooms and the language institute on as near a straight line as the orient can independently muster, had made it doubly appreciated. Would a new venue, once the last mystical drops were consumed, be worth the search's effort? Up to now only convenience and calvados had kept him loyal; and patronising Le Quartorze for anything other than its one declining virtue was not by any means a certainty.

Time passed and the sun inched slowly down from its white-hot zenith. Audible stirrings among the bundled bodies and baskets opposite nudged the street back towards activity. A dog, sagging in every part of its anatomy from hanging head to drooping tail, stood up beneath a café table and with a limp hind claw flicked dejectedly at the air beneath its protruding navel. Shuffling weakly forward the animal sniffed at Jacques' outstretched shoes until exhausted by the effort it lay down again to wait inertly for whatever chance and the passing hours would bring. A taxi, in search of a fare, crawled lumpily in and out of intermittent drains along the pavement's unswept edge. Returning, but still largely unobstructed traffic hooted ineffectively and the creaking taxi bumped laboriously from sight.

In the airless street a flurry of overloaded motorbikes, like greyhounds hot on the scent of a March hare, rushed in a knot from a nearby junction and passed on both sides of a bicycle weaving its solitary way to an unknown destination. The bike rider versed in the indisciplines of Saigon traffic wriggled forward and swerved as one motorbike piled high with bales looped across its path. Sliding unperturbed to the pavement the mounted woman slowed and stopped; one sandaled foot rested on the kerb and several books held on a carrier behind the saddle shifted forward. At the crossroads a falling leaf struck the ground with the deafening thump of drums and cymbals.

Jacques noticed first the sandal; the thinnest white leather straps on a soft platform that looked incapable of supporting more than a child's weight and inside a foot the colour of risen bread. Sensuality lay not in her foot's nakedness, but in an observer's unfettered imagination. The rider was no more than twenty-two and in spite of the precariously loaded and madly driven motorcycle's imposition, not in the least inconvenienced or outwardly flustered.

Jacques' empty glass stopped halfway in its descent. The waiter departed into the cool gloom of the inner café and no one else came or departed on the pavement. The mongrel bitch, as still as death in the merciful shadow beneath the peeling table, lay with legs cast in different directions as if loosely attached to a broken doll's torso.

On her handlebars the young woman set down a *non bai tho* hat and leant back to shake loose thick hair. For a moment Jacques was held suspended in the tumbling black waves. If he had closed his eyes now, every detail, from the tiny silver ring on a second toe, the pale yellow of the *ao dai* contrasting so strikingly with her jet hair, the aura of serenity, and the silk trousers gathered at her waist and ankle, would have stayed imprinted on his consciousness, ready to resurface in the sweat and turmoil of his rented bed.

Dropping his legs from where they rested he stood up and pushed back the chair. The noise of metal on concrete screeched like fingernails on glass and the bitch, as if bitten by a fly, lurched to her feet shaking mangy head and ears. With jaw hung low she cringed in anticipation of a beating and watched Jacques through eyes misted by age and the legacy of many litters. Satisfied no stick was raised and between pants that shook her entire frame she sank back to her resting place on the hot paving slabs.

Jacques could not explain why, but the young woman had about her a sort of glow, as if an inner light radiated through a filter of grace into the mean and filthy street. He didn't turn to see whether others had noticed, so fully absorbed was he by the chance encounter. Not that they had really met. The rider was twenty metres away and he had not seen her face with any real clarity, or she his. Her profile from a little to the rear, however, trapped him as if he were a butterfly lured to death by the colours of a scentless orchid.

A warning gust of wind preceding an imminent downpour swept along the boulevard and pieces of paper and plastic carried up into the air before dropping back into swirling grime. From her red-rimed eyes the bitch looked at the flying debris and yawned. A torn sheet of newspaper slapped against Jacques' trouser leg.

Making up his mind to do something, although he was not sure what, he began walking to the kerb. Behind, Ly Cam, worried his bill was being avoided, thrust his head and neck out from behind the glass door.

Oblivious to the activity she had prompted, the young woman returned the *non bai tho* to her head and pushed away into the roars of returning traffic. For a while Jacques watched her hat weave and bob slowly further and further away until lost in the growing rush of motorcycles and delivery vans.

Emerging from his sanctuary in the café's interior and in growing distrust of his solitary customer Ly Cam noisily cleared the table of its dish and glass. With his thoughts riding off into the distance Jacques put a hand in his pocket and, without precisely counting, rattled several coins into the waiting saucer. Ly Cam looked at the coins and then at Jacques as if to encourage further thought. Among poor people, service, however shoddily delivered, and mercy are inextricably intertwined in a way that destroys the charade of fixed pricing.

Jacques Decamps didn't sleep well that night. The sultry weather and flashes of far-off lightening on the white fly-spotted ceiling disturbed him more than he could remember. He had an odd feeling of being caught frozen in a leap across a chasm. The woman on the bicycle had rattled him. He tried hard to picture her, or rather the half side-view he had seen, but now, inexplicably, the details would not come. In an intellectual way all the features were still there, dainty sandal, colour of her hands and feet, hat, panelled *ao dai* tied in an unbelievably narrow circumference at her waist, silver ring and circle of light surrounding her like a halo, yet he just couldn't conjure up a mental picture and the harder he tried the further it moved away.

If he couldn't bring her back in his mind's eye, he decided to find another way.

Who was she? What was she doing riding the streets at that stifling hour? Perhaps she was a student; the books on the carrier over the rear wheel of her bicycle suggested as much. But her age put her on the outward margin of formal study. More likely she was a teacher, a new one fresh from university graduation, yes, that was it, and surely the fact that she followed the same route fifteen or so minutes after the gaggle of boys and girls in their white school-clothes was all the proof he needed. Jacques found relief in answering his own questions. But not until next morning did the pieces really begin to fit together.

If she were indeed a teacher, then regular hours must follow and a fixed timetable would enable him to intercept her passage. He couldn't exactly remember the time he'd left Le Quatorze, but it must have been somewhere between four and four thirty. His regular routine would need no adjustment to place him in the same spot the following day, but others priorities were beyond his control.

His last lesson ended at three and as the class of businessmen and postgraduates dispersed he hastened to overtake them on the road. On rare afternoons he stayed for an hour or two to mark exercise texts, but today, not wishing to delay, he threw what had accumulated into a leather satchel to work on over a late meal. As he snapped the locks shut, Duc To, the administrative head of the institute, came to discuss an issue, which in Jacques' present condition, was not of remotest interest.

A gnarled, but erudite little man, Duc To was only just on the youthful side of ninety, such were the virtues of a vegetable diet and no official retirement age. He had received a doctorate from the Sorbonne in days long before twentieth century conflicts convulsed Vietnam, and like all old men, had forgotten people younger than he were inclined to be in a hurry, especially when afflicted by affairs of the heart. But at his great age he could afford and, perhaps by his estimation, was entitled, to move at a more deliberate speed.

"Ah! Decamps. I was hoping to find you," he piped in a reedy falsetto.

"Oh! Doctor Duc, I was just leaving."

Ignoring the hint that the conversation could be postponed Duc To continued as if eulogising his profession, "Teaching a language, would you not say, is incomplete when it resides, as it is apt to reside with us, within the confines of vocabulary and rules of structure. My thoughts increasingly turn to matters that make language, all languages, whole and living. We are in an age of technology when machines translate words, but no machine in my considered opinion will ever do the job effectively, or for more than the briefest periods of time."

Not wishing to appear rude, but fearing a unique opportunity slipping by, Jacques looked at his watch; three-thirty already. At this time he was usually well down his first calvados and on a second cigarette. The earnest doctor, despite his age, however, had all the time the world had to offer.

"And," he continued, "we must take notice and respond to the layers of subtlety that build and erode from one generation to the next. I don't suppose, for example, the French you speak is very like that of your grandfather? Hmm? Would I be correct?"

With growing irritation at what appeared to be a developing monologue, Jacques said rather impatiently, "Look Monsieur Le Docteur, this is an engrossing subject, but I have an appointment. Would you care if we resume tomorrow?"

From behind wire-rimmed spectacles, Duc To viewed him suspiciously as if somehow the great obligations and traditions of teaching's high calling were being betrayed.

"We can if you wish," he said in a begrudging and disappointed treble. "But there is one thought I want to leave with you and to which we can return another time. My question goes right to the heart of the concept – is language a simple tool with which we speak and write and imitate the grunts and squeaks of forest animals, or is it a mirror on a culture's moving soul, reflecting its way of thinking, its values, its currency? In other words can I ever understand, really understand the French of France or you, even if you stay a hundred years ever understand, in the deepest sense, the Vietnamese of Vietnam?"

Scarcely hearing the last sentence Jacques flew through the institute's open door and, with satchel bouncing on his hip, heaved into a jog. Unwilling to let him go so peremptorily, Duc To's shrill almost infantile tones carried into the street.

"I will look for you directly after...." but the rest was drowned in the hum and clatter of passing traffic.

At a gentle walk Le Quatorze was twenty minutes away, but at this accelerated speed the corner of Cathedral Square and the red brick of the old church came into view in just half the time. Breathing deeply and soaked from head to foot in sweat, Jacques dumped the bag of exercise books onto a metal chair and took several strides towards the busy street. In the hubbub and churning traffic he could see fading from sight a conical sun hat in a swaying movement as if worn by someone on a carefully ridden bicycle. Only the hat was visible, but he knew without question it belonged to the woman who paused yesterday at the pavement's edge.

The blended, but separate paths of Saigon and Ho Chi Minh City going about their overlapping lives had, for the space of a single moment, lost their power to dismay. Jacques snatched up his satchel and turned in the direction of his rented rooms. With a gaze as expressionless as a Mekong River crocodile, Ly Cam peered out from behind the darkened glass of the café door and waited for another customer.

The next day and the next Jacques waited eagerly to catch a glimpse of the woman in the yellow silk *ao dai*, but on both days he was disappointed. If he had seen her ride by he was unsure what he would have done. Accosting a woman on the streets even in Saigon took some nerve and, in the probability of being taken for one of those sleazy foreigners he so much derided, he needed a better way. A good woman is, after all, a good woman anywhere.

He devised a strategy; he'd look up the schools in the immediate neighbourhood, yes, yes, yes, track back along the direction from where she came and engage her at her place of work on some easily contrived pretext.

The dusty reference books at the language institute's library provided an early answer. In the couple of miles or so to the east of Le Quatorze there were only two possibilities, the 'Great Patriotic War Memorial School' for the children of government officials and 'Giap's Vocational College.' Straining to imagine the entrancing young cyclist as a lecturer in plumbing or electrical installation Jacques decided the high-sounding memorial school was his target. Once the idea took shape and despite the further tedious attention of Duc To troubling him on less than immediate matters, Jacques impatiently set about his task.

On the fourth day, with jacket over an arm and leather satchel in one hand he was out of his classroom in a rush and pushing through departing students as they made for the outer door. In the corridor the frail Duc To stood aside from the babbling surge and clutched at his spectacles. Standing at least a head taller than those around, Jacques had the appearance of a craft caught on a current.

On the fringes of the flood the thin voice of the institute's chief administrator whistled above the drone of conversation, "We must continue our exploration, Decamps, at a more convenient time. I was considering, perhaps a symposium, to which we would invite..." The words grew fainter in the distance and chatter and Jacques did not learn quite what Le Docteur intended, or who was to be invited and besides, his thoughts were already knocking at the entrance of a different educational establishment.

Past the sky's summit the hot sun, now fitfully obscured by clouds, began its long slow descent towards the horizon and night. For respite from the intermittent but still scorching rays, Jacques walked on the south side of the narrow, colonial boulevard in the space between high brick walls and the ever-present plain trees. Lulled by the after midday interlude, only he and a few compelled by necessity inhabited the streets.

After the best part of a soporific hour, fitful thrust and bustle jerked back into the streets and Saigon began to resume its frenetic and obscure business in exactly the place it had left off. Along the road collections of motorcycles began to spurt in all directions as if collectively and loudly spat from the ends of undirected garden hoses.

At the next junction the brick wall against which Jacques had been walking acquired a cement facing grown brown and crumbly with age. Green, blue and white bottle pieces on the upper surface flashed in the sun as if containment of what lay beyond was the primary preoccupation of those in positions of responsibility. From behind the wall the sound of children released from class welled up like the gabber of geese returning at dusk from country fields.

At a wide gate Jacques discovered a sleepy watchman in a wooden box-like office on wheels, lines of cycle racks against an inner wall and a large unintelligible black and white sign, which surely announced the premises were those of the "Great Patriotic War Memorial School". This then was it.

Knowing enough about human behaviour to understand confidence and luck play a bigger role in life than intelligence and hard work, Jacques threw his shoulders back past where they were accustomed to hang and strode though the gate without looking to either left or right. The watchman raised his chin but not his arms from the sill of the glassless window and, without intervening or questioning, observed the visitor's passage.

Through the gate a rambling collection of French-styled buildings occupied the centre of overgrown and poorly maintained grounds. The various constructions were of the same colour as the outer wall, but partially relieved of their unfashionable history by thickly leaved creepers hanging from the roof tops. Trees overarched domed copulas and ornate but broken tiling added to the impression the entire school was a ruin open to the sky, rather than an occupied and functioning place of learning.

Positioned under a rubber tree's trailing roots and shadows, Jacques hid from sight. The twitter of girls and the rougher laughter of boys mixed in a buzz of sound as scores of teenage children poured through the doors of the memorial school and spread like white foam across the grounds. Held only momentarily by animated conversation, they broke and ran towards homes and parents. Save for the presence of a few late drifters, the watchman and the observer under his rubber tree, the garden sank back into empty and shabby tranquillity.

Patterns of light and shade moved across Jacques' face. The watchman withdrew inside his wooden box and the last few students left the bicycle racks for the now booming traffic criss-crossing outside the gates. Minutes passed and far away a clock struck four.

A group of two men and a woman paused on the building's top step. The men were much frailer than the woman and both carried Duc To's advanced years and similarly thin grey hair combed firmly into a place where a little went a long way. The discussion, unlike that in the corridor of the language institute, appeared mutually absorbing. All held books tightly against their chests as if by this gesture they would increase their ability to absorb and retain fleeting knowledge.

Although her back was turned Jacques knew instantly this was the woman he sought. But what now? Should he barge into the conversation, pretending he was seeking direction, or making enquiries of the lessons? In the second he wavered, the group separated. The men with several formal bows and steps backward moved towards the gate and the woman, clothed in the same yellow-tinged *ao dai* as before, walked over the worn grass to the bicycle shed.

Jacques sucked in the warm air beneath the rubber tree and stepped out of the shadows. Under his breath and as if to provide encouragement, he said to himself, "Tout alors." The woman bent to release a rear wheel padlock and showed exactly the same profile as that captivatingly displayed outside Le Quatorze Juillet just four days ago; the same delicate golden hands, the same cascading jet-black hair, the same slender neck and the same ringed foot.

"Pardonez moi, mai…" his unprepared and foreign speech trailed off as he looked into her face and deep, deep eyes. The natural grace and elegance were just as he had at first witnessed from under the faded umbrella. This then was the time he expected to be engulfed; to fall without a remorseful thought like an opium smoker into scented intoxication.

But he stopped short. Instead of finding liberation he was feeling inexplicably bound. At Le Quatorze discovery and promise had filled him with elation, but now it was passing without a backward glance on the other side of the street. If eyes are the passageway to the soul then those in front of him opened the way to an unfathomable well; into underground regions of echoes and sighs, where none he knew had ever trod in all the length of time. He was looking back thousands of years to where he had no knowledge, no sympathy and no comprehension. This time he was without doubt an alien, with all the totality the word conveyed. Her dazzling beauty had for the space of a few days blinded him to reason and now he realised there was no mountain and no cave either for that matter, where they could meet. Old Duc To had begun to understand, but at close to ninety he could with satisfaction feel one truth was at last uncovered. If

Jacques remained in Saigon for a lifetime he would not find, could not find the reality of a truly shared spirit. There was no point in waiting any longer; enlightenment would not come.

"Mademoiselle, je ne…" the beginnings of another foreign and by definition meaningless nicety froze on the tip of his tongue like an icicle in Siberia's winter. Why go on?

Jacques turned away across the patchy lawn to the gate. Unsmiling and incurious the woman's eyes followed. She watched him go as if he were a street water-carrier.

In the boulevard the overhead leaves of the plain trees rattled in a dry wind. With face down against flying dust he turned back towards Cathedral Square. Passing Le Quatorze he stopped to request one last drink. Ly Cam shrugged his shoulders as if to say there was none left. Large raindrops, leaving marks on the hot pavement as big as old franc coins, began to fall, slowly at first and then faster and faster until watery mist as high as a man's thighs covered the entire street. Jacques picked up his satchel and emptied the contents onto a metal table. With jacket held in his fist he walked out into the torrential downpour.

As the sodden figure squelched out of Cathedral Square Ly Cam brushed up the wet exercise books with ink running over their limp surfaces and dumped them in the streaming litter-choked gutter.

THIRTEEN

THE DINNER PARTY

"Tina, be a dear and move the flowers onto the piano, they'll look better there…no, over a bit more behind the photographs. Be careful of the water. That's it…and before anyone arrives open the wine…it'll need to breathe."

From first days in Asia over twenty-five years ago Tina had tirelessly served the Hudson household as cook, child-minder and housekeeper. If not so evidently foreign, visitors might have supposed she was part of the family, a distant provincial relative perhaps, who in return for her keep performed minor chores around the house. But, contrary to casual observations, Tina's labours were as integral to the family's well-being as Edward Hudson's pursuit of his business.

Paradoxically, Tina moved on the margins of domesticity. Her lot was to work, not to participate. The demands on her were for diligence and duty, which, because of her conditioning, were everything she gave. Without her vast unquestioning acquiescence she would have remained where she first began, scraping a humble existence in an impoverished, but gentle, tropical village where people accepted who and what they were.

With no help, apart from minor interventions relating to cost and discipline, and while the Hudson parents concentrated on financial success and social presence she brought up three children. But that was a long time ago and since then the twins had gone on to university and Emma to a career and home back in Asia.

Now, with only Edna Hudson and her husband, the big house and occasional guests to care for, the tempo of life, if not its regularity, had changed and she had time to remind herself that someday she'd stop work altogether and return to her own children and the several – she could not exactly remember how many – growing grand-children to whom she had long been a stranger.

Tina passed a soft, yellow duster over the grand piano's gleaming surface and made inconsequential adjustments to the photographs from which her own likeness was noticeably missing. Beneath today's and every other day's careful hand the shining piano lid stayed open, and the keys and pages of sheet music were readied for players who never came.

She recalled the twice-weekly lessons provided years ago by Mrs Chu, but didn't pause, either then or now, to wonder whether the endless repetition of scales was of any lasting value. She accepted this was the sort of thing children of well-to-do families did and never troubled her head with questions of why. Going to mass was the same. There was nothing to be gained by looking for reasons; it was done and always had been and that was enough.

To be reassured the settings were as she wished Edna circled the table one last time before lying back on the settee; a full summer bee resting on the petals of an open flower.

"Bring me a Campari, there's a good girl," she called, without pausing to consider the incongruity of addressing a woman in her late-fifties in such a way. In spite of living under a shared roof for over a generation, Edna and Tina were of two different worlds that met in distinct although complimentary dependencies, where condescension came as natural to one as consent to the other.

Edna held up her glass to the sparkling chandelier and delighted in the rich liquid's warm, red glow. Dinner parties were her especial joy, even when conversation went a little over her head. But her intellectual limitation was a minor matter when clever people were at her table.

Tonight's small gathering would include, in addition to the Hudsons, Roderick and Alice McPherson, Crispin Cartwright, the Catholic priest from Saint Anne's in the village and Marjorie Phelps, a bright, incisive woman who made a living doing something called online marketing from her spare bedroom. On the surface the mix was nicely balanced, even though the inclusion of Crispin had been forced by an annoyingly late apology from one of Edward's more recent business contacts.

With the exception of spaces at her table, Edna's greatest concern was how communicative her guests were likely to be and substituting names at the eleventh hour unsettled her calculations, except, that is, when a garrulous minister of the church with the ability to talk expansively on any subject was on convenient call. Although she would not have admitted as much, a steady conversational buzz and social agreeability sometimes enabled her incomplete grasp of the topics of discussion to pass unnoticed.

After a second glass of wine and under the steadying eye of his wife, Roderick McPherson was also known to enliven conversation. But instead of the florid elaborations of a worldly Catholic priest, he contented himself with plain Presbyterian views that lost none of their severity for being roundly uttered.

Only Ms Phelps, invited on the basis of reputation and neighbourhood proximity, remained of unconfirmed quality. To assess the suitability of this choice Edna had called on her network, with its history of conservative reliability, before hoping her uncharacteristically hands-off selection would not live to be regretted.

Marjorie's total knowledge of the Hudsons was based on an encounter with Edward at a gathering of local business people and when tonight's invitation arrived in her letter box on customised stationery, she assumed he was indirectly exploring the extent and worth of her marketing services.

Being a woman with different priorities, Marjorie was not familiar with the ways of a calculating and conspicuous hostess and, if she had wondered why some people were asked to dinner and others not, she would have assumed it had something to do with common interests, or familiarity, rather than conformity to a particular profile. Had she been in the least bit self-conscious, her inclusion, smelling as it did of the mid-nineteenth century, would have filled her with suspicion.

Edward had undertaken to be home an hour before the guests were due to arrive, but, being notoriously preoccupied, social punctuality and unproductive pleasure often took second place. Nothing, save the return of the flood, would delay a call on a sales prospect, or impede his unending search for twenty percent annual growth, which, in truth, was all that kept him from retirement and an early death.

Wine glasses on the long rosewood table threw back the chandelier's and log fire's light in a twinkling variety of rainbow colours. Edna allowed herself a satisfied smile. She had a right to be proud. Unlike Edward's marriage to his work, her contentment rested on public approval. His presence, to give a sense of completeness, was preferred, but not, in the final analysis, critical except in so far as he provided some entertainment for her guests. Years ago they had discovered gods of different persuasions; his obliged him to amass, while hers compelled display.

A doorbell chimed and the soft pad of Tina's house shoes preceded murmuring and noisy laughter in the passageway. Crispin Cartwright bustled in.

"Delighted to see you again Edna my dear," he said grasping a limply offered hand. "Good lord, I always seem to be the first to arrive. People will think I never stock any food in anticipation of one of your invitations."

"What an uncharitable thought," beamed the hostess. "You know we appreciate timely arrival. Unfortunately, Edward is again being Edward and has yet to return, so there is time for a little chat while we wait. What then is the news from the cloisters of St Anne's?"

"I wish we could boast of cloisters, but they don't appear often in the 1950's architecture of our noble institution. But…what with…"

"Let me get you something before we become too comfortable. Tina! What will it be?"

"We of the cloth are hard to separate from red wine, so something along those lines would be most welcome and warming too on a night like this."

While Tina waited behind the long settee for more precise instruction, a second ring echoed in the stillness beyond the living room. As she turned to go, Crispin, being the evening's first arrival and having the familiarity of a frequent guest, spread his wide frame and legs in front of the fire.

"Well, a brave evening to you, Edna," boomed Roderick as he bustled into the room and promptly engaged the priest with a hearty, "Hello Crispin; good to see a representative of the apostolic Church standing between poor sinners and the flames."

"Oh, Roderick, already joking before having a glass in hand. But how are you?" Edna smiled at Alice McPherson and in a half embrace mouthed a kiss at the empty air on both sides of the proffered head.

"Do sit down everyone, we all look as if we're waiting for a Calcutta bus."

"And why Calcutta in particular and not Inverness, or Ashby-de-la-Zouch?" Roderick, in addition to his antipathy for Catholicism, hated silly remarks whatever their source. "Because in Ashby, and most places in this country, one boards a bus from a line. In Calcutta people wait, scattered about on the pavement, or in shop doorways. Do you see, we are all over the carpet?"

Being brashly confident, Edna never hesitated to stamp her personality on a conversation. But because many of her utterances appeared slightly dim-witted, listeners were sometimes puzzled how best to respond. In light company and on the right occasion, she could be amusing, but in weightier gatherings, her grip noticeably weakened. Crispin, as a result of the tolerance imposed by his calling, gave her as much room as she wanted. But Roderick and Alice, brought up in the uncompromising world of Scottish Presbyterianism were inclined to call a spade by its proper name.

The last guest to arrive was Marjorie Phelps, who brought with her a bottle of wine wrapped in the logoed paper of a supermarket store where, not thirty minutes earlier, she had purchased her weekend groceries and chosen the bottle bearing a stock label and price upon its neck.

Paying your way was one of those lower middle-class customs Edna had encountered too often in recent years, and it was not one with which she shared affinity. There may be places, she sniffed, where egalitarianism was essential, but in her house an off-the-shelf gift as a prelude to dinner was not a requirement.

"How nice," she said, passing the package without examination to Tina and implying by her gesture that the contents were more suited to coq-au-vin than the fine glassware already shining on the table. "Do please come and meet everyone."

Alice, unlike Edna, made no pretence of contributing valuable insight to a conversation. In any company she contented herself with crisp observations of any issue and of friends and newcomers alike. She examined and pigeon-holed Marjorie in the flash of their greeting and laid away an opinion in the great unread archive of her private thoughts.

Alice had known Edna for many years, including the long period during Roderick's retirement to the old country and while the Hudsons remained in Asia. Now, although the McPhersons insisted on giving half their year to yet older ties in Edinburgh, the families were intermittently united and evenings such as these were the fabric of a relationship that was more marked by longevity than empathy.

Ungenerous pale-blue eyes, which, during the pursuit of his future wife, Roderick had once found so disconcerting, flickered in a raw sparkle behind Alice's glasses and fell on the silver cutlery she and Edna had purchased together many years before.

When she discovered that the tableware was not intended for the Hudson household, but a government minister wavering in his support for a contentious civil-engineering project, she became greatly offended that her minimal assistance had been used to further an immoral objective. When the deal and the minister, whose replacement had altogether different tastes in home décor, fell from favour, her satisfaction was enormous. Now, as her bird-like gaze was reminded of the dinner service's history, she rejoiced that the good Lord did indeed have mysterious ways of negating sin.

Alice's searching appraisal moved across the table to the untuned piano that had not played a single note since Emma's departure, and this, because it was pretence, also failed her test of probity so that she, full of righteousness, could sit a little more stiffly in her high-backed chair.

Everyone the McPhersons encountered was assessed for sufficiency and those who fell below their standard were condemned, either by his scorn, or her unforgiving judgement made on behalf of the Almighty's chastising angels. Together they were a fearsome couple, and so unlike their hosts that others of their circle wondered how the relationship had begun and outlasted so many others.

Without being called, Tina appeared periodically to reinvigorate the glimmer in warming drinks. For her pains she was thanked by Marjorie and Father Cartwright and ignored by the rest.

"This really is too annoying. I hope Edward has good reason for his delay!" Edna's voice had an edge of irritation.

"Whether the reason is good or bad won't matter greatly, or affect our pleasure at seeing him when he does arrive," observed Roderick in a manner brooking no discussion.

"The business world is rife with urgency," suggested Marjorie.

In a far-off corner of the house a grandfather clock intoned eight thirty. A third round of drinks failed to revive the flagging party and the hostess, fretting visibly at her unravelling plan, excused herself and slipped away to her upstairs bedroom.

Crispin's wide-ranging chatter and small ripples of humour were left to hold everyone's interest, but they too began ebbing away on a river estuary's falling tide.

"No doubt we'll hear a very plausible explanation when he does return," Alice, gargoyle-stiff and unblinking, offered in anticipation of another barely credible excuse.

Edna called Edward's mobile telephone, but there was no reply. After three rings of his office number she was informed the business was closed for the day, but that, in the interim, she should endeavour to "have a nice day!" What a stupid, insulting suggestion! Did anyone accept recorded insincerity at more than face value? God! How she hated the sheer banality of Edward's working world. There was no class, no style, no poise and no grace, only trans-Atlantic platitude.

"Edward is simply nowhere to be found," she announced to her guests moments later, "And, as there is no answer from his office, I'd like to think he is on the way home and if that is correct, twenty minutes will see him here. Let us assume the best and make our way to the dinner table." Edna looked at her watch and smiled tautly round the circle of faces. Crispin was the first to rise to his feet, with Roderick close behind.

"Well, I'm ready, if everyone else is."

"We don't doubt the true Church will always lead the way," responded the Scot.

"Crispin," Edna said, standing at one end of the table, "please sit next to me…Roderick on my other side. The two ladies next to them and Alice, you must give up your husband to Marjorie tonight, so the opposite side if you will." Edna, in spite of her smouldering displeasure, was still capable of another wintery smile made possible by her attempted witticism and not because she had confidence in the outcome of her dinner party. At the opposite end of the long table, the place closest to the door was left conveniently vacant.

Dishes came, plates were filled, glasses emptied and between the rise and fall of renewed conversation Tina's meal was consumed. Over her plate Alice watched the diners and cut her meat with the surgical precision of a vivisectionist exploring a sedated cat's intestines. To her fastidious mind the enjoyment of food approached an act of indecency. As if afraid to be caught in indulgence, she inserted into her mouth the tiniest morsels from the very tip of her fork and behind a napkin held to her lips masticated invisibly.

Crispin, however, ate with gusto and mashed his potatoes and greens into a sea of thick brown gravy like a teenager caught in a growth spurt. As his hunger pains retreated, eloquence and inclination to express his many opinions recovered and he swung his eating utensils about in mid-air.

In all the parish's social circles the priest was accepted as a bit of a character and given a degree of licence denied others. But, in this company, the unattached Marjorie, however, was not given the same liberty and her heavy elbow on the rosewood tabletop and a fork used shovel-fashion suggested to Edna her informants had lacked their customary insight.

"And the last but one course will be fruit, or flan, or both if you wish." The hostess was making the best show a flawed evening deserved and her smile passed across the table like an All Souls Eve ghost.

"I'll miss, thanks," declared Marjorie, confirming the now firmly established view that this was a modern woman who did not conform to the right behavioural models."

"No meal is complete without pudding. I'll have the flan...urpf!... if I may," stated Crispin in emphatic tones. His tiny belch went unnoticed, except that the downward curves of Alice's mouth hinting her ears were sharp enough to detect the smallest breaches of etiquette. "Really most unfortunate Edward missed the whole fantastic spread. Should we not congratulate Tina on another splendid accomplishment?"

"At an appropriate moment, why yes, we shall."

At eleven o'clock the women were once again seated by the fire, while the two men remained at the dinner table drinking a final brandy and fencing over opposing church doctrine.

As Roderick's last warming drops were savoured, Alice shifted about on her chair and gave him a look he was expected to read. Through the rim of his glass her raised eyebrows caught him in mid-sentence and, like a field commander peering at the slope of unfavourable ground, he manoeuvred towards withdrawal.

"Well, I think…" he began, before being cut short by a doorbell chime. "Aha! Our much delayed host will at least have the opportunity to wish us all a fond, and well fed, good night."

"I doubt that, unless he has lost his door key as well as a total appreciation of time." Edna's voice hit a shriller pitch.

The lengthy conversation in the hallway was impeding departure and Roderick and Crispin sank back onto their chairs. Marjorie, unaware even farewells have protocol, stood up. In the middle of the uncertainty cold drafts of air wafted in through the door and everyone turned to the fire wondering who would make calls so late.

Outside the dining room the conversation suddenly stopped and a man of about forty erupted in, followed by a profusely apologetic Tina.

"I told him you were entertaining M'am and that I'd have to ask before…but he…"

The new arrival, who carried a stained rain-coat and wore a creased suit too short for his long limbs, looked as if he would be more comfortable patronising a dog-track rather than the lounges of outer suburbia. Alice scanned the visitor and determined in an instant he was a policeman. He, however, following a different process of deduction turned to Edna as the person he had come to see.

"Mrs Hudson? I'm from the CID. I'd like to talk to you please."

"Oh! Why? What about?"

"Not in public, if you don't mind. Have you got somewhere…?"

"What! Oh dear! This sounds dreadful. Is it about one of the boys?" And, without possibly knowing, said to her startled visitors, "This will only take a few minutes. Please wait."

"Do you want me to come?" asked Crispin, who decided his professional skill suited the turn of events.

"Not necessary at this stage," replied the policeman.

"Oh…I see," said Crispin, subsiding again, like a reprimanded schoolboy.

Edna led the visitor back along the hall to a room described inaccurately as Edward's study. Inside, the piled desk, heaped files and laptop computer confirmed that its occupant, when at home, was rarely idle, and also that, because of his reliance on instincts for inspiration and success, the desire or need to study in a conventional sense had never arisen.

"Inspector Foot, Mrs Hudson," the visitor said, picking up the one item in the room that had nothing to do with business. "Is this a picture of you and your husband?"

"Why…yes, but…what has happened? Don't tell me one of them is involved in drugs. I think I'd rather die than have my friends hear that."

"Drugs? Who? Oh, no, it isn't anything like that. We believe Edward Hudson has been abducted." He made the statement as if reading from an official crime sheet at a press conference; "Edward Hudson, a suspected kidnap victim went missing on the night of the tenth, sometime between 7 and 11pm. Further details will be given as our enquiries progress."

"Aah! Oh my God!" Edna sank to her knees, her mouth open as if suddenly deprived of air.

Inspector Foot stepped over the stricken form and summoned Tina from the passage-way. While waiting, he took the photograph from its frame and slipped it into his rain-coat pocket.

"Put her there," he said, indicating to the fluttering Tina her incapacitated mistress and a worn armchair."

The cramped study had only two places to sit. One was the soft pile containing the overwhelmed hostess and the other a revolving pedestal chair at the desk where Edward converted his thoughts into strategies. Inspector Foot decided to sit astride the pedestal and conduct his investigation with his arms and chin on the back rest. He observed Edna's paleness behind her thick makeup and the way she held tightly to Tina's motherly arm and wondered what sort of relationships existed under this roof.

"Have you received any calls tonight, any contacts from anywhere?"

"I, I… what am I to think?"

"Get her a glass of water."

Tina turned to leave, but Edna clung to her with both hands."

"No, don't go."

"Then I need you to answer some questions."

"Yes... yes...whatever you wish," Edna replied, recovering some measure of composure.

"Who are your visitors and how long have they been here? Has anyone other than these people spoken to you tonight?"

"Well...let me see...Crispin was the first, he must have arrived before seven and the others – that's the McPhersons and Majorie Phelps, I don't know her well – came soon after. I've been hoping for a call from Edward to tell us when he would be home, but I've not heard anything from him at all."

"I see. Anyone else?"

"No, I don't believe so... Has there...?" She looked at Tina.

"No, no-one, Ma'am."

"Ahuh, okay." I have to tell you a police patrol found Mr Hudson's car in a ditch out on the Darnford Road. There were scuffmarks and torn upholstery inside and a note on the passenger seat."

Edna almost shrieked, "What did it say?"

"We are expecting you to hear from the abductors. If you've no objection I'll stay around for a while."

"But what about my guests? What shall I tell them?"

Indifferent to the dinner party, the Inspector raised his shoulders. "I'll take their names and a few details and then you can send them home."

He looked round the study and threw his coat over the desk.

"Okay for me to work in here? If there's a phone call I'll prefer you to take it, okay?"

Suddenly Edna couldn't tolerate the presence of the policemen, or the smells of public places hanging about him. Her breathing was being constricted again and she wanted to fling open every window and let in the chill autumn air.

"I'm so sorry," she announced to the dumbfounded gathering as she tottered back into the dining area, "this is simply awful, but Edward seems to have been...kidnapped.... I'm afraid I'll have to ask you to leave immediately after the Inspector has spoken to you."

The four faces stared at her boggle-eyed and then began talking simultaneously.

"What on earth is...?"

"My dear, if I may counsel."

"I'll stay with you. I think another woman in the house would be comforting."

From back along the hallway a steadier voice called, "Who's first?"

"Thank you Alice, but I have Tina."

"Yes, I know, and she will make sure you have everything you need, but someone to talk to will also be important; someone who knows you. I'll just wait here on the settee until you're ready."

Sleep didn't come easily to anyone in the house that night. After the guests were questioned, Inspector Foot closed the study door and could be heard moving about inside. Several times he made a phone-call and spoke to others working on the case. Tina brought coffee and blankets to Alice on the settee and, at Foot's curt request, thick, milky tea to the study.

Edna went to her room, where she had slept separately from Edward for the last fifteen years and all but forgotten the joy and intimacy of a shared bed.

Above her Alice heard the once self-assured hostess pacing round in endless circles. At two o'clock Edna reappeared unannounced, her hair was damp from a recent shower and her makeup wiped away. There were several creases beneath her eyes, of the sort that follow a long illness. She sat down heavily on the sofa and, with a sigh, pulled her dressing gown tightly around her. Her customary pretentiousness and conceit had disappeared.

"Why do we ever get married?" Edna asked, without raising her gaze from the thickly piled rug.

Alice set aside the magazine she had been reading and, as if delivering a lesson from the front of class, said, "Because it is a natural state made holy by the great book."

"Were you ever in love with Roderick?"

"What a strange question! Of course I was; we've always got on extremely well together."

"Lifelong love is really a mirage. It doesn't last you know, even if it was there at the beginning. Was he in love with you?"

"Life isn't a fairy tale, but, yes, I suppose he was. He certainly said so many times and I took him at his word."

"Maybe saying it is enough…but…I've just realized I don't love Edward and I'm not sure I ever did."

"Oh, I'm sure that's not true; you would have, in your own way. But his disappearance has come as such a dreadful shock, none of us know what to think."

"Our lives were intertwined with many things overlapping. The best way to describe us is to say we compared to a motorcar engine. All the parts work together, but were independent and could have been replaced if necessary. You must understand what I mean? He had his work and I my circle of friends where we didn't get in each other's way. But if truth were told there wasn't any serious affection between us; he didn't want me in any romantic sense or I him, but what there was kept a kind of complementary functioning. In years gone by we did spend a lot of time with each other, but then that passed and we lived alongside not as one. I can't remember when we last kissed, or had intercourse and actually the thought of doing so again rather repels me."

"Don't go back to your room just yet, stay down here with me. You won't have had a wink of sleep and my company may do you good."

"Is there a possibility some people formalise their lack of affection with marriage, while others with a towering passion, and for reasons only they understand, never get around to making the same step?"

Somewhere above the dining-room a telephone rang. Alice looked up at the chandelier, but Edna, other than to straighten a fold in her dressing gown, stayed perfectly still. The study door along the corridor burst open and Foot, without jacket or tie, spoke decisively.

"Mrs Hudson, this may be what we are waiting for. I want you to take the call from the office extension. Listen carefully and take as long as you like to answer. We will be working on a trace. If you are asked to take down any details there is a notepad and pencil next to the receiver. Do you understand me?"

Edna looked up wearily and tugged at the cord around her waist.

"Yes... I suppose so," and turning to Alice said, "Please come with me." Alice looked at Inspector Foot.

"Okay, if it will help."

Edna sat on the office chair, but pushed away from the policeman's grubby rain-coat. Foot, committed to observing and deducing, stared into the sunken eyes, while Alice placed her hands on her friend's sloping shoulders. The phone was on its eighth or ninth ring before being taken up.

"Hello…yes…oh…I see…but how will I know," she said and then impassively lowered the receiver onto its rest.

"Damn! Damn! Damn! Well, what did he say?" In the absence of the quick-fire response he wanted, Foot sought to draw answers from her, through sheer force of will.

But in her own time Edna replied with a voice shorn of all its usual superficiality, "It wasn't a he, it was a woman. She asked if I was Mrs Hudson and when I said yes, she replied Edward was being held for an exchange and that I'd hear what to do later."

"When?"

"I don't know. All she said was 'expect to hear.'"

"Anything you can tell me about the voice? Accent? Young, old?"

"A youngish person, maybe…from the South East?"

"Damn! Damn!" Foot was not hearing what he needed.

"Let her rest, or she'll be a wreck. Do you want to go to bed, my dear?"

"No, let's just sit up for a while longer."

Edna's thoughts drifted back to the time when she had met and married Edward. Initially, her parents had disapproved, but as they began to appreciate his qualities, their opinion mellowed. Without question he was a rough and occasionally uncouth character, but no-one doubted he had exceptional ability to provide for a family, not just on a comfortable, but on an almost lavish scale.

In the interval when a lot of men enjoyed university and wondered what to do with their lives, he established a business and made a great deal of money. Edna never denied either to herself or others, that his wealth had been a great attraction. While many of her contemporaries married for love and struggled though years of building a home, she fell into a lap of luxury with one servant and sometimes two, fine clothes and the things many young women only dreamt of acquiring. The burden of bringing up children was delegated and she socialised and shopped in the protective cocoon of a large monthly allowance. Her immediate well-being was not all that Edward considered as his responsibility and he took upon himself the task of securing her future, and that of her children when they came along, with endowments calculated to maintain comparable ease throughout the remainder of their lives.

At first his diligence flattered Edna, but later, she could not say exactly when, the feeling gradually overtook her that the entire family was being treated as yet one more business transaction, with risks assessed and margins, where necessary, squeezed, before being filed away in a corner cabinet for periodic review.

The affinity of Edward's style with Asia brought him opportunities straighter shooters lacked and while still in his twenties and in one of the world's most expensive cities, he bought a large apartment for cash and, as icing on that acquisition, added a smaller one for Edna to rent and to cover short-term investment interests.

But there was a price for so much financial gain. Jokes circulating round the coffee tables suggested Edward only made money for Edna to spend. She had a taste in heavy jewellery and tittle-tattlers, with so much obvious evidence, agreed a significant proportion of Edward's savings hung around her neck. Occasionally, she was aware of the disparaging comments, but as time passed her skin grew as thick as her snobbery and with a sweep of her arm she dismissed the slights as acts of envious people. Hadn't society always been thus, with the successful leaving others behind in an ever widening wake to complain and invent?

Edna got up from the settee and looked through a large bay window onto the lawns where leaves from the beech trees whirled about in clipped, cold darkness. Some way off she could see several lights on the quiet suburban road. Except for the leaves and an occasional branch across the face of a streetlight the neighbourhood was at rest. No fences separated the large houses and she inhaled breaths of wealth and position.

"I wonder if she will call back tonight."

"How did she sound?"

"Very strong, as if she knew exactly what she was doing. I admire self-possession."

"Was there any indication of what she wanted?"

"No, but it must be money. Isn't that all anyone wants?"

"Oh! Edna; there are a few things besides."

"Does anyone doubt that happiness, without the means to support it, is an illusion?"

"If only it were that simple."

"Will you be shocked to hear I married Edward for his money?"

"I don't believe that for a second. I'm sure you were very fond of him," replied Alice matter-of-factly without having the least appreciation, or experience of romantic love, or realising why the past tense had sprung to her lips as readily as Edna's. The only sensation she was remotely able to equate with love was the wholesome warmth suffusing her body when she knelt in prayer before her god and which had similarities to the sanctimonious tingle felt after her before-dawn shower. The hurricane desire for a man that could sweep through a woman's mind and body until she gasped was conceptually beyond her imagining."

The evening's unexpected developments had momentarily knocked a corner off Edna's pretentions, but had done nothing to shake Alice's certainties. Only one question puzzled her; why, she wondered, had it taken a personal crisis of this magnitude to produce so many explicit confidences? Perhaps, in all the years of their relationship, there had never been any event sufficiently intense to provoke such disclosure? And what if there had been? Would that signify any difference in the way the two women related to each other, or their partners?

Despite her mild protest, Alice accepted no real ardour held Edward and Edna together. But wasn't that the reality of wedlock? Weren't all marriages constructions to balance life and provide a platform to pursue greater purposes? The feelings behind Edna's confession were by their very admission unexceptional.

In Alice's view, her own marriage just like that of the Hudsons was as normal as anyone could reasonably expect. She shared a number of interests with Roderick, including the church and a set of simple Christian beliefs, which gave their partnership a sort of efficiency. But romanticism did not get in the way of, or complicate the good-order; and at the end of the road, when one predeceased the other, there would be some readjustment, but no paralysing grief. She could not visualise any loss so crippling that her life or Roderick's would be brought to the brink of incapability. Life would continue with some inconvenient ups and downs until the Creator in his wisdom decided the time had come for the other to follow. Everyone, even Tina, would be able to understand that plain and simple truth.

Before meeting Roderick, Alice had had no worldly experience to speak of. A number of men had made tentative advances, and one had actually gone so far as to use the word love in his letters to her before his enthusiasm ran into a cul-de-sac and he turned to ply his biology elsewhere. For her part Alice had no urge to forge any sort of bond with a man until Roderick came along. Only then did she discern the possibility for a kind of utilitarian joint enterprise.

Her hostess's head was faintly silhouetted in the window by the glow from street and distant residence lights. Alice did not wonder why at this late hour and for this old acquaintance, she had offered her presence. But she did accept a duty to wait, in the manner of a maiden aunt of an earlier generation at the bedside of a sick relative. The threads of her life lay in the severe and unreasoned belief that hands greater than hers drew the map of conduct even to the limit of pointless exhaustion and watching over a woman whose acts slammed on the door of just salvation.

Did Edna's conduct reveal any signs of moral weakness? What, Alice asked, was her true state of mind? Confusion and some distress were reasonable expectations, but although clearly shaken, there was no evidence, other than in the first few minutes of Foot's shocking disclosure, that she was inconsolable. As if weighing carefully all the consequences of the turbulent night, she stared into the deep-folded garden in a reverie of contemplation. Here, Edna seemed to be thinking, was a sudden change of course, a new direction with unanticipated, but not completely unimaginable possibilities.

The study door in the passage opened again and Foot appeared directly from another protracted telephone call.

"We have a team on this, Mrs Hudson. You probably don't appreciate what we are doing, but we've got forensics examining the car and the site and two constables in the grounds for security. Right now and in spite of all the work, we still don't have much to go on, so we come back again to making traceable contact with the people holding your husband. We've let the chance slip once, but it is an essential step to understanding who we are dealing with. I'm going to coach you on what..."

The inspector was interrupted by a distant tinkling of broken glass coming from somewhere above the dining-room.

"What the fu..." he exclaimed and, breaking from his pedestrian rationalising, spun back towards the passage and stairs. Muffled footfalls and bangs of several doors boomed through the ceiling causing the chandelier to jump and sway. An unintelligible instruction was shouted either through an open window, or into a mobile telephone. Tina, hurrying from the kitchen, collided with Foot descending the stairs in great animal bounds. As he crashed out into the garden searching for explanations, damp night and humiliation swept in.

The breaking glass on the upper floor brought Alice to her feet in alarm. But Edna, although looking up quickly, continued her thoughtful brooding.

"That must be the call the Inspector was anticipating," she said with a wry smile. "You would not describe it as a long-distance communication."

Was it possible, in the teeth of her husband's kidnapping, she remained capable of flippancy? Alice nodded to no-one in particular.

"Can you beat that?" said Foot bursting back into the dining-room. "Bastards! Bastards! And right under our noses."

"Please tell us what is going on," implored Alice, taking on the responsibility of ensuring everyone was fully informed.

Through his breathlessness the Inspector replied with commendable passion, "The contact we were expecting came through the window, for crying outloud, while my constables were walking round the house!"

"Ah! And does this…event help us in any way?" asked Edna.

"We've got a stone that looks as if it came from a border in your driveway and a note held onto it by elastic bands. Who knows when the stone was picked up? Could have been today, yesterday, but for sure it was chucked while my two men were watching out front and at the back."

"And the note," pressed Edna.

"Yes, well…I've had it collected and taken for testing. It just said "One million." Not hand-written mind, but letters cut from an old newspaper and pasted on a strip. Someone thinks he's in bleedin' films."

"She."

"Aih?"

"She; it was a woman who called, you remember?"

"Yes...yes, of course it was, but she won't be acting on her own. Bit of an odd way to get a negotiation going, this. They'll be wanting to keep us unsettled by doing the unexpected. That's what it is."

Without excusing himself Foot stumped back to the study and, before making another telephone call, closed the door in another substantial show of emotion.

The night wore on into the small hours of morning and in the half-light of five o'clock Crispin's second-hand Vauxhall drew into the gravel driveway. Alice, whose staring eyes had become even more prominent, went reluctantly home to bathe and change. Crispin sat next to Edna and held her warm hands.

In Alice's absence and on her behalf, they agreed she should move in while events remained confused. Crispin took upon himself the twin tasks of asking her to pack an overnight bag and to instruct Tina that two guests, if the Inspector was to be included, were in need of accommodation and meals for an uncertain period of time.

Autumn winds gusted round the garden and drove dead leaves into small piles in the house's lee. Inside, the mood hung oppressively and the various inmates fell back upon private thoughts.

A young constable joined Foot and manned the study's telephone, while his superior slept fully-clothed in the easy chair. Curious and sympathetic callers were told rather abruptly to ring off. The line, the junior policeman said, was to be kept open for important enquiries. Across the street a small knot of onlookers and local press people gathered by the neat, trimmed hedgerows.

Crispin Cartwright asked Edna if she would like to pray. She looked at the priest and smiled through her fatigue.

"Communicating with the good Lord only in an emergency sounds remarkably like offering business to an insurance agent wouldn't you say? And, besides, I'm long out of the habit."

"There is never a time when it is too late to seek His mercy."

"Crispin, my dear friend, I don't know how you maintain such confidence. You appreciate I'm not a Catholic or anything else that would get a hearing in your heaven, so please don't ask me to change my spots simply because something unpleasant has happened."

"There are more things wrought by prayer..." Crispin recalled an old line, but forgetting the complete quotation faded to an inconclusive stop.

"And if one is going to pray then at least there needs to be clarity in the request, rather than a general appeal for help."

"I suggest Edward's safe release and return would be a good place to start."

"Well, yes, I suppose that's where most people would begin."

The lack of enthusiasm for his solution saddened, but did not greatly offend Crispin. Excessive material well-being, he was sure, often came between people and the Church. In this smart corner of the country even true believers ran the risk of losing their bearings. Under such circumstances a priest had to be content with a counsellor's role, or, when things got really bad, a therapist's. Ah, well, if no-one else attended mass on Sunday, at least he could count on Tina to light a candle.

Suddenly quite exhausted, Edna stood up and returned to her bed to sleep for five straight hours. A trickle of visitors, most of whom were stopped at the yellow security tape stretching across the front lawn, and several nameless plainclothes policemen, came and went. The Hudson household had, in a matter of hours, become a public place and no longer the cradle of Edna's manifest identity.

The day slid into a second evening and in the dimming light Edna reappeared. To escape displacement in her own home she took the similarly refreshed Alice out onto the lawns behind the building. The garden stretched for almost a hundred yards into a small wood. From the damp overhang of almost leafless branches and wet rhododendrons the house could not be seen and it was impossible to imagine this was on the very fringes of outer London, just fifty miles from Westminster.

"If we want to find explanations, gardens tell us everything. Without sentimentality they reveal the true pulse of life... birth, coming to age, death...that's it...there's nothing else. Better, then, to take what's on offer now, rather than rely on Crispin's fanciful dreams. In the rot of autumn we can tell there's nothing to debate."

"In that respect Roderick and I are much closer to Crispin. We don't have any doubts about what lies beyond. Do you want to talk about it?"

"No, not right now, my mind is pretty clear. Do you realise the police are asking me to prepare a ransom. That ghastly man Foot and his colleagues seem to believe it's the way to have Edward returned."

"Are they suggesting the sum that was written on the note? It's a huge amount. Is that even within the realms of possibility?"

"I don't have it in a biscuit tin on the kitchen mantelshelf if that's what you mean," laughed Edna, "But in a day or two, perhaps, yes, it could be done. We are really quite well established you know."

"So what's to happen now?"

"I don't pretend to think like a policeman," Edna said, as if by definition the office was occupied by those with whom one would not want a daughter to associate. "But they do have greater experience of these things, and believe the immediate necessity is to get Edward back and then to pursue the perpetrators."

The two women stood and looked back towards the house. A bird's grating call and an untidy flapping of wings sounded in the tangle of broken branches overhead. Edna stirred fallen leaves with her waterproof boot to reveal beneath the brown vegetation earlier seasons black decay.

"I never realized how sodden this country was until we came back from Asia...and we all know how it rains out there. And worst of all there is no sun to follow and everyone has rheumatism. No wonder people here talk about the weather so much. I suppose they are surprised when they are intermittently dry."

"I suspect we don't miss Asia quite as much as you. You always fitted in so well."

"I'm not really attracted to places, but the way I live is, of course, important."

"Will you stay here after Edward returns? There'll be some uncomfortable memories now in this house."

"I not sure how much of an issue that is, but...you know Alice...." The pause was almost endless. "I don't want to pay the ransom...and...I don't want him released. I've decided there is actually no benefit for me in his return."

Edna looked straight ahead with the same matter-of-fact and unemotional realism as when she had said money was behind her decision to marry Edward. For good reason she was accused of being shallow, smug, selfish; the sins piled up high against her door. But, in pursuit of the things she most valued, there was an unwavering consistency. Of themselves the values were not high-minded, but holding them without deviation though a lifetime was at least honest and not many could claim as much.

"You are just badly stressed by this dreadful business. In a day or so, when Edward is back with us again, you'll feel like your old self."

"Look, tell me what morality is. All I want is to live in a way of my choosing and not according to precedent. You can't say the big rules are God-given, when only a few people like you and Crispin believe such things. Why do we need husbands or wives? Why marriage vows? Why hold on to old pairings designed to bring up children, when the children have moved away? If being human has any value it should be in doing as we want, not in clinging to old habits like the clothes purchased ten years ago. What's the point? I have to say that of all the places known to man the only under-populated one will be your heaven." In uncharacteristic warmth for her subject, Edna almost shouted and her friend's mouth opened wide.

From the thin brittle branches and in a cascade of broken twigs, a magpie dropped heavily onto the saturated ground. With an unblinking black eye it observed the two women before stalking mournfully away into the sanctity of the inner wood.

Their proximity in Asia, not commonality, had held then together and until this day only inaction had prevented them from drifting apart. Things shared long ago were enough, perhaps only just enough, to have inflated their relationship into friendship. But here, in the aftermath of Edward's disappearance, cosy familiarity was called into question and wide gulfs of belief yawned between them.

Alice was puzzled and embarrassed and struggled to absorb fully the bleakness of Edna's vision. The frigid beauty of her own life existed in a single compelling relationship; she meant, of course, the exclusive one enjoyed with her god. Several times a day she spoke to him and luxuriated in an intimacy like no other. In every way he was her king, the lord who possessed her utterly. Outside the rock of this association there was little of any consequence. Wasn't this after all what destiny was about; to give shape and purpose to a person's time on the planet? Her rising in the morning and going to bed at night was accompanied by the internal refrain that it was all for him and done solely in his name. The rightness of her view sanctioned no alternative.

Edna was older, but not in Alice's opinion the least bit wiser. Somewhere along the way there had been a choice and Edna had taken a turn into a place where true love, even the austere sort of her experience, had never been born.

"And will you say this to the Inspector who is doing his very best to return Edward safely to us?"

"Oh yes…well…maybe not exactly in those words. But he'll understand what I am prepared to do. Not that I'm afraid of his judgment any more than I am of yours. He will, however, most likely require an explanation. Answers are, after all, his stock in trade, but, quite frankly, providing them to such a boorish individual would be too tedious to contemplate. I tell you the full details because you have elected to share this event with me, and if, for some reason you are appalled by my choice that, forgive me, will not really matter. The way I think, least of all now, doesn't require endorsement."

Had this woman, Alice asked herself with sudden surprise, always been quite so despicable?

"The air is growing cold again. Should we go in? If anything needs getting used to after Asia it is the sun's disappearance at three o'clock in the afternoon. Why, at this time in the tropics one thinks of evening activities, dinner on the terrace, a swim in the pool, not retreat into one's fortified and unheated stone castle."

Behind them, where long shadows spread into uniform blackness the single magpie rasped and rattled its wings and the woods returned to their rightful owners.

When the two women reappeared, Foot was not in a good mood. "Next time you want to go out let me know."

"Mrs Hudson is under a great deal of stress and your help to get her through these very difficult days would be appreciated," responded Alice with the sort of snappiness calculated to put total strangers as well as the best of friends in their place.

"I am quite up to handling Mr Foot, Alice."

The Inspector frowned at the dismissive remarks. He was used to being treated with greater civility by the people he was helping.

"Perhaps in future," Edna resumed, "You should advise me if the police require us to stay in one place?"

"Look, while you were out we've had a contact. They kept it short again knowing we are here and just said how to deliver the money. Couldn't get a trace, so we'll have to play ball."

"And what do you plan doing about it?"

"My information is that you can organise the payment and then once we've made a switch there'll be evidence enough to track down these villains."

"Ah! Your information, I see. Does your plan include giving me greater detail? Or am I to assume you just need me to provide the means for you to solve your case?"

"Detail? Yeah…right…okay. But in private, if you please."

"Mrs McPherson is sharing the entirety of this event with me."

"Sorry, no, that's where I have to draw the line. We've got to keep this one tight as a tick."

"The police can be quite tiresome. Is it to be in my husband's study?"

"Right, along here then, if you will," and without further explanation Foot led the way into Edward's office and took up a position seated on the desk in the middle of piles of paper that had grown measurably deeper since his first arrival. With a lanky leg he stretched out and kicked the door to.

"Sit down please."

"I'm not in a sitting frame of mind. Please tell me what I am being asked to do."

"The woman called. She wants the money dropped by the sign for Oxfoot Farm on the Snepsford Road at two o'clock the day after tomorrow. Our understanding is you can get it by then. They say your husband will be released after they pick up the bag. You know, they're a smart lot; you can see a mile in either direction from there, with open fields behind and…I wonder if that means they're local? She also said there'll be no discussion and no further contact; except when they tell us where to pick up Mr Hudson. It's risky, but we have to lead them in or we'll be in what you'd call a cleft stick."

"What would be your advice, Mr Foot?"

"You can't go far with a million pounds when the roads are being watched. It might take time, but we'll get onto them. I want you to raise the cash. We'll do the rest."

"Thank you for the suggestion… But… no…I don't wish to raise the money!"

"What? Why?"

"I have obligations that are entirely my affair. It's obviously not a small sum. In fact it's a very large sum and I don't have the ability to raise it and moreover don't wish to raise it."

"See here, Mrs Hudson, if you go down that route I can't say exactly what might happen. We don't have a lot to go on and…"

"Your business is your business; my finances are mine. You are the police; you find the kidnappers."

"This could be obstruction."

"Don't try to scare me. It's no such thing. I repeat again I do not wish to raise the money. Please continue your investigation."

When Foot disclosed this unexpected and, from his point of view, completely unwarranted turn of events to his senior officers they brought pressure to bear on Edna to change her mind, but she remained adamant.

Like the seasonal mists lying on the farmland and woods along the Snepsford Road, indecision and uncertainty settled over once bustling police activity.

Another night closed in and Tina took round trays of food. She chatted to the two constables in the garden and a third waiting morosely in a parked van by the kerbside. In spite of the late hour the press contingent behind the security tape, including a newly arrived television crew and several reporters from the recently alerted national dailies, increased in size.

The sun was not seen to rise next morning and no-one noticed when day began. But a grey light slowly spread across the sky and forced the street into wakefulness. Fine drizzle dampened the huddled crowd and dripped sorrowfully from the leafless beech trees in front of the Hudson residence.

While other occupants of the house had slept, Alice avoided the room prepared for her and spent the long dismal hours wandering fitfully between the settee and Tina's kitchen. A home's daily routine was Tina's greatest comfort. Without custom and fatalism she would have lost her footing in the growing doubt. Boiling a kettle and getting up early to provide for those who had left long years ago were protection against any catastrophe, including hostage-taking.

"What will you do now, Tina?"

"Do? Do when, Ma'am?"

"Why, when this dreadful business is over."

"Oh I'll think about that tomorrow Ma'am. I've got plenty of other things on my mind right now with people coming and going all round."

"What if something even worse should happen; what if Mr Hudson doesn't come back?"

"But why shouldn't he be back?

"I don't really know, but we're dealing with criminals and they must be very unpredictable."

"I belong with the Hudsons, until the day comes for me to go home."

"Are you looking forward to giving up work after so long?"

"Oh, but there'll always be work of some sort, Ma'am, wherever I decide to go. I've put two sugars, but no milk in your coffee. Is there anything else you'd like? Some crackers perhaps?"

In interior warmth, lunch followed breakfast, but outside, fine, uninterrupted drizzle soaked everything under heaven. From time to time the stationary white van disgorged a policeman in a yellow coat with a dog on a short lead. Both man and animal walked several aimless yards up and down the street before hurriedly climbing back behind the van's slammed doors.

For the next two days the uniformed branch of the local constabulary ran unmarked car patrols right along the road to Snepsford and back. The cars drove particular slowly past the Oxfoot Farm sign placed, not to indicate an entrance, but as a farmer's reminder to campers and hikers that this was private land.

Long after the kidnapper's deadline and some way from the farm sign, a south-bound patrol noticed a mud flexed, black saloon car accelerating rapidly in the opposite direction from a point near the old Snepsford Bridge. There was no real reason to be suspicious, but in the absence of any other significant movement on the quiet stretch of country highway, a good policeman was obliged to investigate.

Roughly equidistant from Snepsford Village and the Hudson house the narrow Snepsford Bridge lay among thick clumpy patches of woodland and fields criss-crossed by streams and small rivulets. In the fields and under weeping heavens cattle grazed despondently. Wet clouds scudded low over the copses and in the gullies trees shone and drooped heavily under the weight of incessant rain. Under the bridge a stream flowed in from Oxfoot Farm pastures and fell away into a deep culvert overhung with foliage.

Above the left side of the gully…Police Constable Rees paused… partly covered by a mass of dripping vegetation, was a grey canvas bag knotted at one end. Rees plodded to the south end of the bridge and hoisted himself gently over the rail. He was not a light man and did not want to spoil his weekend's fishing with an unintentional sprain. The descent to the brook soaked his trousers as high as his thighs and he began to wish he had called for back-up. There was, he inwardly complained, proper equipment for this type of search.

In the deepest part of the gully, one end of the bag moved about on swirls of water. Pebbles slid from beneath Rees's heavy tread and when he put out a hand to steady himself his wet fingers closed over unpleasantly soft protuberances in the canvas sacking. He recoiled in revulsion. From beneath his tunic he took out a mobile telephone.

"Inspector, I think you better come up to Snepsford Bridge. There's something here you'll want to see."

An hour later, Inspector Foot looked over the bridge's stone parapet. The sack that Rees had discovered lay under ferns in leaf-stained water and was about five feet long with grotesque bulges in three or four places.

"Max, come with me… now!" he called to the police officer who was coaxing a black Alsatian out of the rear doors of a van that had followed from the Hudson house. "Rees you stay up here."

Instead of walking round the protective railings at the end of the bridge he placed one hand on the top bar and swung over. There was no path down to the stream and he pushed his way into the gloom through plants and bushes that slapped wetly at his legs and arms. Clay and dead leaves collected in growing packs beneath his thick policeman's boots until dislodged by the half submerged gravel below the bridge's grey arches. The dog-handler followed closely behind.

"Open the bloody thing, Max."

The black Alsatian whined and pawed at the tied end of the sack.

"Sit! Sit, god damn you!" The dog gurgled deep in its throat and lay down with ears turned forward. Max opened a folding knife and inserted one end under the knotted cord. The dog backed away up the slope. With a sharp upward jerk of the knife the cord came free, but the sacking, wet and stiff from mud and water, held its position. Foot and Max looked at each other.

"Well, get on with it, for Christ's sake."

Emboldened by superior authority, Max moistened his lower lip and rapidly sliced the sacking from top to bottom. Freed from restraint a body with hands and feet bound behind its back in loops of plastic cord rolled out into the stream. Eyes and mouth were open and a single red hole stained the corpse's receding ginger hair.

"Sweet Jesus!" said Max licking both lips. The black Alsatian stretched out front paws and whined again.

Foot took a creased photograph from his rain-coat pocket and in the fading light examined it and the upturned face at his shoes.

"Damn, damn, damn!" he said.

The news of Edward's murder reverberated through the local community like the rumbling after-shocks of an earthquake. The closeness of the crime created a feeling of involvement, but no-one confessed to real grief. Acquaintances and neighbours gasped, and after gossiping knowingly, returned to what they had been doing.

The unspoken thought in Alice's mind, which she scarcely admitted even to herself, was that those living by the sword would eventually be undone by one. But, because she had a Christian duty, she would stay in the Hudson home until such time as Edna reconciled herself to the widowhood thrust so peremptorily upon her. She need not have worried that the period would be protracted.

Without so much as a word and even while Alice and Edna were eating a carefully prepared late breakfast grapefruit, the police moved out. Their business in the house did not include managing feelings shaped by murder.

"It has been such a long time, but I'm thinking of visiting Asia again. I have so many friends out there, whom I haven't seen in years. I still have the small flat and can take Tina with me. And, of course, Emma too will be on hand."

"That'll help you escape this hideous episode, but what would you do with your home here?"

"I'm not sure there is so much to escape from, but in Asia, you know, the way of life is so much…so much more congenial. And this…? Why I'll just lock it up."

The real shock for Edna, however, was still to come. When Tina was asked to prepare for the journey she replied, "Thank you for wanting me to be with you, Ma'am, but with your permission, I'll take you back and then, if you don't mind, now that Mr Edward has gone, I think I'll be going home."

"Home?" Edna said incredulously. "What do you mean? Isn't Asia your home?"

Tina didn't like confrontation, but beneath her meekness she was firm.

"I can help you find someone who suits you Ma'am, but it's time for me to see my grandchildren."

Weeks later the big house was shut and Alice took charge of the keys.

A gang of handymen came in to turn off water and gas and throw dusts sheets over the furniture. Before locking the main door behind her Alice made a final tour to satisfy herself everything was in acceptable order. She raised the corner of a sheet covering the grand piano and clicked her tongue in disapproval. Why did hired hands never do a job to a standard quite as high as one's own? With a soft bump she closed the lid and took away a single sheet of music to throw it in the rubbish bin waiting for collection in the street outside.

FOURTEEN

SHADES OF GREEN

"You're looking older than I imagined."

"It's been close on fifty years; you can't expect much less."

"So many things have happened."

"Have they? Or has time just moved on?"

At birth the two brothers were separated by eighteen months, but throughout adulthood the distance was half a planet. Today they shook hands awkwardly as if acknowledging the gulf of years that had made them strangers to one another. Not sure whether to hold or let go, the elder Heaver suddenly and self-consciously drew his brother close and threw an arm about his neck.

"By Christ, it's good to see you, lad."

"You should have written more often."

"What was there to say, especially after May died? But you will have seen the two girls?"

"Aye, but they've got lives to lead and what's down here is not for young folk."

They stood back a little and surveyed each other's almost identical face; like a mirror, yet, with differing experiences lying in every crease and wrinkle, quite unlike. The same spare bony features and long straight nose, both heads thick with fine white hair curling at the neck, which on John was brushed straight back to reveal a forehead furrowed with whatever thoughts kept him from righteous sleep. Overhanging a brow unscarred by regret, Tom's unkempt mane was tousled by the wind and gave no indication of having been touched by a comb in weeks. One face was burned brown by tropical suns and the other, save for ruddy cheeks, was as pale as his flying hair.

"How's the farm?"

"Not much changed."

"And people?"

"Children grow and leave and new folk don't come often, so you'll not feel greatly out of place."

John and Tom Heaver were born into the strange calm existing between two great wars, when a continent held its breath and people spoke softly as if afraid of waking mad dogs. In the days of their childhood, the woods and mounded down-land slopes of Sussex were all they knew. Those few idyllic years were compressed into what seemed a short green spring, held precious in memory because such days had never come again. Around them the old order, like a battle-worn knight riding out to undertake a final quest, departed and let in a new dark age.

For rural boys, the events engulfing mankind were initially beyond the sea and in the strangely twisting contrails of the summer skies. But on the day their uniformed father left never to return, their golden beginnings went with him in his kit bag and on the slope of the lane leading to an uncomprehended war.

Once the world half righted itself the two boys, as they only momentarily were, came to manhood. But farming was not for John. Unlike his steadier brother, he was restless from the start and even while still a child wandered further, always wanting to see what lay beyond the next hill's rise. Coming home scratched and bruised from expeditions across the pathless heath-land, he often had a story to tell that left their mother gasping and worrying whether the next outing would end in a fearful telephone call. Tom was the contemplative one whose favourite hideout lay in the forked upper branches of a tall beech tree where he'd write inexpert, but deeply-felt poetry about lost innocence and youths mistakenly sent to jail.

When John was in his early twenties, a letter arrived, which only he had been expecting, offering employment on a Chilean tin mine. Having lost a husband in his prime the mother's heart almost broke at the departure of her youngest son. But she, with the fortitude and resignation of her calling, watched him go while inside she lamented another loss as if a second limb had been severed.

But Tom never wanted to leave; the shrieking gulls and the smell of cattle drinking from Celtic dewponds had entered his soul. He took joy from the changing seasons' ancient cycle of birth and death, which, even in the worst of winters, contained seeds of renewal. On the land at ploughing and harvest time, he'd pick up soil and let it fall through his outstretched fingers. He was at one with the coarse dry humus that had made this free pasture from as long before the Romans as he stood after. Although not given to outward display he knew he was as happy as any man had a right to be and as much a part of the down-land as the cliff-top gorse bushes bent low by Atlantic gales.

"There's a car waiting."

"Will I recognise that too?" The joke had an edge that made Tom frown.

"It's old, but you'll be safe enough."

Realising he had sounded condescending, John regretted his clever words.

"Sorry, that was stupid."

"What was?"

"The humour; you'll think I'm laughing at you."

"And are you?"

"No, I don't think so. I've just forgotten how to be with those I haven't seen for so long. Perhaps we need some time."

"You're my brother; you can say as you feel."

The vehicle was not a car in an accepted sense, but a general-purpose farm pickup used for carrying manure, hay and livestock. Taking John's suitcase Tom heaved it into the space behind the cab already occupied by tarpaulins and petrol cans.

From Brighton station and without urgency the farm was an hour's drive away. To let infrequent traffic pass in the winding lanes, Tom squeezed the pickup hard against overhanging bushes that squeaked and scratched along the already well-worn paintwork. From Jevington to the farmhouse they followed a climbing track still narrower than the earlier lane.

Two border collies ran out barking and jumped at the open widow and Tom's soothing voice. "Get down, get down, or you'll be under the wheels," he scolded gently.

Next to him his brother looked through the dust-streaked windscreen at the farm buildings. "They're still the same. Just a few things lying about that weren't there before. I could almost believe Mum will come rushing through the door, wiping her hands on her apron in a fluster at being caught unprepared by a returning son."

"Well, she's been gone this long while and there's none here at this time of day, but me and the dogs."

"And the ghosts," John said without thinking.

"Why don't we walk over to Crowlink in the morning and stop at a pub on the way back to help you get your bearings?"

There was no central heating in the farmhouse, but a log fire hissed and crackled in the grate.

"I've not seen one of those since I left. Valparaiso got cold at times, but we had steam radiators. Seems primitive now, but no one complained and some thought them a luxury. This is the only country I know of where you can be hot and cold all at the same time; hot in front from a fire and cold on your back with the night coming in behind."

"Did you like Chile?"

"Yes, for the time I was there, but like anywhere that keeps you long enough, it became just another place."

Pulling two stout and worn easy chairs towards the blaze Tom patted one in invitation. The dogs settled among the old men's feet and waited, as if they too had come to hear a tale.

"And after the tin mine?"

"Well, it was off to Brazil and that's where I met my first wife."

"Aye, and the letters stopped."

"There was always so much to do and without children everything was possible. I was not like you to spend hours with a pen or book and be content. You must forgive what was then a young man's selfishness."

"We all forgave; your Mum before everyone."

"None of you would know what it was like; white beaches, brown girls, living for today and not tomorrow. I wasn't weighed down by responsibility or duty. People were not their work. You never heard anyone say this is Jose the baker, or Manuel the tailor." He laughed as if the idea was absurd.

"Did you never want to belong?"

"Belong?" John was puzzled. "To what? I was on an adventure. The world contained so much and I wanted to taste it all."

"I hear there are twenty-seven varieties of banana; how many could you identify?"

"Huh?" John wondered whether it was his turn to be laughed at. "When you have picked papaya and star fruit and seen a tamarind grow I'm not sure how much deeper you want to go."

"On the walk tomorrow, I'll show you the russet tree Dad grafted before he went away."

"I don't remember."

"It's twenty feet high and grows the sweetest fruit. And," Tom went on, succumbing to bitter-sweet memories, "I tie a bunch of heath flowers to its branches every seventh of April."

"Why? What's that?

"It's the last day we saw him before he sailed to France."

John had grown up in this farmhouse and just like Tom had made the surrounding scrub and grassland his constant companion, but now unexpectedly he was an interloper with no honest business being here. The date should have been too remote, too far into a faded past to have any significance, but not knowing of or sharing in the ritual left him with a dull sense of exclusion. There was a private bond between his elder brother and the downs to which he was not party. He didn't believe for a second Tom really remembered with any accuracy all those years ago, because neither of them was more than five or six at the time. But an event had been constructed around the date that rooted Tom to his family and the soil from which John, by his own decision, had long since been cast out.

The thin branch of an elder tree, visible through uncurtained windows in the farmhouse's whitewashed wall, rubbed against the glasswork. Disturbed by the noise, one of the dogs sat up and yawned. The slowly fading light of summer drained imperceptibly from the evening sky.

"I'd forgotten how gradually day passes into night, almost as if it is reluctant to be gone. In the tropics the change comes quickly, like a curtain falling. And then daytime things are put away and twilight takes over. Is that why people here write melancholy books and South American dance sambas?"

"But can living for pleasure be enough? What about indivisibility?"

"You may have changed more on the outside than I expected, but underneath you're still the same old Tom."

In other company the remark could have been either a compliment, or a criticism. But John meant it as neither; it was just a statement of the way things were and his brother accepted it as such. The dog disturbed by the scrapping elder tree stood up and rested his head on Tom's knee.

"We are our story. At the beginning there isn't one of course and we are free to choose, but as we get closer to the end we and it are one and the same, inseparable."

"I hadn't thought of it in quite that way."

"No, I don't suppose so. Tell me what happened to your first wife?"

"You could say she didn't like the way I danced and found someone with better rhythm." John gave a short dismissive laugh through his nose. "Anyway that closed out my interest in Brazil and while I was looking for another tin mine Malaysia came up. That's where I met May and the two girls were born. When she died I thought of going somewhere else, but by then there were too many complications. So now I'm retired and, for the first time since sixty-six, on my own again."

"Is being alone and over seventy the reason why you've come back?" The question was almost cruel.

"You make me sound callous; you think, having given nothing, I'm holding out a hand and asking for forgiveness from those I've neglected?"

"I wasn't going to put it that way. I'd have said that, despite the youthful urge to shake off your beginnings and build something new, the first twenty years formed you as certainly as they did me, and for one last time you want to reassure yourself there is a foundation; that you aren't standing on sand."

From far away a shrill cry pierced the stillness of the farmhouse dusk. Both dogs walked to the door leading to the outside yard and barked two or three times before returning to the warmth of embers glowing in the grate.

"What's that?" said John, uncertainty in his voice.

"Oh, it'll be a fox I expect," Tom said, and with a chuckle added, "They don't just raid chicken-houses like in fairy stories you know. They take whatever they can find including family pets and judging by the scream that one might have been a cat."

Unsure whether this was another joke at his expense, John shivered. "I don't have the stamina I once had. Perhaps I should turn in."

"Mrs Barstow comes up from the village at about six to do a bit of housekeeping. She's a hard woman to restrain, so don't get up if you hear her banging around. When you are about we'll take the track to Crosslink and find an early lunch."

Like all old men John slept lightly, but he was not disturbed by Mrs Barstow's vigorous early morning cleaning and baking, or by the farm hands driving sheep to pasture. But a tractor starting up under his window and crunching away over the yard's loose stones towards a distant field did eventually wake him.

"Well, as like as two peas in a pod, make no mistake. What'll it be dearie?" The home help greeted John with the easy familiarity of every continent's country folk.

"Why, I er...is Tom around?"

"He'll be back directly, just gone down to count the lambs. And my word, you sound just like him too. If I were to close my eyes...well I never. So what would you like?"

"I usually have some fruit and perhaps...coffee?"

"You'll want something more substantial now there's a cold wind blowing and besides we don't have no coffee in this house. A strong cup of tea will put you to rights," and forgetting John's history, continued, "Just you make yourself right at home."

At home; at home; the words echoed in his thoughts like a church bell. Where, he wondered was home? Did he or anyone else for that matter need to claim such a place? Was home an essential part of human existence, or an archaic throwback, which he and others of his sort had discarded; a redundancy similar to worthless hair clinging to a man's body that linked him to his primitive origins and not to a sleek and unencumbered future?

Seen though the window and frail branches of the overhanging elder, several people moved about in the yard. Some of the men carried mucking forks and, John guessed, had been loading the trailer he'd heard leaving for the fields. High-spirited laughter rippled between men and women as if both were teasing each other.

Returning with a well-laden tray Mrs Barstow began arranging the contents on an unpolished wooden table.

"Here you are, dear, get this inside of you and you'll be able to keep pace with your brother."

"Thank you, you're very kind."

Mrs Barstow was used to less elaborate appreciation and looked at him quizzically.

"He talks of you a lot these days, you know?"

"We were close once, but the intervening years, you understand..." his sentence trailed off as if no further explanation was needed.

"It's like my old man, it is. Before he was carried off, God rest his soul, he put up a photograph of his father whom I'd not heard him mention in forty years. It was as if he was preparing to meet him all over again. Uncanny it was. Do you want mustard with that kidney?"

The large willow-patterned dish contained several rashers of crisp bacon, a sausage weeping traces of oil though its pierced skin, two huge eggs, which John suspected were not a hen's, a grilled tomato, a slice of fried bread and resplendent at the centre a fresh lamb's kidney. At one side stood a small basket of steaming bread and a mug of hot dark tea.

"Mustard, yes indeed; that would be most welcome."

She busied away and returned whisking bright yellow powder and water into a paste. By his side she watched John butter a piece of fresh bread.

"What's it like out there? Asia isn't it?"

"Mmm, well, yes..." he replied through a mouthful of bacon, "It's hot and humid and one of many places I've lived."

"Is it home now after so long?" Again the same question.

"I don't think I actually have a home in any accepted sense. I like to see and touch and when it's possible move on again. Everywhere can teach you something; show you something new."

"But don't you have to stay for a long while to get to know things?"

"Of course, you can make a study out of anything, but taking a little from here, a little from there will add up to a pretty formidable experience." The mustard, too thickly applied, buzzed in his nasal passages. "Oh! Could I...possibly...oh dear...have more tea?" He nipped the top of his wet nose between a finger and thumb and held his breath.

The teapot was of the same design as the breakfast dish and Mrs Barstow poured generously from its comfortable round belly.

"Say 'when'!"

"Excellent, thank you," he sniffed painfully.

"So why did your brother stay and you leave?"

"We all live our lives according to our inclinations. Some people like to soak in a bath and sense the shifting temperatures; others like to get in and out. For one the exercise is to ponder, for the other it is to wash and be done. Tom liked to reflect and dissect and still does I suspect. For me there was always a need to get moving to something new. There was never enough time. As for Tom, he has all there is in the whole wide world and he will have it until the end of his days. Ah, the kidney was delightful; would you believe I have not tasted one in half a century?"

"Well, my... and what would they be eating in that place you don't call home?"

"There is rendang and murtabak and flat noodles and..."

"If you were asking me," she interrupted, "I'd be more at home with a nicely smoked rasher or two. Did you know that we..."

In spite of its great weight, the wooden door set with iron fittings swung open almost of its own accord and struck the white wall. Discolouration of the plasterwork surrounding a dark dent suggested the collision was not an isolated occurrence. Tom in mud-spattered green Wellington boots emerged into the warm room preceded by the two collies that bounded up to Mrs Barstow and licked her rough red hands.

"Don't pather around my kitchen with both straight from the fields and all. Be off with the pair of yous," she admonished in a way grandmothers might reserve for particularly favourite children.

"Has he eaten, Mrs Barstow?" queried Tom as if she were the only person present from whom a reliable assessment of his brother's activities could be obtained.

"No appetite to speak of," she said despite the clean plate, "That foreign climate is doing him no good I'd say."

"Well, let's get him walking and we'll see how lunch will look in an hour or two."

From the farmhouse to a five-bar gate opening onto sheep-scattered grasslands was no more than thirty metres, but the unique mud of a South Downs agricultural yard, mixing thin topsoil, dung and chalk, rendered it a tiring slog. Greasy cakes built under the brothers' boots until both stood several inches higher. Despite his age, Tom lay on the top-most bar and rolled his legs across in a move as supple and efficient as any a twenty-year old might accomplish. Viewing his brother from inside the locked gate, John asked in wonder, "How did you do that?"

"Pure unthinking technique, old son, why don't you try?"

"I think I'd knock myself silly." Then from a position astride the top-most rail of the gate, John added, "What makes you so content?"

Without pause and as if he had expected the question, Tom replied, "I don't worry about the state of my mind, so, seeing and accepting the value of what I have, rather than pursuing tomorrow, when it could contain nothing at all, may have something to do with it. I have a past and a present which both mean a great deal. You kid yourself that you have neither and see only an undefined future demanding exploration, which, if you ask me, is where disillusionment and disappointment begin. But there is more to it than that and you half suspect as much or you wouldn't be here, not now, not after all this time."

The two dogs found a hole between the wide gate and a hawthorn hedgerow marking the perimeter of the farmhouse yard and wriggled through. In excitement and, familiar with the way from many previous outings, they rushed to and fro between Tom and a worn upland track.

"That's a pretty big statement."

"Maybe so; tell me if you disagree. That's it over there, where the hawthorn stops."

"What is?"

"The tree, the russet tree I spoke of last night. You and I and it are, in a manner of speaking, all Dad left behind."

"Looks as if it's coped with the years pretty well.... Where do we go from here?"

After the sticky yard the meadow had a spongy feel. From a distance the turf appeared smooth and perfectly rounded, but close to it was hummocked and hollowed with tussocks and rabbit scrapes. Sprinkled droppings broke apart under intermittent sunlight and their half digested shreds blended into the soil until there was no certainty which was which. Bright green shoots of fresh grass broke though the soft lumps in a cycle of decay and renewal.

"Wasn't this all ploughed land years ago?"

"Aye, it was, but pasture long before that and now we are paid to keep it this way."

"Oh? And by whom...aiyah!" John let out a cry as his foot turned in a soft, earthy hole.

"Watch out. I don't want to be sending you back with your foot in a cast. You'll have to keep your eye on the ground and not just the horizon. Did you ever see anything as brilliantly green as morning grass coming up after a rain shower?"

At the back of his mind John did remember encountering such a colour once, but in the sudden discomfort of his ankle he could not quite recall what, or where it had been.

"Ah, that was a bad twinge."

"Are you fit to go on?"

"Yes, I think so. Just have to take it gently for a while."

"There's no hurry, we've no appointment to keep at the other end."

The horizon had indeed caught John's notice. In the far distance the wavy line marking the cliffs' edge was quite distinct, like a pencil slash across white paper, but surrounding it weak sunshine and water vapour mixed in changing shades of yellow and grey as if land, sea and air met and fused together in one combined and insubstantial element.

Following his brother's gaze, Tom said, "In such an empty, wreathing haze as this the world began."

"Do you still write poetry?"

"When the mood is on me," and not wanting to let an unspoken thought slide by unexamined, Tom added, "You'll appreciate people are also part of the landscape and over time become inseparable from their surroundings?"

Although not altogether sure what that meant John had, on reflection, noticed how differently he felt on these blustery northern hills. In the tropics there was nothing in nature that was hinted or implied; rain was torrential, the sun blazed, the night was black and sudden and colours startling.

"I remember now…yes, the green…I have really seen it that bright and brighter too, so much so it was almost too vivid to look at. New rice, before being planted out in a paddy's long straight lines, sprouts in a sort of nursery. I don't know what it's called, but all the seedlings are compacted into a very small area and the dazzling green of germination in a patch of shining water is a marvel."

Yesterday at Brighton railway station they'd looked on each other's similar, but different face and traced in accumulated furrows the happiness and sadness of fifty years. Again they observed one another, but this time to seek out whether a brother's former understanding remained true.

Near the summit of the domed hill, one of the dogs was snorting and yelping into a rabbit hole, while the other ran in wide pointless circles.

"We'll be losing the dogs if we dawdle," Tom said, "How's the ankle?"

"A little sore, but it will hold."

On the other side of the vast green hump of hillside a long gently sloping path wound down between shadowy hollows of juniper and ash clustered together like beleaguered hamlets anticipating a coming storm. Dotting the heath, tiny pinpricks of colour lay strewn in casual confusion as if manifesting God's gifts to an ungrateful planet.

Tom, identifying his brother's thoughts as quickly as his own, said, "It's the result of grazing. Ploughing was destroying plants that only exist in these few square miles and many of the farms hereabouts have returned to keeping livestock."

"They're so small, almost no form, only a dot of yellow or lilac."

"Look closely and you'll see how perfect they are. I bet you've forgotten there are orchids on these hills?"

"Forgotten? I'm not sure I ever knew. All I know of orchids is that they are tropical and of the most flamboyant colours."

As though talking to himself, Tom went on, "This one is a common spotted bee and this; well, well, not an orchid, but a red star thistle. We are undoubtedly privileged; there are not so many of these about."

He bent low to inspect the discovery while John surveyed the indistinct distance.

"What's over there?"

"Three miles straight down this track is Crowlink and if we keep going we'd come to the Saltings, or the cliffs. But much further on," he waved in a general direction, "To the right of the path is Fulking and Devil's Dyke. It's been quite a time since I was over that way."

"Is it just open country, or are there things to see?"

"Oh, there's plenty to entertain, if that's what you have in mind; pre-historic burial mounds, Cissbury Ring and if you want something really up to date we've got the remains of a Norman Castle."

"Can we visit?"

"Not today, but surely, over the ten days you're with us. But don't you remember any of it?" he queried sweeping his arm in a wide semi-circle that took in the narrow combe containing Crosslink and the entire western skyline.

"The farmhouse, yes, of course, but not much out here. The names seem to jog a recollection, but my mind can't dredge up any exact pictures." And, John added with a laugh part self-deprecating and part boast, "May used to say my memory only went back as far as Monday morning, but that's not true either; it's just that I am not strong on details."

In the village pub, Tom ordered lunch for both of them. A stout female, not dissimilar to Mrs Barstow in her blunt affability, served gammon steaks and potatoes at one of three rough-hewn wooden tables in a rear garden. No other customers stopped to eat and only two men, older even than Tom and John, came and went separately and in the course of their short visit drank several glasses of dark, flat beer and gazed out onto the world as if there was nothing under the sun with the power to cause the least surprise.

Rattling cutlery into an empty dish and wiping his mouth on a paper napkin John asked, "Where to now?"

Tom, who was forking a carefully sliced piece of gammon, replied, "Where to? I thought, for your first day, this would be it."

"But the cliffs can't be far off; why don't we keep going?"

At the edge of a perpendicular drop, John, as if he were still a fifteen-year-old crawled on hands and knees to stare excitedly down into the rushing void falling six hundred sheer feet into the surging tide. Sea air heavy with the cries of fulmars and smells of salt swept up into his face and tugged the neat white hair out behind his ears.

"Whoa! Look at this," he called excitedly over the roar of wind to his brother standing a few feet off. "Why's the water so milky and what are those black lines in the chalk?"

"The chalk cliffs are constantly eroded by the current on its way north. The lines are flints deposited in sediment eons ago."

"Is that a lighthouse down there?"

"Yes, it is and it was there when you were a boy."

"I don't remember. Which way is Brighton?"

"To the right, but you can't see it from here."

"What'll we do tomorrow?" he yelled into the teeth of the gale.

For a while the small adventure transformed John from a slightly bored and indifferent man of the world to an invigorated and irrepressible person half his age. On the return walk to the farmhouse above Jevington he talked animatedly of the things he'd seen and done in the half century of travelling. His monologue sped from place to place and one decade to the next in a helter-skelter of yarns. If he were an artist, his brother thought, he'd be applying paint with a roller and not a thin bristle brush.

For the next week John was awake early, often before Mrs Barstow arrived to set about her daily chores, and with a map spread over the kitchen table he planned the day's outing. The two old men ranged widely over all the adjacent countryside to as far away as Harting Down and East Head, without visiting the same place twice. Once Tom suggested they retrace steps to Crosslink and the cliffs, but his brother had no appetite to recreate that only recently past and momentarily engaging experience.

On his final two days John became unaccountably listless and moody and at first Tom thought impending departure was deepening his brother's natural dissatisfaction. He appeared in the kitchen, to Mrs Barstow's puzzlement and disapproval, unshaven and not much before lunchtime.

"You seem out of humour, John. Is there something I should know?" His brother asked solicitously.

"No, there's nothing, except the old ache. It's time I was on my way again."

"Have you not had a good trip?"

"Oh, indeed I have; the very best. But I'm not a peaceful companion. I don't give these things much thought, but last night I lay awake and wondered what was to come next. You know how I was when we were boys?"

"Yes, as well as anyone. But we can grow out of old patterns."

"Not that much. I made the early mistake of surrendering to my restlessness and that is what chiefly grew. Other faculties became stunted and this one thing became the food I could not live without. Like an addiction needing constant feeding. If I'd never gone anywhere, would I have been as content as you? Perhaps not, but nor would I have become so hopelessly unsettled. Looking back I can say I've seen a thousand places, more perhaps than all but a few, but none of them have I known too deeply. Unlike you, who have been almost nowhere, but understand just this one spot to its inner core. It's the same as making love to dozens of women, or really loving only one. I've been the libertine and you faithful to the end. Sorry, but I'll have to go. Will you take me to the station tomorrow?"

"You are always my brother," Tom said as if no other explanation was necessary.

Next day without invitation the two collies jumped in among the pickup's petrol cans, tarpaulins and only momentarily unpacked luggage. At the entrance to the platform they stood on either side of Tom and watched him put his arms around his brother.

"That was a joke, you know, about my first wife," John said.

"What was?"

"I said she found a better dancer."

"Yes, I remember."

"The truth is she asked for stability and at that time I couldn't begin to offer what she wanted. A few years here, a few years there, it was all too much for her. She wanted children, a home and steady income. That's why I had the two girls with my second wife, or I'd have lost her too and by that time I didn't want to be alone anymore."

"Will we meet again?" Tom hoped his brother would say yes, but he didn't expect to hear as much.

"I'd like to say we would and mean it, but who knows what next year will bring. You're a good man, Tom."

Separate lives had increasingly taken them in differing directions and now, approaching their stories' final chapter, what was left from identical beginnings? John's brother held the country's essence in his bones and when death came stalking, as soon it surely must, he'd be reabsorbed into the undulating down-land from which generations of his stock had sprung. Tom was part of a continuum with origins in the people who had dwelt on these chalk and flint cliffs since long before the Saxons came. While John, although of the same blood, belonged nowhere and at day's end would not be taken to any one land's bosom. The particles that made up his being, once deprived of life, would blow forever on the wind over the deserts and mountains through which he'd travelled without ever settling, or finding rest.

As if they heard food being prepared, the dogs stood up and waved their long, black tails. Turning slowly, John walked to the waiting train and as he boarded raised a hand to his temple in farewell. The train rumbled out of Brighton and gathering speed hummed towards the north. The green Sussex downs flashed by more and more quickly until left far behind.

FIFTEEN

RISING SUNS

The tea cup and saucer in the upper right hand corner of his breakfast tray reminded Edwin Potts that habits both blessed and cursed the elderly. Without deliberate rituals to keep his life intact, the road ahead descended bleakly into confusion. Unlike in his twenties, when indiscipline was not just excusable, but expected, today's urge to forgo the morning shave felt like a surrender verging on utter moral collapse. But the tyranny of repetitive and almost comic order ate away at his imagination until residual claims to being a free, thinking man evaporated.

Like any old person, he was caught in a trap where defence of the final barricade was all that stood between him and dotage; once the last parapet was breached, institutional care crept out of the winter trees like a famished wolf.

His mother had once called the fragmentation of life-long standards, including the abandonment of regular baths and a daily change of underwear, the onset of 'old men's tricks'. But while his tired body and more recently tiring mind had strength, he'd never accept there was that yawning cavern opening beneath his feet.

Wednesday morning, for no reason that he could remember, was boiled egg day. In fact, now he thought about it, most days of the week had a prescribed breakfast; Sunday was baked beans on toast; Monday, porridge; Tuesday, after shopping the previous day and as a minor concession to new age eating, chopped fruit and yoghurt. Wednesday's four-minute egg and all the other timeworn fixtures called out for a change to prevent him slipping over the brink. Well, damn it, he wasn't ready to concede anything and would carry the fight to the enemy.

To begin, his breakfast cutlery wouldn't be set out in the usual form and order, but thrown down in a rebellious heap beside his cup. Contemplating the uncharacteristic disorder, he wondered whether his daughters would forgive such wilful octogenarian behaviour. They'd probably say, "You're being silly, Dad."

Not that he was a truly tidy man; the chaos of his house and garden-shed bore ample evidence of muddle, but habits existed even in a mess and some of them were crying out for change. What then would replace the egg? A search of the meagre contents of his kitchen cupboard presented more evidence of comfortable routine, rather than solutions for its overthrow. On the lower shelf three containers marked 'sugar', 'tea', and 'salt', housed an assortment of screws, elastic bands, sticky tape, empty ball-point pens and the inconsequential bric-à-brac he never got around to throwing away. Just once, following his wife's unexpected death, an insensitive daughter had filled them according to their labelling, but that attempt to push an old man into alien patterns soon fell by the wayside and tea and sugar returned to storage in their boxes of purchase.

From a sagging rattan stool the upper shelf offered nothing helpful, containing only a dust-coated book inexplicably marked, "Saint Joseph's Catholic Mission to Seamen"; a length of electrical cable and four or five rattling tins rusting at the hinges.

Being a simple man and these days disinclined to plan too far ahead, he made no effort to stock his kitchen, or to ponder on the consequences of eating succinic acid and xanthan gum from a television meal. If a wrapper said "tomato soup", or "corned beef" and the subsequent experience wasn't offensive, he counted himself satisfied. In his opinion, when the elderly squandered time they committed a far greater sin than eating haphazardly.

Nothing in the gloomy depths of his cupboard struck him as a revolutionary breakfast, but having decided to do something differently, he settled on a tin marked "sardines."

The limp and forlorn spectacle lying on the last surviving plate of a blue and white set, purchased by his wife before their first child was born, prompted Edwin to wonder whether the fish would benefit from heating, or some other type of treatment. An expanding circle of sluggish olive oil suggested improvement was desirable and he dropped two pieces of pre-sliced bread into a toaster. Thank God for toast, he thought, that dependable standby, which had saved him hours of cooking and washing dishes. Years before and as a single man he'd often arrived at a similar conclusion, but then the motivation had been to minimise life's complications not just husband time.

He lifted a half-full tray and, with a newspaper secured firmly under one arm, edged from his cramped kitchen into a spacious garden. The load was set down on a wooden table standing in the middle of a patio he'd built single-handedly at a time when he alone had carried out home improvements. This was Edwin's favourite place and, in the before-sunrise morning, his favourite time of day.

He poured tea, milk and sugar and looked for a teaspoon. Blast! None there. That just goes to show order and regularity have some place after all and if the increased effort of breaking with tradition led to irritation, why bother? Caught in indecision he wondered whether to drag back to the kitchen for a spoon, which in a way was surrendering to the inflexible routine he was trying to avoid, or live with the consequence of change? Not wholly convinced, but because he had already settled into a preferred seat Edwin decided to make do with what he had. If the old widow living with her son in the next house observed him stirring tea with a knife handle she would conclude he'd either lost his wits, or was no longer to be counted on in maintaining neighbourhood values.

Toast with very thickly spread marmalade and a second cup of sweet tea took away the aftertaste of sardines. With familiar flavours restored to his palate Edwin leant back on his chair. This, he thought, was really very pleasant. The sky had been light for a couple of hours, but only now had the sun's disk begun to appear behind the lower branches of trees on the garden's perimeter and shed hatched patterns over the patio. Other living things also stirred in the vegetation and, under bushes planted by Edwin almost fifty years ago, a blackbird, with its head on one side, searched for grubs in the leaf-mould. Apart from these intermittent rustles and a prowling cat, the garden was at peace.

When this house was built, a big garden was as fundamental to a home as garages became to later generations. Now grown to maturity, like the long disappeared children who had once brought games and laughter to the tangled thickets, it seemed resigned and ready to be overtaken.

How many summer sunrises like this were there left to enjoy, Edwin wondered? If three score and ten years were indeed a man's prescribed lot he had over-stayed a long while ago. What if he had only one, or two short summers to go? But, he thought, taking uncertain aim across the barricade, at any age there was always some life expectancy left even if only to the middle of next week.

He moved the newspaper and tray to one side. Today, he was not interested in the world's great affairs and left the pages unopened. At the far end of the garden a rusting child's swing with one rotted wooden plank in its seat creaked in the lifeless air. Looking back across the chasm of decades that had passed in a heartbeat he remembered pushing breathless children, who cried out "more, more," as they arched back and forth. If he closed his eyes tightly he could hear the voices calling from far away.

"Come on Mabs, it's my turn now."

"I'm not done yet and you're too small to be on the swing."

"Dad, Daaad! Tell her to let me have a go."

"One more push Da… and then she can have the silly old swing."

"Come on girls, there's no need to...."

In those days the Potts's home, at least until the children became teenagers and slept as if the world had no end, rose early. Irrespective of parental wishes for longer sleep, young feet rushed about the two cramped floors and lengthy garden, doors swung, toys crashed, laughter howled and shouts, to the annoyance of neighbours, rang. Infant clamour and the start of a new day were so indelibly associated in Edwin's mind that no sunrise came without a flinch while he waiting for bangs and hustle to follow.

In the confusion of old age, his memories had started to collapse one upon another. Clarity disappeared, like in flavours of reheated food. Once, long ago, Edwin had been able to recall events almost hour by hour, but now large slices of his history, where not totally forgotten, were a blur. Even the faces and names of his several daughters had became transposed; he couldn't recollect with certainty which one was the second, whether all or only two were married and where did Wesley fit in? Did he belong to Claire, or Mary? He could remember being amused by the name and thinking the fellow should be in a pulpit, but was that a joke of the time or one that occurred to Edwin years later? Perhaps he was just remembering a memory rather than the event itself.

He tried to concentrate and fix definitively the occasion when he had first seen the sunrise. Young men, he recollected, were apt to experience dawn from the opposite end of the day. Carousing and walking home along wet streets to an accompaniment of clinking milk bottles and the expectations of a fresh day had happened often enough, but in his mind, only one dawn, the one that followed the night he met and bedded Maisy O'Conner, separated with an effort from the vapours of the distant past. Strange to think that event, which, for weeks and months, had consumed his every waking thought and rendered him almost incapable of rational behaviour, was now only a footnote to his life and one he probably was not remembering with any accuracy. The place in his head where recollections were housed or perhaps even his whole brain was, like any aging thing, without elasticity or juice. Edwin felt as if his shrunken memory of that first night and early morning with Maisy were like the screws in his salt pot; saved for a purpose that never materialised. As much as he wanted to squeeze memories of the brief and distant encounter into his mind and recall the hurricane of lost innocence, only a few clouded drops, like stagnant water from a rusted faucet, dripped into the present.

Maisy and a female friend, whose name like so many others had disappeared like mists circling peat heaths in autumn, had come south to the bright city lights. Only after Edwin had spent a night with her did he learn she was married. Whirls of romance and fear left him hollow-eyed and stubble-chinned for weeks. Not that he ever met Ronan, but the fanciful and hopelessly inaccurate images conjured up of a wild, swearing, wife-beating brute, who through neglect and drunkenness had driven Maisy to seek consolation elsewhere, caused him as many sleepless nights as lying next to the man's wife.

For a while Edwin felt as if his life hung by the slenderest thread of Maisy's opinion and arched eyebrow. He rose and fell with her smiles and frowns. But if his intelligence had been equal to his enthusiasm he would have accepted almost at the second of their first meeting that there was nothing to sustain their relationship beyond the occasional sweat-drenched heaving in a rented Great Eastern Hotel bedroom at the end of the railway line from Liverpool. The truth for Maisy was that the affair contained no more honesty than her bad marriage. The only real difference was that Ronan had been given a declaration of fidelity before his and her God, whereas Edwin and a host of other passing ships had not. The value of a promise, and not just one given by Maisy, he concluded, was directly proportional to the worth of the person to whom it was made.

At the time Edwin persuaded himself that his motive, to give an unhappy woman the love she deserved, had been almost honourable. But, if he had removed the question of his own appetite and whether Ronan was a poor lot or not, marriage, he reflected, should have some expectations, if not sanctity. In later years he'd certainly demanded as much in his own. Now, with the heat of the moment so faded and diminished, Edwin accepted his actions had been shallow and self-serving. Increasing age and the disappearance of a young man's imperatives, he concluded, were great incentives to balancing thought. Could he say that he'd outgrown those early flaws of character? Possibly, but that he had never again been an adulterer had more to do with the absence of opportunity than a change of view, or acquired nobility of character.

Maybe the supposedly great truths of right and wrong, of "thou shalt" and "thou shalt not,", that echo in every culture and civilisation, are just a fraud and reflect only the momentary environment in which people live. Are the bad parts of town like that because bad people live there, or do people become bad because they live in a bad neighbourhood? When Edwin looked back over his long life he seemed to have distinct and separate personalities belonging to each time and place. The craven and simpering youth undeterred in his sexual chase, either by the unappetizing taste of pale ale and cheap cigarettes on Maisy's mouth, or the belated revelation of a husband, was not the person who sought to instil virtue into growing and restive daughters, or the almost angrily independent old man, who in the privacy of his overgrown garden, shunned social contact, especially that of women. Each of those cameos in scattered moments of time was of a different person held together by the one frail thread of weakened memory. If that tenuous cord snapped who would be able to say, or even care whether these recollections had once belonged to him?

The evidently more experienced Maisy roused him from sticky sleep at a dark hour of the early morning and insisted he be gone before the grimy hotel stirred to life. Every article of clothing Edwin pulled over his head smelt of stale pub air, tobacco and yesterday's female deodorant, but in the brevity of the moment he felt triumphant and while smoothing his hair in the mirror he exchanged conspiratorial and cocky smiles with that other self. Well, matey, he thought, we did it, not so bad for a first outing. Wonder if she can take the pace?

"Why don't we meet up later in the week, for a meal, or something...?" Basking in his prosaic success, the exit speech's unoriginality was totally lost on Edwin.

"That, dear boy, will not be possible, because I won't be here."

"Why, where will you be?"

"Not that it should concern you over much, but I'll be tending to my dear husband until he's on the road again."

The newly constructed and unfinished fantasy that had hardly mounted beyond the first level of bricks, collapsed on Edwin's head with a crash. The dampness of his skin against underwear, which up to that point he'd rather enjoyed, suddenly felt disagreeable.

"What? Your who?? So what in hell was that all about last night then?"

"It was nice and something we can repeat once in a while if you're well behaved. But," she said laughing in his face, "If I'd known you followed me to take ownership I'd have said I'm spoken for."

Thoroughly deflated for reasons he hadn't expected Edwin sat, or rather fell down, on the bed.

"I thought perhaps...." His voice trailed away.

"And what did you think, silly boy? Look, put your socks on and get off home. Give me a number where I can get you."

"You give me yours as well," he said perking up a little.

"That would not be a good idea. You just leave it to me."

In the quiet and nearly deserted lobby a sleeping hall porter roused into surly action and unlocked heavy outer wooden doors.

"Up early, Sir. Do we have a train to catch?" he enquired with an inscrutable face that showed neither a desire to embarrass, nor an interest in answers to a matter-of-fact question.

"Just open the doors, will you?"

"Yes, Sir," and with a jab born of practice, "That was what the last gentleman said."

"I…!" With weight and finality the doors bumped into place and terminated whatever thought Edwin was on the verge of expressing.

He looked at his watch to give his next moves some context rather than out of real interest in the time and was surprised to read ten o'clock. How could that be? The day was still as dark as the previous night when he and Maisy had arrived at the Great Eastern? Closer examination revealed that, in the rush of departure, he had slipped his watch on upside down. Although the exact hour was of small consequence, at four thirty public transport was still locked up in depots on the fringes of the city. With no one anticipating his early return, because even in those distant days he lived alone, he turned into Bishopsgate and set out in the direction of far-away Edgware in a muddle of conflicting thoughts, ranging from gloating over the escapade with Maisy to not knowing where it was destined to lead. He thought about the excitement he'd felt as he stepped out of the Victorian bath-tub and saw the mounds and valleys of Maisy's naked body lying waiting for him under a single over-laundered sheet, until the same smug grin, exchanged with his mirror image in the seedy hotel returned from passing shop windows. If only Ronan hadn't intruded into the picture and obscured the night's adventure the momentary perfection could have been enjoyed without reservation.

Undefined day crept in and sidled along the streets like methane in a disused coal mine's galleries. Buildings visible only moments ago as two-dimensional shapes in the orange glare of sodium lights began to take form on the opposite side of the street. Apart from an occasionally patrolling police car and a clattering machine cleaning away yesterday's abandoned detritus, Edwin was alone.

As he turned back to look at the eastern sky, there was a suggestion the night was not as complete as it had been once. A thin grey mass that could have been cloud, or just the reflection of lights from a distant part of town, hovered far off. An hour later, a high cirrus bank had separated from the opaqueness and invisibility of the city and along its lower edge a line of orange began to form, as bold and bright as the street lights had been before they went out.

On just four more occasions, at eight, or ten-week intervals and always following her call, Edwin met Maisy. Each time the venue was the same and each time he was dispatched in the early morning as if he was completing a role she had prepared for him. The hotel porter, who carried world-weariness and cynicism on his shoulders like a builder's hod rapidly dropped the "sir" and, for his own amusement, attributed a different name to Edwin on each subsequent visit.

As abruptly as she had entered Edwin's life and after the fifth encounter Maisy disappeared, leaving him with a passion, which for a time was both impossible to satisfy and worthless. Even if Edwin had stopped to think for more than a few minutes he would have acknowledged that Maisy's departure, although perhaps unintended, was her only generous act in their short association.

For the best part of two years, Edwin clung to the fantasy that, if he could find her, something beautiful and permanent would be created. He periodically telephoned the Great Eastern asking for her and on occasions walked the grim streets nearby in the hope of another chance meeting. If only he could find her, he could offer friendship and to be there when help was needed. Recognition that he had been involved in a grubby and transitory affair, which at a time of her choosing Maisy had terminated, was slow in coming. Only after the passage of years and other women through his life had he admitted to a simple, ignoble act that was as common in its circumstances as in its universality.

A warm breeze blew the length of the lawn and rustled pages in Edwin's newspaper. Startled by the sudden noise, the blackbird crossed a fence in a flurry of wet leaves and anxious calls to resume searching further off. Now risen higher than the surrounding trees, the sun no longer threw dappled patches of light onto the patio and wooden furniture. Edwin and the remains of his rebellious meal were bathed in the bright glare of a new day. A very cold cup of tea, which would have been his third, waited untouched in the tray's upper right-hand corner and melted butter and toast crumbs slid thickly together towards the centre of a plate.

Lying back in his preferred chair with eyes and mouth just slightly open Edwin clutched a bread knife as if resting from repelling irresistible forces. Small beads of perspiration dotted his upper lip.

The next-door widow, who had intermittently observed the lengthy breakfast from an upper bedroom window, came down to her garden and called through the bushes.

"You should come inside now; it's far too hot when you haven't got a hat."

A page from the newspaper detached itself and fluttered to the ground and across the gardens a blackbird's song rose and fell.

"Edwin, Edwin!"

But there was no reply.

ADVANCE RESPONSE

With few exceptions, I'm not really a fan of contemporary short stories. Here are some exceptions: the short fictions, in no particular order, of David Foster Wallace, Deborah Eisenberg, Alice Munro, George Saunders, Aravind Adiga, Junot Diaz, Dave Eggers, Adam Haslett, Amy Hempel…and, now, Philip Chatting.

I remember the first time I read DH Lawrence. A fellow undergraduate and I quickly agreed that reading *Lady Chatterly's Lover* was a frustrating, albeit exhilarating, exercise of wearied wonder and repeated relief. "You don't want to read the second sentence because it can't be as good as the first. You don't want to read the second paragraph because it can't be as good as the previous. You don't want to read the second page because it can't be as good as its precursor." And so on forwardly through the rearview mirror; a Beckettian game of checked advancement: "Yes, my progress reduced me to stopping more and more often, it was the only way to progress, to stop" (*Molloy*). We can't, but we can, so we do, and we do, go on.

What is quickly apparent about *The Snow Bridge and Other Stories* is that its author, whose first novel *Harbour Views* was published in 2014, is a master stylist. You won't find clunky sentences like the one preceding this one in Chatting's long collection. And please don't confuse *long* with *tedious* or *tortuous*—or *torturous*. This is not a case at all reminiscent of the philosopher William James's consternation with and chiding of his slightly younger brother the novelist Henry to *get on with it, say it; just say it!* Still, in the same vein, it's also not hard to think of, and then dismiss, a comparison with Camus' comic-relief send up of Flaubert in *The Plague*, wherein the aging Joseph Grand spends years and years recrafting the opening sentence of what is—but only ever was, alas!—to be his first novel.

Almost as fixated upon form as Flaubert, who himself ironically reveals the beauty and brilliance of *les mots justes*— "Human language is but a cracked kettle upon which we beat out tunes for bears to dance to, when all the time we are longing to make music that will move the stars to pity" (*Madame Bovary*)—whatever I read I source for striking phrases and clauses, or for what Walter Benjamin called *Perlen* or pearls. Three stories into the fifteen which comprise *The Snow Bridge and Other Stories*, I realized that if I continued highlighting Chatting's often paragraph-long pearls at this fervent rate my copy of the book would eventually resemble the specious David Foster Wallace annotation of *Ulysses* that recently made the deceptive rounds on social media. In other words, I'd end up indexing and marking up every other word, sentence, and paragraph of Chatting's book. Pearls like the following proliferate:

> From no direction that either climber could readily discern a loud crack reverberated through the air, as if a giant tree felled in the forest had dragged all in its path to chaotic destruction. Echoes boomed from mountain to mountain and then dropped by slow-stepping degrees to a whisper spreading out in ever widening circles until the whole mountain range was engulfed. The ground shook and for a moment the wind appeared to pause. Earth and sky and everything between took breath and listened. ('The Snow Bridge')

> Haggard was a heavy, morose individual, capable of making a burden out of the lightest event. Whatever the time of year, he was a man for whom the month was always November, one whose spirit had been formed under unbroken grey skies and in the slosh of wet streets. ('Lighting up the Sky')

> During the night of the wedding's consummation, the priest took first one and then a second glass of whiskey. The wedding had been an ordeal of participation, but this was ordeal by conjecture. Medieval witches burned at the stake didn't know how lucky they were. Tortured bodies were nothing compared to a tormented mind in which a rustic's hand with black and broken fingernails groped in

the velvety and abominably sensual dark.
('O'Casey's Congregation')

Half way across the plaza Leif stopped. This is crazy, he thought. I've come here to help and yet deny this woman with nothing a chance of making a few miserable pesos. Both she and I know she was trying to rob me, but if survival alone is the goal and only cheating can make it possible doesn't that then become a greater morality? In the absence of order aren't her wits all she has to feed herself and who knows how many dependents? There comes a point where thievery is a kind of honesty, which mercy must allow. ('Visitor to the Barrio')

Edna looked straight ahead with the same matter-of-fact and unemotional realism as when she had said money was behind her decision to marry Edward. For good reason she was accused of being shallow, smug, selfish; the sins piled up high against her door. But, in pursuit of the things she most valued, there was an unwavering consistency. Of themselves the values were not high-minded, but holding them without deviation through a lifetime was at least honest and not many could claim as much. ('The Dinner Party')

We are our story. At the beginning there isn't one of course and we are free to choose, but as we get closer to the end we and it are one and the same, inseparable. ('Shades of Green')

Evident in the page-long series of selections, laboriously culled from a ruthlessly conservative six-page collection, is what we might call the modernist moral centre which guides Chatting's page-turning fiction. Not merely a stylist, the author invests himself in the traumatic conflict, character identification, and ethical complication that sit at the heart of the heart of necessary and affecting social fiction. The author never ever treads near what we should call the three major nonliterary tyrannies: exultant endings, empty moralities, and exhausted truisms.

As badges of this Arnoldian honour, of his writerly resolve to connect with his readers (to delight them) while likewise disconnecting them from facile dismissals or conclusions (to instruct them), Chatting gifts readers with the lovelorn, and as a result self-recriminating, albeit still universally revered in his pastoral parish, Father O'Casey. O'Casey's missionary zeal lands him in a Latin American rustic somewhere and finds him mired in an earthly havoc that most laity would not care honestly to contemplate, much less openly discuss:

> Ah! Celine, Celine, Celine [Casey opines]. Why did you ever erupt into my life? From the moment I saw you in that front pew, my soul has been in turmoil. At every service I look out for you and become by turns elated and cast down. Chance encounters in the town when I'm about my duties are such a whirl of unconfined pleasure, like waves surging freely over rocks on the seashore. When I smile and wave, parishioners say, "Father Patrick is well today." Joining people in conversation, blessing babies, teasing over absences from mass; they all occur with renewed energy, new enthusiasm. Am I not at those times, a better man? And his answer came back *No*. (my emphasis; 'O'Casey's Congregation')

I label father O'Casey a gift to readers because it is a novelty, and a privilege, to identify with such a character, with a man or a woman of the cloth, without this very identification being mediated through the veneration of Kempe, the parody of Rabelais, the contempt of de Sade, the acrimony of Joyce, or the televisuality of Friedkin. And, certainly, the metaphysical work of cleric and poet John Donne presents readers with a balanced complication that revolves around reading his religious sermons in light of his erotic poetry. But with O'Casey readers have the luxury of immediacy, in two senses of the word. O'Casey is our contemporary; plus, we get his story in twenty pages. The priest's context is laid literally bare. To wit, "In all its shabby tawdriness the town stood naked before him and he, contrary to his own assumption, stood similarly stripped." Knowing Father O'Casey and liking him is quite easy, which, of course, ends up being really hard. And this, this identification with and empathy for "The Other" in all of his or her human-all-too-human contiguity is what compelling writing and assiduous reading is all about.

Readers of *The Snow Bridge and Other Stories* will be at once satiated and ravenous as they discover versions of themselves stranded in cold cloud-shrouded mountains, sleeping outdoors in unpoetic urban spaces, mourning un-mourned old age and abduction in cold castles, nattering at rooftop gatherings in view of Victoria Harbour, nursing nostalgic drinks in a filthy Ho Chi Minh café, inciting rebellion in disremembered Puerto Rico, breakfasting in backyards encircled by squinting windows, and many more made-evermore-familiar places. Each story reverses what Richard Powers's eponymous narrator laments in *Galatea 2.2*: "I could do nothing with so perfect a lead sentence but compromise it by carrying it forward." Chatting's readers will witness no such compromise, nor any compromise in terms of character or story. What will be compromised, however, is any secure sense readers might have of unassailable divides between themselves and others—and this disconcertment is all for the better.

Jason S Polley
Associate Professor
Hong Kong Baptist University

Author of *refrain* (Proverse 2010), *cemetery miss you* (Proverse 2011), and *Jane Smiley, Jonathan Franzen, Don DeLillo: Narratives of Everyday Justice* (Lang 2011).

ABOUT PROVERSE HONG KONG

Proverse Hong Kong is based in Hong Kong with long-term and expanding regional and international connections.

Proverse has published novels, novellas, fictionalized autobiography, non-fiction (including autobiography, biography, history, memoirs, sport, travel narratives), single-author poetry collections, children's, teens / young adult and academic books. Other interests include diaries, and academic works in the humanities, social sciences, cultural studies, linguistics and education. Some Proverse books have accompanying audio texts. Some are translated into Chinese.

Proverse welcomes authors who have a story to tell, wisdom, perceptions or information to convey, a person they want to memorialize, a neglect they want to remedy, a record they want to correct, a strong interest that they want to share, skills they want to teach, and who consciously seek to make a contribution to society in an informative, interesting and well-written way. Proverse works with texts by non-native-speaker writers of English as well as by native English-speaking writers.

The name, "Proverse", combines the words "prose" and "verse" and is pronounced accordingly.

THE PROVERSE PRIZE

The Proverse Prize, an annual international competition for an unpublished book-length work of fiction, non-fiction, or poetry, was established in January 2008. It is open to all who are at least eighteen on the date they sign the entry form. Unusually for a competition of this nature, there is no restriction based on nationality, residence or citizenship.

The objectives of the Proverse Prize are: to encourage excellence and / or excellence and usefulness in publishable written work in the English Language, which can, in varying degrees, "delight and instruct". Entries are invited from anywhere in the world. Semi-finalists to date include writers born or resident in Andorra, Australia, Canada, Germany, Hong Kong, New Zealand, Nigeria, Singapore, South Africa, Taiwan, The Bahamas, the Peoples' Republic of China, the United Arab Emirates, the United Kingdom, the USA.

PROVERSE PRIZE WINNERS, 2009-2014, WHOSE BOOKS HAVE ALREADY BEEN PUBLISHED BY PROVERSE HONG KONG

Laura Solomon, Rebecca Jane Tomasis, Gillian Jones, David Diskin, Peter Gregoire, Sophronia Liu, Birgit Linder, James McCarthy, Celia Claase, Philip Chatting.

Summary Terms and Conditions
(for indication only & subject to revision)

The information below is for guidance only. Please refer to the year-specific Proverse Prize Entry Form & Terms & Conditions, which are uploaded in April each year onto the Proverse Hong Kong website: <www.proversepublishing.com>.

The free Proverse E-Newsletter includes ongoing information about the Proverse Prize. To be put on the E-Newsletter mailing-list, email: info@proversepublishing.com with your request.

The Prize
1) Publication by Proverse Hong Kong, with
2) Cash prize of HKD10,000 (HKD7.80 = approx. US$1.00)

Supplementary publication grants may be made to selected other entrants for publication by Proverse Hong Kong.

Depending on the quality of the work in any year, the prize may be shared by at most two entrants or withheld, as recommended by the judges.

In 2015, the entry fee was: HKD220.00 OR GBP32.00.

Writers are eligible, who are at least eighteen on the date they sign The Proverse Prize entry documents. There is no nationality or residence restriction.

Each submitted work must be an unpublished publishable single-author work of non-fiction, fiction or poetry, the original work of the entrant, and submitted in the English language. School textbooks and plays are ineligible.

Translated work: If the work entered is a translation from a language other than English, both the original work and the translation should be previously unpublished. The submitted work will not be judged as a translation but as an original work.

Extent of the Manuscript: within the range of what is usual for the genre of the work submitted. However, it is advisable that novellas be in the range 35,000 to 50,000 words); other fiction (e.g. novels, short-story collections) and non-fiction (e.g. autobiographies, biographies, diaries, letters, memoirs, essay collections, etc.) should be in the range, 80,000 to 110,000 words. Poetry collections should be in the range, 5,000 to 30,000 words. Other word-counts and mixed-genre submissions are not ruled out.

Writers may choose, if they wish, to obtain the services of an Editor in presenting their work, and should acknowledge this help and the nature and extent of this help in the Entry Form.

KEY DATES FOR THE PROVERSE PRIZE IN ANY YEAR
(subject to confirmation and/or change)

Receipt of Entry Fees / Entry Documents	14 April to 31 May of the year of entry
Receipt of entered manuscripts	1 May to 30 June of the year of entry
Announcement of semi-finalists	July-September of the year of entry
Announcement of finalists	October-December of the year of entry
Announcement of winner/ max two winners (sharing the cash prize)	December of the year of entry to April of the year that follows the year of entry
Cash Award made	At the same time as publication of the work(s) adjudged the winner / joint-winners of the Proverse Prize
Publication of winning work(s)	In or after November of the year that follows the year of entry

NOVELS, SHORT STORY COLLECTIONS
AND OTHER FICTION
Published by Proverse Hong Kong

If you have enjoyed *The Snow Bridge and Other Stories* by Philip Chatting, you may also enjoy *The Village in the Mountains* by David Diskin (2012).

You may also like to read the following (all titles in English unless otherwise stated):

A Misted Mirror, by Gillian Jones. 2011.
A Painted Moment, by Jennifer Ching. 2010.
An Imitation of Life, by Laura Solomon. 2013.
Article 109, by Peter Gregoire. 2012.
Bao Bao's Odyssey: from Mao's Shanghai to Capitalist Hong Kong, by Paul Ting. 2012.
Black Tortoise Winter, by Jan Pearson. Scheduled 2015 / 2016.
Bright Lights and White Nights, by Andrew Carter. 2015.
cemetery miss you, by Jason S Polley. 2011.
Cop Show Heaven, by Lawrence Gray. 2015.
Death has a Thousand Doors, by Patricia Grey. 2011.
Hilary and David, by Laura Solomon. 2011.
Instant Messages, by Laura Solomon. 2010.
Man's Last Song, by James Tam. 2013.
Mila the Magician, by Zhang Jian. 2013. (English / Chinese bilingual)
Mishpacha – Family, by Rebecca Tomasis. 2010.
Odds and Sods, by Lawrence Gray. 2013.
Paranoia (the Walk and Talk with Angela), by Caleb Kavon. 2012.
Red Bird Summer, by Jan Pearson. 2014.
Revenge from Beyond, by Dennis Wong. 2011.
The Day They Came, by Gérard Louis Breissan. 2012.
The Devil You know, by Peter Gregoire. 2014.
The Monkey in Me: Confusion, Love and Hope under a Chinese Sky, by Caleb Kavon. 2009.
The Monkey in Me, by Caleb Kavon. Translated by Chapman Chen. 2010. E-book. 2010. (Chinese)

The Perilous Passage of Princess Petunia Peasant, by Victor Edward Apps. 2014.
The Reluctant Terrorist: in Search of the Jizo, by Caleb Kavon. 2011.
The Shingle Bar Sea Monster and Other Stories, by Laura Solomon. 2012.
The Snow Bridge and Other Stories, by Philip Chatting. Scheduled 2015.
Tiger Autumn, by Jan Pearson. 2015.
The Village in the Mountains, by David Diskin. 2012.
Tightrope! A Bohemian Tale, by Olga Walló. Translated from Czech by Johanna Pokorny, Veronika Revická & others. 2010.
Tightrope! A Bohemian Tale, by Olga Walló. Translated by Chapman Chen. 2011. (Chinese)
University Days, by Laura Solomon. 2014.
Vera Magpie, by Laura Solomon. 2013.

OTHER GENRES

We also publish in other genres, including autobiography, biography, children's illustrated books, educational books, Hong Kong educational and legal history, memoirs, poetry, teenage / young adult books, and travel. Other genres may be added.

WRITE TO US!

We are interested to read **your** response to
Philip Chatting's *The Snow Bridge and Other Stories*
and any other of our publications.
Please write to our email address, proverse@netvigator.com,
giving us a few sentences which you are willing for us to publish,
giving your comments on this book.
If what you write is chosen to be included
in our E-Newsletter or website,
we will select another title published by Proverse
and send you a complimentary copy.
Please include your name, email address and mailing address
when you write to us, and state whether or not we may cut or
edit your comments for publication.
We will use your initials to attribute your comments.

FIND OUT MORE ABOUT OUR AUTHORS
AND BOOKS

Visit our website
http://www.proversepublishing.com

Visit our distributor's website
<www.chineseupress.com>

Follow us on Twitter
Follow news and conversation: <twitter.com/Proversebooks>
OR
Copy and paste the following to your browser window and
follow the instructions: https://twitter.com/#!/ProverseBooks

Request our E-Newsletter
Send your request to info@proversepublishing.com.

Availability
Most titles are available in Hong Kong and world-wide
from our Hong Kong based Distributor,
The Chinese University Press of Hong Kong,
The Chinese University of Hong Kong, Shatin, NT,
Hong Kong SAR, China. Email: cup-bus@cuhk.edu.hk

All titles are available from Proverse Hong Kong
and the Proverse Hong Kong UK-based Distributor.

We have stock-holding retailers in Hong Kong,
Singapore (Select Books), Canada (Elizabeth Campbell Books),
Principality of Andorra (Llibreria La Puça, La Llibreria).

Orders can be made from bookshops in the UK and elsewhere.

Ebooks
Most of our titles are available also as Ebooks.

www.ingramcontent.com/pod-product-compliance
Lightning Source LLC
Chambersburg PA
CBHW050921030726
47503CB00007BB/2409